For son Robbie, who might find the recipes useful

"Do there exist many worlds, or is there but a single world? This is one of the most noble and exalted questions in the study of Nature."
Albertus Magnus, 13th century scientist, philosopher and Christian theologian

"And above all, watch with glittering eyes the whole world around you because the greatest secrets are always hidden in the most unlikely places. Those who don't believe in magic will never find it."
Roald Dahl

Chapter 1

Aristotle, the Prince of Philosophers, saith that the science of Magic is not evil, for by the knowledge of it, evil may be eschewed, and good followed. Therefore the science of Magic is a good knowledge.

The Book of Secrets of Albertus Magnus

In the five sublime days between his death and the funeral there was a General Election and Rosie McLeod achieved orgasm nine times, each one reached with a minimum of fuss in the spacious flat above the *Fox and Duck*. She felt energised; a drab cloak lifted from her shoulders. A conjunction of circumstance had gifted her new life and she was holding tight to the unexpected panorama it now offered. She was becoming herself again; her constituent parts being glued back together. Jack's arms were around her, she'd almost forgotten what it felt like to be wanted.

But wait a minute. She was precise about these things – well, to be honest, *all* things. It wasn't nine times. It was eight times: the *bloody* phone had rung at precisely the wrong moment.

After months of crisis, Rosie was making up for lost time.

With Jack's hands upon her and soft words flowing in her ears, an unwanted phone call was the last thing she needed. Like Humpty, she had fallen. Now, she was being made whole again. She'd snatched up the receiver from its cradle by the bed.

'What?' she demanded without civility. Jack sighed and rolled to one side.

'Mrs McLeod?'

She didn't recognise the voice and was in no mood for frivolous distraction. 'Perhaps... who wants to know?'

'It's Graeme Hutchison from Hutchison and Butler. Look, I really am very sorry to bother you, if you are Mrs McLeod.' He coughed gently, a clearing of the throat, as if to buy time. 'Normally, of course, we wouldn't have considered asking you.' His tone was modulated and sombre, a professional's voice attuned to the requirements of the bereaved. Yet Rosie also detected a hint of hesitancy – as if, perhaps, the phone call hadn't been his idea.

She sighed. 'Yes, I do know who you lot are.' It had been in the newspapers, on radio and across every television station in the land. It would have been surprising if Rosie hadn't known who they were. 'And, yes, depending on what you want, I am Mrs McLeod.'

There was a short silence at the other end of the line. Rosie again heard him nervously clear his throat.

'It's just that I was wondering, actually *we* were wondering, if we could ask you something? It's important, you see, that these things are done right. Even in difficult or, more precisely, strange circumstances. Mr Butler and I

2

positively agree on that.'

Rosie concluded that the phone call hadn't been his idea. She felt passion ebb, heard Jack sigh. A trickle of sunlight patterned the ceiling; she realised that a moment stolen was now a moment lost. One of Jack's feet was poking from the end of the bed, and she noticed that his toenails needed cutting. She frowned. 'You have a question, Mr Hutchison?'

'It's a question of flowers, Mrs McLeod. What flowers might be appropriate, you see? I know it's a somewhat unusual question in the circumstances.' His voice had become thin and apologetic.

Rosie couldn't quite believe what she was being asked. '*Unusual* doesn't begin to get close.'

'Look, I do most sincerely apologise if we've inconvenienced you. Perhaps, Mrs McLeod, it was a little insensitive of us to think…'

Inconvenienced? Insensitive? Rosie, now black affronted, was sitting at attention at the side of the bed, toes angrily kneading the carpet. Jack, temporarily forgotten, lay on his back and contemplated the ceiling. 'You want *me* to recommend flowers for that bastard's funeral? You can't be serious!' Yet he'd phoned her up, deliberately waiting in his Edinburgh funeral parlour until she was on the point of bliss. 'You're not *really* serious, are you?'

Chastised, he took a moment to reply. 'Well, it's just that we didn't know who else to ask. No family, you see, no close friends. Mrs McLeod, I appreciate that you may feel that…'

'Just fuck off!' she shrieked into the receiver. Then, remembering, she commanded in a calmer voice, 'Wait! Just

3

hold on a bloody minute!'

What horticultural damnation could she possibly propose? After everything he'd done. Yet he'd also tried to save her in his own way. A friendly foe whose death had given her new life. She had to remind herself grudgingly of that. This moment of furtive passion, while their customers swilled beer and gossip downstairs, was proof of it.

She looked ahead, hearing birdsong, the tick of the bedside alarm clock, and a burst of laughter from the public bar. *I am also young*, she thought. *I was taken to a boundary and in that frontier land, between good and evil, had the sense to go no further*. Rosie McLeod ran a hand through her hair and reached a decision.

'Poison ivy,' she suggested calmly and slammed down the phone.

Yes, eight times. Eight times, *precisely*. What made it all so unnerving, her deliverance, was that two weeks before it had all seemed so impossible.

Chapter 2

There be many herbs that have great virtues of the influence of the planets. The herb of the Sun, which is called Polygonum, *or* Corrigiola. *This herb healeth the passions and griefs of the heart and the stomach. If any man drink the juice of it, it maketh him do often the act of generation. And if any man bear the root of it, it healeth the grief of the eyes. It helpeth also them that be vexed with the frenzy, if they bear it with them in their breast.*

The Book of Secrets of Albertus Magnus

It began, as these things always do, with a thunderstorm.

The Reverend Lionel Kennedy sat in his stationary car, grey hair swept tightly back from a weather-beaten face that looked carved from burnished walnut. He peered nervously ahead as fat raindrops began to fall, the evening turning black under gunmetal clouds. He had clear blue eyes over an imperious nose; it was only the nose that detracted from the overall impression that he might once have been good-looking. He was tall and angular, not quite old but departing rapidly from mid-life and his head pressed against the roof of his trusty Volkswagen Beetle. His hair was lacquered flat like an old-time fighter pilot; a tic pulled at one eye. With nervous hands he plucked a red and white spotted handkerchief from an inside pocket and noisily blew his nose which, being rather large, took some moments. Calmer, he replaced the handkerchief and took a deep breath.

The storm that had been threatening to break all afternoon finally did so in a crash of thunder. The intermittent drops now came in a downpour, an intensity of noise drumming and beating on the car bonnet. Raindrops bounced and exploded against the windscreen, passing headlights making it seem that tears were running down his face. A bus rushed past and Lionel's car shook in its slipstream. He switched on his windscreen wipers and stared intently ahead. The road ahead seemed black and empty.

Even on main beam, it was hard to see more than a few yards ahead. He pressed his nose close to the windscreen and, starting the engine, piloted his way slowly and shakily towards Haddington, the nearest town. It was a narrow road lined with trees whose branches, in places, formed a canopy, making it a dark tunnel, closing him in. Then he could see the lights of the town, its normalcy, and debated whether to stop, then dismissed the idea almost as quickly; the young police sergeant in Holy Cross would know what to do. Holy Cross was also home, and he wanted the safety of home.

The minister had experienced one of those moments when the very fibre and strength of his faith had been tested, unexpected in its suddenness in a pleasant lane in rural

6

Scotland – a juxtaposition of normality and nightmare, like a small child with the eyes of a murderer. Only ten minutes before, in his capacity as a minister of the Church, he had been judging a Women's Institute jam-making competition. He licked his lips, which still tasted unpleasantly of cranberries – a prize winner, though Lionel hadn't voted for it – and swallowed hard.

The rain beat louder on his car bonnet and he slowed, biting his lower lip in concentration. On either side of the road strange shadows loomed and were swallowed in the night, each more menacing than the last. He knew they were only hedgerows or trees or farm buildings but the consuming fear that filled him made each shadow a thing of terror.

Haddington passed in a haze of lights. He saw only one small group of people, a knot of teenagers sheltering in a shop doorway, coats or hoods pulled over their heads. He felt a pang of guilt as he swept past. He again considered stopping and again dismissed the idea. He wanted to put as much space as possible between himself and whatever it was on the road behind him. Holy Cross offered sanctuary and Lionel was not a brave man any more; older age might give some people a kind of heady fatalism – an acceptance of the vagaries of life – but approaching old age had merely diminished him. His Volkswagen beetled homeward like a refugee through the night, bumping and twisting along the small road to Gifford and Holy Cross. Sensing sanctuary, the little car bounded forwards, picking up speed.

By the time he reached Holy Cross he was fairly cantering, not enough perhaps to break the speed limit, but for him a speed never before attempted nor attained. The Volkswagen hurtled into the village as if pursued by all the demons of the underworld – an analogy which he might at that moment have approved – and skidded to a stop, although a very small skid, outside the police station.

The village of Holy Cross is, of course, as internationally well-known as Edinburgh Castle or Loch Ness. Its long association with one of the greatest Christian myths puts the place right up there with haggis, tartan and shortbread as an icon of Scottishness. Tourists, many with metal detectors, come in large numbers from across the world. The village is often referred to as the heartbeat of Scotland – a place of myth and legend, and yet just thirty minutes from Edinburgh. Throughout the year, coach parties visit the small visitor centre and take sugary photographs that are immediately recognised world-wide.

The village takes its name from the fabled Glastonbury Cross that is reputed to have been buried inside the parish precincts when King Henry VIII purged the English monasteries, although local legend has over the years embellished what was probably a doubtful tale. The story goes that monks spirited the cross from Glastonbury as King Henry's soldiers drew near, the original intention being to flee southwards to the coast and, from there, by ship to France or Spain. However, cut off by a detachment of cavalry, the monks were forced to head north to Scotland, a country which then still embraced the Catholic faith. How and why they ended up at Holy Cross is anybody's guess, although the village does lie on the original Roman road linking Newcastle with Edinburgh.

However, as none of the reputable medieval historians mention the cross, it probably never existed beyond the imaginings of local priests and travelling holy men. That, of course, hasn't stopped the village's numerous gift shops from selling commemorative pendants and brooches. Like bagpipes or the Loch Ness monster, the golden cross is good for business.

Unsurprisingly, given the village's legendary association, it is the church that dominates Holy Cross. However, catering also to Mammon, the *Fox and Duck* is conveniently across the street.

Inside the cosy public bar, Mara Thomson, a temporary barmaid, had set a pint of beer in front of Tam Cronin, one of the pub's regular customers, and was automatically wiping slops from the bar's wooden surface.

'It's dead, Tam,' she was saying.

'Trees don't just die, lass.'

'Well, this one did.'

The *Fox and Duck* has been a hostelry since the early 1840s, when the pub had extensive stabling, now converted into a function suite much in demand for weddings and funerals, largely because of its proximity to the church opposite. However, the pub's name only dates from 1942 when a stray Luftwaffe bomb landed one night in the village pond, killing all its finned and feathered inhabitants, including a scavenging fox. At the bottom of what had been the pond was found a medieval stone cross and, following much debate in the village, it was decided to fill in the pond and erect the stone cross in its place. The story of the cross's discovery inevitably made the national press and gave the landlord of the then *Railway Tavern* a marketing opportunity – in those days a branch line ran from Holy Cross through Haddington to Edinburgh. The pub's far wall is dominated by a large and intricately carved wooden fireplace, pillaged from a local mansion house that had also been hit by a Nazi bomb. Nobody can say that the Luftwaffe wasn't generous to the *Fox and Duck*.

The older man looked doubtful and scratched his chin. 'Aye, well, as I said, it's not looking too healthy.'

'No, Tam, believe me, it's absolutely and completely dead.'

Rosie McLeod, joint proprietor of the *Fox and Duck*, swilled glasses in tepid water in the sink behind the bar, then set them to drain, with only half her mind on the debate over the illness, or demise, of the last remaining tree in the beer garden. Tam Cronin, a *Fox and Duck* stalwart, was nodding.

Over recent days, the hazel tree had been going from bad to worse, which was odd because it had always been so sturdy. It was never fed, never watered – although the Scottish climate usually gave it ample water – and in summer, when the beer garden saw more use, beer dregs were poured on its roots. It had stood, stoic and undemanding, since Rosie's arrival years and years before. Then, without warning, its leaves had withered and turned brown; now in the course of an afternoon they had all fallen, swirling in eddies across the flagstones. Mara had been out earlier to sweep them up.

Rosie, now drying glasses and replacing them on shelves, regarded her sourly. Against the brilliant bird of paradise that was Mara, she felt like a dowdy sparrow – an about-to-be-very-old dowdy sparrow, without youth or plumage. Rosie was experiencing a period of bleak introspection, exacerbated by a significant and approaching birthday with all its associated connotations. She wanted to be wanted. She didn't want to be older. Where the bloody hell was Jack?

'Apparently, that tree of yours is dead,' Tam informed Rosie. 'I have it on good authority,' he added, indicating Mara, who had moved down the bar to serve another customer.

'I know it's dead,' she replied. 'Actually, I do know about these things, Tam.' Her eyes lingered on a framed newspaper article hanging on the bar wall. "*Medicine Woman*", said the headline.

'Aye, I suppose you do,' he conceded, noting the slope of her gaze. 'Anyway, how's Mara's mum?' He was in his late fifties, with thick glasses that magnified his eyes and made him appear, head on, like a strange and rather bemused sea-creature. He had a permanently stubbly face and tangled brown hair that rarely made the acquaintance of a comb, and only ever drank Belhaven 70 Shilling from his own pewter tankard which was kept, alongside several others, on a shelf behind the bar beneath a smiling photograph of Jack and Rosie on the day fifteen years beforehand when they'd taken possession of the pub.

'Julie? Back on her feet, sort of,' she replied, frowning. Having earlier watched a wildlife programme on TV, Rosie had temporarily forgotten that a pile of greenery, chopped and washed, awaited her attention upstairs.

Further up the bar, Mara, resplendent in a small black skirt and tight white shirt, was reaching to a top shelf to retrieve a bottle of brandy, much to the gathering interest of the male clientele.

Tam said, 'I'll tell you a wee something. She's got a boyfriend.'

'Don't be ridiculous, she's just had a hip replacement.'

'For God's sake, Rosemary! Not her mother. Mara! Very hush-hush, apparently.' He shrugged. 'Don't ask me why.'

Mara, serene and beautiful, could have any man she wanted, although, so went village gossip, she kept herself to herself as far as romantic entanglements were concerned. She was only helping out in the pub for a few summer weeks as a favour to Rosie and Jack, her main purpose being to look after her mother after the operation. Soon she'd be gone, back to real life in Edinburgh and a PhD to complete. Beautiful *and* intelligent, it really wasn't very fair. No, bugger it, it wasn't fair at all. Full-*bloody*-stop.

'How do you know?' asked Rosie.

'I heard her on the phone yesterday. Canoodling, I think it's called. Well, she couldn't very well deny it what with me sitting at the bar listening. But she made me promise not to tell anybody.'

'You've just told me, Tam.'

'Aye, well. But secrets are no fun if you don't tell

anyone.' He swallowed a mouthful of beer and wiped his mouth scratchily with one hand. 'Don't know who it was, though. Anyway, I suppose I should give you one of these,' he said, conjuring a leaflet from his jacket pocket. Like the rest of him, his jacket – in scuffed brown corduroy – had seen better days, many decades before. 'I'm also supposed to ask if we can count on your support.'

Emblazoned on the front of the blue leaflet was a photograph of a self-satisfied, rather fleshy man in a grey suit. His mouth was set in a thin, determined line and his chin was raised for the battle ahead. Beneath, in big, bold letters, was written: **FORWARDS WITH THE CONSERVATIVE PARTY.**

'I didn't know you were a Tory,' said Rosie with some surprise. 'Or isn't it something that you normally admit to?'

'I'm not really sure I am, which is why I'm in here and not out there delivering these.' Tam's cartoon eyes indicated the pub door; then he deposited a bundle of leaflets on the bar where they spread like spilled water.

Rosie laughed. 'You're a dark horse, Tam... here's me thinking all these years that you were some kind of radical socialist. Now I find out that you're really an enemy of the people. Put your leaflets away before I ban you forever from my pub.'

'In which case I take it that we *can't* count on your support?'

She shrugged, not having given the forthcoming election much thought. 'Maybe, maybe not.'

'Ah, then I'll put you down as an undecided.'

13

'Take it any way you like, Tam. I'm just not sure that I can be bothered to vote, that's all.'

The papers all said that the election, timed deliberately by Downing Street to coincide with her birthday, was a foregone conclusion. A landslide was predicted to sweep the Socialists back to power. Against that overwhelming likelihood, election fever had failed to raise the country's political temperature.

'Emmeline Pankhurst would be proud of you, Rosemary. All those years struggling for emancipation and you can't be bothered to vote. I fear the cause of universal suffrage to be lost.' Tam dipped his nose to his pint.

'Dear Lord, I've just remembered,' said Rosie and consulted a large book that lay on the counter beneath the optics. 'You lot are coming here tomorrow evening.'

Tam nodded, his head still glued to his tankard. 'An election address by our parliamentary candidate. A last pep talk to the party faithful, or some-such shite. You should listen in, maybe learn a thing or two.'

'I doubt it, but thanks for the offer.'

'Beer, sandwiches and a little tedium.' Tam bestowed a small smile on the publican, displaying brown teeth that perfectly colour-matched his jacket, and every other part of him. 'Our candidate is... how shall I put it?... rather renowned for the quantity, rather than the quality, of his speeches. Still, I'm not doing anything else.'

This was palpably true as Tam never did anything except prop up the bar of the *Fox and Duck*.

Mara squeezed past on her way to the cash register and

Rosie suddenly felt old again. She was still on the right side of forty, but now only days away from it – close enough to feel its dead weight and the accusation of middle-age. She knew she had once been attractive and wondered if she still was. Nobody now thought to reassure her on this point, particularly Jack, who hadn't made love to her for weeks – months, even. She had black shoulder-length hair and dark eyes and, in profile could seem serene, even beautiful. Her dark eyes sparkled and she had a gap between her front teeth; usually she had a quick smile. She was small and slight, but possessed of a quick and demanding energy: *when exactly did he last make love to me*? she thought, catching sight of her reflection in the mirror below the optics and seeing only grey hair. Jack was probably organising a surprise party, to whisk her to London or Paris for a romantic break, buying diamonds or diazepam – all very nice of him but not what she really wanted. She was a woman of baser needs. She'd made up her mind earlier, standing in her knickers before the full-length mirror in their bedroom, disconcerted by what faced her. *Things may be sagging but I am still desirable*, she'd told herself, repeatedly saying the words out loud until they sounded convincing. Jack still finds me desirable. He still finds me utterly desirable, even if he doesn't know it. I am not *bloody* middle-aged.

Rosie's mood wasn't improved by the darkening skies outside. The village flag over the church that had clung lifelessly to its pole through the afternoon heat had now flapped to life, an energised Saltire awoken by the approaching storm that the lunchtime news said would be upon them by early evening. Rosie had the publican's professional distaste for bad weather. The beer garden, which had been full all afternoon, was now deserted, a drift of discarded crisp packets swirling around the decaying hazel tree by the back wall. She'd have to get Jack to cut it down.

Just then there was a crash of thunder that momentarily silenced all else; the pub lights flickered and dark shadows chased across the walls. Rain patterned the windows and, in the beer garden, a sudden river gushed across the paving stones. In the distance a dog barked once, forlorn and melancholy, and then was quiet.

'Bloody hell!' said Mara, one hand clutched to her ample chest.

'Bloody hell indeed,' said Rosie.

Tam pocketed his election leaflets, undaunted by the racket outside. 'Perhaps I could tell you about our economic policy?' he suggested.

'No offence, Tam, but no.'

He shrugged. 'To be honest, I'm not entirely sure what our economic policy is. Maybe we don't have one. Perhaps I could ask our esteemed candidate about it tomorrow evening.'

'Did you know,' asked Rosie, 'that a firefly is actually a beetle?'

'No, Rosemary, I can't say that I did know that... not, I hasten to add, that I've ever given it any thought.'

'Well it is.'

'How interesting, Rosie.'

'Ah, Tam, but it is. Not quite as interesting as Tory Party

policy, of course, but it has given me an idea.'

At the bar a couple of younger customers, stalwarts of the cricket team, had retreated from their weekly practice on the village green and were ordering pints of beer. 'Damn shame about the weather,' said one, clearly delighted not to be throwing a ball about, 'but damned odd about the minister.'

Reverend Kennedy had been spotted hurtling through the village not minutes beforehand, and dashing in lolloping strides to the police station. The cricketers, evacuating the village green, had seen him while sheltering under one of the few remaining oak trees beside the river before sprinting to the *Fox and Duck*. 'Bloody stupid hiding under a tree in a thunderstorm, but I'd rather be dead than wet,' remarked one of the cricketers, a nice lad called Liam, if Rosie remembered correctly.

It was indeed odd, thought Rosie, as she served her customers, dispensing as much good cheer as she was able to muster. She knew the old minister quite well from the many functions that the *Fox and Duck* had hosted for happy couples and the recently bereaved, and sometimes both together, and was intrigued to know what seemingly urgent business Lionel Kennedy had with the constabulary. Although she wasn't particularly religious, she sometimes attended Sunday service just to be on the safe side. Rosie also knew Sadie Gallagher, the priest's indiscreet housekeeper. She'd ask her what he'd been up to.

'Big match on Sunday, lads,' Liam was saying to nobody in particular.

'The Battle of the Legends,' replied one of the other

17

cricketers, imbuing the phrase with great significance, whilst also ordering another round of drinks with a sweep of his hand. It was clear to Rosie as she poured pints of beer that team bonding was now well under way.

Rosie looked at the driving rain, trying again to remember when Jack had last laid a lustful hand upon her. *I* am *still attractive*, she told herself firmly. *The dead weight of final accusation is not upon me yet. I am* not *old*.

The legend of Holy Cross relates how Satan rose up from the Lower Kingdom and rebelled against the angels of the Heavens. In the ensuing battle, Michael slew Satan and the emerald from his dark crest fell to earth as a meteorite where it was found by seafarers. The emerald was fashioned by craftsmen into a wondrous chalice, the greatest of all the possessions of King Solomon. His descendant Jesus Christ used the chalice at the Last Supper for the Institution of the Holy Sacrament and, at His crucifixion, the blood of Christ was collected in the chalice by St Joseph of Arimathea. It is said that when St Joseph was imprisoned after the Resurrection, he was sustained in his ordeal by the chalice. Later it was brought to England in the first century AD and, for safekeeping, buried at Glastonbury.

For unclear reasons, the chalice was then taken to Spain, although the legend says that a part of the dark emerald remained in England and was kept in secret adoration by the monks of Glastonbury. Later still, the chalice was taken to the remote country of Prester John in the Kingdom of Kerait in Northeast Asia. After the death of the last king at the hands of Genghis Khan, the emerald was taken to Antioch where it disappeared for ever.

The legend relates how the monks of Glastonbury secretly fashioned a great cross of pale Welsh gold and adorned it with the twelve stones of the Mystical City of the Apocalypse: jasper, sapphire, chalcedony, sardonyx, sardin, beryl, chrysolite, topaz, chrysaprase, jacinth, amethyst and emerald. The horizontal arms of the cross were encrusted with the seven stones which symbolise the Christian church: diamond, ruby, sapphire, topaz, chalcedony, emerald, and amethyst. The upper arm was dominated by a single pearl symbolising the descent of wisdom from Noah, Abraham and Isaac and also representing both the Gospel and the salvation of Adam. The lower arm of the cross was adorned with the stones of the seven planets: tiger's eye for the Sun, quartz for the Moon, crocidolite for Jupiter, agate for Mercury, ruby for Mars, aventurine for Venus, and black onyx for Saturn. In the centre of the cross was the twelfth stone of the Apocalypse, the greatest and most wondrous and magical gemstone of them all: the flawless emerald from the Holy Grail.

The story, of course, is complete baloney.

What Rosie knew is that emotional response is accomplished chemically by neurotransmitters. They work rather like a complex telephone network, telling us what to do and what to think, then hanging up as another neurotransmitter phones up with the next instruction. There are three basic types. The first are small molecule neurotransmitters, the second are neuroactive peptides responsible for our sensory and emotional responses including hunger, thirst, sex drive, pleasure and pain. The third is tumescent nitric oxide, used as dental anaesthetic, propellant in deodorant cans and as an oxidising agent in rocket motors. The low polarity of the gas makes it easily soluble in blood where it acts on the fatty membranes of nerve cells. Without it, sexual intercourse would be quite impossible.

Only after the cricketers had finished talking tactics that none of them would remember, and the last of the pub's customers had departed, was Rosie able to lock up and climb the flight of stairs that separated her two worlds. Downstairs, with its echoes of days gone by, the *Fox and Duck* is – in its own way – an historic place with its original wooden beams and stone floor. Upstairs, in their apartment, all was distinctly modern. Being childless, they were able to indulge themselves with cream sofas, white walls and glass tables. It was, as Rosie liked to say, a complete contrast from the pub downstairs; delineating the domestic from the professional. She helped herself to a glass of red plonk and stood for a few moments looking out over the village green, thinking about love bugs and the physiological effects of natural gases.

Then she remembered about Mara's mother and busied herself in the kitchen, which was where the elusive Jack found her when he eventually arrived home, muttering about bad weather, congested roads and then – unexpectedly – apologising for being late and leaving her to lock up. She paused from stirring a saucepan that seemed filled with weeds and leaves.

'How were they?' she asked.

'Who?'

'Your bloody parents, Jack. These people in Dundee you leave me for.'

'Oh, you know. Bad eyes, bad knees but mustn't grumble. They're busy planning an extended holiday in Greece. Dad bought a book about Greek myths and, well, things seem to have got out of hand.' Jack's father had spent most of a lifetime reading travel brochures without actually going anywhere. Now in his twilight years, he and his wife were making up for lost time. 'They send their love, by the way. I said we'd get them over for a visit. It's been ages since they were last here.'

'Hmm.'

Jack looked over her shoulder as she strained liquid from the green slime and poured it into a bottle. 'It's for Julie Thomson,' she explained, setting the saucepan back on the hob where it hissed and bubbled. 'You know, Mara's mother.'

He wrinkled his nose. 'What's it for?'

'Inflammation.'

In the saucepan, green remnants were boiling rapidly. 'It doesn't smell very nice,' he said.

'It's not *supposed* to smell nice, Jack. You rub it on.'

'Ah, well, OK.' After so many years together, Rosie was well used to her husband's bland indifference to her little recipes. 'Anyway, how was your day?' he asked.

So she told him the bar gossip, about Mara's secret boyfriend, the minister's urgent business with the police, and about the hazel tree in the beer garden that he, Jack, would have to do something about with Walter's borrowed chainsaw. Walter Crosbie, friend or acquaintance – it was hard to tell which – had lent him his chainsaw some weeks beforehand to cut down a rowan tree, the only other tree in the beer garden, which had also fallen sick. Jack had never got round to giving the chainsaw back and he now wondered if Walter had forgotten, or if he bore a secret grudge for its absence.

'Did you know,' she asked, when the small bottle for Mara's mother was finally and tightly stoppered, 'that the firefly is actually a beetle?'

'Actually, no. Is it something I should know?'

'No, I didn't either, which is why I asked. I thought that it might just have been me who didn't know it was a beetle. Perhaps, I thought, everyone in the whole bloody world knows that the firefly is a beetle. Except me, of course.' Seeing her husband's blank expression, she sighed, adding: 'I was watching a programme on TV earlier.'

Later, she watched him framed in the bathroom door: tall and lean and clean-shaven, but with a hint of thickening waist; he still had a square jaw, all his own hair – still brown, if a touch receding – most of his own teeth and firm bum. He had green eyes that sparkled, crow's feet around his eyes and leathery skin. His lips, full and soft, were made for kissing and being kissed, or so Rosie thought, thinking about humble fireflies and the potency of their spark. He saw her looking intently at him and smiled, a little embarrassed, as he swilled out toothpaste. He was two years older than her, but was growing older gracefully; he seemed to accept it.

Rosie was less phlegmatic than her husband; the weight of years lay heavily on her shoulders. The problem she believed was that the chemistry of their attraction was being extinguished by ageing toxins. She loved Jack, always had done, but conditionally; she felt he was walking backwards from her emotionally and might one day disappear off the edge of a precipice and be lost to her. *Or perhaps I'm walking backwards from him*, she thought, remembering their first meeting in – where else? – a pub. She'd just completed her degree and, on impulse, had taken a train back home to the family farm in Sussex. She was rootless and lost; he was on a more considered journey.

She remembered their first proper date, and the week they'd then spent together. She believed everything he told her without question, basking in his smile, believing it when he said how beautiful she was, how they were made for one another, in a match made in Heaven. She'd met the right man and they would stay together for ever and ever. It had seemed so certain although it was also naïve, particularly when Jack went back to Glasgow leaving no forwarding address. She'd been devastated, never imagining he could do such a thing. She'd waited by the door each morning for the post to arrive, running to the phone every time it rang. After three weeks of diminishing hope and rising anger she had begun to give up, believing once again that all men were bastards, when he'd phoned to ask her to marry him. Just like

23

that, typical of the bloody man. Without hesitation, she'd said 'yes'.

Now, years later, he lay sleeping, not having responded to her perfume, a further affront to her much-diminished self-esteem. She'd read in *The Daily Mail* that men were turned on by women's perfume. Jack seemed to be the exception, muttering something in his sleep and turning over.

She stared at the ceiling thinking about the young people they had once been, her approaching birthday and how, when she was little, her mother had taught her to recognise the shaded places where vervain and colewort grew, and the wet ditches where she could gather comfrey and meadowsweet. The shelves in her scullery were packed with tightly stoppered jars and bottles, each labelled with a patch of paper stuck with Sellotape. She arranged them alphabetically with acorn, angelica and averna sativa on the top left shelf, working through bilberry and bittercress to wood sorrel and yarrow on the bottom right.

She slept deeply, an unrequited ache behind her eyes and small pinpricks of dazzling light across her mind.

Chapter 3

The herb is named of the Chaldees Bieith, of the Greeks Retus, of the Latins Nepeta, of Englishmen Calamint, otherwise Pennyroyal. Take this herb and mix it with the stone found in the nest of the bird called a Lapwing, or Black Plover, and rub the belly of any beast, and it shall be with birth.

The Book of Secrets of Albertus Magnus

By morning, the storm had blown itself out, leaving the air crisp and clear, the early sun burning off moisture from the meadows and pastures, so that the village seemed wreathed in rising smoke. Before reaching Holy Cross, the morning sun first touches the high woodland above the village, one of the last ancient woodlands in central Scotland, a majestic place which straddles the river Tess from east to west in a straggling question mark. The majority of the woodland lies on the western bank of the Tess, although, in summer, the river is little more than a wide stream gliding quietly around deep pools. Here and there, gravel deposits cause the pines to thin and green clearings, open to the sun, attract stag beetles and Sweet William. Shafts of sunlight pick out oxlips and delicate archangels and, in the cooler shadows, lime trees attract great swarms of bees so that, in places, the woodland

25

hums like a great machine. Squadrons of insects patrol this frontier zone and magpies, like quick dark shadows, glide in the tree line.

The Tess, which has turned south from the woodland, flows down the valley towards the River Tyne, passing through Holy Cross on one side of the village green – and just yards from the village police station. Inside, Sergeant Richard Walter Scott – Richie to his many friends and one frustrating girlfriend – was making an unsatisfactory phone call.

'Just file it on District, there's a good lad.'

'In other words, do nothing?'

'There's not a lot that you can do, laddie.'

'But suppose…'

'Look, I'm not saying that the minister's wrong… I'm simply saying that there's nothing that we can do.' Big Mac from Divisional HQ in Haddington, East Lothian's seat of all power and influence, seemed sure of that point. 'The fact is, he may well be right… we do get reports like this from time to time.'

'We do?' Not in Holy Cross, to the best of Richie Scott's knowledge.

'The last one was… oh… a month or so ago near Dunbar.'

'It was? I didn't know.' Dunbar, a small coastal town, was only a few miles south of Holy Cross.

'Look, if you want, go and have a nose around. But, chances are you won't find anything. The rain will have washed out any tracks. In any case, if the animal does exist, it'll be miles away by now.' It was clear that Big Mac found the whole thing of little interest.

Richie's office was long and thin, almost a passageway, and his desk was circled by filing cabinets, giving the impression that he was under siege, like a medieval knight in a policeman's uniform. He replaced the receiver and drummed his fingers on the edge of his desk. Perhaps he *could* drive out and take a quick look at the spot. It wouldn't do any harm and the minister *had* given a precise location. There again, the divisional inspector in his Haddington eyrie was also right: whatever traces the animal might have left would have been washed out by the rain.

He made the journey anyway, mostly out of a sense of obligation to the minister who had, after all, sought out his help. On the way, he thought back to what the old man, clearly rattled, had told him the evening before and the dismissive way his report had been received officially. A large animal, the minister had said. A large *black* animal. Definitely not a cow. Or a large dog, no. I *know* what a sheep looks like, officer. It had a long tail so, no, it wasn't a deer. He found the spot easily enough, just past the Gifford turn-off on the road up to Soutra Hill, cobweb lines and insects sawing the air like particles of living dust. On one side of the road, a ditch bubbled and gushed; above him, a skylark called.

He searched along the hedgerows on either side of the road and then in the fields beyond, watched incuriously by a scattering of cows. He searched diligently for an hour, looking for something – anything – before conceding that, even if the old man *was* right, the storm had scoured away the evidence.

Driving back to the police station, he looked closely, as he always now did, at the *Fox and Duck*. To his disappointment, all he saw was Sadie Gallagher in earnest conversation with the publican's wife. The minister's housekeeper was laughing, although it seemed to be a joke that wasn't shared by Rosie McLeod.

In fact, Rosie hadn't found it remotely funny, barely noticing the passing police car and its sole occupant.

'He says that he saw a big black cat,' Sadie was saying, then cackled. 'Probably something that the Women's Institute slipped into his tea, if you ask me.'

'Good heavens!'

'Well, that's what says.'

Sadie Gallagher had a bag of shopping in one hand and a woollen hat perched on her head. She was an engagingly cheerful woman of indeterminate age who habitually wore tweed skirts and equally sensible walking shoes. 'Although,' she added with another laugh, 'it *was* dark and the poor soul isn't getting any younger.'

'Like the rest of us,' replied Rosie, uneasy at the mere mention of old age.

Sadie shifted her bag of shopping to her other hand. 'It certainly gave him a fright, I can tell you. He said it was like an apparition.'

'Where?'

'Up yonder.' Sadie gestured with a tilt of her head to the

28

Lammermuir Hills that separate East Lothian from the Border country.

Instead of returning to the pub, Rosie walked slowly down the High Street, past the cricket ground with its rotting pavilion, and across the humpback bridge over the Tess. Here she stopped and watched the river, thinking she saw a trout motionless by the riverbank. Sweetgale and chanterelle waved in the breeze from the water, swollen by the storm. Two wood pigeons clapped from a hawthorn tree across the river and the trout shivered and was gone, its movement no more than a shift of light. The sunlight was warm and sweet and carried the scent of nettles and honeysuckle. Then, raising her eyes to the upper pastureland and the old woodland, she climbed steadily to a rocky escarpment overlooking the valley. It took half an hour of steady walking, her slight frame bent against the hillside. She did not stop once and only turned when the ground levelled. Here she sat motionless, catching her breath, looking out. She often came up here, usually with a basket to collect ingredients, mostly harmless plants and herbs for bad skin, clogged bowels or sensitive stomachs. Her concoction to boost fertility and aid conception was locally and benignly famous, except at the medical centre which believed it should have a monopoly on all diagnosis and treatment.

From the escarpment, she could see across Holy Cross and Haddington to the coastline. A tanker, on its way to the petrochemical complex at Grangemouth, hung suspended on the water. Across the Forth, the coastline of Fife was clear and defined against the morning sun.

The valley floor was a darker green than the valley walls, the river and main road slicing it like arteries. She had always thought of the village as home, or as a new home, a place of hope, a new beginning. She'd been born in Somerset, the daughter of a tenant farmer and later brought up in Sussex when her father eventually bought their own farm. She'd been happy to move north, the new publican's wife, building a business with her husband, struggling in the early years, surviving: but making plans, dreaming. She supposed she still was happy and smiled thinly with anticipation. Nitric oxide, who'd have thought it! Certainly not her, and she knew a thing or two about nitric oxide. Well, not happy, not really. Approaching antiquity had made her fragile; like a piece of porcelain – one knock and she might shatter.

She walked back to the village, down the hillside and along the riverbank, occasionally stooping to throw a stone downstream, watching the splash buried by the rush of water. As she came down from the head of the valley the river slowly quietened, and she walked beside it thinking about the strange sighting made by Lionel Kennedy, the water becoming a kaleidoscope of light.

She could also have sworn that the river was changing colour. *Distinctly cappuccino*, she thought, although her mind was elsewhere. Yesterday it had been sludgy brown, as it always was. Today it was milky white, although she barely noticed; to the burden of age had been added the unwelcome distraction of an old man's revelations.

30

The exterior of the village church is squat and forbidding, dating back centuries, but much altered by succeeding church authorities; inside, its pillars arch to an elegant and intricately carved ceiling, and a rose window beams a delicate latticework of light. Historians and archaeologists agree that the church sits on a much older place of worship and to one side of the altar, behind some railings, is an ancient standing stone found nearby which bears the markings of a rough and primitive craftsmanship. To one side of the church is the High Street and in its surrounding lanes are medieval cottages, much admired by tourists. To the south, the village ends at the banks of the river Tess that has been fed by other streams just upriver and which now flows in a wide curve, turning southwards to join the Tyne just south of Haddington. The village green, which doubles as a football and cricket ground, borders the river – a local cricket rule is that anyone hitting a ball in the river scores double, a feat usually achieved at least once a season. A wooden pavilion gently decomposes and although regular efforts are made to raise money for repairs, nothing ever seems to get done.

At the church end of the village green – which last featured in a Channel 4 documentary called *Disappearing Scotland* – is the rough stone cross that the Luftwaffe uncovered. It has settled quite deeply into the soil and is much photographed by visitors and wedding photographers, the newly married couple sitting on its horizontal arms. Sitting on it is said to bring good luck, healthy children, or great wealth, depending on which photographer you have hired for the event. Replicas of the cross can be bought in all the bric-a-brac and curiosity shops that now make up much of the High Street, replacing the grocer, fishmonger and butcher's shops that went out of business when the supermarket opened at the edge of the village, promising greater choice and more jobs.

Lionel Kennedy stood before the altar, hands clasped behind his back, and stared long and hard at the wooden crucifix. Behind him, beams of sunshine crossed and recrossed in mid-air while a thin veil of dust excited by the light swirled like wood smoke. Occasionally the wooden beams that arched from pillar to roof – the very spines of the crouching church – creaked and crackled like arthritic joints. Stained-glass windows threw pink and crimson light to the stone floor. The crucifix over the altar burned in a melancholy fire. Lionel sat on the end of the front pew and ran his fingers along the brass railing, feeling its smooth coldness, burnished to a gleam by Mrs Gallagher and her small army of helpers. He scratched his long nose thoughtfully and ran one hand through his thinning hair. Then he picked up a hymn book from the pew and flicked through it, not reading the words, but finding the familiar pages a reassurance. The book smelled of lavender and age, its cracked spine welcoming and venerable, offering only certainties.

It's only an escaped animal, he told himself again, but still heard a dark clamour in his ear, like a forest touched by a breeze. He wondered again whether he should have been more forthcoming with the young policeman, then decided

32

that he'd done the right thing. He had to be sure first and, until then, he would wait. It didn't occur to the old minister that he may have inadvertently set off the very chain reaction that he was seeking to avoid.

Prosaically, thought Rosie, the jars in her scullery gleaming with promise, *I must consider both dosage and the combination of plants and herbs to make it happen.* Specifically, Rosie wanted to greatly boost Jack's production of norepinephrine, a chemical messenger that is essential for arousal. Increased production of this chemical could, she knew, be achieved in a number of ways, including yohimbe bark, from a tree common in Cameroon, Gabon and Zaire. The bark contains yohimbine which stimulates the nervous system and causes changes in blood pressure by dilating blood vessels. It also encourages adrenaline supply, essential for sexual stimulation. At higher doses it has a significant psychotropic effect. Yohimbe must never be taken with foods containing certain amino acids often present, for example, in vegetarian foods. However, as Jack ate meat for breakfast, lunch and dinner, Rosie didn't give this much thought.

Richie Scott had only just returned to the police station when his telephone rang. A traffic accident, not serious, but requiring his attention. He sighed and picked up his cap and car keys.

His office – 'the sharp end,' he called it – was out front, his living quarters at the rear, the line between leisure and duty finely balanced. His back door led onto a small patio with a white plastic table and ring of garden chairs, to a patch of grass that, he noted, needed to be mowed, and to an equally small vegetable patch in which he grew carrots, lettuce and potatoes. If he was a rabbit, he sometimes thought, he'd be self-sufficient.

He had only moved to the village as part of a Police Scotland trial on community policing – preventing crime before it happens, as the chief constable had put it when he launched the scheme. Until then, Richie had been a beat bobby in Edinburgh before requesting a rural transfer. He had been born and brought up in the city; the countryside was a place to visit, not to live in. He was more used to cobbles and tarmac than fields and meadows. His superintendent, suspecting this, had reluctantly handed him his transfer papers and said that he hoped Richie knew what he was doing. His father, recently retired from the same police force, was more volubly disappointed. He told Richie that he wouldn't get noticed. If you're out of sight, he'd said, you *can't* get noticed. Maybe, Richie had answered, I'm not ambitious enough. He couldn't really explain it to himself.

For the first three months he'd been in limbo, caught between the city's bright lights and the duller tempo of rural life. He had struggled in those early weeks to find his feet, to find meaning to attach to his duties. Until that diamond morning when he'd been crossing Market Place, his footsteps sharp and precise, his breath hanging in the air. There was a hint of spring in the air, a sense of warmth returning after the dense cold of winter.

34

She was tall and blonde and was walking slowly and diagonally away from him. She was wearing a long leather coat with the collar turned up, white scarf and black boots. In a split second he had memorised each detail. She moved languidly, seemingly intent on reading the front page of a folded tabloid newspaper that she held in both hands. The clarity of that pure moment was precise in his mind, chiselled into a perfect memory by chance encounter. Long hair, turned golden in the morning sunshine, obscured her face. At that moment his radio had crackled. She'd looked round and smiled.

Chapter 4

The herb of the Moon, which is called Chynostates. *The juice of it purgeth the pains of the stomach, and breast plates. The virtue of it declareth that it is the herb of the Moon. The flower of this herb purgeth great spleens and healeth them. It is good against the sickness of the eyes, and maketh a sharp sight. And it is good against the blood of the eyes. It is also good to them that have an evil stomach, or which cannot digest their meat, by drinking the juice of it.*

The Book of Secrets of Albertus Magnus

There were two conflicting options for the beer garden, and Jack and his wife had reached no definitive conclusion. The *Fox and Duck* was essentially U-shaped, with the public house at the bottom of the U, facing out onto the village green. The restaurant formed one long side of the U and the function suite the other. The beer garden was in the middle, meaning that all the food for the function suite had to either be ferried through the main bar or through the garden. In winter that meant a long walk through a crowded bar or a shortcut through the rain. The beer garden contained a number of wooden tables with red umbrellas embedded in concrete blocks, the whole area paved with flagstones.

The option favoured by Rosie was to leave the beer garden as it was; the *Golf Inn*, their main rival, had no outdoor drinking area. Even the *Golf*'s most dedicated patrons would visit the *Fox and Duck* on sunny days. Jack, on the other hand, preferred the ambitious option of building a conservatory over the entire area and knocking through into the restaurant. It would be expensive, he conceded that, but it would allow them to further develop the restaurant which was becoming increasingly popular now that they'd invested in Sammy, a gastronomic genius, who didn't mind working in the middle of nowhere. However, neither had won over the other, and the matter had yet to be resolved. At the back of the beer garden were well-tended flowerbeds, mainly planted with roses, and the dying hazel tree that Jack, armed with Walter's chain saw, was now in the process of dismembering.

He turned to find his wife silently regarding him. She was dressed to go out, with a green quilted jacket, jeans and walking shoes. In her hand was a steaming mug. 'I thought you might be thirsty,' she said and handed it to him, 'so I made you a nice mug of *lapsang souchong*.'

Jack looked blank.

'Tea, Jack. You like *lapsang souchong*.'

He took the mug from her and they surveyed his work so far. Now that he had cut off most of the main branches, the tree resembled an amputee. Fallen leaves eddied at their feet, swirling under the tables, piling against the back wall. 'Do you know, Jack, I like it better without that bloody tree. It'll let more light in,' she remarked. 'Well, I'm off to see Julie Thomson.' *Ah yes*, he thought, remembering the sludge of green leaves boiled to a frazzle in their kitchen the night before.

He sniffed at the tea she'd left him, and laid it down untouched on one of the beer garden tables. He'd *never* liked *lapsang souchong* and wondered for a moment why his wife thought that he did.

Jack busied himself again with the chainsaw, lopping off the smaller branches and then, perched on a stepladder, started on the main trunk, taking the tree down in sections. Then he sawed the branches and tree trunk into smaller pieces, carrying them to the back of the function suite area where there was a storage shed. Inside, in winter, were kept the beer garden umbrellas and wood for the restaurant and bar fireplaces. He worked slowly and methodically, as he always worked.

Unlike Rosie, Jack trudged. He'd been born in Ayrshire, on Scotland's west coast, and brought up in various seaside towns; his parents had never been quite sure where to live and, just to be on the safe side, moved town every few years. He plodded through school, across cold rugby fields, but mostly reached his destinations eventually. If Rosie was the hare, Jack was a dependable tortoise in comfortable shoes.

His Uncle Bill owned a pub in Largs, also on the west coast, and one day Jack asked him why he sold beer to strangers.

'Because it's nice to run a place where people go to be happy.' As simple as that but, having thought about it, the young Jack was sold on the idea.

Years later, he enrolled at a management school in Glasgow, emerging on the other side of tertiary education with a good idea. Scottish pubs, he had concluded, were largely male-orientated, family-unfriendly and pretty soulless. They catered to a fading Presbyterianism, with over-bright lights and cheerfully tasteless food. English pubs, on the other hand, had more charm. They were warm and welcoming. They had character, selling food that didn't always come with chips and a salad garnish.

With the end of his education in sight, he spent weekends in his small and clapped-out car, crossing Yorkshire, the Dales and the Lake District. What he sought wasn't the perfect pub, rather the ambience of many pubs: an ambience he could distil and take home. A public house to make people happy – with an outside area, a snug bar and real food. Chips would be optional or not at all.

He travelled further to Cornwall and the West Country. He stopped at Thames-side hostelries and watched, from sunny balconies, traversing barges on the Norfolk Broads. He took notes of the places he visited – bar and food prices, calculating cost and mark-up. He noted where pubs did well and what kind of pub had a regular clientele. He visited pubs that were popular with tourists but avoided by locals. He saw the good, the bad and the ugly. He was plodding, he knew it, but he instinctively distrusted instinct.

When his notebook was full and decisions had to be made

he revisited a nice pub just outside Glynde in Sussex, only to have some utterly stupid woman spill her drink down the front of his shirt. Fate, he supposed; for him, it had been love at first sight. Rosie, his rose, who had recently grown thorns. He sighed, remembering that she'd been exactly the same before her thirtieth birthday and would, no doubt, be equally impossible before her fiftieth and sixtieth.

'That's *much* better!' Mara had come outside for a cigarette, blowing out smoke in little puffs. Jack put down the chainsaw and wiped his hands down the sides of his trousers.

'What's much better?' he asked.

'Not having that tree, that's what. It brightens things up.' Jack sensed conspiracy between Mara and his wife. 'Not to mention leaves,' Mara went on, holding her cigarette daintily between thumb and forefinger. 'You won't have to sweep them up any more.'

Jack mopped at his forehead, realising that with the hazel tree gone the small garden was filled with sunlight. 'Well, maybe,' he conceded. 'Anyway, no more trees.'

Mara was still peering at the tree. Now she squatted down and, reaching out to the tree trunk, low down, prised something loose.

'That's odd,' she said. 'Jack, have a look at this. It's a nail.' She handed it to Jack who rubbed it clean and held it to the light.

'I'll be damned,' he replied and squatted to look closely at the hole in the tree trunk, which was weeping sap like a bullet wound. He again fingered the nail. It was a good four inches long. 'I never noticed it. You've better eyes than me.'

Mara's breath touched the back of his neck. 'Actually, it's not just a nail... it's a copper nail.' She nodded towards the tree trunk with a flick of her hair. 'This is what killed your tree. It's a copper nail, and copper kills trees.'

Jack was incredulous. 'You think someone did this deliberately?'

Mara puffed on her cigarette and shrugged. 'Stands to reason, I suppose. A daft prank, Jack... probably kids, stupid buggers.'

Jack frowned at the dismembered tree, turning the copper nail over in his hand. Then, with considerable force, he hurled it over the back wall into the open ground beyond, the shiny nail turning and tumbling, catching the sunlight like a falling star.

Mara indicated his untouched mug of tea. 'Do you want me to take that in for you?'

'It's *lapsang souchong*, apparently. For some reason, Rosie thinks that I like exotic teas.'

'I take it that you don't.'

'Definitely not. But please don't tell Rosie, OK?' He handed the mug to Mara. 'Actually, why don't you drink it? You look like a *lapsang souchong* sort of a person.'

Drive past the *Fox and Duck* heading towards Tranent, past the village green and cricket ground, and you cross the Tess over a new bridge, which replaced a narrow humpback bridge now reserved only for walkers or cyclists. Once over the bridge, turn sharp left towards the Tesco superstore which sits on the edge of the East Lothian Business Park, speculatively built in cubist steel and glass, and which is now home to a variety of small high-tech and design firms. The largest tenant, VirtualPlayCorp, designs computer games such as *Intergalactic Massacre* and *Ghoul Death Craze* for a worldwide children's market.

Once past the business park, petrol station and agricultural hire and garden centre, the road rises in long sweeps through trees to a disused quarry, the village's traditional and largest employer before its closure, for reasons that nobody is quite clear about. Abandoned machinery still litters the site, as if its owners might decide at any time to resume production, and there are giant concrete blocks at the roadside entrance to discourage fly-tipping. The road has a number of concealed entrances leading to quite grand houses. Past the quarry and the road dips once more to the wooded valley floor, along which Richie Scott now drove, blue light flashing. The road traffic accident had been reported by mobile phone to the emergency services and passed to him for routine investigation: no injuries, but tow trucks needed.

The road at this point runs beside the Tess as it tumbles down the valley, falling through a series of small gorges. The river runs faster here and waterfalls have cut rock pools much used by the village children in summer. Courting couples take picnics here and there is a small campsite managed by the National Trust for Scotland. The area has been designated as a Site of Special Scientific Interest, being an established breeding ground for a fast-disappearing species of toad. It is also something of an accident black spot as, unexpectedly, as you continue your drive from Holy Cross, the road suddenly narrows and recrosses the Tess over a humpback bridge almost identical to the one that has been bypassed in the village. Richie pulled slowly onto the verge between road and river, leaving his blue light flashing, and went to investigate.

A blue Mazda sports car was facing him on his side of the bridge, wafts of steam coming from a fractured radiator. The car was off the road but, apart from a long scrape down one side and a dented bonnet, didn't seem too badly damaged. The hood of the car was down and, incongruously, a Rod Stewart tape was playing. Richie reached in and turned it off, feeling broken glass under his feet, before resuming his preliminary survey of the scene, noting skid marks on the bridge roadway and fallen stones from a wall at the far end, dislodged by the other vehicle.

Across the bridge, facing away from him, an articulated tanker truck was also pulled onto the riverside verge, although it sat at a steeper angle towards the river. The tanker had clearly hit hard against the side of the bridge, dislodging stones in an avalanche to the river. The truck had cleared the bridge before leaving the road, tipping sideways on the far side, the cab now twisted at an unnatural angle to the body of the truck. The road, one of his main concerns, was still passable. The tank section of the truck was made of burnished aluminium and sunlight sparkled on its torn surface as the policeman made his way towards the two men who were sitting facing one another on either side of the bridge.

The younger driver – almost a boy – had lank hair to his shoulders and was wearing dark glasses. His arms were crossed and he looked sullenly in the direction of his truck. He was wearing a dark tartan shirt, blue jeans and white trainers. 'Morning, Richie. Officer,' he added quickly, feeling that some formality might be called for.

The other driver, older, fleshy, suited and tied with slicked-back brown hair, looked immediately suspicious at the use of the policeman's first name. 'Adrian Mountjoy,' he announced quickly in a plummy voice and produced a mobile phone from an inside pocket, which he waved at the policeman.

'I take it, sir, that it was you who reported the accident?'

The younger driver snorted with derision.

'It's an offence *not* to report an accident, officer,' said Mountjoy, producing a large handkerchief and wiping at his face in long sweeps. For a moment he looked pleased with himself, like a boy scout who now expects a badge. The policeman looked at the skid marks and made a note in his pocketbook. The river gushed and hissed; the tanker fizzed sunlight. 'Not that it was my fault, of course,' added Mountjoy, dabbing at his forehead and looking around at the surrounding woodland, a small frown on his face. 'I'm a careful driver, you see. I've got a certificate to prove it.' For a moment Richie thought that he was going to reach into another inside pocket and produce that too.

'Careful driver my arse,' said the other driver, whose name Richie now remembered was Duncan Hedges. He took off his dark glasses revealing flinty eyes and rubbed his nose. An estate car from Holy Cross squeezed past on the bridge, a small child in the back pointing excitedly at the flashing blue light.

'It was an accident,' said Mountjoy, looking at the policeman for support. 'It was nobody's fault.'

The younger man pointed accusingly. 'A complete arsehole, a wanker...' he ticked off accusations on the fingers of one hand '... *and* a Conservative!' he exclaimed triumphantly, slapping one hand on the bridge parapet. 'I knew I recognised you from somewhere. You were in the *East Lothian Courier* last week kissing babies.'

'I don't kiss babies,' replied Mountjoy, pursing his lips in evident distaste. 'You don't know who I am, do you, officer?' he asked in a voice that suggested that everyone should know who Adrian Mountjoy was. He drew himself up to his full height. 'I'm the Conservative parliamentary candidate for this constituency.'

'Told you, Richie, didn't I? Bloody Tory!' Hedges laughed humourlessly.

Mountjoy looked at his watch and sighed. 'Damn nuisance, all this,' he said, again looking round and biting his bottom lip. 'Damned odd, too.'

'That's exactly what the farmers hereabouts are going to say,' said Duncan Hedges, a small smile crossing his face for the first time, realising that the large cloud in which he found himself might at least have a small silver lining. 'Not that any of them will be voting for you now, of course. Bloody waste!' He saw the policeman's blank expression. 'Sorry, officer, didn't you notice?'

He led the way to the tipped tanker that still gleamed in the sunlight; on closer inspection, its polished surface was dented and scraped by the bridge wall. Both vehicles had reached the bridge at the same time and neither had stopped. The tanker had scraped along the side of the bridge on one side and against the Mazda sports car on the other before sliding off the road, its downward progress to the river impeded by a large outcrop of rock.

'Bloody hell!' said Richie, reaching for his radio. There were water extraction points on the Tyne downstream.

The impact had ruptured the tanker's underbelly in several places, and gloops of milk were draining into the Tess and swirling downstream in coffee-coloured streaks. Duncan Hedges lit a cigarette and shook his head, while Adrian Mountjoy twisted his handkerchief in both hands. 'Damned odd,' he repeated. 'I was distracted, you see. Oh God, this is going to sound *awfully* silly. A big, black cat, bold as brass, just sitting by the roadside.'

Mara Thomson was born in Edinburgh following an uncomplicated labour, two years and three months after her brother Terry. Her earliest memories were of their back garden in Edinburgh and of being happy there. It offered a haven, sanctuary even, in the heart of a city made for adults. Outside their front door was a world of cars and hurrying people; outside their back door was her world. It was a world that made sense, simply because it was safe. They lived then in a ground floor flat near the Meadows, an area of gracious and genteel tenement blocks, most with shared back gardens. Their garden, theirs and theirs alone, was small but filled to overflowing with flowers. There was a small grass strip, cut every Sunday by her father with a red Flymo, and which was framed on three sides by flowerbeds. Honeysuckle grew around their back door and attracted bees; once she was stung on the leg, but grimly refused to cry. Sunflowers grew against the back wall. 'Giant daisies', she called them, and would sit among them for hours.

It was a happy early childhood although she and Terry spent much of it bickering; sibling rivalry was intense in the Thomson household. She had pale ringlets and, even as a child, was rangy and lean. When she was seven, she fell from the back wall and broke her leg. When she returned home from the Sick Kids she immediately punched Terry on the nose, breaking it, and necessitating another tedious journey to the hospital. She was roundly rebuked, but didn't let on that it was Terry who had pushed her off the wall. From then on, he knew that little girls weren't made of sugar and spice.

It was her mother's fixed habit to knit or sew in the afternoon; Mara could chart the seasons from this mundane activity. In winter, she sat in the front room that looked out onto the street; in spring and autumn she sat just outside the back door on the small patio. She'd usually be wearing one of her own creations, often a cardigan, buttoned tight against the chill. In summer, she'd sit further down the garden on a small wooden bench. Mara would sit among the giant daisies and watch her mother. She thought that her mother was beautiful and serene until, one afternoon, she found her in the kitchen with tears coursing on her cheeks. Mara's favourite grandparents, her father's parents, had been killed in an aeroplane crash. Granny and Gramps. She didn't go to the funeral, but wondered all day what happened at funerals. She knew they were asleep and wouldn't wake up; but death and eternity seemed too permanent. Their deaths did, although Mara wasn't to know, provide them with a substantial inheritance.

Her father became notable for his absence rather than his presence. Tall and avuncular, he had longish hair – well, it was the fashion – and wore bright, patterned shirts. At weekends, he played golf wearing lurid trousers. Mara used to wonder why golfers wore such ridiculous clothes, or if it was a rule of the game. He would arrive home at odd hours and sweep her into his arms. He would bring her presents; her parents often argued. She would listen to them late at night, reciting nonsense to herself to overlay the noise from the front room. Even now, Mara can't remember his face with any clarity. Only his smile and bright shirts, and the smell of his aftershave as he gathered her into his arms.

They moved to Holy Cross when her father was appointed local bank manager. Although a relatively modest appointment, it carried with it a certain cachet: not only is Holy Cross extremely well-known, it was – and is – populated with some extremely wealthy individuals. People with connections who could make things happen. The promotion and inheritance allowed them the luxury of a large house with a driveway; it also gave her father the freedom to dabble in property. Back then, Edinburgh's residential sector was beginning to boom. 'There's cash in bricks and mortar,' he'd say, rubbing his hands together.

At first she missed her Edinburgh friends and, for a time, she was the outsider in Holy Cross primary school. The girls were suspicious and the boys teased her for her golden locks – until, one break-time, she broke another nose. After that, she became popular. She can still remember sitting in the head teacher's office under the exasperated gaze of her mother.

She wasn't musical but she was sporty. She could run and she could play football, beating the boys at their own games. Terry was her opposite; he was musical with two left feet. She enjoyed feeling the wind in her face; often she'd run home from school for the sheer thrill of it. She missed the sunflowers in her old house; she missed her mother's serenity. Her mother still sewed and knitted but something was missing; a spark had been extinguished. Mara became the recipient of expensive and unexpected presents that made her new friends jealous. 'It isn't your birthday, is it?' they would ask, as another highly prized plaything came her way. She supposed that things would carry on much the same but then, just after her eleventh birthday, her childhood ended. Even after all these years it still made her tearful. Tearful and resolute.

'You all right, lass?' asked Tam Cronin, parked as always at the bar with his distinctive pewter mug, packet of Marlboro Lights and red plastic lighter laid out in military fashion on the bar. Everything just so, just as always. There were only a couple of other customers, although it would doubtless be busy later.

She nodded, although her hands were trembling and spots of perspiration now gleamed on her forehead; unbidden thoughts cascading through the horizons of her memory. *Richie*, she said to herself, *what's happening to me?*

Rosie had taken particular care with the periwinkle, used as a folk remedy for hundreds of years to treat diabetes. The plant contains a mother lode of alkaloids – nearly seventy in total. Some lower blood sugar levels – thus easing the symptoms of diabetes – others lower blood pressure and arrest bleeding, whilst two more have anticancer properties. Periwinkle also induces the production of small quantities of nitric oxide.

In that respect, it acts in similar fashion to sildenafil citrate which you can obtain from your doctor. Nitric oxide, or nitrogen monoxide to give it its Sunday name, is a colourless gas formed by the combustion of nitrogen and oxygen – produced in large quantities by cars and manufacturing processes. It is the primary cause of smog and acid rain. The gas also serves as a source of energy for certain bacteria. In the human body, it acts as a chemical messenger with a wide range of functions, but principally for penile erection.

Mara and Richie's relationship had begun three months earlier at Max Smythe's birthday party in an up-market part of Edinburgh's New Town. Max knew people, or thought he did, and his parties were always lavish and well-attended.

She'd known Max from primary school, becoming friendly with him once his nose had healed. Not *friends* exactly, but friendly enough to go to his parties. Max's father, who was as rich as Croesus, had sent his son for state schooling for ideological reasons – the same primary and secondary schools that both Mara and her brother had also attended for completely practical reasons after their father had walked out, and much of their inherited wealth had disappeared in failed rent-to-buy schemes. Max had therefore always been distrusted; the rich kid masquerading in rags and who now made up for his earlier unpopularity by holding parties. Mara had not been particularly looking forward to it, but still felt obliged to go, although Max had fancied her right through school and, even now, years and years later, was still in hot pursuit.

Mara first saw Richie on the other side of the room. He seemed a little lost, and it took her a few moments to recognise him. Like her, he was away from his usual surroundings. He was wearing a red jersey, rather than his customary blue. Mara smiled across the room and with quiet invitation beckoned him over, then handed him a stack of CDs. She explained that she was the evening's DJ. 'Bloody Max,' she said, leaning close to his ear against the noise from the stereo. 'Look at this trash. Boyzone and Oasis...' She threw several CDs to the floor. 'I ask you!'

Richie merely smiled and tilted his head to one side.

'How come you got invited?' she asked.

'Oh, I'm just here to make sure that nobody enjoys themselves improperly. Actually,' he admitted, 'I know one of Max's flatmates. He invited me.'

It was clear that Max was not pleased, puffing and parading jealously around the corners of the room. Max was dressed in cream chinos and had draped a yellow pullover casually around his shoulders. A gold medallion glittered on his chest.

Mara impulsively touched Richie's cheek with the back of her hand.

His face had tingled with the touch – he told her later – and her fingers felt cool against his cheek. 'It's a pity you're a copper,' she said.

'Police officer,' he corrected. 'Pig, if you prefer. I'm Richard Scott. Most people call me Richie.' He stuck out his hand to take hers, bracelets rattling on her wrist.

'I know who you are, pig. All the girls in the village know who you are.' She sipped at her glass of tepid white wine, remembering walking back from the newsagents, reading the front page of the *Daily Express*. She had first heard the crackle of his radio and turned and then, in a moment of pure clarity, seen a young Robert de Niro in a police uniform.

'Strangely enough,' he said, now leaning close to her ear, 'I know who you are as well.'

'I'm not under suspicion, am I?' She pouted, her mouth a delicate oval, taunting him again.

He shook his head, a lock of hair hanging over one eye. 'I've just seen you around, that's all.'

This time it was Mara who felt flattered and, unusually for her, temporarily at a loss of words. 'I suppose,' she said at length, 'I could change the CD and put on something we could dance to?'

'I can't dance,' he admitted. 'All I can do is prance around and look stupid.'

'OK, something slow. Then all you've got to do is shuffle about and look stupid.' She had never flirted with a policeman before – or spoken to one, except to ask directions, come to think of it. A combination of wine and novelty had made her light-headed.

Mara pretended not to notice as Max edged round his party, throwing quick dark glances at them both, his eyes sliding between them with gathering disappointment. His gold medallion glittered on his chest, like a knife in his heart.

Later still, emboldened by Max's punch, they tried less smoochy dancing. Richie had little sense of rhythm. He waved his arms and stamped his feet, then gave up.

'I told you I can't dance,' he said.

'Richie, I do now believe you.'

He led her to a corner of the room where she lit a cigarette, immediately noticing his disapproval. *Oh shit*, she thought, *a fag fascist*.

'I may not be able to dance, but I can do other things,' he said.

'Like what?'

'Like eat, or go to the cinema.'

She smiled. 'That's nice for you. Actually, I eat too. Most people do, Richie. You'll find that eating is quite a common pastime.'

'A simple pastime,' he said, brushing a fallen lock of hair from his eye. She felt a frisson of pleasure at the gesture, 'although much better for the sharing.'

She thought for a moment, her head to one side. 'Is that some strange policeman way of asking me out?'

He laughed a little anxiously. Again, a small tingle down her spine.

'It might be,' he replied.

'Why *only* might?' She looked at him closely; someone with his looks surely didn't expect rejection.

'It depends on your answer.'

'I see.' She sipped from her glass. 'Then my answer might be "yes".'

'Might?'

She laughed, giving up on being hard to get. 'Yes, Richie Scott. Yes, OK?'

But she wasn't yet ready for what he was really proposing. That was forbidden territory, beyond the reach of reason or desire. Everything was mapped out. Except for a tingle of pleasure when a lock of hair fell over his eye, and a scintilla of doubt behind her own eyes.

'Yes,' she said again, more decisively, and wondered if she was being unwise. *I don't want to hurt you*, she thought, *but I probably will*.

Mara thought now about his slightly lopsided smile, the way his hair was never properly combed, and how his eyebrows furrowed together when he concentrated. Such was the clarity of his image in her mind that he could have been

54

standing in front of her. But she was also saddened; she had other plans – to travel the world, maybe work abroad. She wasn't ready for a white knight. You're too soon, she wanted to say. I have a thesis to finish, a world to see.

Her reverie was broken by Tam Cronin who was tapping his empty tankard on the bar. 'Are you sure you're all right, lass?' It was a question he'd asked her several times, seeing her pallor and shaking hands.

'Sorry, Tam, I was miles away,' she said, hurrying to the end of the bar to answer the telephone. She returned moments later, frowning, a scrap of paper bundled in her trembling hand. She placed the piece of paper beside the till and shook her head, crystal images of the young policeman burning brightly in her mind. Unfortunately, she had drunk most of Rosie's exotic tea.

The simple firefly *is* actually a beetle, Rosie was right. There are more than two thousand species of firefly and each has a unique flash pattern. Until recently this was something of a mystery. Then it was found that cells that line the bug's airway produce nitric oxide that causes an adjacent cell structure, called the mitochondrion, to briefly shut down. This releases a pulse of oxygen which triggers another enzyme to turn on the light. When the burst of nitric oxide dries up, the mitochondrion gets busy and consumes the oxygen, turning the light off. All this happens in milliseconds. Drugs such as Viagra, whose active ingredient is sildenafil citrate, are intended to achieve what the firefly does several times a second.

'A nail?'

Rosie sipped on a glass of lemonade and sat heavily at one of the beer garden tables. She felt distinctly uneasy: the old minister's reported sighting and now this; a black box in her mind had momentarily flipped open and dark shapes were beginning to emerge. She swallowed the lemonade, forcing the lid shut, the dark puppets encased again. Jack had finished stacking the logs and was now sweeping dead leaves from the flagstones into a heap by the back wall.

He stopped and leaned on the brush. 'A copper nail, apparently, according to Mara.' He showed her the weeping wound, fingering its jagged edge. 'I threw it over the back wall,' he added. Like any pub the *Fox and Duck* had its share of damage and vandalism. Graffiti in the toilets was the most common, or late-night theft of the hanging baskets that, in summer, adorned the front of the pub. 'Why would anyone want to do something like that?' he asked, almost to himself.

She shrugged. 'A strange sort of prank but, sod it, who cares. OK, maybe it does matter, maybe it doesn't.' Dark hair fell across her face, hiding her expression. Right at that moment she had other things to worry about, and a Rubicon to cross – alone and without a paddle. She'd been worrying about it all morning, amongst other things. 'Just tell me you haven't organised a surprise party, please, Jack.' He opened and closed his mouth, feeling unsure of himself. 'The one thing that I *don't* want is a surprise party.' She looked sharply at him.

'Look, I...'

'... It's just that I couldn't stand it. All those people swigging back our booze and telling me that I don't look a day over thirty. It would be too awful.' She grimaced at the thought. 'Something romantic, Jack – just the two of us. A nice treat, but without surprises or other people, OK?' She looked up at him again, framed against the sun. 'You do love me, don't you?'

He sat beside her, taking one of her hands in his. 'Forty isn't the end of the world, you know. People say that life begins at forty.'

'Only people who are over forty say crappy things like that – a kind of cheery prelude to false teeth and hearing aids. I mean, how *can* life be starting when your boobs are starting to sag? Anyway, there's something else.'

'Ah, something else.'

'The minister, Jack, remember last night? Well, I was curious so I spoke to Sadie Gallagher.' She turned to look at him directly, squinting against the sun. 'He was at the police station to report having seen a large black cat.'

Jack held his wife's hand and felt it tremble. He could hear children playing nearby: raucous laughter and the sound of a ball being kicked. 'It's just silliness,' he said after a few moments. 'You know that as well as I do. Coincidence and claptrap.'

But silly about what? About the dreaded four-oh? She knew she was being daft about that – biological clock malfunction – but significant birthdays had always had that effect on her; she also hated the bonhomie that went along with popping corks. She preferred quiet celebrations with good friends who could be relied upon to say the right things, or not say anything at all. She thought again about grey hair, approaching incontinence, and all of life's other small cruelties.

'Jack, you do know what they say about hazel trees, don't you?'

'Hazelnuts!' he replied loudly.

'Jack…'

'Hazelnuts to all of it!' His wife's angst was beyond him. 'I simply don't want to know, Rosie.'

She examined the tree trunk again, this time wiping away earth and grime, hoping that Jack was right. There really was nothing to fret about: the black cat was just irrelevant coincidence, even if it had ever meant anything at all. If someone had vandalised the tree then it must have been done weeks ago; the cat and the tree couldn't be connected… except for one thing. She now noticed something that both Jack and Mara had missed, carved into the base of the tree trunk. It was only a few faint cuts in the wood. Hardly noticeable, unless you looked hard. XIII. Five scratches, obviously done in haste.

Rosie McLeod knew things and now sat quietly considering possibilities, her fortieth year almost upon her, its talons in her back.

Chapter 5

The herb of the planet Jupiter, and is named Acharonis, *of certain* Jusquaiamus, *Henbane. The root of it, put upon botches, healeth them, and keepeth the place from an inflammation of blood. And if the juice of it be drunken with honey, or with wine and honey sodden together, it is profitable against the griefs of the liver. Likewise, it is profitable to them that would do often the act of generation; and to them that desire to be loved of women, it is good that they bear it with them, for it maketh the bearers pleasant and delectable.*

The Book of Secrets of Albertus Magnus

For the second time that day, Richie drove his police Land Rover out to the scene of the accident, this time armed with a twelve-inch ruler and camera. Both vehicles had, by now, been removed from the crash site, the "POLICE ACCIDENT" signs taken down. The sports car had been put onto the back of a flatbed and taken to a dealership in North Berwick, the milk truck to a specialised repair depot in

Edinburgh. He parked on the grass verge and slowly walked across the bridge checking for broken glass. Both drivers had made statements and a report would now be made to the Procurator Fiscal. The most visible sign of the accident was skid marks on the bridge carriageway and gouge marks on the far verge as the truck had left the road, tipped over and hit the outcrop of rock. Richie walked back across the bridge to the Land Rover, pulled on wellington boots and retrieved his camera from the back seat. The policeman was once again on the trail, unwilling to *file on district* until all avenues had been explored.

Downstream, the river had almost completely regained its true colour with only a thin grey scum at the water margins. Upstream, the Tess tumbled over a small waterfall, a haze of insects swirling over the pool below. Pine and oak trees crowded in and a willow dipped its branches in the water. A kingfisher, light and insubstantial as a butterfly, darted on the surface. Richie slithered down to the water's edge, the river loud in his ears. Mud oozed over his ankles and sucked hungrily at his boots.

He walked upstream, the river broadening, long grass breaking like surf against his legs, a blackbird calling in alarm. The river hissed over another smaller waterfall in a kaleidoscope of shifting light. He climbed around it, one hand on his camera. Mountjoy had said that he'd caught a fleeting glimpse of the creature sitting at the edge of the bridge on his left side. He'd been distracted, understandably, and against the glare of sunshine had not seen, until too late, the milk truck approaching from the other direction. The young truck driver had not seen the animal, insisting volubly that you couldn't possibly take the word of a Conservative. A quick look around that morning had revealed nothing; now in boots he was able to make his way further up the muddy margin of the river. If the creature existed, it would have gone in this direction, away from the bridge, but alongside the river.

It didn't take him long to find what he was looking for, less than twenty yards upstream from the bridge at a point where deep undergrowth tumbled down almost to the water's edge. He looked closely at the paw-print, deep and precisely defined in the soft earth. But what was it? He didn't know. It could belong to a large dog or fox: he was no expert. Or cat? He looked closely; if so, this was no ordinary moggie. He unslung his camera, placed the ruler beside the print, and took photographs from a number of angles. As he worked, clouds momentarily closed over the sun and dark shadows danced between the trees.

Mara brushed a hand over her forehead; it felt hot to the touch. The tremor in her hands was worsening and she now felt distinctly queasy. She went to the loo and splashed water on her face and felt a little better. She scrutinised her face in the mirror. Her eyes were her best feature, clear and blue, set in an oval face, full lips: and all framed by a golden mane. Richie had said that her eyes were like deep rock pools; an odd compliment, but gratefully accepted. She smiled at the sudden thought of him. She pictured his face turning towards her the last time they had been out together, sharing a meal in *Romero's*, the Italian bistro in Haddington. She cared for Richie, but she treasured freedom: she didn't need love; as with all her romantic relationships, Richie had become more a brother than a lover. That was how, with some regrets, she wanted it: without intimacy, their parting would be easier, for both of them.

Romero's had been full; it always was on a Saturday night. He had eaten underdone calamari – complaining that one almost made it off his plate; she had pasta with vegetables. They talked about one day going to Italy, but without enthusiasm. By now, Richie knew it would never happen. She told him that her mother was drinking too much, how her history thesis was coming on and how her flatmate Skye was going to do a sponsored parachute jump when she got back from a holiday in France. Skye's younger sister was called Iona; they had an older brother, Stirling. Their parents had eventually confessed it was where they'd each been conceived. Mara thought it quite a nice way of naming babies, like Red Indian mysticism, but would probably have ended up, knowing her father, being called Bus Shelter or Back Seat of Fiat Uno. She didn't tell Richie this.

'Crazy cow,' said Mara, 'she's scared of heights. Bet she doesn't do it.'

They held hands under the table, her dress so low that when she leaned over the table he could almost see the Promised Land. Except that there was no promised land on offer. He'd tried to move the relationship along, she had only offered platitudes.

'It's me, not you,' she told him. 'I'm just not good at

62

relationships. Richie, *please*, it's not that I don't like you. It's maybe that I need more time.' It was a half-truth, neatly executed, throwing him off the scent. The fact was that she was frightened of relationships. Her strength came from within; she cherished that strength – it gave her balance. She didn't want to lose that steel core; without it she would be a blind woman without a stick, at the mercy of all men and of her own desires. *I don't want to be hurt, like my mother was hurt. I don't want to end up like her, trapped in a crumbling house in a regretted past.*

That's when he'd complimented her on her rock pools. If he was disappointed by her words, he didn't show it. He'd smiled, almost sadly.

She looked again at her eyes in the *Fox and Duck* staff loo – blue with white flecks, her expression steady. *Perhaps he is the one*, she thought, applying lipstick. Perhaps I *can* loosen up a bit, perhaps the world *can* wait. But, no, she told herself firmly. *He has arrived too soon. I do not want to grow old and be bitter. I am too strong for that; I can cope.*

She walked back to the bar and stared stupidly at the handwritten note she'd made earlier, trying to remember who had phoned, and why. It was her handwriting, but written in almost illegible squiggles.

'Oi!'

'Oops, sorry. Same again?' she asked, woken from her reverie to attend to a longhaired youth with dark glasses at the end of the bar. She poured him another large whisky and watched as he drank it back quickly and ordered another.

A memory kept returning, over and over, like a video

loop. It was of her mother fluttering on the front lawn. There were no giant daisies in their Holy Cross garden. A car was skidding, Mara had her fingers pressed to her upstairs bedroom window. It was all so long ago, but still so real and, if she was honest, it was this that frightened her.

Her mind fast-forwarded to Richie kissing her goodnight after *Romero's*, the smell of him, the press of his lips against her mouth, the lock of hair that fell over one eye when he tilted his head.

'What do you want from life?' he'd asked, meaning *from me*. Ah, she'd thought, it always came down to this. The admission of the impossible, followed by stoic acceptance.

'To finish my thesis, take a year off, travel the world, and maybe get a teaching job at the university.'

'You have it all so worked out.' He sounded disappointed. 'Like a computer program or something. Sometimes, you know, life happens in between the bits you plan.'

But tell him what? Tell him again that she had a PhD to complete, a world to explore. Whatever else she wanted could wait. Another image of the skidding car, a child's fingers pressed to the glass, a woman's grief. I am strong, she told herself: I don't want to be hurt, like she was. She again blinked rapidly, feeling dizzy, as a whole range of emotions washed through her.

Get a grip, she told herself, reaching for an optic with a trembling hand.

'There we are, another large whisky,' she said in hoarse whisper, setting another glass in front of the longhaired

64

youth. To cover her embarrassment, she coughed then gave a little laugh and was disconcerted when it emerged instead as a crone's cackle. The longhaired youth seemed not to notice. Having been in a road accident with a bloody Tory and lost his job, he was quite determined to get horribly drunk.

Lionel Kennedy was a rational man with a detached sense of right and wrong that made it reasonable for him to suppose that if the kingdom of God could be systemised in a *Summa Theologiae,* the kingdom of the Devil would also have its *Summa Daemonologiae*. To deny the existence of the Devil was to deny the existence of God, it was that simple. He understood perfectly that in some respects he was more Catholic than Church of Scotland but belief, to Lionel, didn't need boundaries: it simply needed certainties, right or wrong.

He lived across from his church in a sandstone manse that soaked up the sun in summer and froze the pipes solid in winter. It looked out over neat flower beds and, beyond them, to a row of cottages outside which small children played relentlessly and young mothers hung out washing. The spire of his church rose above the rooftops as a reminder of his faith.

Mrs Gallagher had finished the washing and the ironing, chattering to him all the while. She did not ask him what was wrong, and did not expect to be told; she had been his housekeeper for far too long to share more of him than his dirty laundry. Probably that nasty wee fright he got last night, poor thing. At least, that's what she'd told Rosemary

McLeod in the village earlier.

The phone rang.

It was the young police sergeant phoning to confirm that a second sighting had been made of the black cat, this time on the back road past the supermarket, several miles closer to the village.

'So what are you going to do?' asked the minister, feeling vindicated. It had not, after all, been his vision alone. That in itself was a relief.

'Keep an open mind,' Richie replied, 'at least for the time being. It could be an escaped animal, we simply don't know.'

Richie replaced the receiver, undid his tie, and stood by the back door with its view across his unkempt garden and waited for the kettle to boil. He'd emailed his photographs to Edinburgh Zoo, assiduously copied to Big Mac, and by morning the mystery might be solved. He sat at his small kitchen table facing the noticeboard by the fridge, with its reminders about milk and unpaid bills, and a laughing photograph of Mara Thomson. It had been taken two weeks before, on a day trip to Edinburgh, Mara sitting on a picnic rug on top of Arthur's Seat, the city spread out beneath her, a tapestry of houses, sea and history. She was laughing at some stupid joke he'd made, hair blowing from her face, her glacial beauty almost translucent. He touched the photograph, hearing the kettle start to shriek. He lifted the kettle from the gas ring with a dishcloth and poured hot water into a mug.

He often recalled the moment when he first saw her; a

newspaper held in both her hands: a vivid memory made perfect by the disappointment of what had happened since. Although they were close, they were also distant. He knew that commitment wasn't on Mara's agenda; and he knew that she would soon make good her escape: to roam the world, to settle somewhere else but here. Her plans involved single tickets, without the encumbrance of someone else's baggage. But he had already fallen for her and he didn't know what he would do when she finally said goodbye. He wanted to be with her, in every way, but that wasn't going to happen, not now anyway. So he treasured instead his crystal memory: the moment when his radio had crackled and he had fallen in love with a perfect stranger.

It was the habit of the East Lothian Conservative and Unionist Party to meet on the last Friday of each month in different hostelries around the constituency, partly to encourage a sense of Party spirit among the faithful and partly to encourage members to bring along guests and so spread the message of Conservatism. The forthcoming general election, less than a week to go, made such gatherings doubly important in the fight to win back the East Lothian constituency. Every six months or so, it was the turn of the *Fox and Duck*.

First to arrive was the large and florid Clare Derby, with a booming voice that brooked no dissent and who, when on the move, resembled a galleon in full sail, voluminous skirts billowing all around. She carried a clipboard and advanced purposefully on the function suite bar behind which Mara was stationed.

'You must be Mrs Derby,' said Mara. Jack's description left little room for doubt.

'Madam Chair, yes.' She placed the clipboard on the bar and drummed her fingers on it. Mara saw heavy rings on fat fingers; she appraised the diamonds and judged them to be real. 'You don't happen to know if our parliamentary candidate has arrived, do you?' She looked at Mara closely for the first time, quickly deciding that she didn't look like a Conservative. 'You *do* know who he is, I take it?'

'Mr Mountjoy might be a bit late,' Mara informed Madam Chair in a husky voice, having now remembered details of the earlier phone call, and her almost indecipherable handwritten note. Jack had only deputised her to work in the function suite with some reluctance, having kept a close eye on her during the afternoon, noting her pallor, the perspiration on her forehead, and the way her voice seemed to have dropped an octave. If it hadn't been Friday, he'd have sent her home. Jack, of course, could only see the outward symptoms of inner turmoil; inside her head, like a badly wired telephone exchange, neurons were randomly spinning.

Madam Chair looked momentarily nonplussed by this abrupt announcement. 'Mr Mountjoy late, you say? I did so want to have a quiet chat with him before the others arrived.' She drummed her fingers more forcibly on the clipboard.

'He's had a bit of an accident.' During the afternoon Mara had also been speaking to Duncan Hedges, now unemployed, who was still drinking large whiskies in the public bar, and becoming voluble about politicians in sports cars. At least, she *thought* she remembered speaking to Duncan; it had become hard to distil reality from the other turmoil in her mind. But at least she'd remembered the phone call and the squiggled message.

'An accident?'

'A car accident,' said Mara, in her new-found deep voice.

'Good grief!' said Clare Derby whose secret fear was of unexpectedly having to make a speech in place of a wayward guest speaker. Her hands flapped in sudden panic. 'I do hope that it's not…'

'… Serious?' interrupted Mara, fixing her with an unblinking gaze. 'Dunno, I'm afraid. Crashed into a milk lorry,' she added huskily. She now felt curiously alive; each noise seemed magnified but separate: she could clearly hear Madam Chair greet a new guest, a burst of laughter in the public bar. Then she was overcome by a sudden thirst and retreated to the kitchen for a glass of water.

In the kitchen. Sammy, the head chef – on weekdays, the only chef – was stirring pots and slicing a salmon in a blur of activity. Jack looked up from emptying bottles into a cardboard box and scrutinised Mara closely. She was still looking pale and flushed, her eyes red-rimmed. Perspiration shone on her forehead. 'You OK?' he asked.

She nodded slowly, but uncertainly, her eyes hooded. The bright lights in the kitchen were hurting them; she put a hand to her face. It was like a roller coaster: one minute she felt fine, the next terrible, while in the background, like a TV she couldn't switch off, were sequences of images dimly seen, as if through gauze. It was as if someone else had taken her remote control buttons: her thoughts came unbidden. She had tried to turn them off, or to change channels, but she couldn't; she ached with unexpected and unwanted desire.

'What about a bite to eat?' suggested Sammy, looking up from his salmon.

'There's some cold chicken,' said Jack, opening a fridge door and poking about.

'She's a veggie,' replied Sammy. 'Only eats things that can't run away. Isn't that right, pumpkin?' This was news to Jack who pushed the plate of chicken to the back of the fridge and closed the door.

'Maybe just a cuppa,' said Mara, advancing into the kitchen to find her half-filled mug from the morning still on the worktop where she'd left it. The exotic tea that Jack hadn't wanted and which had tasted musty and enigmatic. She popped it in the microwave for a few seconds and then drank greedily, surprised by her thirst, dregs and all. But when she again thought of Richie a small chemical imbalance in her brain had, unbidden, stripped off romantic detachment. To her genuine horror, Mara was presented in her mind's eye with an image of Richard Walter Scott standing bollock-naked, his erect penis as long and hard as one of *Romero's* pepper grinders.

Chapter 6

The herb is named of the Chaldees Lorumboror, of the
Greeks Allamor, of Englishmen Wild Teasel. Take this
herb, and temper it with the juice of Mandrake, every
one that shall drink thereof shall begin anon battle.
And when thou would put it away give to him the juice
of Valerian and peace shall be anon among them, as
before.

The Book of Secrets of Albertus Magnus

Rosie always had plenty of garlic in her scullery; yohimbe
she ordered from a specialist website. Both plants help to
balance natural amino acids – particularly histidine, the
building block for histamines. Histamines are chemicals
responsible for a number of functions, including both male
and female orgasm. Doctors typically prescribe anti-
histamines for inflammations and allergies without advising
that this might have some effect on orgasm.

Men who suffer from premature ejaculation tend to have
high levels of histamine. Women who achieve orgasm easily
or who experience multiple orgasms also have high levels of
histamine. Simply, men who suffer from premature

ejaculation make ideal bed-mates for women with hay fever.

She had been in a fragile mood for much of the day; quiet and thinking about other things, as well she might. The news of the black cat had unsettled her, raking up dark ashes, as had the markings on the tree. A copper nail wasn't the most effective way to kill a tree unless, of course, you wanted it to happen slowly. That was the worst part of it: that it seemed so senseless. She'd been out to examine the back wall again. It was over nine feet high and made of good solid brick. It would have taken both cunning and luck not to get caught. Most likely, whoever did it would have had to carry a ladder down the riverside, cut in across waste ground that lay behind the pub, set up the ladder, climb over – and then repeat the process in reverse. Somebody had gone to a great deal of trouble and risk to hammer home a copper nail and leave their five-incision mark. It was senseless, unless it was personal – a message for her, and for her alone. After all, nobody but *bloody* her would know what the markings on the tree meant.

The XIII was the nub of the conundrum. King Charlemagne and his twelve Paladins; the Danish Hrolf and his twelve Berserks; Romulus and the twelve Lictors of Rome, Jesus and the twelve Apostles, King Arthur and his twelve Knights of the Round Table – Galahad, Bedivere, Lamorak, Gareth, Gawaine, Kay, Geraint, Percival, Tristan, Gaheris, Bors and Lancelot. The thirteen months of the lunar calendar, the number of witches in a coven. The symbol carved onto the tree was a message for her alone, she was sure of it. But what on earth for?

What she did know was that witches had once used the mark as a symbol of recognition, back in the days when being a witch wasn't a healthy career choice. Specifically, it was mark used in Sussex, where she'd grown up, and why she'd known about it. If she'd come from Wiltshire, Oxfordshire or the moon, it would have meant nothing. They'd learned about the symbol at school, from Mrs Beecham who taught history. Mrs Beecham wore black, had unruly grey hair and wild eyes. Rosie and the rest of her class were convinced that she actually was a witch, on the lookout for recruits. Most of the children, including Rosie, kept well clear of Mrs Beecham.

Rosie, of course, was no witch. Her only vanity was to understand the changing seasons and to blend the properties of plants and herbs to her own desires. It was an instinct, beyond her mother's teaching: a gift of healing, not of magic, despite what some people laughingly said in the village. As far as she knew, there was no malice in their gossip; Rosie was almost a local institution, also being joint proprietor of the most popular pub in the area. Whatever was said behind her back – and sometimes to her face – was always said smilingly or tongue-in-cheek: she neither owned a black cat nor a broomstick, unless you counted the Hoover in the under stairs cupboard. She knew, however, that the village had always had a certain reputation, although she'd seen no direct evidence.

Except for the black cat, she told herself, remembering the grisly tales they were laughingly told when they first arrived, although nobody quite knew what had happened, if

73

anything. It was a story without context or ending; a story told to make the village seem more interesting than it actually was. Take away the Holy Grail claptrap, and Holy Cross could be any insignificant village: prosperous and pretty, law-abiding and unassuming – a place, in short, where nothing ever happens.

Most of the tonics she made were crafted from plants and herbs of humble origin; she knew that a few drops of borage in a glass of mead, flavoured also with sweet briar, cloves and mace, would chase away the worst depression, or that an aromatic tea of mistletoe, scullcap and valerian would cure a raging headache. When Jack went off to berate the brewery for a late order she once added quarrelsome catmint to his coffee and, in the evening, a pinch of calming sage, cowslip and valerian. When Jack gave up cigarettes she made it easy for him with crafty snakeweed. She understood the properties each herb or plant possessed and how their properties could be blended or distilled to produce whatever was required. It was an innocent gift. She gave her tonics to friends and relatives, her distillations made from nature itself, using the countryside to cure the illnesses it produced, always recognising the limits of her efficacy.

Some plants she generally steered clear of. Like belladonna, used by 16th century Italian women to dilate their pupils – and hence the plant's name. Belladonna's alkaloids are anticholinergic; they work by blocking nerve impulses involved in the parasympathetic nervous system. It was used to kill the troops of Marcus Antonius during the Parthian wars. Closer to home, Macbeth used belladonna to render

74

insensible an army of invading Danes. Or mandrake, used from the days of Pliny as an anaesthetic. The plant's powerful alkaloid, mandragorine, was the sleeping potion of tragic Juliet. Rosie was no wacko weirdo; she didn't do poison, not really.

By the time she was seventeen, her mother had nothing more to teach her, so she encouraged her only daughter to seek proper training.

She applied, and was accepted, for a BSc (Hons) course in Herbal Medicine at the University of Westminster. The course was accredited by the Board of the National Institute of Medical Herbalists and the British Herbal Medical Association. She packed her bags and headed for London. The bright lights bemused her; she was unused to the crush of humanity all about, the din of traffic all day and night. The city oppressed her; robbed her of her individuality. She flitted from shared flat to shared flat, never quite settling or making close friends. Whenever she could, which was often, she fled home to Sussex.

She did badly in her first year, struggling with pathology and physiology. She argued with her tutors. She disputed pharmacological facts; she had other theories that made them blanch. She strayed often from proven efficacy to mere conjecture, finding new combinations of plants and herbs that, she felt, might achieve better objectives. She railed against the boundaries of her knowledge.

At the end of her first year, she had an uncomfortable meeting with her course tutor, a thin and reedy man called Dr McIntyre. He tried to be positive. 'Of course, you have a natural talent,' he told her, 'but instinct has no place in the syllabus. We have advanced our science in stages, we are slowly gaining acceptance from the medical establishment. We are moving from the fringes to the mainstream. We have to accept responsibility.'

It was a word that her mother often used, making it sound like an icon of faith. *Responsibility*. Such a long word for just doing the right thing. Or the ability to respond in the right way – perhaps that was closer. She sighed and told McIntyre that she would change her attitude.

She found it difficult, of course, to reign in her instincts and stick to the scientific. It seemed to her to be a course without potential, over-cautious and mundane. She persevered, although, in her third year, went off the rails for a while. She discovered the pleasures of cider and enjoyed, if that was the word, a string of ill-fated romances. Her work suffered and she was again summoned to the dimly lit office of Clifford McIntyre. This time he was more understanding; her work was relatively on-track – although she did have problems with the social context of her studies. Rosie didn't know what he was talking about, and didn't ask. He appraised her and said that there was nothing to stop her finishing the course, not now that she had learned responsibility.

Ah, that word again. But, curiously, she supposed that she had. It no longer bothered her that so many herbal remedies were made from only one plant, or that the dosages were often ridiculously low. If compliance was all that was required, then she would complete her degree. She knuckled

76

down and accepted the boundaries of her trade, learning the British herbal pharmacopeia almost by heart. She excelled in biology and ancillary biochemistry. She passed with flying colours, the dux of her class.

To celebrate, she got blind drunk with some other students and slept till midday in her small flat in a deeply unfashionable part of Notting Hill. Her flatmates were all out, there was no milk in the fridge and the cat had been sick on the kitchen floor. The flat felt unkempt and unclean; the air outside was warm and tempting. She phoned her mother and, later that day, caught the train to Lewes. Her mother kissed her daughter's cheek and said how proud she was.

'You're now qualified!' said her mother, gripping Rosie's arm. 'Not like me. You've got a certificate!'

Yes, she did and she pinned it to the wall beside her bed. It had swirly writing and a large red seal. The words on the page were formal and embossed. It was a certificate designed to reassure its readers that she, Rosemary Torrance, knew what she was talking about when it came to the diagnosis and treatment of utterly insignificant ailments.

'I'm not sure what to do next, Mum,' she had said on the platform, the train already fussing from the station. 'I'm just not sure any more.'

The farmhouse felt oppressive the next day, the flapping certificate offering only limited promise or none at all. Did she want to go into practice, providing herbal remedies that she knew were of limited efficacy? She had supposed that was what her future held; now it seemed pointless after so many years of study. There again, she might well change her

77

mind. She often did, to the exasperation of friends and family.

Later, she went to the local pub to see if any of her old friends were there. They weren't but when she turned from the bar some idiot with a Scottish accent spilled beer down her cotton dress.

Now, a lifetime later, Rosie watched as he stocked shelves, checked inventories, and briefed the weekend staff. She looked for clues in his smile and eyes, but he seemed the selfsame Jack that he had been yesterday and the day before, even patting her absently on the bum as she bent over to stock a low shelf in the bar – as you might a small domestic pet. It was a gesture of affectionate habit, devoid of lustful intent. He only kissed her quickly on the cheek when she announced, with fading anticipation, that she was going shopping to Haddington. Her tonic should have been working, but it clearly wasn't.

Questions circled in her mind. The only certainty was that nobody really believed, surely, that she was a witch. The idea, of course, was preposterous.

Madam Chair had moved purposefully to the far wall, and laid her clipboard on the table, a sure sign that proceedings were about to begin. She now stood surveying the room like a sea captain, motioning the prospective candidate to stand beside her. He had indeed arrived late, having been back to Edinburgh to wash and change his suit, then taking an extortionate taxi to Holy Cross. But he'd arrived, much to Madam Chair's relief, fussing over him like a large protective hen.

Behind her, drawn curtains covered their view of the beer garden. Clare Derby had drawn them herself, to make sure that everyone's attention remained on the speaker and now, satisfied that everyone was now seated, she rapped her knuckles on the top table.

'Fellow Conservatives,' she intoned, making them a sect apart, 'and guests. The accent tonight is primarily social, so no long speeches from me, and no points of order from you.' She paused, a scattering of appreciative chuckles from the floor. '*Hear, hear*,' said somebody at the back. The audience was seated at round tables and were scraping their chairs to face Madam Chair and the dapper figure on her left side. 'We are on the brink of an election. An historic election. An election that will turn back the red tide and return East Lothian to the Conservative Party.' More applause, more *hear-hears* from the back of the room. 'One issue, however, has divided our great Party. The issue of Europe. Our candidate is pro-European and his topic for tonight is European integration.' Here she paused again and looked round the room. 'However,' she added to polite applause, 'Europe can also be a very nice place to go on holiday,' thereby consigning a millennium of European history to the level of a weekend mini-break.

Mountjoy placed his notes on the table and carefully put on half-moon spectacles. They were superfluous to requirement; he only needed glasses for long-distance tasks, but he had been advised by Central Office that they gave him a certain gravitas. He looked at his audience over the top of

79

his glasses, noting with approval that they all looked Conservative, and seemed to be drinking either tea or gin and tonic, except for a somewhat dishevelled man at the back who appeared half-asleep and drinking a pint of beer. Mountjoy chose to direct his words closer to the front of the room. 'Ladies and gentlemen, fellow members of our great Party,' he began, to a further scattering of *hear-hears*. 'First, let me say how honoured I am to be the parliamentary candidate for this constituency. The election is now almost upon us and, with your help, we will regain this constituency.' Mountjoy seemed sure of this, although every published opinion poll pointed firmly in the other direction. 'However, the really big issue for our Party, once we are elected, as we shall be, is our relationship with our European friends.'

He rocked on the balls of his feet for a moment. 'What we must do as a nation and as a Party' – waving spectacles – 'is recognise that Europe is a train waiting at the station. We can either get on that train, and influence where it goes, or remain on the platform and watch it leave.' A few more nods from the floor.

Mara, back behind the bar, wondered in a brief lucid moment how you can possibly influence where a train goes.

It seemed that Mountjoy was getting into his stride and that the Conservative voters of East Lothian were in for a lengthy treat. Mara walked unsteadily back to the kitchen through the public bar. The youth with the lank hair was still seated in a corner behind a line of empty glasses.

'It wasn't even my fucking fault. Anyway,' he was saying

to another youth she didn't recognise, 'I need a pee.' He rose unsteadily from his stool, tottered across the room, and returned some minutes later from the toilet, which was located just past the function suite door. He was looking grim. In the course of the day he had been involved in a road accident, subsequently lost his job, and was now very drunk. He had also recognised the voice of tonight's guest speaker.

In the kitchen, all was fuss and bustle. Vegetables boiled, a row of small salad bowls were lined up across one work surface, plated smoked salmon across another. The kitchen was filled with steam and a small rivulet of sweat coursed down Sammy's face. 'No, over there. The stock is kept over there,' he was saying loudly to one of the kitchen staff, a spotty youth called Dave, who smiled at Mara. 'You still look terrible,' Sammy said in a matter-of-fact voice, too busy for sympathy.

'I *feel* terrible,' she agreed hoarsely, opening the back door and seating herself in the empty beer garden, but close enough to the function suite to hear Adrian Mountjoy's speech, and therefore to know when he stopped speaking, at which point her duties would resume. 'Europe represents a challenge to us all,' she could hear through an open window. 'A challenge to think in new ways. A challenge to reach out and sell to new markets. A challenge to make British goods the best there is, because only the best will do in the new Europe.' She imagined him rapping his knuckles and waving his glasses, being cooled by the evening air. She kicked off her shoes, the flagstones cold on her feet. She lit a cigarette, dragging the smoke down deep and exhaled in a long plume. She looked up, seeing a scattering of clouds; behind the back wall children were playing on the waste ground by the river. She heard laughter, the sound of small running feet. Behind her, the kitchen extractor fan hummed.

Mountjoy's voice dimmed, thankfully, as she smoked. She continued to look upward, watching the clouds, an airliner high above leaving a vapour trail. She wondered where it was headed and who might be on it. Businessmen and film stars, sipping drinks from the trolley, settling down to watch a film. Soon she would also be on an aeroplane, her thesis written, the world at her feet. She would travel, perhaps never come back; cut herself free. At this, her mind lurched again; she felt that she too was about to watch a film. It seemed that she was seated in an auditorium and that unseen actors were about to enact a play for her benefit alone. She blinked, feeling scared, now seeing figures behind a gauze screen. They were holding hands in a circle, but they were also looking at her; the ones at the front of the circle nearest her had their heads turned in her direction. They were calling softly to her. Mara felt simultaneously hot and cold, her jangled mind making wrong connections. *Please stop*, she wanted to say to the figures behind the screen. And then, suddenly, she seemed to be flying, able to look down and see herself seated in the beer garden looking up.

Her hands trembled, she stubbed out her cigarette; she made to rise. From behind the screen came a cry of such pure pleasure – beautiful, intense and serene – that it provoked an aching desire from deep within her own body; she looked up to see the curtain parting silently and felt herself drawn up and through the aperture to the waiting figures on the other side. She smiled in warm anticipation, hearing again a cry of pure rapture, and knowing that it had emerged from her lips.

'My grandfather fought for this country in the war. His brother was killed in the war. I know what sacrifices have been made in the name of Europe. My dream is that we now put the past behind us and build a new Europe where such evil can never, *ever* happen again. Some of you experienced that war,' said Adrian Mountjoy and looked around the room, spectacles perched at the end of his nose, noting a few very elderly members, several with their eyes closed.

'What about Bosnia?' asked a voice from the back of the room.

Mountjoy, taken aback by the unexpected intrusion, located the speaker as a middle-aged man with glasses and an unshaven face. 'What about Bosnia?' Mountjoy asked, mentally trying – and failing – to place Bosnia on a map.

'It's just that Kenny here was a soldier, and he was in Bosnia. That's in Europe, isn't it?'

'And Iraq,' added another voice, presumably Kenny, a short red-faced man in a blue sweater. 'A few sacrifices were made there and all. Here, Mike,' Kenny continued, craning his neck, 'you were in Afghanistan, weren't you?'

A third voice joined in. 'Parachute Regiment. I was shot, you know,' he added, turning a watery gaze on the now bewildered parliamentary candidate. This last speaker, a pleasant-looking man with fair hair, had a livid scar on his cheek that he now touched self-consciously. The woman sitting to his right – Mountjoy supposed that it was his wife, one of the twinset brigade – said in a loud voice: 'You can't just talk about sacrifice in terms of the Second World War, you know. My husband got shot in the head, and that's a pretty serious place to be shot. They gave him a medal,' she added helpfully.

Adrian Mountjoy took off his glasses and looked at his notes.

The point he was making about a new Europe emerging from the ruins of war, and how it was their responsibility to build security from blood and ashes, seemed to have been lost. While Adrian Mountjoy debated what he was going to say next, the East Lothian Conservatives all distinctly heard a low and pleasurable moan, although it was not immediately clear from where the sound emanated.

Chapter 7

The herb of the planet Venus, and is called Peristerion, *of some* Hierobotane, id est Herba columbaria, *and* Verbena, *Vervain. The roots of this herb put upon the neck healeth the swine pox, impostumes behind the ears, and botches of the neck, and such as can not keep their water. It healeth also cuts, and swelling of the tewel, or fundament, proceeding of an inflammation which growth in the fundament; and the haemorroids. It is also of great strength in venereal pastimes, that is, the act of generation.*

The Book of Secrets of Albertus Magnus

Mara floated, arms outstretched, over an unfamiliar tapestry of Highland countryside; below her were dark hills and flashing water. Stars in geometric patterns flamed around her. Just by extending her fingers she was able to fly where she chose, carried by warm thermals, the wind catching in her hair, cooling her. She imagined herself as a bird of prey, fingernails as red talons, swooping effortlessly towards a shimmering loch then banking towards the valley wall, a sinking sun bright in her eyes. A part of her watched fascinated from the other side of the dark screen; she soared and wheeled in exultation, carried by the breeze. She was laughing at the excitement of flight, like a dream of youth made real: careening over trees, soaring skywards, strange stars reflected in her eyes. The dreamscape below her was glens and lochs, heather hills and, at one point, a scattering of deer. The physical part of her, feet splayed inelegantly on the stone flagstones, heard once more the cry of pleasure – but this time it was bird-like: a cry of exultation in the fastness of the night sky. The freedom of flight was intoxicating; the rush of cool air on her cheek; every cell in her body seemed energised.

She pressed her eyes closed, feeling the thermals against her fingertips; she turned and wheeled. She traversed mountain ranges, skimming high peaks to soar again far from earth. At the furthest reach of her flight she saw the sea; it was flat and dark, an immensity of tensile stretching water. In it was reflected starlight. She turned one hand outward to turn and head back inland. The sea was featureless and cold; the land below offered contours and warm currents. She soared on eagle's wings; it seemed an eternity.

But then she was falling, the light again in her eyes, her arms becoming heavy. As she fell, she twisted and turned; she was falling towards a circle of light, towards a group of men and women carrying flaming torches that threw long, dark shadows. They saw her and pointed; they were laughing at her ungainly flight: she extended her fingers but her body had also become heavy. She fell into water and sank. The water closed over her but, strangely, she could still breathe. It was cold and silent under the water, but she wasn't afraid. She felt cleansed, alive. When she opened her eyes she saw dark shapes grouped on the surface. The water surface had become opaque; the same illusion of light as the gauze screen earlier. But this time she was at peace; the figures on the surface looked down at her with concern. They seemed to be mouthing something, their torches held high above their heads, but she couldn't hear. She felt serene in the water, she wanted to stay longer, but she knew the figures above were waiting for her.

She broke the surface and, without conscious effort, now stood on the shoreline. She had fallen into a loch, a light breeze ruffled its surface. Above the loch were mountains capped with snow. She was wearing a plain linen dress with a golden belt around her waist. She was barefoot, grass under her feet. The men and women were gathered in a circle around her. They were all young; they also wore white togas; they smiled at her. There seemed to be an equal number of men and women; some tall, others small, some dark, some fair. They looked at one another and then looked towards the lake, as if seeking permission from an unseen figure. Then, as one, they took hold of their torches with both hands and thrust them into the ground, stepping backwards and behind them so that all Mara could now see were flames. She turned slowly in the centre of the circle, feeling that something had been completed, that a journey had been made, as another figure entered the circle. He was naked, except for a golden mask in the shape of a ram's head. Golden horns extended upwards and back across his shoulders. She watched him approach, feeling more alive than she'd ever felt. The man in the mask could be anyone she wanted. He stopped before her, but said nothing. Beneath the mask, she knew he was smiling. She reached up with both hands to remove his mask, feeling his warmth close to her and experiencing, in a moment of pure perfection, the oblivion of complete desire.

Only a few yards from Mara Thomson, whose assaulted mind had now entirely logged off from reality, Adrian Mountjoy felt he had regained the full attention of the East Lothian Conservatives. 'We must learn all the lessons of the past,' he was saying over his glasses, 'in whatever part of the world they take place. Our task as Conservatives is to influence the progress of history, not to be bystanders, from Libya to Ireland, from Iraq to Afghanistan, from the Far East to the Americas.' Mountjoy had departed from his prepared text to include every unreliable regime and military black spot he could think of. His audience nodded in approval, Mountjoy clearly having their support for world domination. 'Many have made sacrifices,' he added, and might otherwise have again mentioned his grandfather's brother who had died of food poisoning whilst commanding an anti-aircraft battery in Liverpool.

But once again, pure and beautiful, came a low moan of such exquisite pleasure that even Madam Chair put a hand to her bosom.

'*Oh God, yes!*' came the voice, seemingly in rapt agreement with Mountjoy's new Europe, followed by a long

88

grunt of animal pleasure.

'We must put our Party's internal divisions behind us, to shape together the institutions of a more democratic Europe.'

'Yes, yes, yes!'

This time the voice became a yearning hiss, trailing off into silence. Several of the East Lothian Conservatives sniggered.

At that point Adrian Mountjoy quite forgot what he was talking about and realised that his audience now didn't much care. He looked down at Madam Chair who was looking about uneasily to determine the source of the interruption and what exactly it was. She knew what it *sounded* like, she had children to prove it, but this was different: this was pleasure on another scale – so undiluted and intense that some of the younger women in the audience were looking whimsically at their partners.

'Europe,' declared Adrian Mountjoy, departing again from his notes to bring his speech to a speedy conclusion, 'is our future. It is our destiny. It is up to us to paint the new signposts of co-operation. It is up to us to teach our children how to read them.' Speaking now off the cuff, the quality of Adrian Mountjoy's presentation was sinking fast. 'Your choice,' he said loudly, both hands outstretched. 'Our choice, one Party, walking together towards a shared future.'

'Oh God, yes!'

This time the voice was louder, but throaty, and seemed to be coming from the other side of the drawn curtains. Adrian Mountjoy stood at full height, his hands still outstretched to his voters; to instil in them his faith in a

Conservative future, when he was saved further speculation. The door of the function suite had been abruptly pushed open and a slurred voice now declared:

'Mountjoy, you are a complete fucking cretin.'

From outside came a series of affirmative grunts.

'And a wanker. Definitely a wanker,' declared Duncan Hedges, wagging a finger at the top table, seemingly assured of this last point.

'Yes, yes!'

He advanced unsteadily into the room and looked around him. Then he placed his hands on the back of a chair and stared balefully for a few moments at Adrian Mountjoy who was hopping with some agitation from one foot to the other. The East Lothian Conservatives shrank back, unwilling to involve themselves in what was, surely, a private matter between their parliamentary candidate and a member of the working class. Duncan Hedges removed his dark glasses, blinked several times and, after two attempts, located a pocket in his denim jacket in which to put them. Adrian Mountjoy quickly put his glasses on.

'As well as being an arsehole, actually,' said Duncan Hedges to an improbably long moan from the beer garden, advancing as purposefully as he could towards the top table behind which stood Adrian Mountjoy, Madam Chair sitting by his side. Before anyone could stop him, not that many were thinking of trying, Duncan Hedges swung wildly at the politician with his right fist. He was not normally a violent man but unexpected unemployment and too much whisky had removed whatever inhibitions he might otherwise have had in assaulting a Conservative parliamentary candidate. Entirely fortuitously – or through bad luck, take your choice – it was one of those glorious punches that seemed to hang suspended for a moment before completing a perfect parabola to its target in slow motion.

As he swung, chairs were scraped back, a couple of women screamed and Jack McLeod, alerted by the commotion, dashed from the public bar in time to see the punch connect with Mountjoy's chin with a dull thud. The politician toppled backwards with comic exaggeration, arms flailing, and fell against the window behind. As he crumpled to the floor, righteous indignation and a smear of blood on his face, he reached up, found contact with the curtains and pulled them off the rail. Adrian Mountjoy hit the floor and a moment later was entirely covered by falling curtains that, being of sturdy material, had hitherto offered a degree of soundproofing.

Mountjoy groaned loudly, a parody of the much louder and more exquisite moan that now came from the beer garden. Its intensity and growing urgency suggested that some climactic event would shortly occur. Jack knew immediately, as he headed at full tilt towards the kitchen, who the voice belonged to. Adrian Mountjoy, Duncan Hedges excepted, was in safe hands.

'Get the police,' he hissed to Sammy who was clattering pots and whistling, virtually invisible in a haze of steam. 'There's been a fight in the function suite.'

'I thought that Tories liked each other?'

'Just phone, Sammy!' Jack hurried past and into the beer

garden.

It took only seconds to locate Mara who was slumped on paving stones in a patch of deep shadow behind the kitchen. She was moaning softly, legs kicked out, her eyes unfocused and half-closed. A film of perspiration covered her face, and she was moving her head slowly from side to side. Jack was filled with instant panic.

'Mara!' he said to her ear. 'Wake up!' He shook her shoulders, but she shrugged away from him, pressing her eyes tightly shut. 'Can you hear me?' He was talking loudly, enunciating each word, shaking her shoulders again with more force. Christ, what was the matter with her! She shrunk away and tried to fend him off with one hand; she did not want reality to reclaim her just yet.

The torches were burning out, the circle of flames less bright; sparks were being drawn high into the night sky and over the smooth surface of the loch. On the other side of the water the ground rose in folds to a series of snow-topped peaks. Above was the canopy of stars, brighter than she had ever seen: strange constellations of stars that were seemingly arranged in geometrical patterns. She felt a light breeze on her cheek, warm and forgiving; the loch shimmered. Lying by the water, within the necklace of light, she was warm.

'Mara, listen to me!'

She heard Jack's voice from a long way off, and looked round the circle of light. The dark figures behind their torches stood impassively, a drift of sparks carried over the dark water. On the surface of the water was reflected the geometric stars and the falling sparks. Again she heard her name being called, this time with more urgency.

'Mara, for God's sake!' Jack was hissing into her ear. She had one arm around his neck and was pulling him down, murmuring softly. 'People are watching,' he added in a harsh whisper, noticing several Conservatives looking curiously from the function suite window. In the gathering evening it was unclear how much they could see of the scene outside. Others were looking downwards at the prone figure of Adrian Mountjoy who, with a sore jaw and one cracked tooth, was being disentangled from the curtains.

'Mara, stand up!' Jack commanded, smelling her breath. She wasn't drunk, that was clear, and Mara had protested that she didn't do drugs. *Christ,* he thought again, *what's the matter with the girl*! Heaving and grunting, he managed to half pull her into a slumped crouch, her upper body leaning heavily against his. She groaned softly, but this time petulantly: wanting him to leave her alone. She wanted to fly, to stretch her wings, to traverse oceans. She struggled against him, her head moving rapidly from side to side. Inside, a couple of Conservative faces remained at the function suite window and were looking impassively on, as if they now expected nothing less from an evening at the *Fox and Duck*.

Now she saw that the dark figures had stepped forward; they reached down and plucked their torches from the grass and, one by one, flung them high in the air; they fell like shooting stars to the loch's surface. They hissed as they hit the water, a few sparks drifting across the water's surface. In a moment, the circle of light and warmth had been replaced by darkness: she ached with longing and unfulfilled desire.

'For God's sake try to help!' she heard a voice say, felt his breath in her hair. The figures in their white togas looked to the shoreline, as if towards another figure, then turned and walked away, disappearing into the night. She looked up at the stars, suddenly seeing them as they really were. She frowned, circuits in her mind reconnecting; she felt herself lurch upwards and downwards, sucked back through the gauze screen to her physical self. She felt disappointment, she ached inside: she could still feel his caress.

Jack now had her almost standing, one arm draped round his neck. She was moaning softly, but shaking her head more purposefully now, as if to clear it. He located her other hand and realised what the problem was in getting her to stand up straight. Her right hand was inside her knickers, her fingers working furiously away. This was no illness he'd ever come across before. He smelled her breath again: cigarettes. She moaned loudly.

'Christ, Mara!'

'Oh yes, baby!'

He glanced towards the function suite and hoped that nobody could see precisely what was going on. Then he reached down to her right hand and, as decorously as he could, pulled it smartly out of her knickers. She tried to resist for a moment, making small mewing noises, then let him sling that arm around his neck as well.

'Please don't stop!' she implored, half biting his ear.

'But I'm not doing anything,' replied Jack, loudly, just in case anybody was within earshot.

He half-dragged, half-carried her to the kitchen door, his progress watched with mounting interest by several Conservatives. Mara's arms were tight around his neck, her mouth against his ear. She was mouthing something that he couldn't make out. Her breathing was fast and shallow, and he felt sticky wetness from her fingers on his cheek.

'I've called the cops. They're on...' Sammy stopped and looked open-mouthed from Mara to Jack. 'I thought she was in the function suite?'

Another piece of circuitry reconnected. 'Don't worry, Sammy,' she said automatically, her face now pressed to Jack's shoulder. 'I'm just coming' – which, she then promptly did in a series of juddering thrusts against Jack's knee.

Chapter 8

The herb is named of Chaldees Mansesa, *of the Greeks* Ventosin. *Of the Latins* Jusquiame, *of Englishmen Henbane. Take thou this herb, and mix it with* Realgar *and* Hermodatalis, *and put them in the meat of a mad Dog, and he will die anon.*

The Book of Secrets of Albertus Magnus

It didn't take Richie long to arrive, having only to drive a few hundred yards. He'd not long finished supper – Tesco's curry, which he vowed never to eat again – and was just washing his plate when the call came through. He parked in front of the pub, leaving his blue lights flashing, to find only remnants of the party faithful still in the function suite. The rest had either left, or like Tam Cronin, moved to the public bar. Two larger members had been deputised to guard the function suite door, just in case the drunken youth reappeared. Duncan Hedges, perhaps realising that he had assaulted a local dignitary in full view of several dozen witnesses, had sensibly – although slowly and erratically – made his escape.

It took some minutes for Richie to ascertain the full facts, and to take several witness statements.

'And then he hit you?'

'Grievously assaulted me, yes.'

The politician was sitting at the function suite bar, his mouth sore, a bag of frozen peas pressed to his chin. He smiled weakly at Richie Scott who was, for the second time that day, writing Adrian Mountjoy's name in his notebook.

'A most diverting evening altogether,' Madam Chair said sourly for Rosie McLeod's benefit. She'd been upstairs bathing herself in fragrant oils when Sammy had phoned upstairs on the internal phone. She had been anticipating love and reassurance, a bottle of vintage champagne chilling in the fridge. None of your *méthode champenoise* tonight, when anything was possible.

'Why can't Jack sort it out?' she'd demanded of Sammy, to be told that he was taking Mara home. She had taken ill, it seemed, although Sammy was deliberately vague as to its nature – having been told by Jack in no uncertain terms *not to say a bloody word* to Rosie. Now, with her hair still wet, feeling damp and again depressed, she surveyed the damage to the function suite. The curtain rail had been pulled from the wall – nothing too serious – and some glasses and plates had been broken. The two bouncers, now Richie had arrived, were in the public bar, where there was much excited debate. Upstairs, lacy underwear that she'd bought that very afternoon was still in its carrier bag. Rosie put a hand to her forehead feeling that events, once again, were conspiring against her.

'Let's hope that the little thug gets his just desserts,' said

Madam Chair and placed a consoling hand on Mountjoy's shoulder. 'Are you sure you don't want to see a doctor? It might be best, you know.' Madam Chair had spent a lifetime knowing what was best.

Mountjoy shook his head, feeling the inside of his mouth with his tongue. 'He was clearly drunk, of course. Could hardly stand up, as a matter of fact.' Mountjoy pressed the peas to his chin, his self-esteem at a low ebb.

'I take it,' asked the policeman, 'that this assault is connected to what happened earlier?'

Mountjoy put on his glasses, finding that one of the legs arms was bent and that his spectacles now sat squint on his nose, removing whatever gravitas they were supposed to confer. 'He didn't say as much, of course. Just swore and then lashed out. What happens now?' he asked.

'What happens now, sir, is that I have a quiet word with Duncan Hedges. And, Mrs McLeod,' he added, turning to Rosie, 'I'll need an estimate of damage, if I may. Routine, I'm afraid, but we do need all the facts in the event that this goes to court.' She nodded, looking at the broken plates and fallen curtains.

'What do you mean *in the event that?*' asked Clare Derby, who found the conditional tense quite absurd. Nobody, to her mind, should get away with assaulting politicians.

The policeman replaced his cap and buttoned his notebook into his tunic. 'First, madam, I'll go and talk to him. On the other matter,' he added, turning to Mountjoy, 'we found some animal tracks at the crash site. It's too early to tell, but it does seem to support your story. I'll know more tomorrow,' he said, replacing his cap. 'First, however, I'll go and have a word with Duncan Hedges.'

'Not that you'll get much sense out of him tonight,' said Mountjoy, and looked edgily at Madam Chair in whom he had not confided.

'Animal tracks?' she asked with exaggerated precision once the policeman was out of earshot. '*Animal* tracks, Adrian?'

'I saw a cat,' said Mountjoy.

'A cat?'

'That's why I was distracted, you see.'

'A cat?'

'It why I didn't immediately see the milk truck.'

'A cat, Adrian?'

Clare Derby had known only about the car crash and the milk spillage, hastily gleaned from Mountjoy on his arrival at the pub earlier. Now she looked closely at him, his bag of peas once again clasped to his chin like a child's comforter. Mountjoy removed it reluctantly.

'A rather large, black one,' he said, cleared his throat and shrugged.

'A rather large black cat?' echoed Madam Chair, raising a hand and letting it plop moistly to her clipboard which she promptly picked up and clutched it to her chest. She looked closely again at her political candidate, weighing up collateral damage, and turned her eyes skywards for a moment. 'I think you should have told me about this earlier, don't you?'

Mountjoy acknowledged this rebuke with a grim smile, while Rosie sagged against the function suite bar.

Connections, connections, she was thinking. The white river and the black cat were connected after all – and if the cat and the river were connected, what of their dead tree? She looked outside at the stump, its boughs and branches neatly stacked away, and said: 'I'm sorry that your evening was spoiled. I can honestly say that we've never had anything like this happen before.' She knew also that the *Fox and Duck* was at least partially responsible, having presumably sold Duncan Hedges too much liquor during the afternoon. She'd have to make enquiries, lay down policy – this kind of thing could affect their licence, for Christ's sake.

'Oh, I think it was pretty much ruined before then,' said Mountjoy, removing his bag of peas. 'Those noises, while I was speaking…' He looked at Madam Chair, seeking female intuition, having little experience in such matters. 'Clare, they weren't what I think they were, were they?'

Rosie McLeod looked perplexed.

'Most diverting,' said Madam Chair, fixing the publican with a thin and humourless smile, 'if a little unfortunate given the circumstances of our meeting. It quite ruined everything, including Adrian's little speech.' She waved one of her hands, seeking delicate phraseology. 'It was a bit like *When Harry Met Sally*, if you understand me, only more realistic,' which didn't immediately mean anything to Rosie. 'It came from outside,' added Clare Derby pointing to the beer garden with a bejewelled finger, 'and then I saw your husband carrying in one of the barmaids.' Madam Chair smiled sweetly, quite determined that, with her evening ruined in the *Fox and Duck*, its proprietors should also be made to suffer.

But surely not, thought Rosie, as she offered apologies and refunds to the East Lothian Conservatives. Madam Chair sailed out into the night, skirts billowing, a chastened Adrian Mountjoy following in her wake, still clutching his bag of peas. Jack and Mara? She almost snorted with derision at the thought then realised that there were enough interesting substances coursing in his veins to give an elephant an erection for a month. Why wouldn't he act out his fantasies with Mara, who was young and beautiful, rather than share a marital bed with his dowdy and, she reminded herself, soon-to-be fossilised wife?

On the pavement, her mind in turmoil, watching Clare Derby and Adrian Mountjoy drive off in her large Mercedes, Rosie saw the minister walking slowly to his church. He fumbled with keys and disappeared inside.

Then she remembered the allusion to *When Harry Met Sally* and became very still. Tam Cronin had said that Mara was canoodling with a secret new boyfriend. *Boy*friend? Jack? He was old enough to be her father! No, ridiculous! If there was anything going on she'd have noticed. Anyway, he simply wouldn't do that to her, *and* with a member of staff who was also a family friend. So what had the sod been up to in the beer garden? Confused and angry, she strode into the kitchen and informed Sammy that she was going upstairs and that Jack could bloody well lock up by himself later.

She retrieved the bottle of champagne from the fridge and

hid it at the back of a cupboard, then consigned the afternoon's other lacy purchases to the bottom of her knicker drawer. She wondered if they might come in handy another time. She didn't really believe that Jack was having an affair but, in his condition, maybe something *had* happened – there were enough grounds for reasonable suspicion. Everything seemed to be crowding in on her all at once. Why would Jack be unfaithful to her? What did Mara have that she didn't? – then answered her own question with a long list of evident charms and attributes. *Reality versus fantasy*, thought Rosie, realising that – whatever the truth – her plans were going awry.

Jack stopped the car at Mara's driveway, leaving the engine running. 'Are you feeling better?' It seemed a lame question given what she'd only minutes earlier done against his leg. He looked straight ahead, not looking at her.

She nodded, also looking straight ahead. With her brain now logging on, dim memories were beginning to return, including being half-dragged into the kitchen, feeling that her insides were about to explode in a scary kind of ecstasy. She shuddered, wondering how much of a fool she had made of herself, and why.

'You're sure?' After the episode in the kitchen she'd come around almost immediately, run to the loo and been copiously sick. She'd emerged looking sheepish, not meeting anyone's eyes.

She nodded again. 'Must have been something I ate. Sorry, Jack.'

Her memory of the last hour was patchy, overlaid by other images. She remembered being in the beer garden and of Jack carrying her in, but her memories were dislocated – as if they had happened to someone else. The dark loch and the torch-carrying figures were more real to her; the canopy of strange constellations and the pleasure of surrender; of flying on a warm breeze across jagged Highland mountains to a place of shared peace. Her memory resembled a broken mirror with a myriad of distorted reflections; she remembered crying out with pleasure, of knowing that the voice was hers. She bit her lip.

'Do you want me to come in?' asked Jack.

Mara looked at the house lights. 'Don't worry, I'll be OK now.' She opened the door and swung herself out. 'Thanks for the lift.'

She walked slowly up the driveway to the rambling old farmhouse. It had once been home to a happy family, or she supposed that it had. The gravel crunched under her feet; the downstairs lights were still on. Her mother had kept on the house as a kind of vengeance; hardly sensible given its size but, to Mara, an understandable revenge. The house was doubly inappropriate now that Mara and Terry had flown the nest. Her elder brother, who still could behave like a delinquent teenager, was now in London working in the music production business, his name credited on a Kylie Minogue album. She now only saw him infrequently for occasional birthdays or Christmas get-togethers. Being in Edinburgh, it had fallen to Mara to look after their mother when she fell down the stairs, necessitating some minor stitching and a needlessly complicated hip replacement.

Mara hadn't minded, not really. She'd been planning a long summer break, and her doctoral thesis was nearly finished. Soon she'd be *Doctor* Thomson. She needed time away from it, to consider its conclusions. She already had a degree in politics and economics from Edinburgh University and was now completing her study on the rise of 20th Century European nationalism. Not the most riveting of subjects, certainly, but one that would be published and widely read. After that, who knew what possibilities could be turned to opportunities. Soon she would be free, her bags packed, saying her goodbyes. At this she stopped, remembering also the dark loch, and the man in it, and her hallucination of a naked Richie, stripped of everything except evident desire. She took a deep breath, and scrunched towards the front door.

She'd known Rosie and Jack since childhood, her father being their bank manager. It had been her dad who got the new publicans off the ground financially. They often ate as a family at the pub – her dad called it looking after my investment – and they had become friends. And then, coming back to look after her mother, Mara had bumped into Rosie in the supermarket. There was a staff crisis at the *Fox and Duck* – one person off with a long-term illness, another on maternity leave – and would Mara like to help out? She had done so often enough, both as schoolgirl and undergraduate, waitressing or working behind the bar. So why not again? It would get her out of the house, now that her mum was well on the road to recovery. It was something to do.

Julie Thomson had been dozing in her chair by the Aga when she was woken by Sammy's phone call that simply said that Mara was unwell and that Jack was driving her home. She put the phone down and lit a cigarette. The French carriage clock on a high shelf by the back window geared itself up to strike the hour in a series of clicks, like a frantic dog scrabbling on cobblestones. She flicked ash in the general direction of an overfull ashtray by her chair. She had often tried to give them up but had never succeeded for more than a few hours. It wasn't a simple matter of addiction, they were a kind of comfort, and she was beyond worrying about the damage they might be causing. She had experienced too many realities to worry about possibilities. She sometimes also treated herself to a small drink; nothing fancy, nothing excessive. She drank in nervous sips, and then put her glass on the kitchen table; she pulled at her cigarette and smoke burst against the ceiling in a long explosion.

She heard the front door banging shut.

Mara dropped her keys on the table, kicked off her shoes and helped herself to one of her mother's cigarettes. 'Sammy phoned,' said her mother. 'Said you were ill.'

Mara glanced sharply at her mother, her cigarette held daintily, remembering a little more of what had taken place. She remembered crying out several times, slipping the linen dress from her shoulders, how she'd stepped out of it, how the circle had been completed. Her toes curled at the thought. 'Something, I ate, Mum,' she replied, running a hand through her hair. 'It made me feel a bit, well, strange.'

'Sammy said you were ill.' Her mother was insistent.

'Sick as a dog,' she agreed. 'But only after feeling odd all afternoon.' She noticed her mother's blank expression. She also now remembered with more clarity the episode in the kitchen, with Jack trying to hold her upright and Sammy looking on, although that memory was also overlaid with images from beyond the veil. It was difficult to say where her dreams began and ended. What on earth could she have eaten? 'But I'm OK now,' she added.

'What you need is a hot bath and a good night's sleep.' This had been her mother's prescription for every ailment from broken bones to chickenpox. Curiously, it usually worked.

Mara nodded and sat at the kitchen table, on the seat nearest the window which had always been hers. Nobody ever sat in that seat, except her. 'All in all, a strange day,' she said reflectively, and then told her mother about Mountjoy and the puma, or whatever it was, his car accident with the milk truck, the white river, the fight, and the hazel tree.

Julie poured herself another small glass of port. Mara had by now regained some of her colour; she felt better. Her hands no longer trembled. She also noticed a small green bottle on the kitchen table with a white label in Rosie's neat handwriting.

'They say something about hazel trees,' said her mother unexpectedly, moving slowly to her chair. She was a tall woman, now stooped, and she walked with one hand on the small of her back. 'An old saying, or something. Do you know it?'

'No, Mum, I don't.'

Her mother sighed. 'Well, I'm buggered if I can remember either.'

The Reverend Lionel Kennedy often came to his church to write his sermons. The peace of the place settled him; its stones and arching beams seemed to guide his thoughts. On the way, he'd seen the police car outside the *Fox and Duck* and had inwardly shaken his head.

He'd been unnerved by the black cat, how it had simply sat by the roadside, its head turned towards his car, its eyes reddish-green and venomous in the headlights, as if it had been put there specifically to be seen by him. Now that Adrian Mountjoy had seen the cat – and who better as an eyewitness than a Tory politician – it could now be placed back in perspective. *It's probably just an escaped animal*, he told himself with a lot more confidence than he'd felt the night before; then, his imagination had run riot, now it was under control. He picked up his pen and hunched over his leather-bound notebook; his sermon was coming together slowly but surely. He looked up as a car passed, its headlights throwing beams of green and amber light through the stained-glass window above the altar. He could see the shifting light through the open vestry door, making his church seem ethereal, giving translucent life to the frozen figures in the stained-glass. The window depicts – what else? – a group of brown-robed monks carrying on their shoulders a jewel-encrusted golden cross. From the centre of the cross the fiery emerald radiates green shafts of light; the monk at the rear has his head turned, looking backwards for signs of pursuit. It is much photographed by visitors.

Then he put down his pen and listened, his head to one side.

It was only a small noise and he might have missed it had he not known every creak the old church made as it settled for the night, its wooden beams and stonework crackling like distant gunfire. He had lived in harmony with the sounds of his church for many years – and the sound he had heard came from outside. *Probably someone fooling around*, he thought, picking up his pen once more. Then he heard it again.

It was definitely coming from outside and it sounded faintly metallic, an urgent scraping of metal against stone. He stood up and walked into the main body of the Kirk; the length of the church was in darkness. Another car passed and, momentarily, the pews were bathed in saffron brilliance. The silence after the car passed was doubly quiet, intimidating him with unresolved self-doubts: the cat from the night before filled his mind for a moment. Another car passed and the crucifix above the altar burned ochre. He waited for the noise to restart and, just as he was about to go back to his desk, he heard it again – more urgent now, as if the passing cars had frightened whoever was outside.

He shuffled down the aisle, laying one hand on the back of each pew, as if for support. The noise seemed to be coming from the north wall and he put his ear fearfully against the plasterwork. The scraping seemed louder through the wall, almost frantic now, stealth turning into panic.

Whoever it is, he thought, *is as nervous as I am*. His imagination whispered a warning.

He kept a torch in his desk – to light his path homeward – and he retraced his steps to collect it. First he tested it, carefully shielding the light by putting one hand across the glass. His fingers glowed pink, the torch was working. His chest heaved with repressed excitement as he worked loose the bolts on the west door, then leaned against the woodwork to calm his flustered breathing. Whoever was outside seemed to have given up any pretence of stealth and, so it sounded, was now hammering away – as if whatever he was doing – why did he assume it was a man? – was nearly finished and he was anxious to be away. He gripped the wrought-iron handle of the door and gently pulled it open. He slipped through into the darkness.

Ten yards separated him from the corner of the north wall and, for a moment, he contemplated running forwards and catching the culprit red-handed. Then he dismissed the idea. He was slow-moving – age had rendered that kind of run impossible – and the ground was pitted and uneven. He would be heard before he could cover the distance, or he would trip and fall, and that would be that. Instead, he edged along the wall, feeling his way like a blind person, the torch held in front of him like a weapon. The hammering reached a crescendo then stopped.

'Who is it?' he demanded, his voice sounding weak. 'Who's there?' he demanded again. His torch stabbed round the corner. Tombstones gaped back at him. Whoever it was, he had gone. For a few moments he leaned back against the cold stonework, letting his heart and breathing settle. Then he skirted round the graveyard, shining his torch as he went, every noise a threat. An owl hooted and he nearly dropped the torch in fright.

He retraced his steps to the north wall, shining his torch all the while, scanning the ground for footprints. Reaching the church once more, he then shone his torch in long sweeps across the wall, trying to determine the exact spot where he had heard the noises. He moved slowly up and down the wall, his torch beam lingering on the stonework.

It was the chipped shavings on the ground he saw first; he slowly shone the torch up the wall, his hands shaking. An area of stonework about a foot across had been chipped and mutilated and he looked at it disbelievingly for a moment as a rush of panic welled upwards.

Rosie was pretending to be asleep when Jack came upstairs. She heard him wash and brush his teeth, undress and climb in beside her. She noted that he had pulled on pyjamas; *no passion intended*, she concluded. She rehearsed all his other physical failings: his spreading paunch, creeping jowls, the lines that were collecting on his face, the receding hairline. But it was no use contemplating Jack without also thinking about herself; age and gravity were doing much the same to her. She sighed, instinctively moving closer to his now sleeping back. She had expected to be in his arms, drinking champagne when his ardour permitted, feeling loved – being told that she was loved – and looked, incidentally, half her age. She wanted to believe that her imminent birthday didn't really matter – that it was only another small step along life's path, not a bridge to be dragged across. Now she felt cheated; what she had put into his morning cup of tea would have woken the dead.

Her mother had told her that she had first to respect the natural world before she could understand the healing process or how the potency of plants and herbs could be bent to her will. Only much later did she also teach her how to flavour wine with madwort and feverfew and the secrets that transformed cowbane, foxglove and deadly hemlock into good and powerful tonics. Those lessons would have given old McIntyre a seizure. It was a gift she was being given: the secret of transforming poisons and using them for good use. After all, the hyoscine hydrobromide in henbane had been used by Crippen, and Circe used it to turn the crew of the Odysseus into pigs. Or hemlock, maybe hemlock most of all, needed the greatest of respect and not a little preparation. It was the poison that killed Socrates and which was used in ancient times to keep the breasts of virgins small and make them chaste. Yet even hemlock has its uses. Or wolfsbane, the froth that dripped from the jaws of the triple-headed Cerberus when Hercules dragged him from the underworld, and which was used to kill the Emperor Claudius; that too could be used to great effect, its powerful aconitine alkaloids a recognised and potent stimulant. Rosie knew that in World War I, distillations of wolfsbane were stocked against falling reserves of morphine. Or mandrake, of biblical infamy, passionate and enticing, with its heady cocktail of scopolamine and hyoscyamine – alkaloids not to be trifled

111

with, particularly in the art of love. Everything has its good and evil side; the secret was one of understanding and of arranging the conjunctions between conflicting properties.

Pondering all this, Rosie had moved even closer to Jack, hoping still to entice him into action. She snuggled close and laid her face against the back of his head, before recoiling, smelling Mara's perfume on his hair. She knew it was hers! She smelled it every *bloody* time the damnable girl squeezed past to the cash register! Rosie's thoughts turned bleak for a few seconds; then she concluded, reasonably, that a whiff of perfume meant nothing. Mara had taken ill in the beer garden and Jack had carried her in. It was entirely reasonable that a trace of perfume might still be evident.

Reassured, she now bent her nose to his neck and this time sat bolt upright, her eyes wide and staring. In her nostrils was an earthy tang of something distinctly vaginal and utterly inexcusable. In that transfixing moment of shaken incredulity she reached a conclusion, and damn the consequences.

Julie Thomson had meanwhile been dozing in the easy chair by the Aga, placed there for that very purpose. Sometimes she couldn't be bothered going upstairs: too many reminders and, anyway, her leg still pained her. Too many memories, and too many stairs. Mara had long since gone to bed. Julie suddenly woke, blinking round the room for a few moments, wondering what could have disturbed her. She'd also remembered what they said about hazel trees.

They don't grow near a witch's house.

Chapter 9

The herb is called Arnoglossus, *Plantain. The root of this herb is marvellous good against the pain of the head, because the sign of the Ram is supposed to be the house of the planet Mars, which is the head of the whole world. It is good also against evil customs of man's stones, and rotten and filthy boils, because part of it holdeth Sperma, that is the seed. Also the juice of it is good to them that be sick of the perilous flux, with excoriation or razing of the bowels.*

The Book of Secrets of Albertus Magnus

Next morning, Jack woke with a jolt, thinking for a moment that the pub or their flat was on fire. All he could smell was smoky dampness: an earthy smell, reminiscent of autumn bonfires. He sat up, sniffing, tasting cloying decay. The space in the bed beside him was empty. Then he heard a pot being clattered in the kitchen.

He dressed, realising what must be going on. On his way along the landing, he paused by the kitchen door. Rosie had her back to him, hair unkempt, furiously chopping what looked like weeds, and feeding them into a large and bubbling saucepan. Steam was billowing around the kitchen; the smell from her broth both pungent and acrid. An overflowing wicker basket sat on the kitchen table. Incongruously, Rosie was wearing wellington boots over a pair of jeans. She must therefore have been out already, thought Jack, putting two and two together and shaking his head. *Saturday morning, for God's sake*!

Jack crept down the stairs, quietly unlocked the front door, and headed to the High Street to buy the newspapers. The sky was dull and overcast, although the forecast was for better weather later. On the way back, rather than face a kitchen full of desiccated weeds, he stopped for a coffee in one of the village's many cafes. Despite it being early morning, one of the other tables was occupied by an overweight American family, two adults and two children, all of whom had cameras around their necks. The two boys, barely teenagers, and both probably weighing more than Jack, were unwisely eating doughnuts. He watched them surreptitiously as he scanned the headlines. The father was reading a guidebook, throwing out nuggets of information in a loud voice to the rest of his family. First they would see the church. Then go see the visitor centre. Then maybe have a scout around and find the golden cross. Wouldn't that be real neat? To find the Holy Grail! Then we'll have lunch. The children had finished the doughnuts and were looking bored, but perked up at the mention of lunch. Then, unable to procrastinate any longer, Jack headed back to the *Fox and Duck*.

Miraculously, the kitchen was now spotless, although a faint whiff of decayed vegetation still remained. All remnants of earlier activity had been disposed of. Rosie had also removed her wellingtons. Jack now saw that she wasn't looking particularly happy.

'I really don't know why you keep buying *The Daily Mail*?' she informed him, looking at the newspapers Jack had laid down on the table. 'You don't read it and I certainly *never* read it.'

'You do read it. It's what you always buy.'

'No I don't. Not since, well, ages ago.'

This was news to Jack. 'I didn't know that.'

'Exactly!' said his wife in a meaningful way and poured hot water into two mugs which she then clattered down on the table.

Jack felt threatened, without knowing quite why. 'Rosie, if you *had* told me, I wouldn't have bought it.' There was a crackle in the atmosphere, and a glint in her eye which Jack didn't much like.

Rosie deposited two slices of brown bread into the toaster. 'That's not the point.'

Jack sat warily at the large oak table that dominated their kitchen-cum-dining room. It was much too large for the room – a cast-off from Rosie's parents when they moved to smaller accommodation – and getting anywhere in the kitchen meant a lengthy circumnavigation. Jack now sat at its furthest point, keeping a safe distance, and unfolded his newspaper. 'Well, maybe I didn't tell you,' she conceded after a few moments, staring intently at the toaster. 'Honesty in a relationship is so important, don't you think?'

'Of course,' he replied slowly, fairly certain now that they weren't discussing newspapers.

She sat facing him, pushing hair back over her ears. 'Well, at least you agree on the importance of honesty. That, I suppose, is a start. However, the trouble with veracity is that it involves communication.'

'Veracity?'

'A rather long word for the truth which is, I suppose, a rather small word.'

Jack paused, his coffee mug poised mid-way to his mouth. This had been said so portentously – clearly rehearsed – that he instinctively guessed what the real subject was. Perhaps he should have told her last night but, then as now, he didn't quite know how to phrase a plausible explanation. Rosie had of course spoken at length to Madam Chair, and he could only guess what she'd been told. He also had to presume that, despite being sworn to secrecy, Sammy may have also filled in a few other juicy blanks. Rosie could be exceptionally persuasive when it came to wheedling out information. Jack tried mentally to frame his defence. *Mara was masturbating in the beer garden. My hand was in her knickers because I was trying to force her fingers out of her*…what? What biological or scatological description best fitted where Mara's fingers had been working so dextrously? *When I was carrying her into the kitchen she had an orgasm against my leg. At that point, m'lud, my hand was nowhere near her knickers. I ask you, ladies and gentlemen of the jury*…

'About last night,' he said, not really knowing how to begin but realising, what the hell, that it would all sound improbable anyway. 'I can explain, Rosie.'

She held up a hand. 'Actually, I don't want to know, I really don't.' She didn't now want to be told any lies, to see him squirm or avoid her eye. That would be too awful now that phone calls had been made and plans put in place. She still, in her heart of hearts, didn't believe that Jack was carrying on with Mara, but the evidence did seem to suggest otherwise. Having vaginal secretions all over him made Jack guilty of something. 'Right now, Jack, the police want an estimate of damage, the Tories want a refund and God knows what the licensing people are going to say. After all, we did ply that damnable youth with whisky all bloody afternoon.'

Jack thought back to the moment he had burst into the function suite: Clare Derby clutching her bosom and Mountjoy succumbing to the weight of curtains. Even the most elderly of the Tory faithful were awake, including Tam Cronin, having rarely seen so much violence at a Conservative gathering, and certainly never so early in the evening. Jack drew his newspaper closer to his chest, as if it might offer some protection, as his wife fired another salvo. '*And* it was me who was left to apologise to the Tories *and* deal with the police. I've never been so bloody humiliated in my life!'

'Well, someone had to —'

'*Anybody* could have taken Mara home! Sammy, one of the bar staff – me, even. But no, in a moment of crisis, you chose to desert the sinking ship. Bloody typical!'

This seemed to be going a bit far, although Rosie wasn't entirely cognisant with all the facts of Mara's strange affliction. 'Under the circumstances,' he began, finally admitting defeat and putting his unread paper down on the table. 'Under the circumstances —'

'Bugger circumstances!' she replied with some feeling. 'I really don't want to discuss it further.' Rosie stood at the window with her back to him, hands on the sink, looking down into the beer garden. Under the circumstances, thought Jack, the weekend wasn't getting off to a very good start.

Mara was also awake but still in bed, her hands knotted behind her head, her unblinking gaze on the ceiling, watching trickling light and chasing shadows. Everything was the same, but something was different. In place of certainty, a doubt had crept in. Her single-mindedness remained the same, but the journeys she had planned now seemed perilous. She no longer felt as strong; what she might find elsewhere now had to be balanced against what she would be leaving behind.

She also felt utterly awake; a forensic wakefulness that painted everything in crystal-clarity. When she did get up, crossing to the window and pulling back curtains, the line of hills above the village seemed like a jagged knife-edge cut against the sky. She looked around and saw each object as if for the first time, from a new perspective. Everything seemed defined and, somehow, altered. For a few minutes she walked around her bedroom, picking up an ornament here, fingering a framed photograph there. The embarrassment at the *Fox and Duck* was far-distant, as if it had taken place long, long ago. Like a memory of childhood. She remembered, but dimly, Jack carrying her in from the beer garden, her mind a cocktail of other-wordly thoughts. *Unfortunate circumstance*, she told herself, wondering again what could have caused her soaring journey and humiliating landing. Something had shifted in her mind; she shook her head to clear it. She felt alive, different, new. Her thesis seemed to matter less; something else did. Ambiguous memories filed across her mind in slow motion. She had, she realised, experienced a diversion so extraordinary that it was beyond rationalisation.

She looked at herself in the mirror, feeling new liberation. A chemical imbalance had been shifted. But what did she now feel? In her dreamscape, in the beer garden, he'd whispered endearments to her ears, his breath light and insubstantial on her cheek. His arms had held her tight and tighter, as she too had clung to him, wanting never to let him go. This was the memory that now stopped all thought; the final – and best – realisation to all that had gone before: that at the furthest edge of pleasure, when every fibre has served its purpose, there remains only love.

This thought was so powerful and utterly disturbing that it dared to put a contradiction together, like a jigsaw piece suddenly making a picture clear, or a camera coming into focus to reveal an unexpected vista. In a sudden moment of shifting chemicals, she recalled a primal sense of belonging so intense that she said his name out loud, then realised that her mobile phone was bleeping.

It was a text from Richie. There was a funfair at North Berwick. Did she want to go?

It was like being released by a starting gun. *Yes*, to everything, she thought, remembering what had gone before and the purity of what remained.

Back at the *Fox and Duck*, Rosie McLeod was making an unexpected announcement. 'Anyway, I've decided to go to Edinburgh for the night.'

'Edinburgh?'

'Scotland's capital, Jack. It's a big city, you must have heard of it.'

'But –'

'Look, it's all arranged, please don't be tiresome. I'm staying with Betty and we're going to see *Les Miserables*.' Betty Fullerton, old friend, now newly divorced, lived near Waverley Station in reduced circumstances with the whine and fizz of electric trains filling her small flat.

'*Les Miserables*?'

'Jack, you're becoming an echo. It's a musical about the French Revolution, and you would positively hate it. You *know* how much you hate musicals. Anyway, it's only for one night so I'm sure you'll survive. I'll be back in the morning.' Rosie, now washed and wearing make-up, had even flicked through *The Daily Mail* before realising that she didn't now like it. Once she had liked it, now she didn't. In between articles on illegal immigrants and the iniquities of socialism, it seemed full of advertisements for incontinence pads and anti-wrinkle creams, products that she dared not contemplate.

'It's just that this all seems a bit sudden,' he said, trying to sound reasonable, and wondering when he had suddenly stopped liking musicals. As far as he knew, he had always liked musicals. 'Anyway, who's deserting the ship now?' He felt he was being punished for an unmentioned crime of which he was entirely innocent.

'Not deserting, Jack. Neither of us works on Saturday nights. You know that. House rule.' On Saturday evenings, Sammy ruled the kitchen and restaurant and a rota of under-managers looked after the bar and function suite – all designed, of course, to give the joint proprietors of the *Fox and Duck* some much-needed time together. *Fat chance of that*, thought Rosie sourly. 'Anyway, you know how much I've been wanting to see *Les Miserables*.'

'I have?' asked Jack, realising that there was quite a lot he didn't seem to know about his wife. 'Look, has this got anything to do with last night?'

'Good heavens, whatever makes you say that!' She smiled sweetly, again not really believing that Jack could have been unfaithful with Mara, but also weighing up the potency of the chemicals in his veins and once more smelling the musty and unmistakable odour of her sexuality on his cheek. Not to mention the allusion to *When Harry Met Sally* and Jack carrying in Mara from the beer garden. Sammy had been suspiciously evasive when she'd interrogated him before coming up to bed. 'One of Betty's dogs died last week so she's feeling a bit low. I thought I'd pop up to town and cheer her up.'

'You haven't been very cheery yourself lately,' Jack reminded her and looked down at the table which was now strewn with bills from the cash and carry and bar receipts. He wanted to tell her that he loved her, even drawing breath to frame the words. But something stopped him, as it had also stopped him reaching out to her recently. Of course he had wanted to make love to her, but hadn't, although Rosie wouldn't have understood. Over-anxiety made Rosie volatile and fragile; if she felt herself to be cast from porcelain, Jack saw himself as the person clumsy enough to break her apart. His seeming indifference was his way of protecting both of them; she had to resolve middle-age by herself: he couldn't risk fracturing the person beneath. He bit his lip, trying to reconcile conflicting thoughts, while his wife fizzed energy from across the room.

'Don't worry,' he said instead, tapping a calculator with the end of his biro. 'Somehow I'll survive without you.'

'That's better,' she said and unexpectedly circled the kitchen table to plant a kiss on his forehead. 'I've defrosted you a chicken pie – please eat it, Jack, it won't keep. Oh, and I've put a bottle of your favourite in the fridge. Eat, drink and be merry,' she said kindly enough, although it did seem that there was also a flash of malice in her eye.

Richie also saw the large American family as he walked from the police station to the manse. All four were standing outside the church and talking photographs of each other, no doubt using wide-angle lenses. Then the two children went and sat on the arms of the stone cross, one each side of the

122

upright and probably making the whole edifice sink further back into the duck pond.

Sadie Gallagher answered Richie's knock with a minimum of civility, looking him up and down with her mouth in a thin line. She was wearing a floral apron and carrying yellow rubber gloves; she was plainly not pleased to have been interrupted from more important tasks. Sadie, normally friendly and outgoing, was evidently not pleased to find the constabulary on the doorstep.

'I phoned earlier,' said Richie.

'I know,' she replied. 'It was me you spoke to.'

She asked him to wait and pointedly closed the door, leaving the policeman on the doorstep for several minutes. 'He'll see you now,' she said on her return, and stood aside, allowing him to squeeze past into a narrow hallway that smelled of cabbage. Sadie led him down the passageway and into a small study.

The minister shook his hand, bending his long frame towards the policeman, then waved him to a chair by a large walnut desk that dominated the room. He suggested that Mrs Gallagher might like to bring them tea and some of her Black Forest gateau if there was any left. Richie now saw her chilly civility as a form of protection; like an elder sister who believes her young brother is mixing with the wrong sort. Her expression suggested that it would be a mistake to waste good chocolate cake on police officers.

'You mustn't mind my housekeeper,' said the minister when they were alone. 'She worries overmuch, that's all.' The room was in semi-darkness, heavy red satin curtains half-pulled across a French window that opened out to a lawn garden and houses beyond. A garish yellow oil painting dominated one wall; on the minister's desk were framed photographs of a younger Lionel shaking hands with a number of church dignitaries and Bob Geldof.

'Saint Bob,' said the policemen, impressed.

The other man shrugged. 'He was kind enough to visit a children's project I had set up in the east end of Glasgow.' It was said offhand, self-deprecating, a reflection perhaps as to why he'd never achieved, or sought, high office in the ministry.

The minister settled himself into a wingback leather chair behind the walnut desk. 'You'll be here about the cat,' he said.

The minister was wearing dark trousers and a white shirt opened at the neck. Richie looked at his own jeans and blue polo shirt; it seemed that both of them were out of uniform. 'Well, for what it's worth, you were right. According to the zoo, the tracks were most probably made by a puma.'

The minister raised his eyebrows, seemingly preoccupied by something else. 'So what's a black puma doing in East Lothian? They're not exactly native to Scotland, are they?'

The expert from the zoo had been voluble on the subject. 'Sorry to say, minister, but sightings of big cats are quite common. Well, not common; but not uncommon. The zoo believes that, maybe, a breeding pair got loose from a circus. Years and years ago. They've been sightings over the years from the north of Scotland to the south of England. This particular animal was seen near Dunbar just a few weeks ago. The same cat, maybe a different cat.'

'So it does exist.'

'Yes, minister. It certainly does.'

Sadie Gallagher had soundlessly reappeared carrying a tray in both hands which she deposited wordlessly on the minister's desk. Richie noted that there was no chocolate cake although she had found it in herself to lay out a small plate of digestive biscuits.

The minister looked down at his jumble of papers, and abruptly pushed them to one side of the desk. He was a humanist and his great fear was that he now faced a moral absolute that he barely understood. 'Mrs Gallagher,' he said with a conspiratorial smile, 'has a rare form of gastronomic dyslexia that makes most of her cooking almost inedible. But digestives are quite safe, if you'd care for one.' The Reverend Kennedy delicately lifted a biscuit off the plate and nibbled thoughtfully. 'Is it dangerous?' he finally asked.

Richie shook his head. 'Dangerous, no. At least, that's what I've been assured.'

'And these things get sighted all over the place?'

'From time to time.' The policeman shrugged, having had several long conversations with the big cat curator at the zoo, 'although it is something of a mystery.'

'Quite so,' the minister agreed. 'So what are you going to do?'

'Keep an eye out for it. Nothing more that we can do.'

The minister placed his half-eaten digestive down on the table. 'That's all? It's not exactly comforting to know that there's a dangerous animal on the loose.'

'I'm told that it's not dangerous,' Richie said again. It was the question that he'd asked the cat curator, who spoke in a Welsh accent and who laughed off all suggestions that the animal could pose a threat. Richie, who didn't trust anyone with a Welsh accent, had pressed him several times.

'So, case closed,' said the minister. Richie couldn't decide whether it was a statement or a question.

'Case closed,' he agreed, having also spoken to Big Mac, who had also spoken to higher authority in Edinburgh.

The minister picked up a sheet of paper on which Richie saw scrawled notes in blue ink. 'Except that it's not closed. Not for me.' The minister put the sheet of paper down and looked up sharply. 'It may just have opened. In fact, if you hadn't phoned this morning, I was going to phone you.'

'About the cat?'

'Not about the fact of the black cat,' said the minister after a few moments. 'It's what it represents. That's what's worrying me.'

The policeman sipped at his cup while the minister picked up other pieces of paper and peered at them. 'It's not really a police matter, although a small crime has been committed. Nothing dramatic, I assure you,' he added quickly. The minister rose from his chair, crossed to the window and clasped his hands behind his back. 'I suppose I could have been a bit more forthcoming with you the other evening.'

'You reported having seen a large cat.'

'I reported the fact of a black cat.' Outside, across the back fence, a line of washing flapped in the breeze. Richie could hear children's voices and the sound of a football being kicked.

'You also said something about a crime.'

'A very *small* crime.' The minister had returned to his chair and now held up his hands like a fisherman and spread them very wide. 'It may, however, be a symptom of a rather bigger problem. The trouble is that, in matters of religion, problems do not always have easy solutions.' He crossed his legs and brushed biscuit crumbs from his knee.

Richie had no idea what the other man was talking about. 'It's the same in law,' was the best he could come up with.

'Nearly, but not quite. You see, in your job you can at least admit the possibility of injustice. Happens all the time, doesn't it? The appeal courts are full of wrongs being put right.' Lionel placed both hands on the desk, palms downwards, as if about to push himself upright. 'The difference between us is that I have to deal in absolutes. The laws of the Church are not endlessly sub-paragraphed like yours.'

'Then that should make it easy.'

Abruptly, the old minister did push himself upright. 'Come, I'll show you. You see, officer, the black cat has come back and I'm rather worried that history may be about to repeat itself.'

Mara had taken her courage into both hands and, despite it being her day off, was calling in at the *Fox and Duck*. She felt that it might be better to clear the air sooner rather than later. She still keenly felt the humiliation of the night before, but she also felt what it had gifted her: a new energy and a changed perspective. She no longer knew who she was, or what she felt; the dark loch and its cast of characters spilling in and out of her mind.

She found Jack alone at the kitchen table, which made it easier. She could only guess at what Jack might have told Rosie, and what the latter's reaction might have been. 'I just popped round to say sorry about last night. I don't know what came over me.'

Jack looked embarrassed, squinting down at a VAT return, which should have been sent in the week before. 'You're feeling better, I take it?'

'Jack, it must have been something I ate,' she suddenly gushed, feeling her cheeks turn crimson. 'I don't usually…' She trailed off into silence.

'No, no, of course not,' replied Jack, remembering the press of her groin against his thigh.

'Something I ate,' she repeated, now feeling a prick of tears behind in her eyes, and willing them not to spill out. 'Jack, it's never happened before. To be honest, I can't really remember what happened. All I know is that I'd been feeling ill for most of the day.'

Jack cleared his throat. 'Well, yes, I suppose you weren't looking too good.'

There was an awkward silence.

'And then I felt boiling hot, like someone had poured hot water over me, and that's when I went into the beer garden.'

There was another difficult silence.

'Anyway, thanks for the lift home.'

'No problem,' said Jack.

Mara blinked rapidly, forcing back tears. 'Rosie OK, is she? What with the police and everything?'

Well, Jack had to concede, *probably not*. He'd waved her off, feeling again that he was the innocent victim of a miscarriage of justice. He also had a sneaking suspicion that she was up to something; trips to Edinburgh weren't suddenly arranged just like that. Rosie also hated dogs; canine bereavement would not have moved her to drop everything and rush to the side of a rather distant friend. He suspected that the real reason for her absence was standing in front of him.

'It's just that I don't really remember anything between going into the beer garden and waking up in the kitchen.' Mara bit her lip; she did faintly remember pressing herself to Jack's leg, and of being drawn backwards through a veil. But it was also as if it had happened to someone else; she had decided on the way to the pub that amnesia about the whole incident was probably for the best.

Jack looked relieved. 'You don't remember anything?'

'Not a thing,' replied Mara with wide eyes.

'So you think it was something you ate?'

'I don't know, but yes, probably.'

Jack was looking worried again. 'Something eaten here, you mean?'

'Look, don't worry. It's done with. End of.'

'In which case,' said Jack, crossing to the fridge, 'perhaps a small gift is in order. An apology from the *Fox and Duck*, just in case it was us who made you ill.' He turned from the fridge with a wine bottle that he held up to the light.

129

'Rhubarb and elderflower,' he said.

'Jack, no apology needed.'

'Perhaps not, but take it anyway.' He held out the bottle to her.

Mara peered at the label, grateful for the change of subject. 'A Rosie special, is it?'

'Apparently it's my favourite.' Mara put the bottle down on the table beside the bar and restaurant receipts. 'Actually, she's gone to Edinburgh to see *Les Miserables*. She's always wanted to see it, apparently.'

Mara noted his small frown. 'That's nice,' she said.

'Well, no it's not, actually.'

Mara's smile flickered momentarily.

'I mean this wine that's supposed to be my favourite.' He picked up the bottle with its white inscribed label. 'I don't know where she gets her ideas from, I really don't. To be frank, I positively don't like her home-made wine. I only drink it to be sociable. But don't tell her that I said that,' he added hurriedly, thinking again of his wife's recent departure and her hastily made plans. 'Here,' he said to Mara, pushing the bottle towards her. 'Eat, drink and be merry,' wondering again what his wife was up to.

The minister led Richie the short distance to the church and showed the policeman the defaced stonework. A five-pointed star, roughly hewn and obviously carved in haste. Richie ran a finger down one of the irregular markings, and then stood back. It barely measured a foot in either direction.

'This happened last night,' said the minister. 'I was inside the church, you see, and heard it being done. At first I thought it might be something to do with the pub across the road.' He pursed his lips, remembering the police car outside the *Fox and Duck*. 'Then I decided to take a look. But I wasn't quick enough. Whoever it was had scarpered.'

The policeman was frowning. The village did see vandalism and graffiti from time to time, but not something so precise, and never anything that required more than a can of spray paint.

'It's a Star of David,' said Richie eventually.

The minister was standing close to Richie. 'See here,' he said, and pointed to the bottom of the star. 'See this bit?' Richie looked more closely; two of the chipped lines didn't quite bisect. 'That's probably when I disturbed him, or them. It's not quite finished.' The minister let his arm drop to his side. 'Actually, it's not a Star of David. It's a pentangle.' He had lowered his voice, as if worried that they might be overheard. Richie looked around but there was nobody in sight. 'Or a pentagram, take your pick. It was once a Christian symbol, officer, representing the five wounds of Jesus Christ. In Judaism, it's called the Seal of Solomon. It's also still a religious symbol in the Baha'i and Taoist faiths, so I understand.' The minister indicated a wooden bench nearby, looking over the cricket wicket to the *Fox and Duck*, and they sat side by side beneath a spreading elm tree, framed in a mosaic of light and shade, while the minister composed his thoughts and Richie Scott looked at his watch.

'So why carve a religious symbol onto your church wall?' asked Richie.

The minister took some moments to reply. 'Because it's not a religious symbol, that's why.' The minister bunched his hands in his lap, his fingers twining and untwining.

'I thought you said that it was?'

'Not in the accepted sense, no. It's a wiccan symbol.' The minister saw that the policeman was looking blank. 'Witchcraft, officer. It's a wiccan symbol of faith.'

Richie had an urge to laugh. 'You honestly think a coven of witches did this?'

The minister sighed. 'I am a man of reason, officer. Not a crank. Yes, I believe that someone associated with the cult did this. Is that so fanciful?'

In all Richie's briefings before taking up the Holy Cross posting, witchcraft activity had not been mentioned. 'Sorry, minister, but yes. In one breath you tell me it's a Christian symbol; in the next, a witchcraft symbol. It can't be both.'

The minister was still twisting his fingers into impossible knots. 'In witchcraft, the pentangle represents earth, air, fire, water and the human spirit.'

'Look, it's just a bit of stupid vandalism.'

'But a rather *precise* bit of vandalism, wouldn't you agree? On a church, of all places? It last happened twenty years ago,' said the minister with sudden venom. In profile, his face looked craggy and avuncular, the lines on his face deep and precisely defined. 'I was told it might happen again, you see.' He took a deep breath and exhaled slowly. 'Did you know that it was once a heresy not to believe in witchcraft?'

Richie shrugged. 'A long time ago maybe.'

The minister rubbed his chin. 'The last Witchcraft Act was passed in 1951. That's not so long ago.' He turned to look directly at the policeman. 'In my lifetime, officer.'

'But not in mine,' replied Richie.

'That's why our laws disagree. Simply because an act of parliament makes something legal, that doesn't make it right.' He said this with conviction and retrieved a large handkerchief from his pocket, which he proceeded to twist between his fingers. 'Adam Campbell, my predecessor, warned me, you see. He was quite specific about it. He said that it all started because a large black cat was sighted near the village.'

Richie was holding up one hand, like a traffic policeman. 'Hold on... what started?'

'Twenty years ago, officer. That's when the cat was last seen around here. By a local farmer, apparently... even fired his shotgun at it. You see, it doesn't really matter whether the cat actually exists or not. It's what people want to read into it.'

'You've lost me, minister.' Twenty years ago he was in primary school, the apple of his mother's eye. The minister needed a historian, not a policeman. 'So what happened? Twenty years ago?'

The minister visibly deflated. 'I'm not sure if Adam Campbell really knew,' he conceded. 'He simply said that the witchcraft cult had never died out in the village and that the black cat was the sign to watch for.' The puma, if that's what it was, had been his vision first, he reminded himself, and the pentangle carved on the wall of his church was the second proof. He wasn't going to deny the evidence a third time. 'The sighting of the cat and this bit of vandalism can't be coincidence.'

'Minister, nothing happened here twenty years ago.' Richie was positive about that. 'I've read all the Holy Cross incident files. Nothing, I can assure you, has ever happened here.'

'My predecessor believed that something rather bad did happen.'

'And?'

'He didn't know what. He merely suspected.' The minister's hands were back in his lap, forming and reforming complex knots. 'He died some years ago.'

'Then I don't quite know how I can help,' said Richie.

The minister turned sharply on the bench, his face close to the policeman's. 'Open the files again, officer! That's what I'd like you to do. Settle this once and for all!' Flecks of spit had gathered at the corners of his mouth. 'If I'm wrong, then I'm wrong. But if I'm right, something equally bad may be about to happen.' He held up a hand. 'No, I don't know what, officer.' He unfolded his handkerchief and wiped the spit from his lips. 'But I do believe that the cat and my vandalised church are connected.'

Richie was shaking his head. 'Look, I'm sorry, but if no crime was reported twenty years ago, then there's nothing to investigate. There aren't files to be reopened.'

'That,' said the minister, 'is what I was afraid you'd say.' He smiled wanly and then sighed loudly. 'It was the reason I wasn't more forthcoming with you when I reported seeing the cat. It would have sounded, well, implausible.' The minister gestured towards his church. 'Then that happened.'

'It doesn't change anything,' said Richie. 'If a crime wasn't committed twenty years ago, there's nothing to be done.'

'No old files to open? Nothing?'

'All I can do is file a report with Division. Beyond that, there's not a lot I can do. However, if it helps, I will ask around,' Richie promised. 'Discreetly. I'm sorry,' he added. 'I thought that being proved right about the cat would solve things.'

'Well, we'll have to see about that, won't we?'

Lionel Kennedy then sat by himself by the spreading elm tree, the light patterning his grey hair. He hadn't been surprised by the policeman's reaction; it was no more than he had expected. But he'd felt obliged to raise the matter formally; to share his concern. This was his parish, temporal and spiritual, and he had a responsibility to it and its inhabitants. Something was going on, he knew it, as his predecessor had also known it. But witchcraft, here? Lionel had never seen any sign of it, and he had kept an eye out. *It's never died out here*, that's what old Adam Campbell had said. Despite suffering from an advanced and incurable cancer, he wasn't daft. He believed what he was saying, although unable to fill in any detail. He didn't know what had happened in the village. He couldn't even hazard a guess. Like the policeman, Lionel had long concluded that, probably, nothing had happened. Holy Cross simply wasn't that kind of place. Until the moment when he'd turned a bend in the road, a storm threatening to break, and been faced with the contrary evidence: the distinct possibility that a shadowed cult might exist in the village. His vandalised church made *might* seem probable. So what to do now?

The minister was faced with a situation requiring tact and delicacy. At all costs, he wanted to avoid opprobrium. He wanted the matter to be taken seriously but, handled badly, knew that he would be made to look ridiculous. Also, he had no desire to stir things up unduly. The villagers were a conservative lot and liked neither change nor trouble. Say the wrong things to the wrong people and the consequences might be, at best, unforeseen. No, he needed an ally – someone who knew people, someone well-connected and influential: someone, he suddenly thought in a moment of lateral clarity, who had also seen the animal and might therefore understand his concern. Someone with authority who could get those old files reopened. Someone who could impress upon the chief constable himself that something needed to be done. After all, they had both shared a vision of the improbable. Adrian Mountjoy, his political star in the ascendant, might turn out to be the ally that he needed.

Rosie McLeod drove westwards towards Edinburgh thinking about strange omens and the nature of infidelity, a frown gathered on her forehead. She still couldn't bring herself to believe that Jack had been unfaithful, even in his aroused state *and* in their beer garden *and* with a family friend – however attractive that family friend might be. Nor could she quite believe that the young and beautiful Mara would want to have sex with a man who, for all his raffish charm, was old enough to be her father. That thought, sad and forensic, was also a reflection on her. She and Jack were both roughly the same age, each old enough to be Mara's parents.

On the other hand, there was the undeniable evidence of someone's vaginal scent on his skin and, on the balance of probability, that someone was Mara. *Christ*, she thought, *how do you get someone to rub their private parts against your cheek by mistake*? In her experience it could only be achieved in a limited number of ways – none of them remotely accidental, and none of which had happened to her for months and bloody months. And Jack, she reminded herself, had come to bed without even trying to make love to her. No arm around her shoulder, no knee pressing against her buttocks, no kisses down her spine – the usual tell-tale signs of impending passion. Ergo, he must have satisfied himself elsewhere and with another woman – another woman who, she remembered, was canoodling in secret, if Tam could be believed.

In his defence, she considered, Jack's physiology had never had to contend with such a potent cocktail of chemicals as he'd been subjected to the day before. The mandrake alone would have given a corpse an erection. Perhaps having sex with Mara had been no more than a biological necessity, like having a pee, and should therefore be forgiven. It would have meant nothing, a simple exchange of bodily fluids, and back to work as if nothing had happened.

I couldn't help myself, she imagined him saying, like a small boy caught with his hand in the sweetie jar.

Rosie pursed her lips and narrowed her eyes: something had happened. What she had to do was define what that something had been and only then decide how forgivable it was.

Her anxieties, of course, went beyond her husband; she also felt queasy about the black cat and the markings on the hazel tree. Jack, of course, had said *silliness* to all of it. Whatever had happened, *if* it had happened, had taken place a long time ago.

Jack's dismissal of her worries might have been less condescending if he'd known about the carved XIII, but she hadn't told him about that. She'd kept that to herself; it had seemed a personal message addressed only to her, and Jack wouldn't have understood. The enigma was that it could either have been carved as a friendly warning or a threat. Friend or foe, or someone still in the process of making up their mind. It made no sense.

She stopped at traffic lights near Meadowbank Stadium, feeling the crush of the city's population and feeling anonymous among their numbers. A young mother was pushing a buggy crossed the road; Rosie smiled. Maybe they should have had children. Maybe it wasn't too late. She might be on the brink of terminal decline but her reproductive cycle, if under-utilised, was still relatively intact. *I'm only thirty-nine*, she told herself, trying to feel positive, like a child reminding herself that she's nine and

138

three-quarters. She frowned again and bit her lip. Neither of them had ever really wanted children; they weren't nurturing types. It had been one of their first agreements, after she'd said 'yes' to his overall proposition of marriage, but before she'd agreed to the fine detail. Like a beautiful but inaccessible country, motherhood had never seemed worth the bother of getting there.

She would have been even less sanguine had she known that her contingency plans were not going quite as expected.

Chapter 10

The herb of the planet Mercury, which is named
Pentaphyllon, *in English Cinquefoil or the Five-leafed*
herb; of others Pentadactylus, *of others* Sepedeclinans,
of certain Calipendalo. *The root of this herb brayed*
and made in a plaster, healeth wounds and hardness.
It putteth away also the toothache. And if the juice of it
be holden in the mouth, it healeth all the griefs of the
mouth. Moreover if any man will ask any thing of a
king or prince, it giveth abundance of eloquence, if he
have it with him, and he shall obtain it that he
desireth. It is also good to have the juice of it, for the
grief of the stone, and the sickness which letteth a man
that he can not piss.

The Book of Secrets of Albertus Magnus

Adrian Mountjoy was meanwhile being berated by his
constituency Chairperson, and wasn't enjoying the
experience. Clare Derby had the unnerving ability to be
always right, and in a tone of voice that made him feel like a
toddler who has just peed on the floor.

'But — '

'But nothing, Adrian. The whole episode is not going to do us any good at all, mark my words. In such matters I do have quite considerable experience.'

Adrian Mountjoy tenderly touched the side of his mouth and held the telephone a little way from his ear. Clare Derby ploughed on, her voice sounding both shrill and metallic at the other end of the line. 'I also don't have to tell you that our Party's main economic policy is to get young people back to work. The government's current policies are a dog's dinner and their record on education reform even worse. Youth unemployment is a national scandal and we, our Party, have a new and alternative approach. The issue of youth unemployment is *the* key battleground of the election. Not Europe, Adrian, however much you like our foreign friends. The opinion polls tell us that, Adrian. Adrian?'

'Still here, Clare,' he replied from his kitchen chair. Madam Chair had obviously been speaking to someone in greater authority. Normally, Clare Derby wouldn't have given two hoots about youth unemployment.

'So it doesn't look very good if our political candidate actually does the opposite and puts one of these young people *out* of work. You see the problem, I trust?'

'It was an accident,' insisted Mountjoy, with as much conviction as a sore jaw and loose tooth would permit.

'I appreciate that it was an accident,' said Madam Chair in a softer voice. 'I don't think anyone will accuse you of having a car crash on purpose. That would be plain silly, wouldn't it? However, you do know that a report will have

141

gone to the procurator fiscal and they may decide to charge you with stupid driving, or whatever people like you get charged with.'

People like me? 'Careless driving,' he parried, trying to keep the irritation from his voice. What right had she to be his judge and jury? 'Anyway, the local policeman said it was unlikely.'

Clare Derby sighed theatrically. 'It hardly matters, Adrian. What matters is that you have had a car accident, the PC is considering bringing charges against you, and a young man has lost his job.'

'A young man, don't forget, who just happened to assault me.' Mountjoy felt that his association chairperson was being more than a little unreasonable. 'I'm the real victim here and I've got a sore mouth to prove it.'

'Yes, yes,' said Clare Derby, brushing aside his protestations. 'That may be so, but my concern is solely with our reputation and, therefore, with your chances of being elected. Anyway,' she added in a more conciliatory tone, 'have you at least considered what the Safer Lothians Roads Campaign is going to say?'

He hadn't and almost groaned out loud. 'Well, you should, Adrian. You are the campaign's chairman. Your car accident isn't a very good personal advertisement for road safety, is it?'

'That's hardly fair, Clare,' protested Mountjoy. 'I'm the victim here and, in the fullness of time, young Duncan Hedges will be found guilty of assault. Justice will be done,' he added in his best parliamentary candidate's voice.

Clare Derby disagreed. 'Poetic justice has already been done, Adrian. The sympathy of many people will be with the underdog, now unemployed. Frankly,' she intoned, 'what we need is a bit of spin.'

'Spin?'

'A new version of the truth that puts you and us in a better light.'

'Clare, I'm an accountant. I don't know how to spin.'

'Then learn, Adrian, and learn quickly,' said Clare Derby, replacing the receiver.

Richie Scott picked up Mara in his pea-green MG sports car and they drove to North Berwick. She felt his presence like a charge of electricity. Her world had tilted on its axis. The man in the dream, from whom she had removed the golden mask, was beside her. The countryside seemed lush, the air succulent; patterns of thought had altered. She was both strong and vulnerable; she didn't need to escape to be free. The lesson from her dream was unambiguous: at the end of everything, there is only love. She squeezed his leg, making him turn and smile. She had crossed through a veil and been returned.

'I thought you might have been on duty today,' she said. 'Making the world a safer place, or something.'

'Ah, so that's what I'm supposed to be doing... and here's me thinking I was just a humble copper.' He changed down a gear and negotiated a tight bend. 'Apart from which, I haven't been to a fair for years. I thought it might be fun,' he added, glancing anxiously at her. 'You do like funfairs, don't you?'

She smiled. 'I do now, Richie Scott.'

The steam fair comes to North Berwick for one weekend every year, setting up their marvellous contraptions on the rugby club's playing fields just up from the town centre, conjuring up a panoply of noise and colour. The Forth was steely grey, a cruise liner heading upstream. Around the basalt fastness of the Bass Rock hung swirling gannets.

The most popular attraction was the roundabout with its rearing horses, each horse the same yet different from the one beside it. They galloped round in wooden circles, heads reared and teeth bared, as a hurdy-gurdy man fed music boards into the machine which devoured them as quickly as he fed its appetite. The operator was a thin unsmiling man who had cotton balls plugged into his ears and delicate hands that caressed his music machine. He stacked the wooden boards in neat piles and fed them through the hurdy-gurdy in regimented batches, over and over; sometimes he hummed along.

The man who worked the roundabout was his opposite: a great, fat man who sat on a metal stool beside the engine, one hand encompassing the regulator. He had a grey face and his small eyes were like shiny coins. When he opened the regulator, steam hissed from the cylinder and the greased piston turned the horses faster and faster, until they danced in a stampede. Occasionally he touched another lever and made the engine whistle, a spurt of steam condensing on his face. The funnel from the engine rose vertically through the centre of the roundabout blowing neat smoke rings that the younger children pointed at excitedly.

Mara and Richie whirled around, his arm encircling her and his eyes half-closed: the people around the roundabout were a revolving blur, like a video on fast forward. She squealed with delight each time their wooden horse, like a stallion gently bucking, rose and fell on its retaining pole.

There was another steam engine nearby, with a cradle for about twenty people that went backwards and forwards, higher and higher, like a child's swing. Each time the cradle reached its zenith there was a cacophony of screams, and then it swung downwards and towards the sky again.

'That looks like fun,' she said, dragging him towards it. 'C'mon, let's have a shot.'

'That all depends on your definition of fun. To be honest, the one thing I'm not good at is heights.' It was the first time he had admitted to weakness; once again he glanced at her anxiously.

'Fiddlesticks! You, Richie, are supposed to be a superhero. So if it bothers you, just close your eyes. That way you can't see how high up you are.' She narrowed her eyes; seeing each bolt and rivet of the steam engine in sharp focus, the gleam of oil on the piston.

The engine fussed and the cradle moved. It started slowly then, building momentum, rose higher until their legs hurt with the effort of preventing themselves falling under the safety bar.

'Shit, this is awful!' she squealed as the cradle reached a new height, trembling for a second before plunging down. She added, 'I feel sick,' gripping tight to his arm: talons digging. The cradle swept downwards and across the fairground, missing the grass by inches.

Afterwards, her knees felt like water. 'Maybe it wasn't quite so much fun after all,' she conceded. 'Here,' she said, pointing to a shooting gallery that had air rifles that fired little balls, 'I challenge you to a duel. Metaphorically, of course.'

His first shot completely missed the little metal target and clanged harmlessly against the retaining wall. He snapped open the gun barrel and pushed in another pellet. He clasped his teeth together, a quacking hiss escaping.

He handed over the gun; she aimed, her face screwed up in concentration, and hit the target first time. She was almost as surprised as him. And more: she enjoyed it – the power, the dull *clunk* when the pellet struck, the feeling of invincibility. A weapon: another kind of weapon. She looked at its scratched blackness – so harmless-looking – and wondered: but I have something else. The gun suddenly felt heavy – its muzzle a sightless eye: it made no moral judgements.

Richie then missed with his last pellet and put down the gun feeling crestfallen.

'Don't worry,' said Mara. 'You can't help being hopeless. Thank God our policemen aren't armed, that's all I can say.'

Then they bought candyfloss and sat on the grass at the edge of the fairground, giggling as the candyfloss stuck to their hair and faces, watching the crowds pass; youngsters pulling parents from one delight to the next; older children pretending the fair was really rather uncool; and grandparents descending to a second childhood, remembering it all with eyes as filled with wonder as their grandkids.

'I used to come here as a teenager, you know... me and my pals. Friday nights out on the town in North Berwick's hot spots. We were pretty sure that, this far from Holy Cross, nobody would recognise us getting shitfaced. Not, of course, that there was much to do except sit on the beach and drink vodka. Strange, but I've never drunk the stuff since. Keys,' she suddenly demanded and fetched a wicker basket from the car, into which was packed a selection of sandwiches and a wine bottle on which was stuck a white label. They carried the basket away from the steam fair and the bustle and set it down at the edge of the playing fields, with a view across the town's rooftops to a small island around which gulls wheeled and dived. She made a great show of spreading out a tartan rug onto which she set meat pie and a bewildering array of sandwiches in brown and white bread. 'I didn't know what you liked,' she said, 'so I made everything.'

She opened the neatly labelled bottle and filled two plastic cups. 'It's probably revolting. A Rosie McLeod special. Rhubarb or bison grass or something.' She sipped and swallowed. 'Actually, it's not too bad. Have some pie,' she commanded. 'I've even got some good English mustard. None of that French muck.'

'I thought you were veggie?'

'Only by choice. Unlike you, I'm not a fascist. I really don't mind if you like killing and eating cuddly animals.'

'I'm not a fascist.'

'A *smoking* fascist, Richie. Depriving other people of a simple pleasure because *you* don't approve.'

'OK, OK.' He wasn't sure if she was being serious. 'Anyway, cows aren't cuddly.'

'Yes they are… they have big sad eyes. Like they know that, someday, they're going to be made into meat pies.' She held out a paper plate on which were spread several slices of pie in a pastry crust. 'But don't let me put you off.'

He reached instead for the lettuce and cucumber.

'Good boy,' she said approvingly and refilled his glass, feeling flushed, a slight tremor running up and down her spine.

He watched her eat, feeling that a boundary was inexplicably being crossed. It added piquancy to the moment: an extra tension. She felt it too: red spots on her cheeks. Mara sniffed and ate her sandwiches in companionable silence, lifting each corner to examine the filling. 'Watercress,' she'd sniff then, later, 'Chutney!' She nibbled at her food, working her teeth like pincers – examining everything first, then frowning, then nibbling. When she swallowed, he could see its passage through her gullet. As she swallowed, she tilted her head backwards like a bird. He almost expected her to squawk and flap her arms. Instead she sniffed and muttered 'Cheese!' or 'Onion rings!'

She drank the rest of her glass and refilled it, holding out the bottle to him. He declined. The wine was definitely going to her head; for no reason, she was being transported years back, remembering mornings when the air crackled with broken promises – and both her parents pretending everything was OK for her sake, as if she was blind or deaf. It was the pretence she hated most of all, the painted smiles and, all the while, the paint becoming chipped. Her mother grew indifferent, as if everything all around was a bad dream, and Mara would sometimes wonder if the arguments and tears weren't part of a strange adult ritual, or a habit, like her cigarettes. If so, if was a ritual that slowly killed their marriage, but so slowly that only she noticed. She also remembered the giant daisies, how they nodded and waved and how she'd hide among them, aching with longing to one day grow up to be like her mother.

With a start, she realised that she must have said some of this out loud.

'She's divorced, isn't she?'

'Dumped and abandoned, Richie. Traded in for a younger model. Not a blindingly original script.'

He put a hand on her arm, causing another electrical storm down her spine. 'Do you ever see your father?'

She shook her head.

'Do you miss him?'

'Questions, questions, Richie. What are you, a copper, or something?' She looked down and again shook her head, remembering with renewed clarity what it had really been like. 'I did to start with,' she said, then felt her head throb. 'I felt all sorts of things and then I felt nothing.' He took one of her hands in his and was surprised to find it moist, as if she was crying all over except from her eyes.

The truth was, his leaving had been the best bit. They had competed guiltily over her, their only daughter, and Mara was for a while spoiled with sweets and pocket money. Her friends played jealously with her toys and said how lucky she must be, not knowing that there are some things that you pay for twice. And then he was gone, with her mum running around on the lawn, fluttering this way and that, not knowing what to do next – as if she believed that he might have forgotten by mistake to take her with him. 'Bastard!' her mother had eventually screamed when he was too far away to hear. Mara watched from the upstairs window, biting her lip. There were posters of rock stars on the walls, a red Mickey Mouse alarm clock on her bedside table: she could hear it tick in the unnatural silence that followed her father's skidding departure. She was wearing a blue smock dress, white ankle socks and her long hair was tied back with an elastic band. On her dressing table beside a candleholder was a posy of primroses in a small glass vase. She could smell them from across the years, and breathed deeply; she was also holding a hand to the window, but didn't know whether she was waving her father goodbye or beckoning him back. She knew that he'd seen her in the rear-view mirror, but he didn't return the wave. After fluttering and shouting, her mother sank to her knees on the lawn and put her head in her hands.

At first she missed her father and then realised that she especially missed the presents he gave her, and felt guilty about it. The Barbie doll they said was indestructible came apart in her hands one morning and she had cried all day, unsure why she was upset or what she was crying over. She had been touched by her father's anger and his leaving; she had come to terms with it, adopting a selective longing that remembered only what was good, and pushing aside the rest, telling herself that nothing like it was ever going to happen to her – until a dazzling police sergeant had put a hand on her arm and suddenly she could recall with complete clarity the jumbled-up thoughts of an eleven-year-old child.

'Where is he now?' he asked.

'He moved to Birmingham years and years ago and got shacked up with another woman. The *Hon* Jessica Barrowclough. Imagine, daddy with an aristo! He now only communicates by solicitor's letter and doesn't bother visiting. Damn him,' she added, then regretted it as pain momentarily bloomed behind her eyes. *Consequences*, she thought, *always consequences*.

'I'm sorry,' he said. 'You've never talked about it before.'

'To be honest, it still pisses me off. The whole fucking pointlessness of it all. Anyway, I'm not remotely sorry,' she said flatly. 'He never sends enough money and my mum's frightened of rotting away in a fancy house that we can't really afford. No pennies, Richie; even the central heating's on tick.'

In her mind's eye the car was skidding on the drive, a hand was outstretched, his eyes were averted after seeing her at the window: a small child in a blue dress with one hand raised. 'I don't know why I'm telling you all this,' she said, looking at the sky and the churning clouds. 'Life sometimes happens in between the bits you plan. You told me that, you bastard.'

Adrian Mountjoy's office in Edinburgh's New Town, close by his small flat, was bathed in afternoon sun, an unfortunate and unforeseen occurrence that had transformed him into a rather colourful chameleon.

The illusion of Mountjoy as a small tropical creature was partly his own fault as he had approved the final design. His firm had only recently employed a local advertising and design agency to update their crusty image; to help present Mountjoy, Newbattle and Brown as a dynamic and forward-looking organisation at the start of a new millennium. Accountants, the design agency told them, had an old-fashioned reputation, albeit one of probity and diligence. In seeking a new image for the 21st Century it was important to maintain the strengths of the past whilst building a new image for tomorrow's customers. The design firm, understanding the problem completely, worked up a number of options, utilising their experience in graphics and industrial and social psychology, finally recommending a change of typeface for the stationery and a new logo in bright and contemporary colours. To Adrian Mountjoy's untrained eye, the new company logo represented the colours of dawn and sunset, of different shades of opinion working together within one integrated whole – a concept of modernity that the agency had also put forward to explain the seemingly random splodges of colour that could have been painted by a small child but which became the new corporate image of Mountjoy, Newbattle and Brown.

The new design was approved, with some reservation

from Brown – Newbattle was colour-blind and unable to contribute much to the debate – and quickly applied to the firm's stationery and promotional material. It was also represented on a large advertising blind that obscured the top half of Mountjoy's tall window in his second floor office and which, on sunny afternoons, beamed in a confusion of light and colour. Mountjoy's desk faced the window and, as he bent his face to his papers, he resembled either a chameleon or a Biblical Joseph, depending on your point of view.

His political obligations meant that he often had to work at weekends simply to keep up with his clients' financial demands. The small but distinguished firm of Mountjoy, Newbattle and Brown, business advisors and chartered accountants, had been founded by Mountjoy's father some fifty years before and, albeit in a modest way, had prospered ever since – enough, certainly, to ensure his son's progress through Glenalmond School and Cambridge. Mountjoy Jnr, an only child, had gladly accepted his progress through some of the country's finer educational establishments with due gratitude and, as a debt of honour to his father, had never considered any other career but the family business. His father now retired, Mountjoy was senior partner. He looked at his in-tray and estimated how much he had moved to his out-tray. Right now, and more prosaically, he had to finish auditing the accounts of the Sun Lai Chinese carryout.

He lived within walking distance of the office in a modest two-bedroom flat in a Georgian block; it suited his needs admirably and Mountjoy was not an ostentatious man. He was unmarried and, given the political whirl in which he lived, was probably unmarriageable. He paused from the Sun Lai's problems with the Health and Safety Executive, his torso – encased in a white open-neck shirt – turning bright red and his face bright green.

As the afternoon passed he found it increasingly difficult to concentrate. The earlier telephone conversation with Clare Derby was turning in his mind, offering him a bleaker analysis on events that he had hitherto imagined. OK, having a car accident wasn't clever – particularly since he was chairman of a road safety group – but he had been distracted. The sight of a large puma-like creature would have distracted anyone and, as the police sergeant had told him on the phone, the animal had now been identified. Not only had he good reason to be distracted but his story had been proved. OK, it was also unfortunate that the ensuing accident had caused a milk tanker to leak its contents into a small river and for the driver of the tanker to lose his job, but neither of those connected events could be laid at his door. The police sergeant had also said that it was unlikely that he would be charged in connection with the accident – it had neither been stupid nor careless driving – so he should be in the clear. The main fact of the accident was that it had been just that: an accident.

A distraction, he decided. That's what was needed. A distraction that would take people's attention away from his car accident. As he pondered this, the phone on his desk rang and he picked it up warily, expecting Clare Derby, to hear instead the measured tones of the Reverend Lionel Kennedy. Mountjoy was at first brusque – phone calls from ministers usually meant invitations to church charity events, and Mountjoy was not at that moment feeling charitable – then intrigued and, in slow degrees, positively effusive. A wide smile spread across his fatty jowls and his pen scribbled furiously.

After hanging up, Mountjoy poured himself a whisky and settled once more in his swivel chair, the firm's visionary logo colouring his face a steely grey and making him appear bold and resolute. He reached for the telephone with an indigo and peach arm, dialled a number in Glasgow and waited to be put through to an old chum on *Look North Tonight*.

Chapter 11

The herb is named of the Chaldees Iterisi, *of the Greeks* Vorax, *of the Latins* Proventalis, *or* Pervinca, *of Englishmen Periwinkle. When it is beaten unto powder with worms of the earth wrapped round it, and with an herb called* Sempervivum, *in English Houseleek, it induseth love between a man and woman, if it be used in their meats.*

The Book of Secrets of Albertus Magnus

Jack had spent the day finishing his VAT return, sweeping the last of the leaves from the beer garden and rehanging the function suite curtains. He'd also made a brief inventory of the damage, which didn't come to much. He was just about to settle down to a gin and tonic and the early evening news when his wife phoned.

'Jack.' Rosie always started phone calls by saying the other person's name, as if they might have forgotten who they were. For some reason, she never introduced herself first.

'Yes, my love.'

'Jack, it's me.'

'Yes, Rosie, I *know* it's you. I thought you were going to the theatre?'

'We're just waiting for the taxi. I must say I'm ever so excited. It's simply yonks since I've been to see a show. You'll never guess,' she added, dropping her voice to a stage whisper, 'what Betty's done.'

'Got married? Had a baby? Invaded Poland?' suggested Jack, at a loss to know what Betty Fullerton did at any time.

His wife hissed at him from the other end of the phone. 'Don't be *silly*, Jack! She's bought herself a new dog to replace Bones, that's what. It appears that the stupid thing got run over by a milk float. From Betty's description it wasn't very pleasant.' *Especially for poor Bones*, thought Jack, but was sensible enough not to share this with his wife. 'It's some kind of terrier, I think,' she added, sounding doubtful, before resuming her normal voice. 'You're managing without me, I take it?' His wife was being unusually solicitous having only deserted him hours beforehand.

'Shouldn't I be?' he asked.

'Well, I've left you chicken pie in the fridge and a nice bottle of wine, so you should be.' In the background he heard a doorbell ring and a yappy dog barking. 'What will you do? Have a quiet night?'

'Oh, I expect I'll get drunk, seduce a gypsy woman and elope to Gretna Green. The usual kind of thing that men get up to when their wives are away.' Rosie didn't sound amused, making indistinct small noises between her teeth whilst, off-stage, the yapping grew louder. 'On the other hand, I suppose I could just stay in and eat chicken pie.'

'Sorry?'

'Chicken pie,' he repeated loudly. 'I said that I might just eat your chicken pie. Apparently, I like it.'

'Sorry, Jack, but it's this blasted terrier thing. I can't hear myself think let alone have a conversation. She got it from some animal sanctuary place, so I suppose you have to make allowances. It's come from a broken doggie home, according to Betty.' Her voice dropped to a stage whisper once more. 'Promise me one thing, Jack – don't ever, *ever* buy me a dog. No surprise parties and no surprise dogs, got that?' She sounded genuinely concerned, as if he might have sneaked off to a pet shop in her absence and bought forty Great Danes for her birthday.

Jack now poured himself the generous gin and tonic he had promised himself, safe from whatever home-made wine had been left in the fridge, and safe too from the chicken pie which he had handed on to Sadie Gallagher to give to the minister. *It'll save you the bother of cooking*, he'd told her. *Lionel looks to me like a chicken pie sort of person. But not a word to Rosie, all right?* Sammy had fish stew on the evening menu, and that was his favourite.

He thought fondly of his wife although this fortieth birthday nonsense was becoming tiresome; so too this black cat business. They'd heard the stories, of course, such as they were, apparently put about the village by the antiquated idiot who had been the village minister. They hadn't been in the village twenty years before: like everyone else, they didn't know anything. Nobody did, of course, although Lionel's predecessor had apparently stirred up all sorts of rumours. He shook his head and wondered if Rosie would enjoy *Les Miserables,* which she had always wanted to see, apparently. Actually, this sudden flight to Edinburgh was typical of the woman. Rosie, it had to be said, was unpredictable and randomly obsessive: deciding to leave at a moment's notice for Edinburgh was entirely logical simply because it *was* utterly unpredictable. Likewise, the feigned grief over a distant friend's dead dog was equally implausible.

He remembered when they first met and the idyllic few days together in Sussex before he returned north to finish college. She'd been going out with some fellow student, temporarily out of the country on a student exchange, and had said that she'd choose between them once Jack went back to college. She said that she'd decide whose absence made her heart grow fonder. So he'd given her his address and phone number and she'd promised faithfully to contact him with her decision. But she didn't contact him, of course, and was then angry when he eventually phoned her some weeks later, because *he* hadn't contacted *her*. *Bloody woman*, he had thought then – and still often did – but had asked her to marry him nevertheless. He might move slowly but he got there in the end.

Her unpredictable obsessions all came together in her herbalism, the kitchen forever filled with the heady aromas of boiling foliage, the shelves in the scullery lined with jars containing God knows what. She worked at odd hours, sometimes in the morning, sometimes at dead of night if she couldn't sleep, scouring the countryside for herbs and plants.

This single obsession had remained throughout their marriage, a harmless enough hobby – except for her wine that Jack only drank out of sufferance – although some of her remedies did seem to work, if you could believe what you were told, of course. She was also qualified, he reminded himself. Sadie Gallagher, for example, swore by his wife's remedy for lumbago, and Arthur Grimshaw, who owned the *Old Curiosity Shop*, hadn't been near a doctor since she prescribed some of her bramble laxative. She maintained a small but regular band of customers, some of whom admitted where they received their medicines from and, over the years, Rosie had developed a certain benevolent reputation in the village. In his own way he was quite proud of her modest accomplishments although, when in need, he preferred the attentions of old Dr Murray at the health centre. Jack had faith in pharmaceutical advancement, all safely tested on rabbits and other small animals, and wasn't going to trade his neatly packaged medicines for something plucked from a hedgerow and boiled to a mush in his kitchen.

The local paper had written a story about her some years beforehand, calling her – what else – *Medicine Woman*, an epithet that caused much local mirth and underlined her benign reputation in the community. Her university certificate, now behind glass, hung in the scullery. The newspaper cutting hung in the public bar. There were a few villagers who grumbled about her – including the good Dr Murray who believed with some justification that the practice of medicine should only be carried out by those more suitably qualified. The secret, Rosie would say, is to know what boundaries of treatment not to cross.

Mara and Richie walked down to North Berwick's small harbour, and then over rocks towards the harbour's furthest point, the west sands on one side, the east sands on the other. Family groups sat on the sand and children paddled in the water's margins. They could just hear the hurdy-gurdy up on the playing fields and see splashes of smoke from the churning steam contraptions. On the water, a cargo ship lay low in the water, its deck piled with containers, heading towards Leith. On either side, spread out behind the beaches, was the genteel town itself. Behind them was the conical volcanic plug of North Berwick Law, a pyramid of a hill, a whale's jawbone marking its peak. A light breeze had sprung up and waves sucked gently on the rocks. In the afternoon sun, the Bass Rock shone white, clouded by gannets that, from the harbour, were as small as insects. Richie followed her along the man-made concrete pathway that leads to a small lighthouse on the point, aware again that something had altered. She had been telling him about her thesis and why she had studied history; trying to convey something of herself by conjuring up stories from the past.

'Think of history as a book,' she said. 'A story that's continually changing. To understand where we fit in, you have to understand the previous chapters.'

'That's too clever for me.'

'*Everything* is too clever for you, that's your trouble.' She pointed backwards past the Law. 'Did you know that there once lived a king called Loth who lived up there in the

Lammermuir Hills? No, of course you didn't. He had a daughter, whose name I forget. She was a Christian, he wasn't. OK, no problem there, until king wants her to marry some nobleman. Instead, she runs off with her real love, a local shepherd, and gets pregnant. Definitely, not OK. By way of punishment, King Loth has her chucked off Traprain Law, and that should have been the end of it. But, miraculously, she survived the fall, and the king gets suddenly worried in case there might be something in this Christianity thing. So, he put her in a coracle and set her off up-river without a paddle. She landed over there.' Here she pointed, coming close to him so that he could look along her arm to the talon of her extended forefinger. 'Near Culross in the Kingdom of Fife, to be precise. Anyway, she had the baby, called it Mungo, and he later converted the west of Scotland to Christianity. He gets himself canonised and into the history books as St Mungo, the Lothians get named after a king who tried to kill his daughter... and I can't remember the mother's name. To history, you see, she isn't important.' She brushed hair back from her eyes, squinting across the water. 'What I'm trying to say is that most of history is about the big stuff, the really important things. I like the little stuff... the details that make up the real story. Me, I want to know what happened to the mother. I'm not explaining myself very well, am I?' She smiled wanly, leaning against him, still looking over the water towards a place where a small boat had once landed.

'Maybe she went back to her shepherd,' he suggested.

'No, I don't suppose that it would have been possible.'

No, she thought, *you can't always go back*. She had a choice to make but, really, it had already been made.

Later, seated cross-legged on the grass in Richie's small and unkempt garden, Mara shielded her eyes and looked up, hearing what sounded like a child's cry.

The buzzard was so high it was no more than a small dot against the cloud base, or a speck of dust on the lens of a camera; it floated as motionless on the updrafts as if painted on a photograph of the sky. From up there it would have seen northwards across Fife; south, across the rolling hills to the English border; west to the Wallace Monument and east across the horizons of the North Sea. Looking down, it would have seen a beautiful young woman in faded blue jeans and borrowed rugby shirt, an edge of memory in her expression as if also remembering the gift of flight.

'I don't think I've ever met a man who could cook before. Except Sammy, of course.' Still shielding her eyes, she watched as a second buzzard joined its companion with a cry of exultation or adulation, then turned and wheeled across the village and, bending their wing-tips against the thermals, dived like fighter planes towards the old woodland above Holy Cross. She paused to light a cigarette, grimacing at his look of disapproval. 'Richie, *please* don't be a fascist. I promise to give up, OK?'

'When?'

'Soon.'

'When exactly is "soon"?'

'Soon means soon. Anyway, maybe you're only telling

me you can cook to impress me.' She blew smoke at the sky and regarded him with a small smile.

He had opened a bottle of white wine and now poured two glasses, one of which he handed to her and then lay on the grass beside her, glass balanced on his chest. 'Shellfish and salad isn't difficult. The tricky part was the mayonnaise. I had to go to Tesco's for that. Anyway, I didn't say I could cook. What I said was, why not come back for supper. But, yes, the shellfish was definitely to impress you.' He looked momentarily worried. 'You can eat shellfish, can't you?'

'I told you, I don't eat cuddly animals.'

'Shellfish aren't cuddly.'

'A distinction I also happen to agree with.' She pulled on her cigarette, making the end glow. From somewhere in the village came a burst of rock music, swiftly silenced, and the blare of a car horn. In her. He sensed both danger and desire: her painted fingers like claws that could either tear or caress.

She drank from her fluted glass, squinting against the low sun, and again remembered her transformation; the soaring journey of free flight to the dark loch where anything was possible. She looked at the young policeman and touched his face with the fingertips of one hand.

He could feel each blade of grass against his neck, the dying sun on his cheek, the call of songbirds darting between trees. Hesitantly, she put her head on his chest, lustrous hair cascading. He put an arm around her, somehow knowing that, at least for now, she was tamed. He felt her weight and the soft whisper of her breath. 'I dreamed about you last night,' she said. He squeezed her shoulder, saying nothing, sensing a threshold. She frowned, another fragment of memory returning. She now recalled that, behind the circle of light, in the half-shadows beside the loch's shore, another figure had been standing quietly. This figure, also dressed in white, had simply stood and watched. At her throat was a necklace of sparkling moonstones. She bit her lip, trembling slightly as the sun edged lower. The moonstones had caught the light from the torches and made another half circle of light, reflections from the flames on the dark loch. Why hadn't she remembered her before? She remembered her presence almost as a shadow, and then the falling torches momentarily illuminating her face – her own face. In the circle of light, Mara had been both spectator and participant.

'C'mon, let's eat,' she said suddenly, sitting up, a hand to her brow, as falling torches filled her mind. She touched his face again with the tips of one hand, grateful for the sudden memory and of her other self, just beyond the circle of light, raising a hand in silent blessing.

Richie too felt altered but supposed it was just too much sunshine and home-made wine. He felt energised but also sad; conflicting emotions seemed to be piling up, without discernible rhyme or reason. He watched her as she chopped lettuce: the curve of her spine, the swell of her buttocks encased in tight jeans, her long and shapely legs. She was barefooted, kicking off her shoes the moment they had come inside, her feet soundless on the lino floor. She looked over her shoulder and saw him watching her. She smiled.

'What did you dream about?' he asked.

She looked back at him again, then chopped furiously at a cucumber. 'It was a very odd dream,' she said after a pause. 'I dreamed that I could fly. Fly anywhere, I suppose.' Her hand stilled on the knife; *but I chose to stay*, she realised. I could have flown anywhere but I *chose* the dark loch.

'Does that mean it was a rude dream?' he teased.

'Hey, I've got the knife, remember,' she replied, waving it at him. She scraped chopped salad into a bowl and wiped her hands on a dishcloth. The dark loch was both a place she had visited and a place within herself that she had unexpectedly found, beyond reproach or explanation.

She poured a glass of wine then noticed her photograph pinned to the notice board by the fridge. It startled her somehow, an image of herself pinned to his wall; her eyes narrowed and her expression become still. The face in the picture was hers, but it wasn't. A twin sister, another person, dressed in her clothes. She touched the photograph, feeling confused.

'Arthur's Seat,' he said, coming up silently and giving her a small fright. 'You pointed out every one of the city's landmarks and told me all about them in complete and utter detail. Remember? That's when I started to believe you were into history.'

She remembered. 'It's a gift. I could bore for Scotland.'

'Actually, I believe you. Later we went to Haddington and you tried to push me in the river.' He watched her touch the picture, a frown on her forehead; in the photograph her head was turned to the camera, her body in profile, billowing blonde hair partly covering her face.

'Do you know,' she said after a few moments, 'that you look a bit like a young Robert de Niro? No, don't laugh! It's true! It's what I thought when I first clapped eyes on you. What's a young Robert de Niro doing here *and* in a police uniform, I thought.'

'You, I remember, were crossing a road and reading a newspaper. Do you ever look both ways before crossing roads?'

She sniffed, arms rigid and heavy by her side. The photograph now seemed faded, like a snapshot from an ancient album brought out to amuse the grandchildren. 'Anyway, I expect you deserved to get pushed in.'

Richie too now studied the photograph. The bright girl in the photograph was witty and glittery; filled with energy; the person next to him now was the same but not the same. He tried to put a finger on what had changed and couldn't. He'd sensed it earlier as well, lying on the grass and feeling each blade on his neck, her head on his chest, her clean smell filling his nostrils. He blinked, simultaneously feeling hot and cold, his emotions peeling back like onion skin. He took a deep breath, tasting Rosie's wine as he exhaled.

They ate at his small table in the kitchen, laughing at each other's jokes and, with a new intimacy, spoke of things not previously shared. She felt inexplicably relaxed: no, more than that. She felt absolved from the past and, without its weight, absolved too from the present. She felt as if this moment was a vacuum in time: a capsule within which there was no right or wrong. As she ate, small tremors ran up and down her spine.

Richie too felt a shift in perception; he again supposed it was Rosie's home-made concoction. He'd never drunk rhubarb or bison grass, or whatever it was. He had always loved Mara, of course; right from that defining moment when she'd turned from her newspaper. He'd seen *The Godfather*. He knew that lightning could strike the heart in one breath-taking moment. He'd had his share of girls – compulsory given his good looks – but this was different: in a flash of a turning head and cascading hair, Richie had been pierced to the quick. He had, of course, engineered his invitation to Max's party.

'You did what!'

'I invited myself. Told Jamie – that's Max's flatmate – that I needed to meet people. I don't think he believed me. Still, it did the trick, didn't it?'

She was flattered and said so.

'Don't be,' he replied. 'You know I'd slay dragons for you.'

'No more dragons left, Richie. Too many white knights. Too few damsels in distress.'

He was biting his lip, feeling suddenly hot. 'There are always dragons. Metaphorically, of course.'

Outside, the sun flamed and died; he fetched candles from a cupboard in the hallway and she placed them in a circle on the table between them. He again sensed that she could be either lover or predator, her sharp fingernails dextrous on the shellfish. He felt both peaceful and threatened, a circle of candlelight in her eyes and her gaze steady and unblinking. *But I have tamed you*, he told himself, no longer trusting what he felt. The onion of emotions was still unfolding; he felt tears prickle his eyes although he didn't now care what animal she might become.

Afterwards she simply dumped the dirty dishes into the sink. 'Your house, your mess,' she informed him, opening another bottle of wine. They told each other about the Edinburgh they'd known as children, how they could conceivably have bumped into each other at the National Gallery or the cinema. She told him about her work – dull, *dull!* – her friends and flatmates – one sunning herself in la belle France – and how, again, after years and years, her banker father had finally made good in a property deal and then promptly made off to a new life in Birmingham, the bastard.

'You see, dragons.'

'Dragons?' She didn't immediately understand.

'Your dragons. The dragons that live on the inside.' He tapped the side of his head for emphasis.

She was trembling again, but not from troubled memory. The car was skidding, but she wasn't beckoning or waving at the upstairs window. This time, she was simply looking on. It was history: ancient history, without resonance or meaning; she could now look, without pity or judgement, across the vista of years.

'No more dragons, Richie. Dead and gone. Promise.' She smiled sadly, looking to his notice board and her picture which was surrounded by pinned up milk bills and useful numbers. The detritus of normality surrounding an image from another place and time.

'Why did you become a copper?' she asked. Such an obvious question, but she'd never asked it before. Now that he knew things about her, she wanted to know things about him. Real stuff, like the fact that he was afraid of heights. The kind of things that explained him; made him human: the fault lines that she could then trace with a finger and recognise his silhouette next to hers.

He shrugged. 'I grew up with it, I suppose. My dad was a policeman, so it was an easy decision for me to make.' He looked off into the middle distance. 'I guess that I never found anything else to do. It's a living, I suppose,' he said, sensing an unwanted memory seep towards consciousness.

'You're frowning,' she said. 'Anyway, what made you come here? After all, Holy Cross isn't exactly an epicentre of crime. Or were you simply looking for an easy life?' She smiled wickedly. 'Please don't tell me that you're really a wimp, Richie!'

He couldn't immediately reply; couldn't smile back. The memory was taking shape, a swirl of smoke at the edge of his mind. Within its shifting outline he was able to discern faces. He shuddered, suddenly cold.

To blot it out, he told her about his Uncle Ned who once nearly burnt the house down with a dropped cigar, about Frank, his best friend through school, who ran off to join a circus, and then, unable to stop the flow of words how, hardly more than a year ago, he'd found a small boy who had fallen from a third floor tenement, his hand still clutching a grey teddy bear. He was dead.

At that he became still, the fragment of memory now

jagged and sharp. Then he took a swig of wine and laid the glass down between them. She noticed that his hand was shaking. He raised one hand from the table and turned it over, palm upwards. Then he made a fist and laid it back on the wooden table top.

'That,' he told her with surprise, 'is when I decided to leave Edinburgh.'

She looked at him, her expression blank. 'Does that mean you're running away?'

He took one of her hands in his, shaking his head: he had never admitted that moment to anyone before, least of all to himself. Explosions of memory burst inside his skull in flashes of bright colour. That night he'd gone out with some mates for a few beers and a curry. He'd not given it a second thought; he had a job to do. She felt his hand tremble again, saw tears in his eyes.

'Dragons, Richie. Your dragon.'

'I'm sorry,' he said. 'I have absolutely no idea what made me remember that.'

'Because it matters to you.'

His mind was clearing. 'No. Well, maybe. I dunno. Or maybe, until now, I didn't realise it.' He laughed but instead, to his consternation, found tears on his cheeks. Christ! What the fuck was happening to him? He wanted to apologise, to cover his face. Instead, he said in a thin voice: 'He was only small, Mara. I had to go to the hospital.'

'I know.' Her voice was only a whisper.

'God, I don't know why I'm telling you all this.' He took a deep breath, trying hard to be the action hero. The memory

171

of the small child was clear; he could look back with detached clarity, feel the pavement under his feet – as clearly as he'd earlier felt each blade of grass. He took a deep breath and smiled wanly.

He could also remember the smell of the hospital, the rushing nurses, and their bustling efficiency. There was nothing anybody could do; at the end of life it simply remained for a formal identification to take place and for the correct forms to be completed in triplicate. Then he was free to finish his shift, change into civilian clothes and, over a few pints, decide what curry house most deserved their patronage.

'It all seemed such a waste. A small child, his head split open. I felt so useless. There wasn't anything I could have done.'

She had one hand pressed on his. 'Is that why you came here?'

He uncertainly shook his head. 'Do you know, I really have no idea. Until now, to be honest, I didn't really know why I applied to come here. To be somewhere different, that's what I told myself. Maybe, too many bad experiences. That was the worst.'

'You don't have to be strong all the time, Richie.'

'Then what should I be?'

'Just to be decent,' she said. 'Like the other night with Dunc Hedges. You drove round the village until you found him, didn't you? Then you took him to Haddington where you could have banged him up for the night. Instead, you took him home, made sure he got in safely. Had a cup of tea

172

with his girlfriend and explained what had happened. You didn't have to do any of that.' She stroked his hair gently.

When she came back from the loo, he was still sitting at the table, hands bunched in his lap, a lock of hair over one eye. She remembered the freedom of flight and a place of silent judgement where anything was possible. She stepped forward towards the dying candles and pulled the rugby shirt over her head, dropping it to the floor. Her gaze didn't leave him. In the loo she'd already removed her jeans and underwear, tucking her bra and panties into her jeans pockets. She stepped forwards again, into the candlelight, shadows dancing over her translucent nakedness. At the ends of all pleasure there is only love, she thought. She blew out the guttering candles.

He rose from the table and held tightly to her. She placed a finger to his lips.

'Mara —'

She shook her head, kissing him, and took his hand.

What she had to give had no price attached and she didn't want to be told anything that he might regret, or that she might regret believing. They placed a new candle on his bedside table and she watched him undress. She lay down uncertainly, a perfect object of desire, her hair billowing across the pillow.

Every Saturday, the Reverend Kennedy visited the sick and lonely in his congregation, providing whatever solace that he could in difficult circumstances. It was still a relatively tight-knit community, despite the best attentions of tourists and weekenders, and he took his pastoral duties seriously: it was expected of him. So he'd visited the sick, calling in on the cottage hospital, travelling as far as Dunbar to see an elderly parishioner now confined to a care home.

On his return he'd found a note from Sadie with precise instructions on how to warm through the chicken pie, peas and boiled potatoes that she'd left, instructions simple enough for even him. He ate in front of the television, watching an old western. He enjoyed its moral certainties: the good guys in white hats against the bad guys in black hats, with men having to do what men have to do and John Wayne getting his girl. In an advertising break he rose and fetched second helpings, balancing the tray on his knee: Sadie had excelled herself. It was a taste straight from childhood.

His father had been an infantry soldier in World War II and had fallen for his mother who was serving as a nurse in Normandy: he was shot in the leg and she was charged with his recovery. She was a Yorkshire lass – no *nouvelle cuisine* in their household – and the young Lionel had been brought up on vast portions of wholesome country fare. By the time he had finished his second helping, his mood had so improved that he poured himself a large brandy, John Wayne setting off down-river on a raft. His sermon was complete, the sick ministered to, and he had been – for one gastronomic moment – transported back to childhood. He sighed with fond memory as sticks of explosive blew up the last of the bad guys and John Wayne rode into the sunset.

Normally he would have gone straight to bed. He was a

man of fixed routines and it was now, precisely, time for bed. He got up at the same time each morning, ate fish each Friday, roast beef on Sunday, and retired to bed at set times. He supposed it was one of the by-products of older age or of living alone. Tonight, however, he didn't feel like going to bed. It had been a strange and confusing day, a day of half-formed worries and unopened files that the young policeman said would remain closed. He crossed to the window, drew back the heavy velvet curtains and opened a window. Over the village were the lights from other houses, other lives. His parishioners.

He poured himself another brandy, the chicken pie now heavy on his stomach, and watched the news. It was dominated by an earthquake in Japan and, inevitably, the imminent general election. Voter apathy was the issue, what with Scotland now having its own parliament. Why bother voting for that lot at Westminster when most decisions are made here and, anyway, Labour seemed to have it in the bag. 'And finally,' said the TV announcer, a broad smile on his face, 'it appears that hubble, bubble, toil and trouble may be about to hit Scotland's best-known village. Where else but Holy Cross in East Lothian where, so the story goes, a bit of the Holy Grail is buried. It's been alleged that recent sightings of a mysterious puma-like cat in the area may be about to trigger a re-emergence of witchcraft – as it did, apparently, twenty years ago when another large cat was seen. If you're not already behind the sofa, Mark Fisher has the details…'

Presenter: *The village of Holy Cross just east of*

Edinburgh is probably one of the oldest inhabited places in central Scotland. Old it may be, but it also has the strangest of histories. Damian Andersen is an archaeologist at Glasgow University.

(Cut to middle-aged man with a shaved head, large moustache, and a tweed suit). *The village marks the spot where, reputedly, a piece of the Holy Grail, embedded in a golden cross, was buried by monks fleeing from King Henry VIII. Of course, (*the archaeologist smiled and waved his arms about*) despite this being a very well-known story there is no hard evidence that the cross ever existed.*

(Cut back to presenter who is standing beside the main road to Edinburgh. Behind him is the village's roadside sign). *Holy Cross's reputation as a place of witchcraft worship dates from the seventeenth century when East Lothian was famed, or infamous, for it. Nowadays, visitors come here from all over the world, mostly unaware of this other side to the village's reputation. Edwina Tomkins is a spokesperson for the Pagan Society.*

(Cut to dowdy woman with staring eyes in a green cardigan*). The village lies on a profusion of ley lines running between the northern isles, the Outer Hebrides and St Andrews, linking Holy Cross with Canterbury, Rheims in France and Tromsö in Sweden. It is certainly therefore a place of some mystic significance and may, who knows, actually be the final resting place of the Holy Grail. Pagan worship, including witchcraft, was, of course, well known in the village and is, indeed, much more common today than most people suppose.*

Presenter: *Recent sightings of the large cat have been reported by Adrian Mountjoy, the Conservative candidate for East Lothian and the local Church of Scotland minister. Local rumour is that the black cat may mark a resurgence of witchcraft in the village. It last happened two decades ago, apparently, when a similar cat was spotted. What is certain is that witchcraft symbols have been found carved onto the local church, leading some to believe that events – whatever they were – may be about to repeat themselves. Police sources confirm that animal tracks have been found in the vicinity and are asking people to be vigilant.*

(Cut back to studio, where the grinning anchorman is stacking papers and winking at the camera). 'Thanks, Mark. That's it for tonight so, if you can, sleep well…'

Lionel Kennedy listened in appalled disbelief. He had been betrayed by someone in whom he had placed his trust. The report did not mention Mountjoy as the story's source, but who else could be responsible? 'Dear God,' he said aloud.

Richie Scott had entered a dark corridor along which he walked steadily towards a blue light, his footsteps echoing on a floor that smelled scrubbed and antiseptic. The walls, curiously, ran with a sticky substance and he heard drips falling from the ceiling. He looked back; the corridor behind him was empty. On each side were closed doors. He walked on more uncertainly, the blue light closer, a translucent partition between him and the hurrying figures he could now dimly see on the other side. He paused, listening to his own laboured breathing, and placed a hand momentarily on the wet corridor wall. He heard their voices now and telephones ringing and again walked towards the filament that separated him from the hurrying figures. He reached forward to find that he was touching some kind of plastic door that yielded to his touch and slowly opened. He stepped through, a blaze of light blinding him.

He opened his eyes slowly; he stepped backwards and again steadied himself against the wall. He was in a hospital corridor – some sort of treatment area. He was wearing his police uniform. A large West Indian nurse hurried by, her eyes averted, carrying a metal tray on which gleamed surgical instruments. On either side were treatment rooms and, in front, a desk behind which sat other nurses with telephones to their ears. Some of the beds were empty; others were occupied. In one, a small girl lay still, a bandage on her face. In another, an old man writhed, a drip feeding one arm. A third was closed off by curtains.

He became aware that between him and the desk was a long bench on which sat a young woman. She was unnaturally still, as if frozen. He stepped forwards. She had brown wavy hair cut short in a bob and was dressed in a green jogging suit. Eyes cast down, she sat in the centre of the bench, her knees pressed together and her hands bunched in her lap. She looked up as he approached, hearing the crackle of his radio, and reached up to him, searching his face with desperate eyes. Then she was standing, clinging to him. Her fingers dug into his back and she wailed with such misery that it was almost beautiful.

In Mara's mind other worlds were colliding; the dark figure on the shoreline, her other self, was nearby. She heard her breath in the breeze that moved the trees outside and saw her own shape in the drift of curtains pulled shut against the open window. In her translucent hand was the moonstone necklace and she laid it quietly down, somewhere beyond the foot of the bed, and then turned and left, her departure no more than a cloud passing across the face of the moon. On the dark shore she had watched herself watch herself from beyond the circle. She knew that her dream had offered her a choice, and she had finally chosen. She accepted him gladly and without condition, her cry of ecstasy so intensely beautiful that it could also have been pain.

Chapter 12

The herb is named of the Chaldees Algeil, of the Greeks Orum, of the Latins Lingua canin, of Englishmen Hound's tongue. Put thou this herb with the heart of a young Frog and her matrix, and put them where thou wilt, and after a time all the Dogs of the whole town shall be gathered together. And if thou shalt have the aforenamed herb under thy foremost toe, all the Dogs shall keep silence, and shall not have power to bark.

The Book of Secrets of Albertus Magnus

Holy Cross, with its history of witchcraft and the Holy Grail, was transformed overnight from a nationally treasured backwater into the wiccan capital of Europe, if some of the racier tabloids were to be believed. Adrian Mountjoy had thought that a little harmless TV exposure – jocular and light-hearted – would generate enough heat to turn the political spotlight elsewhere. He certainly hadn't quite anticipated the public's appetite for the occult – especially when mysterious animals and the Church of Scotland were also involved.

The News of the World and *The Sunday Mail* both ran the story as their main front page headline, but with scant regard to the few pertinent facts that they possessed, concentrating instead on the village's association with the Glastonbury Cross and the legend of the Holy Grail.

If the same story had broken in a small village of no historical significance in, say, Yorkshire – a place about which the national press knows little and cares even less – it would have died a quick and happy death. However, given the particular circumstances, even *The Sunday Telegraph* managed to cover the story on its front page, having roused a professor of medieval history at Aberdeen University. Their coverage of the story had more historical accuracy, even listing the various archaeological excavations that have taken place over the years to locate the elusive cross. The evidence suggests, their story concluded, that the cross was probably an Augustinian invention to throw King Henry's troops off the scent of other treasures. Still, it added brightly, a lot of innocent folk from the area *were* burned at the stake. However, even *The Sunday Telegraph* couldn't resist running this sober analysis under the headline "SALEM COMES TO THE LOTHIANS".

This, it has to be said, was preferable to *The Sunday Sport* that simply featured a naked woman astride a broomstick under the banner "TEN THINGS YOU DIDN'T KNOW ABOUT WITCHES" – "Witches like to fly with their familiar black pussies. *Sunday Sport* readers like black pussies..." *The Sunday Times* chose to ignore the story altogether, the only national newspaper to take the view that what goes on in the privacy of rural Scotland should remain there.

Tam Cronin, wearing a stained white coat, worked in the village newsagents on Sunday mornings. It wasn't exactly full-time employment but it was, as he explained, a small diversion from doing nothing. He sold out of every newspaper by nine o'clock – even *The Sunday Sport*, the overnight story giving the married men of the village a perfect excuse to buy it. Some of the older villagers handed over their money grim-faced, not wanting the unwelcome attention that the media would inevitably bring in its wake. The village already attracted a fair number of cranks, many with metal detectors and shovels, others with long hair and beads. Like a Mecca, Arthurian and pagan societies from across the globe beat a path to the village. From the glare of publicity, more would undoubtedly be on their way.

Tam handed over Jack's newspapers. 'You'll have heard the news then,' he remarked. It was a statement rather than a question. By then, almost everybody had heard the news.

Jack counted out change and shrugged.

'So what do you think?'

Jack shook his head. 'Do you know, Tam, I don't think anything at all,' he replied, wondering how his wife would react when, eventually, she came back from Edinburgh. Of course, like all long-standing village residents, they'd been told about Adam Campbell's ill-judged sermon denouncing the evils of witchcraft, and which had precipitated his retirement from the Church. Nobody that Jack had spoken to had ever taken the minister's sermon seriously. Nobody, that is, except Rosie. She took everything seriously, even things that were patently nonsense.

Returning to the *Fox and Duck*, newspapers under one arm, he was surprised to find that she had already returned and, not having listened to a news broadcast, was probably the only person in Scotland not to know about the village's national notoriety. This he surmised almost immediately as Rosie kissed him frostily on one cheek and enquired solicitously about his bowels.

'Adrian, you really must consult with me before talking to the press.' Clare Derby was greatly displeased, enunciating each word carefully. 'We have an election upon us, and it's an election we simply *must* win. The country is depending on us.'

'I thought I *had* consulted with you. You told me —'

'I didn't advise you to turn a small local difficulty into national news,' she said sharply. Her disappointment oozed down the phone line. The small media torch he had diverted was now being replaced by a battery of extremely large spotlights, any one of which might shine unkindly in their direction. Mountjoy, in his small New Town flat, distinctly heard her diamond-encrusted rings tap the receiver for emphasis. 'You should have phoned me last night *before* talking to your journalist friend. Adrian, really!'

'You told me to spin,' he said defensively.

'Honestly, Adrian! Witchcraft, I ask you! It's not the kind of thing that the Conservative Party usually gets involved with.' Clare Derby sounded pained, as if Mountjoy had trodden dog dirt into the house.

'I agree it's preposterous, but the minister —'

'Please don't interrupt when we have important matters to discuss,' she said, tapping again at the receiver with her jewelled rings and reaching a decision. 'You, Adrian, are going to have to lie low for a while.' She said this emphatically, making him sound like a bank robber. 'Do you understand me?'

He sighed. 'Clare, we have an election to fight. I have to canvass. I've meetings to attend. I've got a speech to make in Gullane —'

'You've been assaulted, Adrian… grievously assaulted by an oik. It takes time to recover from these things, to regain composure. We want the voters of East Lothian to sympathise with you. The good people of Gullane know that you'd much rather be speaking to them than lying, bruised and sore, at home.'

'Actually, I'm fine.'

'No, you are not fine!' Clare Derby placed a full stop between each clearly enunciated word. 'Most assuredly *not* fine. You've been assaulted. I simply don't want a bad situation made worse. I don't want it inflamed. I want you to lie low.'

There was a short silence. 'I do wish that you hadn't seen that cat, I honestly do. Really, Adrian, you shouldn't have reported it to the police. It makes us look so, well, *silly.*'

'I had a car accident,' he reminded her. 'I had to report all the salient facts and I'm afraid, Clare, the cat was a salient fact.'

Clare Derby cleared her throat, unconvinced that Conservatives should report seeing improbable wildlife, but didn't say anything.

'No, of course I haven't read the newspapers, Jack. I've just driven down from Edinburgh, and I can't read and drive at the same time. Anyway, bowels, Jack, it's a simple question.'

To his certain knowledge she had not asked such a question during all their years of marriage.

'They're fine, thank you,' he said after some moments, feeling that some further response was required but quite unable to think of one.

She was pottering aimlessly by the sink, lifting up plates and saucers, then replacing them on the draining board. She was clearly distracted and on the prowl. He glanced down at the stack of newspapers neatly piled on the kitchen table. 'You did eat that chicken pie, didn't you?' she asked at last, facing him from across the room. 'Honestly, Jack, I go to all the trouble of making you —'

'It was delicious!' he lied gallantly, knowing that this would generate further chicken pies, its place as *Jack's favourite* firmly fixed in his wife's mind. Right at that moment it seemed easier to lie, what with everything else that was going on. 'Anyway, how was the theatre?'

Rosie was looking at him speculatively, an ignited spark in her eye. 'Betty sends her love, by the way, although I don't know why. She knows you don't like her.'

This was news to Jack who had only met Betty on two brief occasions, both years beforehand. He didn't know Betty well enough to know whether he liked her or not. However, he let it pass, keenly aware that his wife remained strangely agitated. 'Actually, there's something that I want to ask you,' she said, opening the fridge and poking about inside. Then, abruptly, she closed the fridge door with some force and advanced towards him. 'It's a simple question, Jack, and a simple "yes" or "no" will suffice. OK?'

He shrugged, settling himself on a kitchen chair. The newspapers would have to wait until Rosie's interrogation was complete. She was still, quite obviously, in a foul mood. *Les Miserables* had not changed that.

She looked closely at him, her dark eyes troubled, her small mouth pressed in an oval. 'The question is, Jack, whether or not you still love me? It's something that's been worrying me.' She sat on a chair facing him and leaned her elbows on the table. 'Well, that's the question, Jack, and I'd like an honest answer. As I said, it's a straightforward question requiring only a "yes" or "no".'

Ah, so that was it. More reassurance as the clock ticked down to year zero. 'Yes, of course I do,' he said, meaning it, and would have placed a hand on hers had she been close enough. Rosie, however, was keeping a safe distance.

'Not, *of course*, Jack,' she snapped, drumming her fingers on the table, pondering again on what may have taken place in the beer garden – and why it hadn't happened to her, her lacy purchases still hidden at the bottom of a drawer. 'That makes it sound insincere. I clearly explained that you had to say only "yes" or "no".'

Clearly explained? This was pedantry, even by her precise standards. 'Look,' he asked. 'You didn't get drunk last night and have a girly chat, did you?' Rosie did have a habit of going to girls' nights out and returning home with strange ideas on love and relationships, usually gleaned from women whose own marital relationships were in tatters.

'Yes or no, Jack?'

'Yes,' he said.

'Cross your heart and hope to die?' But it seemed that a distant spark in her eye had been extinguished.

He bit his lip. 'Does this by any chance have something to do with what happened on Friday night?' he asked, thinking about Mara and the small group of Conservatives at the function suite window. It was time to come clean. 'Look, Rosie, there is a perfectly simple explanation,' he said, and would have tried – somehow – to explain it, had Rosie not pulled a rectangular blue box from her handbag and extracted a pair of glasses. She saw his surprise and squared her shoulders, daring him to laugh.

'I went to one of those glasses express places,' she said vaguely, pulling *The Sunday Telegraph* from the top of Jack's pile and studying it intently. 'You won't have noticed but I'm getting old and going blind. Like a bat. God, it's depressing.' She frowned at the paper, then looked sharply at him over the top of her new glasses. 'Next week, just to be on the safe side, I may also get false teeth.' She took off her glasses and ran a hand through her hair.

'It's just a birthday, Rosie.'

'It's my fortieth bloody birthday! Christ, what a fucking, *fucking* mess!' she said and started to cry. 'Jack, you wouldn't lie to me, would you?' It was a stupid, *stupid* question, blurted out in a moment of weakness. She wanted reassurance, to be loved. She wanted to be desired, to feel that she could be young again. But the complete and utter bastard hadn't eaten the chicken pie – that much was evident from a lack of crockery on the draining board. Nor had she found the remnants of home-made wine in the fridge, or the empty bottle in the recycling box under the sink.

Jack came round the table and held her close as she sobbed, although it was unclear whether she was crying about her impending birthday or the fact that Holy Cross was now the witchcraft centre of the universe and, as everyone knew, Rosie was the resident witch.

'I'd never lie to you,' he said softly. 'I've always, always loved you, Rosie – right from the moment you spilled your drink over me. That time when we first met, remember?'

Of course she remembered, the large oaf apologising for his clumsiness. She could have corrected his false memory, but chose not to, her tears falling to the newspaper where they formed small dark circles.

'All this,' he said, gesturing to the newspapers, 'is nothing.'

'It's something, Jack,' she replied, her face in his shoulder, and her mind beginning to frame a dark and threatening canvas.

Chapter 13

The herb is named of the Chaldees Glerisa, *of the
Greeks* Isaphinus, *of the Latins* Rosa, *of Englishmen a
Rose. Take the grain or corn of it, and the corn of
Mustard seed and the foot of a Weasel, and if the
aforesaid powder be put in a lamp, and after be
kindled, all men shall appear black as the devil.*

The Book of Secrets of Albertus Magnus

Something small but profound had changed, something
subtle able to move mountains. The shift had happened to
them both. No more dragons. Slain. All gone. *Dragons*, he'd
said, touching the side of his head. *Metaphorically*. He'd
watched her as she slept, her hair cascading across the
pillows, the soft sound of her breathing.

'I can't lose you now,' he told her. 'Not now that I've
found you.'

'You won't,' she replied.

'Promise?'

'There's nothing to promise.'

Oh, but there was. In his dreamscape of tortured loss,
Richie remembered the haunted disbelief in the young

mother's eyes. She had loved and lost; no salvation or the promise of hope.

He remembered Mara stepping into the light of the flickering candles. 'I dreamed this moment,' she had said, putting a finger to his lips.

No, it had already happened before that moment of pure clarity. He had known it from the moment she stepped into his car on the way to the fair at North Berwick. He had sensed that a tenet of her being had been changed or cast aside. The night before in his bedroom had only been a fulfilment of a previous journey. A journey completed in candlelight downstairs and – standing at its edge, nervous but certain, a rite of passage to be completed.

They had talked for much of the night, kissed and made love. Then, before dawn, he found tears on her cheeks.

'Why are you crying?' he'd asked.

'I'm not really crying,'

'Then it's a girly thing, is it?'

She nodded, holding him tight. She had dreamed this moment, only to find that she could make it real. She *had* made it real. She had *chosen* to make it real. She could have flown anywhere. Instead, she'd chosen *him* and to remove his golden mask. She slept with one arm extended over the edge of the bed, new toxins in her bloodstream and nerve endings sizzling.

In the morning, Richie told Mara that he loved her. That he had always loved her. The dawn chorus was in loud symphony and early sunshine cast moving streamers.

190

'I bet you say that to all the girls.'

'Never. Only once. Now.'

Another decision, except that she had already made it. 'And I you,' she replied, feeling alive but again tearful. Simple words, but with consequence attached. This wasn't what she had planned. She was now on a road that she had always avoided. It had no signposts, no certainties. It didn't end at the Great Wall or Tibet. It didn't have a destination; she could be hurt, like her mother. The words made her vulnerable, the child with her hand to an upstairs window.

She felt fearful but also liberated. She had chosen her fantasy and made it happen. She had chosen dangerous words and spoken them aloud. The consequences could wait.

She touched his face with one hand, tracing its contours. She was frowning. 'I just don't know what happens now. It's a little unnerving.'

'Breakfast might be a good idea.'

Her brows were still furrowed. 'I mean after breakfast. Tonight, tomorrow.' She drew back from him sharply. 'It did mean something, didn't it, Richie? Please say it did.'

Strangely, he couldn't have lied to her if he tried. He felt utterly unable to say anything, except the truth, and would have done so but for the police station doorbell ringing downstairs in the sharp end. 'It's OK,' he said, unfolding his godlike body from the bed and pulling on a cream dressing gown. 'I'm off duty. I'll be back,' he intoned, in a gravelly voice.

To his surprise it was Big Mac himself, here in person and not in a good humour, informing him that he was unexpectedly back on duty and that, as Richie was off duty and had put his phone on divert, nobody had been able to contact him.

'I'm sorry,' said Richie, hearing another voice take over, 'but I was in bed with my girlfriend.'

Rosie read and reread all the newspapers, except *The Sunday Sport* which Jack tactfully hadn't bought, and gradually composed herself. She supposed that, now the whole sorry mess was out in the open, things could resolve themselves – whatever those *things* were. *I am not a witch*, she told herself firmly. *The villagers may laugh, but I am not a witch. I am a professional practitioner, with a certificate to prove it.* So what was she worried about? The dead hazel tree, certainly. The XIII, definitely. But what did it add up to? Something, that's what she'd told Jack. But what that something was she didn't know. She put on her glasses on and reread an article in *The Sunday Post* that helpfully listed a number of other black cat sightings made over the past decade, including for good measure a fuzzy shot of the alleged Beast of Bodmin, one of the original sightings in the south-west of England.

Like many people in the village, Rosie felt a positive need to go to church that morning and hear what the Reverend Kennedy had to say. She'd never made a point of going to church on a regular basis, and didn't have strong religious beliefs, although she did sometimes make the short journey from pub to church on a Sunday – just to be on the safe side, as she'd tell Jack. Her faith in the turning earth, with its seasons and generous gifts, was enough for her. First, Imolg and the spring equinox, Bealtaine and midsummer, Lughasadh and the autumn equinox, Samhain and the winter solstice. They were harmless things in which to believe. They made a kind of sense to her. When she did consider the existence of God, she saw Him in the landscape or in a pattern of clouds. Whatever He was, He certainly wasn't the white-bearded old buftie in a grubby loincloth with lightning jumping from his fingers. She wasn't sure whether this made her a believer or an unbeliever.

She concluded that events were gathering pace, although she had reached no conclusions about anything, searching once again through the kitchen, only to find that Jack had taken out the rubbish, finally disposing of the evidence – or lack of it. She sighed theatrically and looked again at the lurid headlines with their sordid implications of impropriety. *I am innocent*, she wanted to say, but didn't know why or to whom. Well, innocent of *almost* everything.

'You look all spruced up,' said Jack who had padded in behind her with a calculator in one hand and a bunch of receipts in the other. He had decided to look busy and so avoid any difficult little chats.

'I'm going to church,' she informed him. There was no point asking Jack to go with her. The last time he had been in church was on their wedding day. Then she put a hand to her mouth. 'Oh my God, you're wearing carpet slippers!'

He looked at his feet and wiggled happy toes. 'I bought them last week. Got them in that funny shop in Haddington. You know, beside Mason's.'

Rosie looked at him over the top of her new glasses. He couldn't help but smile. 'It's not funny, Jack! Old people wear slippers. Please don't tell me you've bought a cardigan as well.'

Jack looked crestfallen. 'No, only these. You don't, um, seem to like them.'

It was, of course, only a small disappointment in the scheme of things. She wanted roses and champagne, to be kissed all over, to feel loved in a tangible way. She wanted to be young and vulnerable, to be physically wanted. She didn't want to be shrivelled and *un*wanted. *Actually*, she thought, *sod the roses and champagne*.

'I neither like nor dislike them. I do, however, dislike the fact that *you* like them.'

'That doesn't make any sense.'

'It's not supposed to,' she parried, hands on hips, and her glasses perched perilously. 'Why don't we make love any more?' she asked, fixing him with an intent look.

'That's a question and a half,' he replied, neatly evading it.

'It's not a question and a half. It's just *one* simple question.'

'Well, it's not that simple,' he said, looking uncomfortable in white shirt, blue jeans and carpet slippers. He hadn't shaved that morning and Rosie noticed that his paunch was definitely on the increase. 'We're not getting any younger, I suppose.'

'What's that supposed to mean?' she demanded. 'Please don't confuse me with an old-age pensioner just yet, although,' she snapped, 'you're the one wearing *slippers*!' She spat out the word, her nostrils flared, a sure sign of impending pyrotechnics. 'Jack, only very old people wear carpet slippers or cardigans. Please promise me that you'll never buy a cardigan.'

'Well, you've just bought reading glasses. That's a sign of something, and it's not a sign of getting any younger.'

'My eyesight has always been bad. You *know* that! I just decided to get some glasses because, well, that's what I decided to do.' She stared intently again, daring him to disagree. 'Anyway, you haven't answered my question.'

'Because they're comfy,' he replied, moving towards the door and freedom.

'No, the other question,' she said, raising her voice to his retreating back, although it wasn't clear whether or not he'd heard.

Mission unaccomplished, she pondered whether to follow him downstairs and confront him again but decided that, what with everything else, this probably wasn't the best time for a marital heart-to-heart.

Walking to the church a short time later, Rosie's fraught mood wasn't eased by a cheery voice behind her. The dowdy sparrow found herself joined by the bird of paradise. Mara was wearing a blue summer dress, a leather belt encircling her perfect waist and a golden necklace around her perfect neck. Rosie again felt the heartfelt pang of unfortunate comparison as the younger woman fell in step beside her.

'Oh, hi, Mara. You're in a good mood this morning.'

'I am,' she said, slipping an arm through Rosie's and putting her mouth close to her ear. Rosie could positively smell the vitality of youth, remembering also the yeasty tang of possible infidelity. 'I think I'm in love.'

This was something of a jolt for Rosie in whose imagination dark thoughts had remorselessly gathered. 'Oh,' was all she could immediately reply, before summoning back her senses. 'Anyone I know?'

Mara smiled broadly. 'Richie Scott, the village policeman. I'm in love with a superhero! Please tell me that you think he's gorgeous.'

'I didn't know about you and him. How exciting!' She actually *did* feel pleased for the girl, remembering the raw zest of her own youthful emotions. 'You must tell me everything, no details spared. Well done!' she added for good measure, beginning to believe that Mara and Jack couldn't possibly have been at it in the beer garden.

'To tell you the truth we've been going out for a couple of months, but only really got it together last night.'

Rosie remembered when she first got it together with Jack and wondered, again, when she might next get it together with him. Damn him for buying carpet slippers! How could he be so unfeeling? Arm in arm with Mara, she couldn't help but feel approaching dotage. Through the pressure on her arm, she felt the exuberant bounce in the younger woman's step and, when she turned towards her, the glow on Mara's skin that didn't need moisturiser or all the other beauty products that cluttered Rosie's dressing table, all recommended by *The Daily Mail*, which she didn't now read.

To Mara she said, 'That's *really* nice for you. I am pleased. Actually, I knew you were seeing somebody. I just didn't know who.' If Mara's disclosure let Jack off the hook, at least as far as Mara was concerned, there were still other hooks ensnaring him. He might be innocent as far as Mara was concerned, but he wasn't yet innocent of all charges. He was certainly guilty of not desiring her enough, of not planting kisses down her spine, and of buying carpet slippers. He was also guilty of not knowing that he *shouldn't* have bought carpet slippers. He was therefore guilty of both action and omission.

'Tam, I suppose?'

'The very same. He heard you canoodling on the phone. His word, not mine. Anyway, why were you keeping it a secret?'

'Not so much keeping it secret as being discreet about it. You know what people round here are like for gossiping.'

Rosie thought about it for a moment. 'Well, I suppose, what with him being the local superhero... but, yes, I suppose, he is just a wee bit gorgeous.' She looked at the crowd around the church, several of them carrying notebooks or cameras and shook her head. She suddenly had a need to confide. 'Mara, could I ask you something? A little something that you might think is a bit odd.' She hesitated and took a deep breath. 'It's something personal, I'm afraid. No, not personal... a bit embarrassing, really...' She ground to a stop physically and verbally.

'Just ask, Rosie.'

'It's, well... it's to do with the stuff in the newspapers. God, this is going to sound very silly but, well... does anyone around here *really* think that I'm a witch? I mean, a real one, rather than a joke one.' This said, she did immediately feel silly.

Mara laughed and squeezed her arm. 'Of course not! You're *Medicine Woman*, remember? Scourge of acne and athlete's foot! It's a ridiculous thought.' She was quiet for a few moments. 'Anyway, why do you ask?'

Rosie waggled her head and sighed. 'It's just that I don't really know what to think. Maybe I'm just being menopausal.' She smiled wanly.

'Ah,' said Mara, 'approaching birthdays.'

'Has it been that obvious?'

'Like, yesterday, you hid all your birthday cards under the bar. Rosie, they could have got binned!' She smiled impishly. 'Or was that the intention?'

Mara threaded her arm through hers and drew her away from the church towards a wooden bench under a spreading elm tree. Patterns of light played on the ground while songbirds jumped in the branches. A breath of wind again lifted Mara's mane of hair. 'Richie's furious about all this. He was supposed to have the weekend off, his first weekend off for ages. Now he's having to stalk the streets like Batman. Making sure there's a police presence, that's what his orders are.' She giggled. 'It also buggers up his cricket this afternoon. The mighty cricket team will have to do without my superhero.'

Rosie again felt diminished against the younger girl. 'I'm

pleased for you. Pleased for both of you. He's a good lad,' she added, having seen him at work in the function suite with Madam Chair and Adrian Mountjoy. She'd also referred to him as a *lad* – the old dinosaur, ancient beyond redemption.

The bottle of home-made wine that she had carefully given to Jack the day before had been absent from both the fridge and waste bin. A thought occurred to her. 'Mara, in a spirit of honesty, could I ask you three simple questions?'

Mara nodded a little uncertainly.

'One, have you ever had a fling with my husband?'

Mara was staring at her wild-eyed. She shook her head emphatically.

'Two, do you know of anybody who has?'

Again, an emphatic shake of the head. A small child on a squeaking bicycle pedalled past. Rosie took a deep breath.

'Three, what exactly were you doing in the beer garden on Friday night?' There, the question had been asked. Jack's final absolution hung in the balance.

Words formed in Mara's mouth, an explanation of being unwell and going into the beer garden for a cigarette and a sit-down. The explanation would either have involved the time of the month or food poisoning, or a combination of the two. In the milliseconds it took for her mind to put the explanation together and frame the correct words in the right order, she felt unbidden words spill from her mouth. 'Rosie, I'm really sorry. It just came over me. A strange feeling. I needed to… oh God, Rosie, please don't ask me to be explicit!'

This silenced the older woman for a few moments until

another small piece of the jigsaw that was her failed scheming slotted neatly into place. Jack's *lapsang souchong*. Bloody man! Incapable of even drinking tea. 'Rather loudly, by all accounts,' she said, remembering Clare Derby's Hollywood allusion.

'Oh God!' whispered Mara, utterly and completely mortified.

'Don't worry about it. No, really. We've all done it at some point in our lives, although perhaps not so publicly,' she added. 'I doubt that many of the Conservatives who were watching really saw what was going on. They're a pretty unimaginative bunch, or so I've found.'

This much veracity had to mean something. 'I take it Jack gave you a bottle of home-made wine yesterday and that you drank it?'

The younger woman nodded. 'He said that he didn't like it. Rosie, please tell me what's happening?'

'In a moment,' she replied, now having another charge to lay at her errant husband's door. The charge of not liking her wine, when he had always *bloody* told her that he did. Like a presiding judge, she now sought final closure to the strange case of McLeod v McLeod. 'Tell me, on the morning before you were, um, in the beer garden did you by any chance drink a cup of tea that I'd left out for Jack?'

Mara's long hair was blowing over her face. Her plumage was slipping. 'That's five questions,' she said eventually, her voice barely a whisper, then nodded. 'He doesn't like your tea. What's happening, Rosie?'

'Don't worry, you'll be OK,' she replied, putting a

friendly hand on the younger woman's shoulder. 'I'm only sorry that you drank it, I really am. It was meant for Jack. A herbal thing. Not really intended for the likes of you or me. It was for his bad back,' she added, although Mara hadn't asked and was looking doubtful. 'It's rather good for arthritis… but not really intended for us women. Anyway, he *bloody* well does like *lapsang souchong*! The sod keeps telling me that he does!' She wondered why everything seemed to have gone wrong. 'He didn't by any chance also give you a chicken pie?'

Mara blinked several times, and then shook her head. 'You didn't honestly think I was having an affair with Jack, did you? For Heaven's sake, Rosie, he's nearly old enough to be my father.'

'Well, maybe. I honestly didn't know what to think. All I knew was that strange noises had been heard coming from the beer garden and it was Jack who carried you in. Anyway, by that logic I'm also nearly old enough to be your mother.'

To which Mara then said the most remarkable and, for Rosie, the very best thing possible. 'Not you, Rosie, not you. You're still much too young.'

It was therefore in a state of some serenity that Rosie entered the church a few minutes later, an explanation of sorts given to Mara, and the final fate of the chicken pie temporarily banished from her mind. *I am not a witch*, she could now tell herself with some justification, *and neither am I old*, the truth of her continued youth confirmed by someone unable to tell a lie.

In a career ministering in Glasgow council estates, the Reverend Kennedy had seen a few things. Things he'd rather not have seen, witnessing at first hand the hopelessness of lives at the bottom of the pile. This hadn't been noble poverty, enriched by servitude or decency or community. It was grind, made worse by bad health and petty larceny. Real life in tooth and claw.

Now he was faced with something else entirely. His current worries had no flesh and blood. He couldn't reach out and touch them. He'd tried to call Mountjoy several times, of course, but the politician was either out and about or not answering his phone. Each time he got as far as Mountjoy's answerphone before replacing the receiver with a sigh of exasperation. He'd confided in the man and had been let down. What on earth was he going to tell his congregation? More to the point, how was it going to affect his relationship with them? Even worse, what was it going to do to the village's reputation? The Holy Grail nonsense was nothing more than harmless fun. He'd always felt honoured to minister in such a well-known place, but had never really believed in the fairytale. Visitors liked asking his opinion about the Grail and, occasionally, journalists and TV crews would come to his door. He'd been on Japanese TV once, saying with a smile, *well, we can't prove the story, but we can't disprove it either.* However, whatever he had done in confiding to Mountjoy was done – the cat was out of the bag, so to speak, heralding nothing or something.

Mountjoy definitely wasn't answering phone calls and

was, for different reasons, feeling equally unhappy about the passage of events. Here he was, a politician on the brink of an election. He should be out there shaking hands, making speeches, exhorting voters to use their votes wisely and return him as the duly elected representative for the East Lothian constituency. Instead, what was he doing? Skulking in his flat and screening phone calls on the orders of Madam Chair. Apart from the minister, several friends and journalists had phoned. It was all, he conceded, getting a bit out of hand. He didn't dare check his e-mails. He'd also been phoned during the night by the *New York Post* and, earlier that morning, by *The Sydney Morning Herald.* Mountjoy now picked up the phone to nobody, not sure who to trust, and wondering bleakly how so many journalists had managed to discover his home phone number.

Others had been to his flat in person. His door buzzer had rung several times. Each time, looking at the little security screen by his front door, he saw only strangers carrying notebooks. He had declined to answer any of them, leaving it all to Madam Chair to sort out. He hoped fervently for some new and cataclysmic event to occur: another Japanese earthquake, typhoon or shipwreck – something so awful that the press would all chase off in another direction. He then inwardly winced at this uncharitable thought. He didn't want to be *here*, lying low; he wanted to be out *there* in East Lothian, winning hearts and minds, folding their votes to his purpose and to the greater vision of Conservatism: of Scotland's secured place within a United Kingdom at the heart of a new Europe.

He looked in the fridge to see what provisions he had to eke him through his imprisonment. Instead of edibles, mostly inedibles. He tossed an ancient and half-eaten lasagne and a Tupperware carton of rotting stew into the bin. He was left with a wedge of stilton, two onions, half a pint of milk and a limp carrot.

As he pondered what to possibly do with these ingredients, his phone rang again, the Reverend Lionel Kennedy leaving another exasperated message.

Having once more endured Mountjoy's answerphone, the minister replaced the receiver and irritably shook his head. The man was impossible! He'd phoned Mountjoy to ask whether, being a politician, he could possibly persuade the police to look again at their files. If something had happened all those years ago, there might still be evidence of it. Something that might tell them what to beware of now. Instead, Mountjoy had gone to the media and, not only had he broken a confidence, he hadn't had the decency to phone and apologise – although, he conceded, his own phone had been off the hook since the unfortunate TV programme the night before. But unlike Mountjoy, who was under orders to lie low, Lionel Kennedy couldn't suddenly go AWOL on a Sunday morning. This was his one big day of the week.

He guessed that the pews would be rather full. He also guessed that there might be several unbelievers from the media as well. Whatever he said might therefore have a wider impact than was normally the case with his sermons, which were usually delivered to a few near-death old people.

The pile of notes carefully written during the week added up, in the present circumstances, to an inadequate explanation. But where to start? He sat at his desk and looked at the framed photograph of a younger Lionel Kennedy shaking hands with Bob Geldof. He reached for his pen and was about to start writing when he felt a sharp pain in his lower abdomen. Rising from his desk he crossed to a cupboard and extracted a couple of Rennies which he swallowed with a sip of his now-tepid cup of tea.

He really shouldn't have eaten so much of Sadie's delicious chicken pie, a favourite of his own mother's, its exquisite flavours conjuring up memories of long ago. Among Sadie's more usual culinary disasters, this had been a real gem.

Chapter 14

The herb is called of the Chaldees Luperax, *of the Greeks* Esifena, *of the Latins* Viscum querci, *of Englishmen Mistletoe. This herb with a certain other herb, which is named* Martagon, *that is* Silphium *or* Laserpitium *as it is written in the Almain language, openeth all locks. And if the aforesaid things, being put together, be put in the mouth of any man, if he think of any thing, if it should happen, it is set on his heart, if not, it leapeth back from his heart.*

The Book of Secrets of Albertus Magnus

The current church at Holy Cross was founded in the early 15th Century by Sir Thomas Macgregor of Saltoun, one of some forty collegiate churches built across Scotland between the reigns of James I and James IV. Their stature as places of worship was assured by the magnificence of their construction although, sadly, little now remains of the original Holy Cross structure. However, the rough-hewn standing stone beside the altar suggests that the site has much older religious significance. This is likely, given the village's position on the main Roman road from Newcastle to Edinburgh and at a natural ford on the river Tess. People would have lived there for a thousand or more years.

Sir Thomas's collegiate church was itself built on an older Christian structure that appears to have had connections with the Knights Templar, a brotherhood of warrior soldiers formed in the 12th Century under the protection of the Pope. The Knights' connection with Scotland stems from later persecution by Philip of France, by which time the Knights had become too big for their boots. Excommunication followed; persecution became execution. In the rush to escape, Scotland was the ideal destination. King Robert the Bruce had also been excommunicated and wasn't therefore going to enforce Rome's Order of Suppression against the Knights. As was King Robert's wont, with Knights as well as spiders, he turned their cloud into a rather good silver lining. The core of King Robert's cavalry at the Battle of Bannockburn – Midsummer's Day and the Feast of St John the Baptist – was composed of fugitive Templar knights.

The Templar link, long suspected, was proven when a Templar seal was found in the Luftwaffe bomb crater that also unearthed the village's stone cross – two knights riding on a single mount. In a later excavation under the north wall, a sword blade was found with the inscription *Non nobis Domine, non nobis sed Nomini Tuo da gloriam* – meaning: Not to us, O Lord, not to us, but to Your Name give the glory – the snappy motto of the Knights Templar. Although a complete survey of the foundations has yet to be completed, one theory is that the original floor plan of the church may be a replica of the Temple of Herod in Jerusalem. Both the seal and sword blade can, of course, be viewed in the small Holy Cross Visitor Centre and Tea Shop.

The newer collegiate church survived both the Reformation and occupation by Cromwell's troops, only to be burned down as idolatrous and popish by an Edinburgh mob. It was rebuilt soon afterwards but the original magnificence was lost. Some speculate that it might even have rivalled Rosslyn Chapel in Roslin, just round the Edinburgh city bypass – another collegiate church, albeit one that has survived. Underneath the Holy Cross Kirk, stretching far beyond the church's original west wall, are extensive deep vaults, largely unexcavated, although there are plans to conduct further surveys, Historic Scotland and Church authorities willing.

There is a brass plaque just inside the church, donated in 1974 by the Earl of May, the local hereditary bigwig, to commemorate yet more renovation work. On it is inscribed in bold copperplate – what else? – the last verse of *Sir Galahad* by Alfred, Lord Tennyson.

"The clouds are broken in the sky,
And thro' the mountain-walls
A rolling organ-harmony
Swells up, and shakes and falls.
Then move the trees, the copses nod,
Wings flutter, voices hover clear:
'O just and faithful knight of God!
Ride on! The prize is near.'
So pass I hostel, hall and grange;
By bridge and ford, by park and pale,
All-arm'd I ride, whate'er betide,
Until I find the Holy Grail."

The Reverend Kennedy usually found the words reassuring, an affirmation of a quest worth making, even if it was a search doomed to failure. It was the quest that was important, as he felt his own had been through the misery of Glasgow's slums. He had tried to make a difference, to make things better, to speak up for those at the bottom of the pile; a journey in the service of others less fortunate. He touched the brass plate, his eyes closed, reading the words with his fingers.

Outside, two photographers who had taken pictures of him arriving at the church now sat on the stone arms of the old cross, unaware of the possible effect this might have on their fertility or good fortune. The crowd that had been milling in small groups outside now sat in whispered contemplation inside. There was a low murmur of anticipation. The minister looked down the aisle to the stained-glass window through which weak sunlight spilled, the monks carrying their wondrous cross, the last man in the group turned fearfully to look behind. The window had also been gifted by the selfsame Earl of May.

Lionel tuned his ears to the packed pews, his fingers still lovingly reading the last lines of the unfulfilled quest. The noise level suggested standing room only, a fact confirmed when he advanced purposefully down an aisle that now seemed unexpectedly long and fearful. Familiar and unfamiliar faces turned as he approached. Some smiled, some nodded. Others, those he didn't recognise, looked merely curious or stared blankly.

Not everyone in the village felt compelled to go to church that morning, among them two young men dressed entirely in white.

'What we've really got to decide... what we've *really* got to ask ourselves, of course, is who we put in to bat first. What risks we take early on to get a few runs. Not having Richie, quite frankly, is a bit of a blow batting-wise.' Liam Connarty, tall, lean and dark-haired, leaned on the heavy roller that lived inside the rotting pavilion. His companion, Eric Middlemiss, also helping to pull the roller over the village cricket square, was shorter, rotund with curly red hair.

'Actually, if you don't mind my saying so, I don't think that it is a question of batting order,' Eric said, a contrary opinion to his captain's that he would never have expressed in front of the rest of the team. 'The important thing is to keep their score down. That means keeping some of our better bowlers in reserve to get rid of their tail-enders.'

Cricket, it has to be said, is not a national sport in Scotland, despite what the Scottish Cricket Union optimistically claims. The sport is *de rigueur*, of course, in the posher schools but enjoys little favour elsewhere. However, there are small pockets of interest: Fife, for example, in the shape of little Freuchie, is a former British village champion; so too East Lothian which boasts several national league sides and its own village league. On Sunday summer afternoons, East Lothian's villages battle it out in cricket whites and the weaponry of willow bats. A Holy Cross home fixture, if the weather holds up, can be well supported by patrons sitting outside the *Fox and Duck*. It has not been unknown for bored outfielders to slip away unnoticed to the pub, sometimes never to return.

'OK, OK,' said Liam, irritated by Eric's lack of

support in his captaincy. 'I agree that we hold back a couple of our better bowlers. But we're not going to win this if we can't put runs on the board. Well, are we? That means rearranging the batting order now that Richie's out of it.' Richie Scott, hopeless bowler, was the team's star batsman, regularly hitting the ball full toss into the Tess for twelve runs. This quaint local rule means, of course, that teams have to deploy an inordinate number of fielders to guard the river – leaving gaps elsewhere that batsmen of Richie's calibre can take rich advantage of.

The pews were packed. His church hadn't seen such a gathering since the Earl of May's eldest daughter's wedding to a rock musician, which had barely lasted until the end of the honeymoon. It was standing room only at the back. The church door creaked continuously as latecomers arrived. Reverend Kennedy's gaze encompassed them all, from the solitude of the pulpit.

'Some of you may have read the newspapers,' he began, to some relieved laughter, then frowned at an unbeliever in a white T-shirt who was fiddling with a tape recorder. 'I suspect that some of you here today may even write for those same newspapers.' He fixed his eye momentarily on another unbeliever who was scribbling furiously, a reporter's notebook open on his lap. 'My friends, although what I have to say today may be reported elsewhere, my sermon is for this community... and for this congregation alone.' He paused, his hands gripped on the edge of the pulpit, light from the stained-glass window illuminating his hair, making it glow with divine sincerity. 'First, however, let us consider what this village really is. What it *really* stands for. Because I am proud to be the minister of this fine, upstanding village and its good and decent people.' This drew a smattering of applause from the younger members of the congregation who didn't usually attend church and who were therefore largely unaware of its etiquettes.

He spread his arms wide, his vestments making him seem like an underfed bat about to fly. 'The history of this village is known throughout the world.' Here he gestured back at the stained-glass window; the monks bent under the weight of pale Welsh gold. 'Perhaps there is much truth in the story. Maybe the cross does exist. Maybe, my friends, just maybe, it is buried here.' For emphasis, he pointed downwards at a flower decoration below the pulpit which a photographer duly photographed. 'Many have searched for it, none have found it. Perhaps one day it will be found, and, perhaps, at its centre there will be that fragment of sacred emerald. My friends, I hope that it won't be found,' he added with a small smile, momentarily folding his arms across his chest, 'because the quest for the Holy Grail

213

would then be over. A mystery solved. You see, the real story of the Holy Grail involves a simple lesson. A lesson for us all. What is it? Merely that it teaches us how important is the quest.'

His abdomen was beginning to hurt now that the Rennies were wearing off, and he'd forgotten to put the packet into his pocket. 'The Holy Grail is really a parable and, as a parable, the story of the Holy Grail is *absolutely* true.' A couple of unbelievers leaned forwards, their pens poised for tomorrow's headline. 'We are all, throughout our lives, on a quest, even if we don't know it.' He nodded towards the younger element on his right. 'For most of the time, of course, it might just be a quest for love, or a qualification, or a job. But it's also a quest for fulfilment – happiness, even. In my younger days, as many of you know, I ministered in parts of Scotland that were a great deal more disadvantaged than here. I know how difficult the quest for contentment can be. I also know,' he added, dropping his voice, 'how the grace of God can be found. The important thing is to keep looking for Him. Keep seeking Him out. That's what the Holy Grail teaches us... how important is the quest for the answers that we all seek. So, does the Grail exist? Well, maybe.' He smiled wanly, his stomach muscles bunched tight. 'However, the Holy Grail is also in all of us, in our hearts... and that is where we must look, today and daily.' He tapped his own heart rather sharply for emphasis, hoping to dislodge whatever it was that was clogging his digestive tract. His stomach was becoming distended; pressure was building.

He ploughed on, feeling nauseous. 'Nowadays, we welcome visitors from all over the world. We show them round our church and our village. We enjoy their interest and we are proud of our village's place in a famous legend. At the same time, my friends,' he said, again dropping his voice and reaching a hand towards his congregation, 'this village is also our community. It doesn't belong to all those who come here from the four corners of the world. It belongs to us, the good people who live here.' Here he paused again to fix the unbelievers with a beady eye. 'That is why the publicity this morning was so hurtful to me and, I know, to you also. It only told about the Holy Cross that is in the history books. It didn't describe the village I recognise. It didn't tell of a place filled with decent, ordinary people. *That* is the Holy Cross I recognise.' He decided to repeat this last point, hoping to encourage the younger element into further applause. He wasn't disappointed. Lionel Kennedy held up his hands like a chat show compère to still his audience, unable to prevent an inaudible fart from escaping.

'Although history is forever being repeated in newspaper headlines, our community's place in the

215

history books was written many, many years ago. The golden cross is an ancient legend. The *real* story of this village now is that we don't make the news. We are an ordinary community made extraordinary by a quirk of history.' He paused, feeling momentarily unwell. An utterly nauseous smell had now filled the pulpit, drifted over its edge and reached the noses of those at the front of the congregation, several of whom glanced furtively at one another.

Lionel Kennedy clenched his buttocks with such force that his eyes watered, making it difficult to read his notes. 'A few days ago, my friends, I was judging a jam-making competition. Some of you, I know, were in that competition,' he said, recognising Mrs Galbraith from the Post Office and Mrs Saunders from one of the village's several tea shops. 'Ladies, I voted for all of you,' he said through clenched teeth, another inaudible fart escaping.

Beads of sweat were now on his brow. He pulled out his trusty spotted handkerchief and mopped his brow. 'Later, that evening,' he said, tucking it away, 'I saw a large cat standing in the road. It was momentarily mesmerised by the car's lights, I suppose. Then,' he said, banging on his chest with one hand to dislodge the remnants of chicken pie, 'it was gone.' This merely put added pressure on his sorely afflicted abdomen, forcing unwanted and unnecessary pressure downwards. This time, the minister's fart was like a wind instrument badly blown by a three-year-old. Again, a nauseous cloud eddied over the pulpit ramparts to assault all in its path. Mrs Galbraith, he noted, was looking sourly at her husband – having been, presumably, guilty of previous sin. In an uncharitable moment, Lionel Kennedy also looked sourly at him, attempting to apportion guilt elsewhere.

The smell, it has to be said, was awful – doubly so since it was emanating from a man of God, who was now hopping from one foot to the other, dabbing at his eyes and clearly in distress. He was also speaking in hesitant jerks, teeth clenched, unable to prevent further noxious fumes from escaping. He relaxed for a moment, the wind section finding sudden voice.

Several of his congregation now had handkerchiefs to their noses. Frankly, who could blame them? Some of the younger element were grinning broadly, not entirely sure who to blame. The noise that to Lionel Kennedy seemed like a sonic boom was, to everyone else, somewhat muffled. The culprit was not so easily identifiable. The pulpit shielded him; its contours deflecting sound. He looked meaningfully again at Mr Galbraith, feeling wretched. The congregation saw the slope of his eyes, noting where blame lay. *Ah*, they were thinking, *for a minute there we thought it was the minister.*

The charade, of course, could not go on for much longer. The pressure in his abdomen was worsening. He could feel internal organs gurgle. Gas in large quantity was building up. Like a pressure valve on overload, his clenched buttocks could not stem the tide indefinitely. 'I felt that the black cat might be, you see, a kind of warning. I was told that by my predecessor. About what, I don't know. All I was told is that witchcraft had never died out in the village. I wasn't sure what to believe, but I did report the matter to the police.' He looked round his congregation, seeing signs only of collective nausea. More than a few in the congregation now had handkerchiefs to their faces and several youngsters were loudly giggling and wafting their hands ineffectually. Some were staring balefully at Mr Galbraith who was shifting uneasily on his seat, a sure sign of guilt. Another muffled blast, more giggles, and the pressure momentarily eased.

'The lesson I have learned from the past day or so is to choose friends wisely and not to confide unwisely. My friends, I did not confide in the media and I most certainly did not invite them here today.' It seemed an apt way of turning confession into salvation; an admission that life's lessons could still be learned at any age. 'Life,' intoned Lionel Kennedy in a jerky squeak, 'is about learning difficult lessons.' This would have carried some gravitas if it hadn't also been accompanied by a triumphant blast, the trumpet now being played by a virtuoso. It started somewhere around top C and played faultlessly down the musical scale to bottom G. All eyes were now turned rather suspiciously towards the minister who was again hopping from one foot to the other and mopping at his face with the spotty handkerchief.

The smell had become intolerable for one very aged man in a wheelchair who was perhaps reliving the unwelcome experience of being gassed on some distant battlefield. His carer, a pretty young woman in a light blue uniform, had seen his distress and, gently turning his chair, now pushed him down the supply trench to the safety of the rear line. A low murmur again assailed the minister, his congregation wanting the guilty party to be found and ejected. A few watched the old soldier's departure with some relief, believing that he might be to blame.

Lionel clutched his abdomen, trying to loosen his belt. 'Maybe the black cat was also a warning for us all. A parable. Like the story of the Grail, perhaps the black cat is a reminder that the past should remain buried. Like the Grail, if it exists, buried where nobody should ever find it.' Although his words were coming out in rough formation, their delivery now left a great deal to be desired. Not only had his voice risen still further, his teeth were now so tightly clenched that he had difficulty opening his mouth. The words were therefore only audible, and hardly discernible, to those at the front of the congregation. A few parishioners at the back were now shuffling their feet; not only had the stench reached them, but the minister had become incoherent.

If Lionel Kennedy could have stopped, he would have. He wanted more than anything else to apologise to his congregation, explain that he was feeling unwell, walk with dignity back to the manse and lock himself in the downstairs toilet. However, he was also physically unable to move. Or, to be precise, he was unable to move without slightly unclenching his buttocks and that, he concluded, would unleash the whole orchestra. He had no idea what was happening to him, his affliction so unnerving and completely sudden. His only hope was that, if his condition had appeared so quickly, it might disappear as suddenly. He refused to contemplate the option that it might get worse – which it promptly did, his intestines filling with more dense fumes, the pressure cooker now dangerously overloaded. 'My friends, we hold this place dear in our hearts. We hold our village's history dear in our hearts. We must learn from the past and apply those lessons in our day-to-day lives.' Under the circumstances, the fact that Lionel Kennedy could speak at all was a miracle of sorts. However, the words were now indecipherable to the bulk of his congregation, many of whom were now looking at him with both nausea and concern. It was clear that not all was right with the ageing minister. The smell of corruption was in their nostrils.

He spread his arms wide, as he had at the beginning of his sermon, his task now to turn earthy homily into the written words of God. His vestments stretched out on either side, and Lionel Kennedy again seemed about to fly – an impression underlined by the sound of a jet engine starting up. Unlike the previous trumpet solo, this started as a low whine, almost inaudible, the turbine in his bowels slowly spooling up until, with internal pressure now critical, the after-burner kicked in with some ferocity.

This time there was no disguising what was happening, and no time to waste unless he wanted to avoid an even more humiliating fate. Lionel Kennedy, clutching his stomach, made his way slowly and painfully from the pulpit, his progress on each step marked by a triumphant fanfare. His embarrassment was total; his bewilderment complete. He had come here to speak to his congregation; instead he was assaulting them. He saw how they shrank back as he passed, handkerchiefs to their noses, eyes wide and disbelieving. He couldn't believe it himself; this was like no other infliction ever experienced. He walked slowly down an aisle that seemed even longer on departure than it had on arrival, the jet engine in his abdomen sensing a runway and applying full throttle.

Liam Connarty and Eric Middlemiss, still lovingly engaged in rolling the cricket square, were first alerted by the sound, before they saw the minister make his way painfully, bent almost double, in the direction of the manse, his slow progress made audible by the echo of retreating trumpets.

It took Rosie McLeod some minutes to regain her composure, gulping down fresh air and breathing out slowly. After the minister's ignominious departure there had, of course, been a stampede for the doors, old friends and neighbours jostling each other to be out first. The church seemed filled with a green miasma; the monk in the stained-glass window was no longer looking fearfully over his shoulder at advancing soldiers, but recoiling in horror. It had not been the most dignified of church services and what made it all the more galling for Rosie was that it was her bloody husband's fault. He must have given her chicken pie to the minister. Rosie gritted her teeth, breathing deeply. Why couldn't he have just eaten the damn thing, as she'd asked him? Why couldn't he have shared it with the person he was carrying on with? He'd always, *always* liked her chicken pie – *and* her home-made wine.

It did mean, however, that she would have to offer

Jack some sort of explanation. The minister's affliction would by now be common gossip, and no doubt her chicken pie would be blamed. Likewise, her mostly harmless bottle of wine. Jack *liked* her home-made wine. He often said so. So why hadn't the bastard drunk that either?

Back at the *Fox and Duck* there was no alternative but to tell the truth, however painful Rosie found it. First, she poured him a gin and tonic, then she poured herself a large brandy, even though she didn't much like brandy. 'Jack, you are completely hopeless, inconsiderate, and utterly unreliable,' was her opening gambit. 'I don't know why I bother cooking for you, I really don't.'

'You don't usually,' he countered, sitting at attention in an easy chair in their lounge and wondering why a large gin and tonic had been thrust into his hand. 'Usually we get something from downstairs.'

'That's not the point,' said Rosie, nostrils flared. This was all his fault, every last noxious whiff of it. OK, she wasn't *entirely* blameless, but Jack was mostly responsible. 'I have something to tell you,' she informed him, then knocked back her brandy and poured another.

'What have you done?' he asked in a low voice.

'What do you mean, what have I done,' she demanded, the brandy watering her eyes. 'Why should I have *done* anything?'

'The only time you drink brandy,' he replied, 'is when you're feeling guilty about something.'

'Guilty? Guilty! It's you who should be feeling guilty. Not me! Christ, I was nearly sick in church. The smell!'

Jack was looking at her blankly.

'You haven't heard?' she asked. 'Oh shit!' Rosie sat down heavily onto their settee. 'Jack, I have something to tell you.'

It took her some minutes to explain things in her own way, repeatedly blaming him for carpet slippers, unconsumed exotic tea, chicken pie and wine. By the end, when she'd run out of accusations and excuses, he was rigidly sitting at attention, his glass of gin untouched. 'Anyway, it's probably all nothing really,' she optimistically concluded.

'Nothing *really*!' Jack McLeod was beside himself with anger. 'You've poisoned three people and you have the effrontery to say *nothing really*! God, woman!' he said loudly, running a bemused hand through his hair before being assailed by a sudden thought. 'Rosie, you haven't poisoned anybody else, have you? Please say "no".'

'I simply gave you a little, um, stimulant in a cup of tea and Mara drank it by mistake. I then gave you a bottle containing something to, um, encourage veracity —'

'A rather long word for the truth —'

'which *you* gave to Mara! None of this is my fault, you know,' she said with some conviction.

'I simply gave her a bottle of wine. I didn't know that it was poisoned.' His expression darkened. 'What exactly was in it?'

She sighed. Jack's casual generosity was so infuriating, so too the pointed condemnation of her professional skill. 'I don't do poison, how many times do I have to tell you that?' Her nostrils again flared in righteous indignation, before she relented. 'A mild sort of sodium pentothal. Sort of,' she added.

'And what exactly does sodium pentothal do, *sort of*?'

'It encourages the truth, nothing more. Unlike you, Jack! Never saying anything nice, never wanting to touch me, and secretly buying geriatric footwear!' She stared at him angrily.

But another thought had forcefully struck him. 'Oh God, her boyfriend is our local policeman.' She had informed him of this fact earlier as a prelude to further disclosure. 'Rosie, you could get arrested.'

Somehow, she rather doubted it, although she hadn't thought of this before. 'Jack, chicken pie is your favourite. Honestly, how could you?… and to the minister, of all people.'

'Actually, I gave it to Sadie Gallagher. However, let's get one thing straight. Chicken pie is *not* my favourite. It never was and it never will be! Rosie, I don't *like* chicken pie!' He shook his head, trying to clear the nightmare that was his wife's scheming, then realised that he was holding his glass of gin and tonic. He took a gulp, feeling reality slip. 'I don't know where you get your ideas from, I really don't. What on earth made you think I was having an affair with Mara? Christ, she's young enough to be my daughter!'

'Well, that might have been part of the attraction, Jack. She is very pretty, you must admit that. She was also heard making –how shall I put it? – noises of a sexual nature in the beer garden. *You* were seen carrying her in. Clare Derby said it was like something from *When Harry Met Sally*. I simply put two and two together and got —'

'Five, for God's sake! She was, um —'

'Playing with herself. Yes, she pretty much said that.'

'She *told* you?' In Jack's experience this was not something that people casually admitted to, before remembering the home-made wine, and its promise of veracity. 'What else did she tell you?'

Rosie emptied her glass, feeling revived from the smell of decomposing chicken. 'She said that she wasn't having an affair with you. She also said that you were old enough to be her father. She seemed rather shocked by my question.'

'Can you blame her? Well, can you! My God, Rosie, you can't just go around asking people questions like that!' At least, most people couldn't. Rosie danced to other tunes and believed in straight answers to blunt questions. 'The chicken pie, I suppose, was just a bit of insurance, in case I shared it with my secret lover. Sudden flatulence to condemn us both.'

Rosie poured another glug of brandy into her glass, washing the vestiges of Lionel Kennedy from her lungs. 'Something like that. It's just that I thought you'd drunk the tea.'

'And was at it with Mara in the beer garden. Christ, Rosie!'

'Jack, you can hardly blame me.'

'Blame you? Blame you!' Jack's voice was on a rising curve. 'You've now tried to poison me three times in as many days. Instead, let's see, you've poisoned an old family friend... no, you've poisoned her twice... *and* you've poisoned the village policeman. Why the hell *shouldn't* I blame you? Oh, and let's not forget the bloody minister! What's he going to say about it?' It wasn't really a question and she didn't bother to answer. Instead, her glass brimming, she leaned back into the settee. 'Anyway,' he asked, again running a hand through his hair, 'what was in this mild stimulant concoction thing?'

'A few herbs, a bit of this and that.' She was being defensive, not meeting his eye.

Jack had no idea what a bit of *this* and a bit of *that* actually added up to. 'What kind of stimulation are we talking about here?' He thought back to Mara's afflicted state in the beer garden, agile fingers, and Conservative faces at the window. 'A stimulant, presumably, that makes young women comatose and then makes them masturbate in public. That's hardly a *mild* stimulant in my book.'

She sighed theatrically and placed her glass on a small table beside the settee. 'Jack, you do still find me attractive, don't you? Just a little bit adorable after all these years?'

Jack held up a hand. 'Right now, I'm not going to discuss this nonsense any further. Neither of us is getting any younger and we both may as well just get used to it. You've tried to poison me and you've ended up poisoning half the village. Rosie, *please* don't snort! If you thought I was having an affair, why didn't you just ask me? That's what normal people would do! But no, that would have been too easy, wouldn't it?'

He did have a point, although she wasn't going to admit it. 'I didn't want to be told lies,' she said.

Jack didn't appear to be listening. 'Right now, I'm going downstairs to help Sammy with the Sunday lunches. I'm also going to make damn sure that there are no home-made bottles of wine lying around.'

She thought to ask further questions of his retreating back but then thought twice about it. Really, the man could be impossible! *Poison,* I ask you! OK, the very, *very* mild stimulant in his tea had contained small – very, *very* small – quantities of mandrake, but she knew what she was doing. She had been taught well; she had a gift – everyone said so, even old Dr Murray in his lucid moments. She wondered what adventures had befallen Mara. They should have happened to her, the bastard, leaving his mug of tea lying around for anyone to drink.

But she hadn't told Jack about the XIII carved on the tree or its possible significance, and she wondered again at its ingenuity and ambiguity. A warning or a threat? She felt again that events were out of control and that other hands were at work – carving symbols on the church and her tree, and all because of a large, black cat. The effrontery of it almost made her laugh, except that it was no laughing matter. Someone had taken a risk to deface the church. As a prank? Someone – the same someone? – had taken an equal risk to kill and deface her tree. A someone who knew about ancient symbols and the significance of the black cat. Strangest of all, the XIII had been carved weeks before – long before the appearance of the bloody animal. Rosie shook her head. She could see no logical pattern.

However, she did concede that baking the chicken pie had not been one of her better ideas. She might now have a bit of explaining to do. At the very edge of her Jurassic period, Rosie admitted that the pie had, actually, been a very *bad* idea, particularly if you had second helpings. The required dosages were difficult to control and she supposed that Lionel Kennedy's titanic reaction meant that he rather liked chicken pie. Perhaps she'd phone him later once enzyme balance had been restored.

Her motives may have been innocent – to be loved and to discover possible infidelity, but she had mishandled her gift. It seemed to her that she was crossing a line between worlds and could no longer discern where the frontier lay.

Chapter 15

The herb is named of the Chaldees Ango, of the Greeks Amela, of the Latins Lilium, of the Englishman a Lily. If thou wilt gather this herb, the Sun being in the sign of the Lion, and wilt mix it with the juice of the Laurel, or Bay tree, and afterward thou shalt put that juice under the dung of cattle a certain time, it shall be turned into worms, of the which, if powder be made, and be put about the neck of any man, or in his clothes, he shall never sleep. And if thou shalt put the aforesaid thing under the dung of cattle, and wilt anoint any man with the worms breeding thereof, he shall be brought unto a fever.

The Book of Secrets of Albertus Magnus

The question of what had, or hadn't, happened in the village was also troubling Richie Scott as, on the orders of Big Mac, he displayed a police presence around the village, mainly reassuring parents that their children were safe from predators. He felt light-headed, a shifting clarity amplifying each sound. His footsteps sounded unnaturally loud and he walked slowly, aware of each tree's bough and leaf, each roof tile or curtained window. Everything he saw seemed packaged in its constituent parts; not a whole but a compilation of bits – like seeing a completed jigsaw with all its pieces clearly etched. He was also disconcerted by the number of visitors the story had generated. He was also thinking about Mara, the shape and taste of her; the way she had stepped into candlelight, a finger to his lips.

But the lurid headlines had at least achieved Lionel Kennedy's objective: Force HQ in Edinburgh now wanted definitive answers. The chief constable didn't like surprises, and this particular surprise came packaged with politicians, church ministers and that damnable bloody village. A review had been ordered. Old crime records were being consulted, so too the deliberations of Haddington Sheriff Court. Computers were being interrogated.

Richie walked slowly down the High Street, the sun bright in his eyes, each footstep amplified, and turned into Market Place. Here, he saw that the visitor centre had unusually decided to open its doors on a Sunday and that the small car park was already full. Several souvenir shops were also open for business.

'I hear that you're not playing today.'

Tam Cronin had his white coat over one arm, his morning exertions in the newsagents now complete. Tam regarded him balefully. 'I mean, that's not very good, is it?' Tam had been a stalwart of the cricket team in younger days and was now a regular umpire, making as impartial a job of it as inebriation and bad eyesight allowed.

'Duty,' replied Richie. 'Orders,' he added, feeling the other man's magnified eyes on his face.

'Aye, well it's still not very good, is it? I mean, what good are you doing *on* duty when you could be doing some good *off* duty?'

'I'm maintaining a police presence.' He indicated the visitor centre car park, where a small knot of Japanese tourists was bowing to one another and laughing. 'What with the newspapers, Tam. You know how it is.'

'Well, it's still not good. This, laddie, is our biggest match of the year. The battle of the legends, and all that guff. We don't like them very much and they, frankly, have every reason to hate us. This, Richie, is the one fixture that Holy Cross *has* to win.' Tam regarded Richie sourly, making it his fault. 'To underline how bad things are, I'm off to see if Jack McLeod can take your place.' This small duty, involving a trip to the *Fox and Duck*, did have its compensations, although Jack McLeod was no cricketer.

Richie's scalp felt suddenly itchy under his cap and he removed it for a moment to brush back hair that had fallen over one eye. 'Tam, could I ask you something?'

'Aye, but no guaranteed answers.'

'It's just that you've always lived here.'

'Since time began,' said Tam, one hand scratching at his chin. 'Born and bred.' He said it proudly, a badge of honour that he had his place on earth.

'Well then, maybe you can fill me in. All this stuff in the papers. Everyone speculating and getting nowhere. I also had a chat with the minister. Or, rather, he had a chat with me.

He seemed rather worried.'

'Our flatulent minister probably has other things on his mind right now.' Tam guffawed. All village news travelled through the newsagents, for onward transmission by Tam Cronin.

'Maybe so,' said Richie, who had also been stopped in the street by several churchgoers. 'But that's not what I'm talking about.'

'Ah,' said Tam with some emphasis. A door banged in the visitor centre. 'Pussycats and witchcraft, is that it?'

'Something like that, yes. Well, can you help?'

'I could, but it's all pish. You shouldn't bother yourself with it.'

Richie's earlier encounter with Big Mac had not gone well, his superior officer making it clear that, as the resident police officer, Richie *should* know what was going on, otherwise he had no bloody right being the village police officer. 'Humour me,' said Richie.

'OK, OK,' said Tam. 'But like I said, Richie, it's all pish. Pish and ancient history,' he added.

'The cat, Tam.'

'Aye, the cat.' Tam turned his big eyes upwards to rolling clouds and blue sky. 'Last time around it was big Gordie Stuart who saw it. Pig farmer. Farmed up by Stenton.' His face creased open in a smile. 'Big Gordie, I tell you! Huge fellow, all of six-six and built like a shithouse. Played rugby for Scotland a few times. Then busted a leg and had to retire. God, did Gordie milk that story! Told it over and over. The cat, of course, getting bigger each time. He was out shooting pigeons and came across it at the edge of a wood. Boy, could Gordie drink!' added Tam reverentially, who was no slouch himself.

'That's it?'

'Of course, that's it.' Tam shifted his coat to his other arm. 'What more do you want?'

'Some kind of an explanation for all this.' Richie gestured to the High Street where several vans with satellite dishes were now illegally parked.

'The plain fact is that nothing happened here twenty years ago. A big cat was seen, that's all, and for no reason the minister gets his proverbials in a twist. Starts spouting off about satanists taking over the village. A complete arsehole, Richie!' Tam poked Richie in the chest for emphasis, again shifting his umpire's coat back to his other arm. 'We didn't know it, but he was on his last legs. Completely mad. Then he died, end of story.'

'Mad?' echoed Richie.

'The man was bonkers. He even turned the bloody cat into a sermon. I wasn't there, of course, having better things to do on a Sunday morning. The crux of it, so I was told, was that it seemed as if history was repeating itself.'

'History?'

Tam regarded him balefully, duty and the *Fox and Duck* loudly beckoning. 'You really don't know much about local history, do you?'

'History? What history?'

Tam put a kindly hand on his arm. 'Don't ask me, ask a historian. Ask Mara. She'll tell you.'

East Lothian is a place of history – you can't get away from it. It lies in broken castles strung along the coast, battlefields neatly annotated on the map, the Roman road that has transported kings and paupers for a thousand years and more. Even the annual cricket match between Holy Cross and Athelstaneford is something of a battle of the legends, which goes some way to explain the keen rivalry between the villages.

Battles have been fought across East Lothian. Armies have crossed and recrossed its fertile fields. Haddington has been besieged, Aberlady held off a sea-borne invasion by the English, and the Bass Rock was the last stronghold of the Covenanters. Way back then, Glasgow didn't really exist, Edinburgh and Stirling were Scotland's seats of power, and all routes north and south were across the county. It was an area where old scores were settled.

One such battle involved King Athelstane, a Northumbrian nobleman, and the local monarch, King Angus. It should have been, in the scheme of things, an insignificant fight between two warlords except, of course, that it didn't quite work out that way. Before battle commenced, King Angus looked up and saw blue sky crossed with a cloud formation – a white cross painted on the heavens. It was therefore a good omen and, of course, King Angus triumphed. This meteorological phenomenon later became the Saltire, Scotland's flag. The flag flies outside Athelstaneford's church and there is a large plaque that tells you of its provenance and about the local battle. Unlike Holy

Cross, Athelstaneford has real and authentic history on its side. Athelstane and Angus were *real* people, the battle *actually* took place there and the Saltire *is* Scotland's flag. However, Athelstaneford doesn't have a visitor centre and its one souvenir shop, selling Saltire flags and pendants, also doubles as the village Post Office and general store. The annual cricket match is therefore something of a grudge fixture; real history versus the fairy-tale nonsense of Holy Cross.

The big roller was now back in the pavilion and the stumps in place. Hefty ropes marked the boundary on three sides, the inviting Tess with its offer of double runs on the fourth. The wooden tables outside the *Fox and Duck* were full and families sat on rugs behind the roped-off field of play. A makeshift scoreboard had been carried from the pavilion and set up as close to the pub as possible. This made it difficult to read from the cricket square itself – and quite impossible for the likes of Tam Cronin – but did offer close proximity for the scorers to the *Fox and Duck*.

Liam Connarty had still not finalised the batting order, preferring to wait until his team had gathered. On the right breast of his cricket shirt was printed *Holy Cross Cricket* in swirling gothic script. On the left breast was a cartoon embroidery in red and black of a fox and duck, the fox standing on its hind legs, one foreleg around the duck in friendly embrace. The design had been commissioned by Jack, on behalf of the pub, the cricket club's shirt sponsor. He could usually be relied upon to help out.

'At least it's a nice day,' remarked the opposition captain, a wiry fellow with an angry spotted face, turning a cricket ball in his hand and looking at the sky for signs of rain. 'The forecast's pretty good. Makes a change, I suppose.' As often as not cricket matches in East Lothian are rained off. 'Anyway, I'm just going to enjoy being a celebrity.' He gestured towards the High Street where a number of TV cameras on tripods had been set up, their lenses turned to the cricket square. The electronic media, alerted to the battle of the legends, and having been banned from the church service earlier, needed footage of something – *anything* – for the evening broadcasts, even if it was just a cricket match. England might be playing Pakistan at Trent Bridge, but the match of the day was definitely taking place further north.

Rosie had by now accepted that events were entirely out of her hands, and that she owed explanations to a number of people, not least the Reverend Kennedy. She'd tried to phone him, to apologise for an errant pie that should have been thrown away – and should never, *ever* have been given away by her stupid, *stupid* husband – but his phone was constantly engaged. Jack, of course, had once again abandoned the sinking ship, announcing with bad grace that he was needed instead by the cricket team.

Lionel Kennedy had only just made it back to the manse. Floodgates were about to be breached. Luckily, the dam burst only as he gratefully lowered himself to the toilet seat in the downstairs loo; a torrent of relief that was so utterly gratifying that, for a short while, he was able to forget his complete humiliation in church. He felt light-headed and dizzy, like any new mother having just given birth. His peaceful sojourn in the downstairs loo was broken by trumpet solos and other orchestral flourishes – from a vaporous mixture of nitrogen, oxygen, carbon dioxide, hydrogen and methane, and several other components in lesser portion, most notably methylindole, skatole, hydrogen sulphide and methyl mercaptan. He had, as Rosie suspected, eaten far more chicken pie than was good for him.

He emerged at length from the loo to find that Mrs Gallagher had called out the doctor and that Dr Murray was waiting patiently in his study.

Dr Murray examined him, listened to his heart, and took his blood pressure, which he pronounced to be a little high. He explained that of the three nutrients – carbohydrates, fats and proteins – carbohydrates are the most effective gas producers. He asked Lionel a few questions about his diet, and what he had most recently eaten. The doctor managed a laugh when he explained that modern dietary advice was to eat more carbohydrates – adding fuel to the fire, so to speak. He advised against fizzy drinks and, for the time being, to cut down on such things as cabbage, bran and onions. 'I could also do a blood test,' said the doctor, 'or take a stool sample.' – suggestions that the minister in his worn state considered to be further and unnecessary humiliations. The doctor, now without diagnostic alternative, prescribed anticholinergics and antacid tablets that Mrs Gallagher, looking concerned, was dispatched to fetch from Haddington, where there was a chemist open on a Sunday.

On her return, Lionel Kennedy was sitting behind the desk in his study. The TV was on and he was watching the start of the Test match from Trent Bridge. He was still looking green around the gills. 'Mrs Gallagher, I rather think I've made an idiot of myself. I confided in someone I thought I could trust, and we now find ourselves being made fools of in the media. And then, this morning, well…' The effort to finish the sentence was too much.

She forced tablets on him and watched as he washed them down with a glass of water. 'Dr Murray thinks that it was probably something I ate.' He shifted uncomfortably in his seat, his abdomen not fully recovered.

Sadie Gallagher paused from her ministrations. 'Don't you go worrying about what other folk might think. What's done is done and you can't change what's in the past.'

This, he had to concede, was palpably true. 'In particular, Dr Murray thinks it may have been induced by chicken pie. Absolutely delicious, I assure you, but regrettably explosive.'

'Jack McLeod gave it to me,' she said. 'His wife had made it for him but she went off to Edinburgh to see a show. She thought that Jack liked chicken pie but it turns out she was wrong. Jack thought that you might like it instead.'

Sadie Gallagher had, of course, already made it absolutely clear to everyone she knew, and quite a few who she didn't know, that she had never cooked chicken pie in her life.

The game of cricket is, depending on your point of view, either a lengthy exercise in psychological and physical combat or a complete waste of time. The majority of Scots tend to the latter view and, it has to be said, so too the majority of residents of Holy Cross. However, the proximity of the cricket square to the *Fox and Duck* does encourage a healthy support on warm days, giving spectators a justifiable reason for spending Sunday afternoon at the pub.

There are rules specific to East Lothian village cricket. Each match is limited to twenty overs, batsman retire if they reach twenty-five runs and no bowler can bowl more than three overs. This last rule means that each team must use at least seven bowlers, a local rule that was still vexing the Holy Cross cricket captain as Liam Connarty led his team onto the field of combat. The question, of course, was when to use his better bowlers – at the start against their more competent batsmen, or later on against their poorer tail-enders? Normally, such tactical decisions came easily to him. He was comfortable with the mantle of captaincy, but not today. Not with photographers and TV crews pointing cameras, and a larger-than-usual gallery camped outside the *Fox and Duck* and becoming boisterous.

The opening Athelstaneford batsman started brightly enough, blocking the first two deliveries and then edging the third behind second slip for three runs. A smattering of applause greeted this less than convincing shot, repeated more loudly when the second batsman knocked the next delivery for four on the leg side – which he then proceeded to repeat on the fifth and sixth balls. Liam Connarty's decision to hold back his better bowlers was not paying immediate dividends.

After her humiliating confession before church, Mara should have been furious with Rosie but, with exotic vegetation still coursing in her veins, anger didn't seem worth the effort. She felt calm, serene even, as she poured drinks, took plates out to the beer garden, and cleaned tables. A trick of eyesight made her register small details: a pink carnation in a women's lapel, the shape of a cloud as it passed across the sun, the shimmering feathers of a starling perched in an elm tree by the church. She felt light-headed and hot, sweat gathering on her brow and back. The bar and beer garden were full, with much lively discussion about the minister, and a growing crowd spilling down the gentle grass bank overlooking the cricket square.

She saw that Richie was also on the grass bank, a hand on his uniform belt. Her heart missed a beat. She wiped her hands and walked over. As always, a lock of hair was over one eye, his smile lopsided. 'I just came by to see what the score was. Oh dear, Jack's missed a sitter!' There was a collective groan from the Holy Cross players as a slow delivery was edged to first slip, and dropped by Jack McLeod. Liam Connarty was shouting at his team to pay attention. The runs were inexorably mounting; chances were being squandered. 'Actually, I was also wondering if I could ask you something. In your professional capacity as Scotland's most boring person.'

'Thank you for the kind endorsement.' She smiled, squinting against the sun. 'I take it that you're still prowling the streets?'

He smiled. 'Mostly reassuring mothers that their kiddies aren't about to be eaten.' He turned to look at the cricket. 'Jesus, they're not giving the bowling to Jack, are they?'

Jack McLeod had not been expecting to bowl; he hadn't played for the cricket team all year: he was rusty, out of practice. He was also a port of last resort, willing only to make up numbers if there was a last-minute crisis. To be fair, Liam Connarty had not intended to offer Jack any bowling duties; they had, however, managed to keep Athelstaneford's score within an attainable total and Liam was grateful for Jack's help. He tossed the ball to Jack for the nineteenth and second last, over.

Jack, in his younger days, had been quite a good cricketer. He liked playing at slip – usually he had dependable hands. Today, of course, he'd dropped the only ball to come his way. The dropped batsman had gone on to score the mandatory limit of twenty-five runs and been cheered from the wicket by his team-mates. Jack had also been something of a reasonable medium bowler, although he hadn't bowled a ball in anger for over a year. This probably explained why his first delivery was judged a wide even by Tam Cronin's forgiving standard. There were ironic jeers from the *Fox and Duck*, the spectators sensing that a new level of incompetence was about to be reached.

They weren't disappointed as Jack's second ball sailed several feet above the wicket and several feet above the gloves of the stretching wicketkeeper. The ball continued on its path to the boundary rope.

His third ball was another wide.

Tam Cronin looked at his watch. 'This could take some time,' he remarked to nobody in particular.

His fourth and fifth balls were, miraculously, on or near the target, stopped by defensive strokes. However, overconfidence led Jack to push his sixth ball down the leg side where it was hit for four. Overcompensating, his seventh went well outside the off-stump and was batted away for another four.

Jack's last delivery was on target, but it was near the end of the innings and the batsman was in no mood to end it with a whimper. This was clear from the little edging movements he made towards the bowler, his bat at full swing behind him. Jack tried to fool him with a slightly faster delivery. This time the ball pitched short, just on the leg side, and began to swing in towards the stumps. The batsman swung at it, connected, and sent it across the boundary rope for another four runs.

'Over,' said Tam. 'Eventually.'

Richie and Mara had walked further round the cricket ground, towards the rotting pavilion, during Jack's disastrous over. Richie cast an anxious eye at the scoreboard that hadn't changed for some time, the scoreboard operators having disappeared inside the pub.

'You had something that you wanted to ask,' she reminded him. 'In my professional capacity.' Richie was looking at the wicket where Tam Cronin was myopically peering down the crease, his borrowed butcher's coat stained with the remnants of other slaughters.

'I still love you, by the way.'

She smiled. 'That's not a question.' She leaned against him for a moment and laced her fingers through his. She wanted to kiss him, but didn't know if kissing police officers in uniform was allowed. She brushed hair from her eyes, smiling stupidly; seeing the precise design of his uniform buttons, a fleck of dust on his collar, the way he hooked one thumb over his belt.

'It's just that I bumped into Tam this morning,' he said eventually. 'My superiors, you see, aren't exactly pleased with my total lack of local knowledge. So I asked Tam about the cat.'

'And he said to ask me.'

'Even mentioned you by name,' said Richie.

A ball bounced close to the river, stopped on the very brink of disaster by a sliding outfielder. Richie clapped and shouted encouragement. Liam Connarty was dashing about the wicket slapping his team on the back, one hand in a fist, instilling his faith in them.

'Richie, you really don't know anything about anything, do you?'

He shook his head which caused the lock of hair to again fall over one eye. She pushed it back for him. 'Can't have you looking scruffy, can we?' she said, turning her attention briefly to the field of play where a fast ball had narrowly missed the batsman's stumps. A collective groan went around the ground. There were a few jeers from the direction of the *Fox and Duck*. The locals, becoming anaesthetised

245

with beer and sunshine, were – against their better judgement – beginning to enjoy the game. 'You must, at the very least, have heard of the North Berwick witches? Oh God, Richie, *everybody* knows about the North Berwick witches.'

'Except me, apparently.'

'Except you, patently.' She shook her head, smiling. 'Do you want the long version or the short version? OK, unfair question. I'll give you the *very* short version. No need to bore you to death. I'll ask questions later, mind you,' she said and wagged a finger.

On the cricket field, in the last over, another batsman had been dispatched, caught behind by the wicketkeeper. A ragged cheer echoed from the pub.

'It happened when James VI was on the throne – you know the one, the Scottish king who also became James I of England? No, then what exactly *do* you know? Christ, Richie, did you actually *go* to school? Anyway, a local worthy from Tranent, can't remember his name, decides that one of his servants is a witch. In a dream, he'd seen her riding on the back of a large, black cat. So, when he wakes up he has her tortured. She, of course, confesses and implicates a whole lot of other people. The great thing about being a witch finder was how easy it was! You simply put thumbscrews on a poor unfortunate and, pretty soon, she's implicated everyone she ever knew. Easy.' There was a burst of laughter from the *Fox and Duck* as an easy ball bounced between the legs of fielder.

'One of the unfortunates who she named was the Earl of

246

Bothwell. Now, that was an unexpected bonus for King James! Bothwell, you see, had a claim to the Scottish throne if the king died childless. So, what better way to get rid of a rival? One who could now be tried for treason. One of the claims, you see, made against the North Berwick witches was that they had tried to place a spell on the king's ship as he sailed back from Denmark. Witchcraft *and* treason! Bothwell, however, managed to escape and legged it to Italy.'

She paused, watching the breeze move his hair, noticing for the first time a small scar behind his ear, the way his cap was slightly squint. She took a deep breath. 'Others weren't so lucky. A whole bunch of people were executed. Some of them from Holy Cross. The village, apparently, was full of the unfortunates.'

'They burned them here?'

'Mostly in Edinburgh. Bigger entertainment value, I suppose. They even burned a schoolmaster whose only crime was to own a black cat.' She smiled brightly. 'There, that was the short version. Like I say, I can do long if you'd like me to.'

'I still don't see the significance of the cat.' He seemed to have missed the point.

'The black cat in the servant's dream was taken as a sign of local witch activity. The trial judge went as far as to say that the cat was the definitive proof. He said that it was *the* sign to watch out for in future. It proved, you see, that everyone was guilty.' She shrugged. 'So, when the black cat was seen twenty years ago it did make for some light-hearted banter. Satanism reborn, that kind of thing. The definitive proof had returned.'

It still made no sense to him. The only evidence of wrongdoing was a prank symbol carved onto the church wall. Nothing had ever happened in Holy Cross, apart from burning a few witches, and that was hundreds of years ago – Tam Cronin, Mara, court records and several computers were all now certain of that – and nothing was happening now, if you could lay aside volcanic flatulence and the attention of the international media.

Chapter 16

The herb is named of the Chaldees Celayos, *of the Greeks* Casini, *of the Latins* Melissophyllum, *of Englishmen Smallage; of the which herb* Macer Floridus *maketh mention. This herb, gathered green, and casten with the juice of the Cypress tree of one year, put in gruel, maketh the gruel to appear full of worms, and maketh the bearer to be gentle and gracious, and to vanquish his enemies.*

The Book of Secrets of Albertus Magnus

While admitting that her plans had not gone exactly to plan, Rosie McLeod, like an unrepentant alcoholic, was now considering the stormy properties of the humble foxglove.

Wily foxglove, so called because its flowers look like the fingers of a glove, given to the crafty fox by bad fairies to muffle his footfalls and help him hunt. Foxglove is used for congestive heart failure and atrial fibrillation; the cardiac glycosides in the plant blocking an enzyme that regulates the heart's electrical activity.

Or happy St John's Wort, she considered, serving another

customer with beer and smoky bacon crisps, weighing up its many constituents. No, she concluded, it also needed something more calming. Valerian root, perhaps? – although she'd never much liked the plant with its pungent volatile oils. But the root does contain several unstable but useful esters. Valerian is effective in reducing depression: in a chemical combination not yet understood, its active ingredients somehow work in calmative partnership. Like the flight of a bumble-bee, valerian root shouldn't work, but it does. Its chemical composition is remarkably similar to Valium, which Rosie now badly wanted and in large supply.

Like valerian root, the gift of healing is to combine the properties of plants and herbs so that, in combination, you arrive at a required result; of knowing how alkaloids interact with seemingly inert ingredients and what the end result will be.

However, the obligation of knowledge, as Rosie well knew, is to use it wisely, and having seemingly crossed a boundary, Rosie McLeod now wondered whether she could return. Although Jack's marital innocence had been established, he *was* guilty of carpet slippers. The jury was still out on the charge of love. She now looked on her gift in a different light – it offered a shifting landscape of possibility. The XIII had been her sign, she was now sure about it. Her warning. Perhaps also the defaced church wall. She'd look after herself, but in her own way.

'One hundred and twenty isn't impossible,' Liam was telling his team in a corner of the function suite set aside for cricket teas. Rosie set down two trays of sandwiches prepared that morning by Sammy. 'We only need an average of six runs an over. Guys, we can win this, we're *going* to win this.' He smacked a fist into the open palm of his other hand.

Nobody doubted him, the cricket team nodding solemnly. 'Putting Jack into bowl wasn't a very good idea,' said Eric Middlemiss, *de facto* vice captain because of his duties with the roller. He took his cricket seriously and looked at Jack accusingly.

Jack held up his hands. 'OK, OK. Sorry. Bit rusty. First game of the season.'

'But it's still an achievable target,' repeated Liam, casting his eyes around the small group. 'We *can* win this match! Here's the batting order.' He laid a piece of paper on the table, the players listed one to eleven. Jack was firmly at the bottom of the list, potentially surplus to requirements.

In the public bar Tam Cronin was lubricating his dubious eyesight with a welcome pint of Belhaven. Apart from one disputed LBW the innings had gone quite well, except for Jack's dropped catch and wretched bowling. 'Ah, the very man,' said Tam, holding out his pewter tankard as Jack reappeared from the function suite. 'It's thirsty work this standing around business. I take it that Liam is firing up the lads for the battle yet to come.'

Jack held Tam's tankard under the beer tap. 'Something like that. Giving his usual pep talk, slapping their backs. You know what he's like. Still, we've beaten them before.'

'I also remember being beaten by them last year. Smug

bastards!' said Tam, drawing a hand across his stubbly face. 'The people I dislike more than bad losers are bad winners. And they, Jack, are *very* bad winners! Didn't even have the good grace to buy the umpire a pint. It won't, of course, affect my impartiality.' Tam drank deeply from his tankard and looked at his watch. 'Well, I suppose we'd better go and entertain the masses. He turned his pebbly eyes to Jack. 'I just hope that your batting is better than your bowling. Could I ask you something?'

Jack followed him to the open doorway, the rest of the team filing out. The opposition were already out on the field of play. Tam extracted a Marlboro and lit up. 'Is it true,' he finally asked, once sufficient nicotine had entered his system, 'that you don't like chicken pie?'

The Holy Cross cricket team emerged from the *Fox and Duck* to a ragged cheer, some ironic catcalls, and a scattering of applause. The presence of TV cameras and the intake of alcohol were having a positive effect on the team's supporters. Liam handed the batting order to the scorer and then had a motivational few words with the opening batsmen, instilling in them the certainty of victory. The opposition players generously clapped the two men in. In Richie's absence, the first man in was Eric Middlemiss, a pugnacious and dependable batsman who compensated for a lack of style with dogged determination. The strategy was for Eric to remain in for as long as possible, allowing other batsmen to hit out and score the needed runs.

To a howl of derision from the *Fox and Duck*, Eric

Middlemiss was clean bowled on the second ball, remaining rooted with disbelief at his crease for some seconds. The Athelstaneford infielders were high fiving with the bowler who was grinning sheepishly. Nought for one.

'Looks like you might be needed after all,' remarked Rosie, as she passed Jack on her way to the cash register. In a gesture of conciliation, he'd offered to help out in the bar until – or if – he was needed to bat. Despite all her other worries, Jack's innocence of most things had imbued her with a meagre optimism. Everything else was a mess, but her husband, carpet slippers and waning libido aside, seemed largely innocent.

By the end of the third over, Holy Cross had lost a further wicket for a grand total of ten runs. Despite this, a mantle of faith still hung from Liam Connarty's shoulders. 'Just go in there and do what's necessary,' he was saying to the incoming batsman, a large and cheerful farmer called David Petrie, although it wasn't entirely clear to Big Dave what exactly his captain was asking of him. The spectators were noisily demanding a home victory, the growing gallery at the *Fox and Duck* spilling further down to the boundary rope. Big Dave nodded, suitably energised, his bat held under one arm like a spear. Two minutes later he was back in the *Fox and Duck* and ordering a pint of lager.

'Not looking good,' remarked Eric to his captain.

They were sitting a little apart from the team to keep a close eye on the scorebook. It wasn't unknown for occasional runs to be forgotten as scorers lost interest or concentration, or simply departed for the public bar. The rest of the team was lolling by the boundary rope, bottles of beer in their hands.

Liam's articles of faith remained intact. 'Never say die,' he said firmly.

Adrian Mountjoy's feeling of political impotence was made worse by gnawing hunger pangs. Closer inspection of his kitchen cupboards had thrown up a tin of peas, half a bag of rice and a stale packet of digestive biscuits. Unable to eat, he sat sullenly in front of the TV and watched the Test match. The mouldy digestives had tasted of cardboard. He ate two and then consigned the packet to the bin alongside the other detritus from his fridge. He'd spent some time on the phone earlier, explaining his absence to the local Party hierarchy and activists – the faithful on whom the country depended to return a decent Conservative administration, although everyone seemed to have been briefed already by Madam Chair and were sympathetic to his plight. *Let's hope the young man gets his just desserts*, seemed to be his Party's consensus. He promised them that he would be back in the thick of things by tomorrow, knocking on doors, handing out leaflets, glad-handing the good people of East Lothian. He now returned phone calls from several friends who had called earlier but deleted all messages from journalists. The assault was now *sub judice*. Clare was right, lying low for the day was probably good advice. Later still, he phoned Lionel Kennedy, feeling that an explanation might be in order.

He heard a thin female voice at the other end.

'Reverend Kennedy, please.'

She seemed to hesitate before answering. 'He's indisposed,' she informed him gravely, a noise like thunder in the background. 'I rather think that he may be indisposed for some time.' Adrian looked out the window. At least the weather in Edinburgh was still fine.

Liam Connarty's thoughtful strategies for success were, he believed, being entirely undermined by his team's poor execution of them, thereby deflecting all blame to the other ten men in the team. Eric Middlemiss should not have been out second ball. He was supposed to be still hanging in there, a safe bat to allow the big hitters to make runs. Nor was it in the script for Big Dave to give an easy catch to the wicketkeeper off the first ball. The crowd, however, was enjoying the spectacle and, despite their almost total ignorance of cricket, were also sensing that things weren't going entirely to plan. By the end of the twelfth over it was fifty-nine for six, and there seemed little possibility of achieving a winning total. The game had become a kind of stalemate – bowlers unable to hit the stumps and batsmen unable to hit the ball. Ironic cheers greeted every delivery, the patrons of the pub wanting better action than this. They wanted nothing less than victory and lustily sang the chorus of *Simply The Best* before descending into laughter.

And then, like a slow osmosis, the alchemy of the crowd's support found its way onto the field of play. The Athelstaneford players, not used to a sizeable gallery, became nervous. New bowlers were jeered and made uncharacteristic errors. They felt like outsiders, outnumbered. Holy Cross, on the other hand, now felt the burden of expectation. Deep breaths were taken, the ship steadied. By the end of the sixteenth over, the village had scored ninety runs for the loss of only one more wicket. Four more overs, thirty-one runs for victory. It was, maybe, just possible.

Liam took his place at the crease, hearing the crowd chanting the village's name over and over. A TV camera panned from the crowd to the cricket square. His inclusion down the batting order was the last piece of his strategic jigsaw; apart from Richie Scott, he was the team's best batsmen – and he now faced, because of the limited overs rule, the poorer opposition bowlers. Other strategies had failed. This one *had* to succeed. He noted the position of each fielder, twirling his bat, telling himself it was possible. The bowler, grey-haired and asthmatic, offered a slow ball down the leg side that he pushed away without fuss for four runs. There was a rousing cheer from the *Fox and Duck*. By the end of the over he had added two more boundaries, to the obvious chagrin of the Athelstaneford captain who now ordered all his players to the outfield. The opposition no longer cared about the single runs that Holy Cross could score. To secure victory they only needed to prevent the ball crossing the boundary rope.

Despite the batsmen's best efforts to reach the boundary, this they were simply unable to do, taking only four single runs off four balls and disaster on the fifth. Liam's batting partner, Zac Morrison, a local plumber, called the run, the ball bouncing smartly towards the river. An outfielder, charging in, scooped the ball on the move and hurled it to the wicket. It was both skill and bad luck combined; the stumps in front of Liam's stretched bat shed bails and, seemingly, all hope.

He departed the field to a scattering of applause and ribald catcalls from the direction of the pub. The spectators, sensing imminent loss, were in no mood now to tolerate defeat quietly. The new batsmen, one of several make-weights in the team, dangled his bat at the last ball of the over, not making contact.

'You're supposed to hit it!' someone shouted to a burst of laughter, and another chorus of *Simply The Best*.

The rest of the team had now grouped together to yell encouragement. Liam Connarty, back at base camp, was deeply regretting his decision to give Jack a bowl. That one disastrous over had propelled the Athelstaneford score beyond reasonable reach. The mantle of his optimism was slipping – tail-end batsmen, two overs to go and fifteen runs required. In that penultimate over, Holy Cross managed just three runs and with the last ball of the over, Zac Morrison was clean bowled.

Jack, of course, could not immediately be located, much to the amusement of the *Fox and Duck* clientele who started a slow hand clap. There was therefore a short interlude during which search parties were dispatched to the pub, its elusive owner found and escorted to the cricket square to be padded up.

A measure of the captain's steely optimism had returned. 'We only need thirteen runs,' Liam was whispering to Jack's ear as he fiddled with straps and Velcro, making it sound ridiculously easy. 'I *know* it's your first game of the season. I *know* you're a bit rusty. But just go in there and hit out.' It was meant to be inspirational. Instead, it simply served to remind Jack of his limitations. He trudged onto the field rather like a doomed gladiator, catcalls and cheers from the coliseum gallery, and took station at the bowler's end. Tam Cronin, six coins in hand, raised large eyes to the sky.

The Athelstaneford players were pumped up for victory, dancing on the boundary ropes and yelling meaningless encouragement to the bowler, a great bull of a man who was almost pawing the ground with excitement. The other batsman, clearly nervous, edged it away through where first slip should have been – first slip, all the other slips, and everyone else now being on the boundary. The wicketkeeper dropped his gloves and scampered after the ball, allowing Holy Cross to add another run.

Jack now had to face the bowling. He had never enjoyed great prowess with the bat, was now hopelessly out of practice, and found himself in the unenviable position of losing the annual battle of the legends in front of a sizeable crowd and at least two TV crews. He was aware of Liam shouting inane advice from the sidelines and a chorus of good-natured jeering from the *Fox and Duck*. He missed the first ball, the wicketkeeper clapping his hands, Tam Cronin inscrutable behind his pebble glasses.

Slightly panicked, Jack swung wildly at the next ball

which connected sharply with his left pad. The bowler appealed for LBW, but Tam Cronin simply transferred a coin from one hand to the other. A shake of the umpire's head and a collective cheer from the crowd. With three balls to go, there was still the faint hope of a miracle.

All hope then seemed lost when Jack missed the fourth ball and only managed to push the fifth back down the wicket to the waiting bowler. Opposition players were whooping and yelling, victory now assured. On their playing shirts was stitched a Saltire, a reminder of their place in Scotland's *real* history, unlike the Holy Grail garbage of the home team. The bowler now rubbed the ball against the small flag on his chest; a good-luck gesture for the last ball of the match and an affirmation of their true iconic status.

Thoroughly unnerved by his inept performance, Jack simply wished for everything to be over and to be able to retreat to the safety of the *Fox and Duck*. The bowler was eyeing the wicket speculatively, anticipating the great shout that would greet this last ball and final victory. He was smiling, almost a grimace.

However, being a newcomer to village cricket, he didn't know about the Holy Cross local rule. Nobody had thought to tell him, a fact that he angrily made clear afterwards. Had he done so, he would have been more careful not to put the ball down the leg side which, unfortunately, he did. Jack, unnerved and confidence shredded, swung wildly at it, eyes tight shut.

His bat connected although it wasn't immediately clear to him where the ball had gone. He saw fielders by the river looking skywards and edging back towards the riverbank so, presumably, the ball was in the air. *This is my fate*, he thought: *over and out on the last ball*. There was an eerie hush from the *Fox and Duck*, spectators straining their necks to follow the ball's parabola.

Jack's ball had discovered the freedom of flight and soared gloriously over outstretched hands to splash down in the Tess for twelve runs. The *Fox and Duck* erupted, Holy Cross players ran onto the square to embrace him. Jack held his bat over his head, the gladiator victorious, as Athelstaneford players sank to their haunches with disbelief. Only the bowler danced with delight, only realising by degrees that not all was well. Jack turned to face the crowd, the villain of the bowling now the hero of the last ball.

There was, of course, an immediate and vociferous outcry from the opposition team. Their not unreasonable argument, succinctly and loudly advanced by their captain, was that local rules should not apply in a league match. It was important that every team in the league played to the same rules. Jack's last ball should therefore only be counted as six runs, and the final outcome reversed. However, the merit of this argument was undermined by the Athelstaneford tail-end bowler who was now angrily blaming his team-mates for not telling him about the rule. Pretty soon it descended into an internal squabble, making it easier for Tam Cronin to impartially decide that the local rule should stand. This decision was greeted by a loud cheer from the sizeable gallery still camped outside the *Fox and Duck*. Tam then took off the stained butcher's coat, removing his official cloak: no further appeals allowed.

'Well, it's still not fair,' muttered the defeated captain.

'Life isn't fair, laddie.' Tam had more liquid thoughts on his mind.

Most of the Athelstaneford team drifted off once their kit was packed away. There were only a few grudging handshakes. The winning ball was carried downstream; a small search party failed to find it.

'Well, that's the bastards sorted for another year,' remarked Tam as the last opposition car departed to some good-natured boos from the gallery. Honour intact, it was time to celebrate.

Euphoria wasn't universal. The Reverend Kennedy was still feeling bloated and uncomfortable; his innards fizzed and grumbled. However, the worst was over; the thunderstorm had passed. Not for the first time that day he put his head in his hands and groaned. He reread Rosie's pious apology… "*destined for the bin… it was entirely my husband's fault… husbands can be so infuriating… he can't apologise enough.*" The note had been pushed through his letterbox earlier, relayed to him by an unsmiling Sadie Gallagher. It seemed to Lionel Kennedy that Rosie was protesting overmuch. She was the pie's creator; Jack guilty only of generosity. He laid the note down on his desk, rose stiffly from his chair and poured a large brandy.

After several pints, the team collectively agreed that it

had been a fairly straightforward win. After a couple more, they agreed that the match should have been won much earlier. Only bad luck had prevented Holy Cross from giving them a complete drubbing. However, whichever way you looked at it, you couldn't get away from Jack's mighty wallop at the death, the trajectory of the ball far above grasping hands. It was, they agreed, a legendary finale to the battle of the legends.

Tam Cronin, back at his appointed place at the bar, had already consumed an heroic amount of Belhaven. 'I'm not saying that it was a lucky shot, Jack. I'm just saying that it was fortuitous. After all, having missed several balls, hitting the bloody thing into the river was the only shot you had left. There just wasn't an alternative. It was all or nothing.'

Jack was enjoying his sobriquet as action hero. 'I know that it was a lucky shot,' he readily agreed, bending to the tap to refill Tam's tankard. 'However, cometh the hour, cometh the man.' He set Tam's tankard in front of him and then, what the hell, poured himself another pint.

A lit candle on the bedside table was burning in Mara's eye and making her seem again like a wild or untamed animal. In the flicker of its flame, she looked translucent, without inhibition. Riche lay beside her, running his tongue across her breasts, across the soft flatness of her belly. She folded her legs around him, abandoning herself, a blinding light of pure pleasure behind her eyes. She cried his name, her back arched, then lay still.

Richie Scott held her in his arms and ran a finger down

her spine. He bent his mouth to her hair, drinking in the smell of her. She moved her body to his, moulding to him.

The sexual act involves the autonomic and somatic nervous systems, the peripheral circulatory system, the spinal and central nervous systems and the endocrine system. Sensory receptors in the skin, mucosa and subcutaneous tissue start numerous sympathetic and parasympathetic reflexes, including the release of hormones from the posterior pituitary gland. These hormones include oxytocin and act peripherally to make sexual organs more sensitive to nervous stimuli. Testosterone, converted to oestradiol, is also involved and ejaculation is controlled by oxytocin and vasopressin, facts of which both Richie and Mara were entirely unaware.

'What's wrong?' she asked.

Richie was frowning, assaulted by a sudden, unlikely and uninvited thought.

'Can I ask you something? It's a history thing.'

In the aftermath of love he suddenly felt foolish. 'Mara, what exactly *did* they do to witches?'

Once more, unprompted, he had remembered the fallen child.

The boy had stolen matches; the mother was on methadone. The small fire he had started wasn't serious – a waste bin, nothing more. His mother was only out for a few minutes buying groceries. It was concluded that panic and smoke were probably to blame, the small boy climbing onto a chair to open a window. Toppled out. A tragedy, end of story. Or maybe not.

Chapter 17

The herb is named of the Chaldees Isiphilon, of the Greeks Orgelon, of the Latins Centaurea, of Englishmen Centaury. Witches say that this herb hath a marvellous virtue, for if it be joined with the blood of a female lapwing, or Black Plover, and be put with it in a lamp, all they that compass it about shall believe themselves to be witches, so that one shall believe of another that his head is in heaven and his feet in the earth.

The Book of Secrets of Albertus Magnus

Next morning found Rosie pondering the significance of several herbs and their chemical composition.

She was also thinking about the complexity of our feelings and how our responses are controlled by dependable phenylethylamine that speeds up the flow of information between nerve cells. Also involved in the process of attraction are dopamine and norepinephrine, kissing cousins of amphetamines that massage our limbic systems. These three chemicals combine to form a cocktail of passion at the start of a relationship, when partners can talk and make love for hours. Dopamine, produced by the action of nitric oxide, makes us feel good and norepinephrine stimulates the production of adrenaline, thereby increasing heart rate when your loved one is nearby. Vasopressin gently encourages us to be faithful – once initial infatuation passes – while endorphins, similar to morphine, make us yearn when apart from those we love. Oxytocin makes us more responsive to the feelings of others and is also important for sexual arousal, lactation and labour contractions. In women, arousal and orgasm are also controlled by rising levels of apomorphine that controls blood flow to the vagina. Prostaglandin, testosterone and the amino acid L-arginine allow blood vessels to expand. L-arginine also comprises 80% of sperm cells. Production can be enhanced by either saw palmetto or *Sida cardifolia*, the active ingredient of which is a natural amphetamine.

She had almost removed all trace of cricket celebration when she encountered her husband looking dishevelled. He was carrying a black bin liner filled with rubbish. She followed him outside.

'I'm still not pleased with you.'

Jack, feeling wretched, dumped the bag in the bin and pulled the lid shut. 'Why, for God's sake?' was all he could muster at this early hour.

'For trying to make love to me.'

'I thought that's what you wanted me to do?' Really, the woman could be so unreasonable, particularly first thing in the morning.

'Sober, Jack. Sober! Not staggering around like a demented gibbon!'

He couldn't immediately bring to mind what a gibbon looked like, demented or otherwise, and made no reply.

Rosie remained on full throttle. 'You were drunk!' she said sharply, making it sound like a capital offence. 'It's a simple fact! Don't you see how upsetting that is?'

The last hours of Jack's Sunday evening were somewhat hazy, with rounds of beers being consumed, and Liam Connarty having to be carried home. 'I may have been a little —'

'And the rest, Jack. Really!' She'd wanted to be woken slowly like an enchanted princess, rising to wakefulness to the accompaniment of kisses – not having a great paw thumped into her midriff and his beery breath on her cheek.

It was impossible to reason with Rosie when she was in one of her moods. He had thought that she would have welcomed amorous pursuit, the flat upstairs smelling unpleasantly of boiled cabbage. OK, he'd had a few more beers than was good for him – but he had been the team hero. Instead, he'd been shouted at and chased naked to the spare room.

He groaned inwardly, details of his ignominious retreat to the chaste single bed coming back to him. 'You're going out,' said Jack, noticing her warm coat.

'Of course I'm going out. I don't dress like this to stay *in*.'

She now walked over the humpback bridge across the Tess, raindrops patterning its surface. She looked up to the high ground above the village, bending her small frame against the chill wind. She climbed steadily across the open grassland, rabbits darting for cover, towards the woodland. Here she stopped and sat on a stone dyke, her face to the drizzle from the Forth. West lay the smudge of Edinburgh, north the indistinct outline of Fife. A red supertanker, seemingly motionless on the steel river, headed towards the open sea. Sheep grazed at the woodland margins; a blanket of grey cloud promised more rain.

She stooped at the woodland edge to dig up nettles and place them in her basket. The woodland dripped; it was gloomy under the trees. She trod carefully on the wet ground, brushing branches from her face. Weak sunlight reflected in moisture on spiders' webs. She supposed that she should have been grateful for Jack's advances, however brutish – a reminder that she could still be an object of attraction, even under the influence of alcohol.

She was careful to wear gloves. The hollow hairs of nettles contain four active ingredients that cause them to sting. Ironically, the juice of a stinging nettle also acts as an antidote to the sting – an example of natural balance: pain and healing within one plant. The humble nettle is useful in all sorts of ways, not least in restoring cytokine balance – important for fighting all immune disorders from flu to cancer. Nettle root also inhibits sex hormone-binding globulin, which considerably boosts testosterone metabolism in both sexes.

Even the winsome buttercup has a part to play as it contains oestrogenic sterols that are the beginnings of steroid hormones like oestrogen, progesterone and testosterone. Buttercup causes levels of follicle-stimulating hormone to fall, thus improving the lining of the vagina.

It was wily, but poisonous, foxglove that she principally sought to bind the properties together and she found a patch in a small clearing by a towering oak. The favourite haunt of honey bees, foxglove contains digitalis, a cardiac stimulant. The first thing it does is to constrict the heart and arteries, causing a rise in blood pressure. The second effect, in conjunction primarily with periwinkle, is to excite the production of nitric oxide and oxytocin.

Rosie's basket was filling with the last ingredients she needed, which she planned to boil to a mush and strain lovingly through two layers of muslin.

With some misgiving, Richie Scott had taken his suspicions to higher authority. He was probably wrong, he knew it, but the memory of the falling child had been so vivid, his still body on the pavement and his mother on her knees, screaming.

'I know it sounds unlikely, sir, but that's just the point. A number of unlikely things have been happening in the village.'

The divisional inspector, Ronald MacDonald, Big Mac himself, was a large and garrulous islander from Coll with wiry grey hair and puffy jowls. He suffered fools less than gladly and was naturally suspicious of fast-track young sergeants with bright ideas. The buttons on his crisp shirt, too tight for his generous girth, were strained to breaking point.

Surprisingly, when he spoke it was with a soft Hebridean accent quite at odds with his considerable proportions. 'Unlikely, I agree,' he said, clearly not believing a word of it. They were in the inspector's hot and cramped office in Haddington, and by arcane diktat the radiators had been on overnight. The room was fetid, the window closed. Outside, clouds scudded. Richie sat at attention, his collar burning in the overheated room, having only been granted a limited audience.

'But I do believe that it's worth pursuing. The possibility remains that a crime may have been committed.'

The inspector sipped tea from a china cup and returned it crisply to its saucer. Richie had not been offered any such generosity. 'A crime? But what crime, sergeant?' He raised his eyes to meet the younger man's eye.

'Maybe nothing,' conceded Richie.

'Ah, nothing.' Badges of rank glittered on his shoulders. 'I remain to be convinced,' he said, reaching again for his cup. 'Bloody waste of time! Complete nonsense! Four detectives – *four!* – spent most of yesterday double-checking. And what do they find? Nothing, sergeant. Precisely bloody nothing! Police records, fire records, court records,' he said, holding up fingers. 'Even the local rag. Fact is, sergeant, nothing has *ever* happened in Holy Cross. It's a place where nothing does ever happen. Not since dinosaurs roamed the earth and even they probably found the place utterly dull. Well,' he conceded, finally running out of steam and narrowing his eyes, 'not until this weekend.' On his desk were the morning newspapers. "WITCHCRAFT

SUSPECTED IN ICONIC VILLAGE" said *The Scotsman*. "HOLY STINK" said *The Sun*. "HOLY CROSS WINS TENSE CRICKET MATCH" said *The Sporting Life*.

'Exactly, sir,' suggested Richie, 'although I do agree it's unlikely.'

'We're back to that word *unlikely* again,' said Big Mac and leaned forward in his swivel chair, an action that gave his shirt buttons some temporary relief. 'Give me one good reason, sergeant,' he asked, 'why I should authorise any more time on this nonsense?'

In Richie's mind's eye was the hospital corridor, the inconsolable woman, and the small child's doomed flight from the tenement window. 'After twenty years,' he replied, 'perhaps the truth.'

The truth was also on Rosie's mind, although a different kind of truth, foraging in the undergrowth with rubber gloves and secateurs, a steely glint in her eye. Her quest to discover the facts about Jack's possible infidelity may have been entirely ruined by his stupid *bloody* incompetent generosity, but she was now embarked on something even more personal. She was in danger; she could sense it, although who would believe her? She could hardly believe it herself, telling herself not to be so bloody stupid, but couldn't ignore mounting evidence to the contrary.

This sober analysis merely reinforced her change of perspective; an altered view of herself in the onward march of circumstance. A dark shadow hung over her head, the clouds low on the higher hills; drizzle scoured her face and her basket felt heavy.

She was thinking about love. Her love for Jack, the wayward bastard, and how couples in love have low levels of serotonin, underlying the sad fact that true romance is merely the result of a chemical imbalance. New lovers in the first flush of infatuation produce high levels of a trace amine that releases friendly dopamine that, in turn, produces sexy oxytocin – causing blood pressure to soar. The infatuation of attraction is simply the action of neurotransmitters communicating signals to nerve terminals. Love may be blind but it's actually clever, shifting chemistry – and in humankind heady infatuation doesn't last. Only about four per cent of the animal kingdom is programmed to be monogamous, including a variety of African vole.

Once they mate, chemical imbalance is there for good and no other vole gets a look in. Human beings do not form part of the four per cent, apart from Rosie McLeod.

She had passed a staging post within her mind; her feet still on the ground, but her head in the clouds. Between worlds, no longer sure to which world she belonged. Again, she felt the dead hand of accusation for a crime uncommitted in a time long ago. *I wasn't here then*, she wanted to say – *I too remain innocent*. But say it to whom? But, she supposed, maybe innocence won't last for much longer, her basket under one arm, her long coat buttoned to the chin. The gift of new perspective brought with it a price. *If I am being accused, then make me guilty*. Out on the Forth a tanker mournfully sounded its horn.

She was walking back down the hillside, thinking about

love and accusation, when she was startled by a loud voice.

'Ah, Mrs McLeod.'

To her dismay she was joined by Dr Murray, out walking his black Labrador. The dog was pulling at its leash, breathing heavily, and eyed her suspiciously. Dr Murray, of the old school, doffed his flat cap. His green Barbour jacket was zipped up tight; a heavy raindrop hung on the end of his nose. Rosie resisted the temptation to flick it off. Archibald Murray, closing in on retirement and the prize roses he planned to grow, looked without expression at the unusual contents of her basket.

'I was just out for a spot of exercise,' he said and indicated the panting dog.

He and Rosie had never really hit it off, being of different views on her talents. He seemed on the point of saying something, then changed his mind. 'Perhaps I could escort you home?' he instead suggested, tugging on the leash. 'I take it that's where you're going. My wife's dog,' he said. 'Toby. Him not her. Me, I'm not really a dog person. Terrible day.' he added.

Rosie nodded agreement, untangling herself from the circling animal's lead.

Archie Murray was tall, had thinning grey hair, a bushy and unkempt moustache and long face. Under craggy brows his blue eyes regarded her thoughtfully. 'I saw one of my patients yesterday,' he said, finally getting to the point. Rosie had the sneaking suspicion that this meeting was not entirely coincidental.

'Ah.'

'The Reverend Kennedy to be precise. He was, as you know, a bit under the weather.' Dr Murray felt that this neatly described the matter, pulling again on the dog's lead. 'Bloody animal! Toby, not the minister,' he added with a small laugh.

Rosie cleared her throat. 'I did hear, yes. Actually,' she said, 'I was in church, so heard everything rather too well.'

They walked a little way, down to the river into which Jack's ball had plunged to save the day. 'I don't see much of you at the surgery,' he said at length.

'Is that a good thing or a bad thing?' she replied reasonably, thinking that civility might be the best option. It had been, after all, her chicken pie that had set tongues wagging. 'I rather think it's a good thing, don't you?'

'It's just that most women of your age require a bit of attention,' he suggested, an affront to Rosie's afflicted self-esteem. 'A few running repairs to sort out the ravages of time, that sort of thing. You, it seems, are made of sterner stuff.'

Most women of *my* age? Bloody man! 'Since when was self-reliance to be disdained?' she asked sharply, feeling a heavy hand of mortality on her shoulder and deciding that civility, even with medical practitioners, had strict limits. 'I don't often visit your surgery because I'm not often ill. Hardly any point bothering you when I'm well. Or am I missing something?'

Dr Murray seemed to find this amusing and laughed in wheezing gulps. 'That wasn't what I was suggesting, Mrs McLeod. But seriously, can I ask you something?' She'd already worked out what the question was going to be. Hardly rocket science. 'I'd just like to know, as a medical professional, what was in the minister's, um, last supper?'

'Chicken.' Rosie felt that stating the obvious might be a good place to start.

'Chicken,' the doctor echoed, reining in the Labrador which was eyeing up a nearby rabbit. 'Toby! Heel! Damned dog,' he added. 'Never does anything I want him to. That's dogs for you. Anyway,' he continued in a more conciliatory tone, 'the minister's reaction was, in the circumstances, both unusual and extreme. I just want to know what he might have ingested, apart from chicken.'

The doctor probably knew, or had once known, that food has to be broken down into small units to enter the bloodstream. Protein is broken down into amino acids, fats into fatty acids and carbohydrates into glucose, or equivalent, molecules. By the careful preparation of fennel and other assorted herbs, Rosie had merely inhibited the action of the enzyme lactose, thereby allowing most of his meal to pass undigested into the large intestine. Here, bacteria get to work and produce, among other gases, methane, hydrogen and pungent hydrogen sulphide. The old fool must, of course, have eaten far more of the pie than she'd estimated for one portion – turning what should have been a minor complaint into an orchestral triumph. Frankly, it hadn't been very difficult to achieve.

'I've already apologised to him,' she said. 'Most unfortunate, of course. My husband's fault, really. Stupid man! It should have been thrown out. Not fit for human consumption.'

Dr Murray had another raindrop on his nose. 'Yet Mrs Gallagher says that *you* gave the pie to your husband. She rather supposes, you see, that it was intended for him.' He smiled encouragingly, looking once more at her filled basket that she now shifted from one arm to the other. Toby again wrapped his lead round her legs and forced her to an unwelcome halt.

'You are presuming, doctor, and that's never a good thing for a medic to do.'

'You'd know, of course.' There was a flinty edge to his smile. 'Foxglove, if I'm not mistaken, nettles and…'

'… Garlic,' she said, meeting his stare. 'Doctor, I don't know why Jack saw fit to hand out our food willy-nilly. A misunderstanding. Unpleasant, I agree.'

The doctor untangled the lead and they set off at a brisk pace. He thrust one hand in his jacket pocket and shook his head. 'It really was most unusual,' he said almost meditatively, 'and, quite frankly, I've never come across such a severe case before. You must therefore appreciate my professional interest in the recipe.' He fiddled with car keys in his pocket, and then removed his hand to brush the raindrop from his nose. 'You do, after all, have a certain reputation hereabouts.'

Rosie couldn't dispute the fact of her reputation, having agreed many years before to the newspaper interview that was now framed in the bar. 'Well, it's not something that I particularly relish right at the moment.'

The doctor seemed surprised. 'How so?' he asked, an

inflection in his voice. 'I thought that you enjoyed your benign trade. I may not agree with what you do, but I don't judge you harshly for it.'

Benign, benign. New ingredients in her basket to fuel other possibilities. She had been found guilty *in absentia*, she knew it, and now faced retribution from a person or persons unknown. Now, it seemed, she was also being made a scapegoat by the village doctor. 'I rather thought that you did,' she suggested sourly, deciding that she'd been civil for long enough.

Again, he seemed to find her riposte amusing and laughed in wheezing bursts. 'I'm not completely ignorant, Mrs McLeod. Many herbal medicines were around when I started practising. The difference between us is that I know what's in them. You, I rather fancy can't, or won't, tell me what was in a chicken pie.'

The flintiness had returned, so too the dog's lead wrapping itself around her legs. 'Chicken,' she repeated, feeling trussed like a chicken herself, the doctor tugging the recalcitrant dog back to order. 'It should have been chucked out,' she added pointedly, 'whatever Sadie Gallagher says.'

The doctor wasn't being entirely fair about her medical knowledge. Rosie knew a great deal more than he chose to believe, although her science was a different kind of science. Hers was a gift of the living world, not artificially synthesised in laboratories.

'I apologise if I've offended you,' he said, Toby panting loudly through the constriction of his collar.

'I have a degree, you know.'

'I know that, Mrs McLeod.'

'Well then. No offence taken,' she replied. 'Maybe I should get ill more often. Then we could have more of these little chats.'

He laughed warily, noting again the contents of her basket. 'Garlic,' he said flatly, his free hand back inside his pocket and jangling keys. 'I hope that you're not planning any more chicken pies.'

She smiled brightly, the pub nearby, a pot of green mush requiring her attention upstairs in the scullery, and a basketful of new ingredients to prepare. She calculated again the likely dosages required to fire the first reaction, a precaution that pleased her – particularly since she had found such a profusion of wild garlic.

'If I am,' she asked, 'should I invite you and your good lady wife?'

The doctor grimaced. 'Not if you want company,' he said without apology and stopped to pass the lead from one hand to the other, the Labrador pawing the ground in frustrated escape. 'I don't think I'd like to be poisoned.'

Poisoned? Poisoned! She faced the doctor squarely, nostrils flared. 'See over there?' She pointed to his left. 'Water mint, good for hiccups and flatulence. Perhaps you should pick some for the minister.' She pointed again. 'That's yellow iris. It's cathartic and astringent. Over there is meadowsweet. Its salicylic acids can be synthesised to aspirin.' She pointed to his right. 'Over there is bogbean, good for arthritis. Beside it are some thistles, excellent for ulcers. That stuff over there is viper's bugloss, an aphrodisiac and diuretic. Those are forget-me-nots, for the treatment of bronchitis. Beside that is a clump of speedwell, once used to treat measles. I concede, however, that you are better able to treat measles than I am.'

'Thank you,' said the doctor, doffing his cap.

'But look over there,' said Rosie, again pointing. 'That, doctor, is wild parsnip.'

'Especially lovely with Christmas dinner.'

'Also known as hemlock water dropwort. It can cause skin inflammation.'

'Ah, well… maybe not so lovely.'

'Quite so, doctor.' She pointed to her left, a small knot of anger in her stomach. 'These are snowdrops. They contain three different poisons.'

'I'll have to take your word on it, Mrs McLeod.'

'One of those poisons, galantamine, is now being used to treat Alzheimer's disease. Did you know that, or can't you remember?' The doctor merely pursed his mouth, saying nothing. Rosie pointed to her right. 'Over there are bluebells,' she informed him. It was once thought that bad fairies used bluebells to trap small children, but she didn't tell the doctor this. 'They contain glycerides that cause diarrhoea, vomiting and cardiac arrhythmia.'

'I can't say that I knew that either, Mrs McLeod.'

'Then you also won't know that bluebell juice disrupts proteins surrounding the HIV virus. Poisonous but a life-saver, doctor.' She could also have educated him about the witches in Shakespeare's Macbeth, chucking eye of newt and toe of frog into their cauldron, herbs used in a contemporary cough remedy, or that everything, people and plants, are made from light and darkness. How castor oil might be good for you but just one seed from its plant can be fatal. Or yellow bird's-foot trefoil, not native to Scotland, alas, whose leaves and flowers are filled with cyanide. 'So I can assure you,' she said, feeling breathless, 'that if I ever want to poison somebody, I know precisely how to do it.'

To her disappointment, the doctor didn't seem to take offence. 'He did enjoy your chicken pie, you know. The minister. He said that it reminded him of childhood.'

'Ah, childhood,' echoed Rosie, remembering a time when youth was eternal.

'If it's any consolation,' said the doctor, 'I'm a little further away from it than you.'

This was, of course, true enough although Rosie saw age in a different and more personal light. On the sideboard when she'd left were more garish envelopes, her name handwritten on the front. Inside would be jokey cards, inscribed with good wishes and reminders that life begins at forty. 'Not from where I'm standing,' she replied. 'In a couple of days I'll be forty. Hardly a great age but a milestone I could do without.'

The doctor nodded sagely, not entirely at ease with this small, dark woman who crackled with nervous energy and whose lotions cured piles and eczema when recommended medications failed. He noted puffiness around her eyes and pallid skin. 'You are all right, aren't you?' he asked, professional solicitude kicking in.

She felt enormously depressed by this question. 'The joke

is I'm a witch,' she said, clutching her basket to her midriff in both hands.

'Yes, but it is just a joke,' he agreed, straining on the lead as Toby's paws scrabbled in a frenzy.

'Not a very funny ha-ha joke.'

'No, I suppose not,' the doctor agreed. 'By the by, are you?'

Actually, this was a difficult question to answer. In the space of a few days she had crossed ethical boundaries, and although ethics weren't something to which she ever gave much thought, she certainly didn't intend to be lectured on the subject by a condescending old fool of a GP.

She said instead: 'Tazmanian chimps eat aspilia plant, did you know that?'

'Probably not, Mrs McLeod.'

'Aspilia plant has no nutritional value, that's what was so puzzling. Why should the chimps bother? Then it was discovered that the plant contains Thiarubine A. It protects them, you see, against gastrointestinal parasites.'

'Quite so,' agreed the older man. 'Your point being...?'

'That even monkeys believe in herbalism, Dr Murray.'

'Touché, Mrs McLeod. Touché.'

'No offence intended, Dr Murray.'

'And none taken, Mrs McLeod.'

Her basket suddenly felt heavy, the rain seeping behind her collar and down her back, chilling her. 'One of the last witches in Scotland was burned near here,' she said after a few moments. 'Did you know that?'

'Once again, Mrs McLeod, your knowledge has me

stumped.' This said with a cautious smile and a sharp tug on the lead.

'A long time ago, of course,' she added.

She was wrong about that, but wasn't to know.

Chapter 18

The sixteenth herb is called of the Chaldees Carturlin,
of the Greeks Pentaphyllon, of the Latins Serpentina,
in English Snake's-grass. This herb put in the ground,
with the leaf of the Three-leaved Grass, engendereth
red and green serpents, of which if powder be made,
and be put in a burning lamp, there shall appear
abundance of Serpents. And if it be put under the head
of any man, from thenceforth he shall not dream of
himself.

The Book of Secrets of Albertus Magnus

'The wind machine returns.'

Tam Cronin chortled, pewter mug lined up alongside his cigarette packet and lighter. Rosie looked at him balefully.

The *Fox and Duck* served unpretentious local fare at lunchtimes and Rosie, looking around, saw that the restaurant was doing reasonable business. Sammy's speciality was seafood. Crabs and lobsters were bought from the quayside in Dunbar, other fish from the market in Musselburgh. Meat and vegetables were also sourced locally.

The *Fox and Duck* earned a good mention in the *Taste of Scotland* food guide. Holy Cross has more than its fair share of retired wealthy bankers and the bored wives of rich lawyers. The village is therefore brim-full of people who like to do lunch, and the *Fox and Duck* is just the place to do it.

'Not funny, Tam.'

'Don't take it to heart. It's really very funny.'

'Frankly, not funny. Definitely *un*funny.' She heaved off her coat and hung it on a peg beside the bar, then placed her basket out of sight under the counter. 'You haven't seen Jack, have you?'

'Our sporting icon went out. Quite where, he didn't say. Anyway, you really mustn't worry about the minister. He'll get over it.'

'Tam, it's embarrassing. For him *and* me. I've had people asking me about chicken pie all morning. Even people I don't know have been asking about it. Edie Grant from the hairdresser's wanted the damn recipe. She wants to play a trick on someone.'

'And did you give it to her?'

'No, I bloody well did not! It was a mistake, Tam. A stupid, bloody, bloody, *fucking* mistake!'

'Ah, so it was a mistake then.'

She poured herself a mug of coffee from the machine beside the till and ran one hand through her dark hair. 'Dr Murray also wanted to know what was in it. I suppose for more understandable clinical reasons.'

Tam chortled again. 'I suppose it has been something of a talking point.'

'Precisely!' she said sharply. 'A talking point that I don't want to *be* a talking point, thank you very much.' She glanced at his neat stack of blue leaflets. 'You're not being much good in here, are you? I thought you had an election to fight.'

Tam indicated the rain-smeared window behind him. 'It's too wet for democracy,' he replied brightly. 'Conservatism only flourishes in the sunshine. We're like a rare and delicate orchid. That's my excuse anyway.' He sipped from his tankard. 'I'm supposed to be leafleting this afternoon,' he added for good measure, 'on the orders of our constituency chairperson who, I rather think, still holds Friday night against you. She was going on about it again this morning.'

'Oh God!'

'How it *quite simply* has blown her election plans off course.' Tam did a reasonable impression of the formidable Clare. 'Complete pish, of course. Having that idiot for our parliamentary candidate is the real problem. However, for reasons unknown, she's seems quite smitten with him. Motherly, you might say.'

Rosie groaned inwardly. 'Tam, I could really do without all this fucking aggro. Where's Mara?' she asked, remembering who was supposed to be on duty behind the bar.

'Getting me a prawn baguette, I hope.'

On cue, Mara appeared from the kitchen with a plate and cutlery wrapped in a paper napkin that she set on the bar in front of Tam. Mayonnaise oozed onto a generous portion of salad. Rosie regarded her sourly for a few moments, perched by the bar with the basket of weeds at her feet. 'Do you know where Jack is?' she eventually asked Mara.

'Out.' Mara shrugged. 'He didn't say where he was going.'

'Well, he *should* have said. He's no right being out, wherever *out* is. I'm going upstairs,' she added, retrieving her basket and taking it to the scullery. She breathed in its mustiness, its combination of heady aromas offering all kinds of salvation. 'I am not guilty,' she said aloud to the stoppered bottles. 'I have never been guilty.' *But I am guilty now*, she reminded herself, as she got to work cleaning and chopping the contents of her basket and setting it on the stove to boil. *I am guilty of something, although quite what, I don't yet know.*

Also in Rosie's bubbling saucepan was a large handful of saw palmetto berries, mainly because of their oil which contains a variety of fatty acids and phytosterols which inhibit the conversion of testosterone. In conjunction with other extracts, most notably periwinkle, nettle, garlic, foxglove and ginger, saw palmetto also reduces levels of epinephrine, dopamine, cortisol and growth hormone – something that happens naturally when we laugh.

Jack McLeod was in Edinburgh's George Street, a swish Georgian boulevard of trendy restaurants and expensive shops. His nose was pressed close to a plate-glass window behind which gleamed expensive jewellery – the kind of minimalist jewellery that Rosie liked. Small spotlights picked out each ring, necklace and bracelet. Nothing was priced, the assumption being that if you could afford to shop here, the mere detail of price was irrelevant. The shop's name was equally minimalist and spelled out in burnished aluminium above a heavy glass door that could only be opened from inside.

The interior of the shop was reassuringly air-conditioned; diamonds gleamed like ice in glass cabinets. The shop assistants – if you could describe the inhabitants of such genteel sophistication as 'shop assistants' – were impeccably and soberly dressed. Discreet cameras looked down from each corner. The lighting was soft and dignified; the carpet as lush as summer grass. There were no other customers. A grey-suited man approached Jack and looked him up and down, presumably sizing the content of his wallet and the level of his motivation. The jeweller wore a crisp red silk tie and smiled to reveal large teeth.

Jack pointed uncertainly at a particular glass cabinet.

'It is a most beautiful piece, I *quite* agree.' Jack, however, hadn't said anything. The jeweller's teeth loomed like a New York skyline. Jack wondered why he couldn't just say ring. In his vocabulary, a 'piece' was something carried by a Chicago gangster. However, Rosie needed the reassurance of a love continued and what better than an eternity ring? For Jack, unversed in the arcane practices of romance, the actual purchase of the *piece* was the hardest part.

'Our finest emeralds are crafted only from three mines in Colombia.' The jeweller imparted this information almost in a whisper, as if the shop might be bugged by a competitor. 'Only three mines in the world produce emeralds of such

luminosity and perfection. Perhaps you might allow me?'
Jack was led to a glass table on which sat a magnifying glass
on a bending metal stem. A light built into the frame allowed
Jack to view the piece – ring – in close-up: a gold band of
emeralds interspersed with small diamonds. 'As you can see,
the stones graduate in colour,' said the jeweller. Jack hadn't
noticed but now nodded vigorously. 'Look here,' the jeweller
pointed to the outer emeralds. Jack saw his finger in close-up
and noted that he bit his nails. The evidence of at least one
bad habit somehow cheered Jack up. 'These are from the
Cosquez mine and are a lighter green. These,' the jeweller
sighed in pleasure, his finger trembling against other stones,
'are from either the Muzo or Chivor mines. These three
mines date back to the Incas. The emeralds they yield are of
the finest quality, as I'm sure you appreciate.' Jack saw
bluish-green luminescence, the cut and contour of the stones
sparkling under the light like distant constellations.

'Only three mines?' he asked, stalling for time.

'The stone of Cleopatra.' The jeweller was evidently
pleased to share his arcane knowledge. 'She simply *adored*
them. 'Of course, there are other sources.' He was obviously
less happy discussing inferior products. 'The main supplier
of lesser emeralds is now Zambia.' A link of saliva joined his
top and bottom lip. 'I could, of course, show you some of our
other pieces, if you would prefer.'

'I thought that Colombia only produced drugs.'

'Drugs *and* emeralds. A surprising combination, I agree.
Rarer than diamonds, did you know that? And, of course,
fine emeralds of such quality as these are like...'

'... Hen's teeth?'

'Quite so, sir. Can you see the growth patterns in each stone?' Jack saw whelk-like swirls radiating through each emerald. The jeweller's breath was against his cheek. 'We call these trapiche emeralds. The growth patterns are perfect, the chromium content giving just the right amount of colour. Does your partner appreciate such quality, sir? A woman of exquisite taste, is she? A *very* special anniversary?' He was moving in for the kill, adding guilt to Jack's other afflictions.

'Just how rare are we talking here?'

'Extremely rare, sir.'

'We must therefore be talking pricey.'

The jeweller spread his hands on the glass table. 'That does, of course, depend on how much you consider exquisite beauty to be worth.' His voice was reverential; Jack wasn't sure if he was referring to the ring or his wife, or both.

Jack thought of a figure, multiplied it by ten, and had a strange urge to laugh when the jeweller told him the price. The Colombian drug cartels were clearly in the wrong business. 'It is, sir, a most reasonable price for such rarity.'

'Exquisite rarity,' replied Jack, stalling again and wondering whether his wife would know the difference between a Colombian trapiche emerald and some tawdry rubbish from Zambia. Emeralds were her favourite gemstone – something they had always found amusing given the Holy Cross legend. Rosie, he concluded, probably knew everything there was to know about emeralds. He now had the choice of purchasing something of lesser quality, and risking her disappointment, or incurring her wrath for buying

288

something ludicrously expensive. She might also see his generosity as a guilt offering rather than a token of love. However he looked at it, a sword of Damocles hung perilously above his head.

Jack, cast as Mark Anthony, now had a decision to make regarding his Cleopatra. The jeweller smiled in hopeful anticipation.

The science of herbalism involves plants and herbs working either in harmony or sequence. No problem: the ingredients had been boiled and sieved through muslin. But it also involves the administration of correct dosage, a problem that Rosie, frankly, couldn't get around. The minister's flatulence was evidence of that.

I am doing this only because I have to, she told herself repeatedly. Because I have to! Full-*bloody*-stop! All she now needed was a detailed plan of the village's water supply and a few ingenious mouse clicks would see to that.

After his unsatisfactory meeting with the divisional inspector, Richie had had an uneventful day. Constantly on his mind was the fallen child. He didn't know why the memory had returned, eloquent and vivid, remembering also how he had laid down in the grass in his garden with Mara and precisely felt every blade. In the evening, off duty, waiting for Mara to finish her shift at the *Fox and Duck*, he opened a bottle of beer and stood at the open door to his garden. The sky was still grey, a steady drizzle falling. The air smelled damp and rich.

Then his phone rang.

It was Big Mac himself. 'The bad news, laddie,' he said without preamble, 'is that you may be right.'

Chapter 19

The herb is named Aquilaris, *of Chaldees, because it springeth in the time in which the Eagles build their nests. It is named of Greeks* Valis, *of Latins* Cheridonium, *and of Englishmen Celandine. This herb springeth in the time in which the swallows, and also the Eagles, make their nests. If any man shall have this herb, with the heart of a Mole, he shall overcome all his enemies.*

The Book of Secrets of Albertus Magnus

A press release was issued late that night once the sparse facts had been checked and double-checked. A tenuous link but enough for the chief constable to be roused and consulted. Holy Cross, after all, isn't just another blip on the map; a mosaic of national identity pieced from errant monks and a slice of legend. The duty press officer received enquiries all night.

The press statement, through informal channels, soon reached Clare Derby, emailed to her home in the small hours. She'd taken it to her study, no longer a shared study since her husband's death, and considered its implications. Johnny's passing had left a small void in her life, but a manageable void: she was a practical woman and had simply transferred her devotion to her Party – her personal loss was Conservatism's gain. Her fingers tapped against the single sheet of foolscap, considering how it could be turned to their advantage, even as polling day beckoned.

In the morning, early, she phoned the *Fox and Duck* and made a booking. A man answered the phone, awake but only just, and wrote down the details.

Had Rosie answered the phone she would politely have refused to take the booking, suspecting rightly that Clare Derby was no ally of the *Fox and Duck*. But she'd been having a shower, which was a pity, having been up for half the night locating the village water main and pouring into it several demijohns of colourless liquid.

Then Clare Derby phoned her parliamentary candidate, rousing him from sleep.

'Adrian, don't grunt. You were right!'

It was still dark in Mountjoy's bedroom and it took him a few moments to come to life. 'I was?' It was all he could think of, then after a pause, 'About what?'

'You have an *instinct*, Adrian, and instinct is so important in a politician.'

'I do?'

'You *span*, Adrian. I asked you to spin and you span, or whatever the word is. You were right, after all. I apologise.'

'You do?' He was sitting up by now, his feet on the warm carpet. He was wearing red pyjama bottoms. Raffishly, he never wore a pyjama top.

'Unreservedly!' His constituency chairperson and election agent seemed in an ebullient mood. 'Now is the time to make political capital. To reap what you, Adrian, have sown!'

Mountjoy now located his alarm clock and pressed the little button on the side that lit up the dial. Just after seven o'clock. *Jesus Christ*!

She seemed to guess his uncharitable thoughts. 'Early birds get the worms, Adrian. The election is this week. Even at this late hour we have work to do.'

'But I've got —'

'You have engagements to *cancel*, Adrian. We have new plans to make! Specifically, we have a press conference to plan for. A sober suit, I rather fancy.'

He rubbed at his eyes and blinked rapidly. He then located his spectacles, realised that he didn't actually need them, and sat back on the bed.

'A press conference to make clear your dedication to this constituency! To make the voters realise that your heart is in East Lothian! To tell them what a great detective you are! You'll come at once, Adrian. We have much to discuss.'

'Detective? A press conference?' he echoed.

'*Vindication*, Adrian! Just desserts and the fruits of hard endeavour. Come right away, won't you! No slipping back between the sheets!'

Mountjoy was now wide awake and needing the loo quite badly. 'Vindication, Clare. Good,' he said without having the slightest clue what she was talking about. Among Clare

Derby's more irritating habits, and there were a few, was an inability to actually get to the point. Instead, like a large sailing ship, she tacked around subjects, sometimes getting close then zig-zagging away. 'Where, may I ask, are we holding this press conference?'

'Where else but in Holy Cross?' she replied, then added with grim pleasure, 'In that ghastly pub where you were so grievously assaulted.'

A deranged accident of history, that was Richie's first thought, and he knew that his incredulity was shared by everyone else in the room. After twenty years, a new version of events was emerging.

Big Mac, shirt buttons strained to breaking point, had been usurped by an unsmiling CID superintendent from HQ in Edinburgh. The mythology of Holy Cross meant that the big guns were being brought in.

Two police forces were now at work to sift fact from fiction and find some binding coil of evidence. Yet it had all happened so long ago, almost a generation past; *surely too much water under the bridge*, thought Richie, as the superintendent rapped his knuckles on the table. He was a grey man: grey foppish hair, grey suit and grey tie: his skin was colourless. He had thin lips and glittery eyes.

Apart from the superintendent and Big Mac, around the main Haddington conference table were grouped two other detectives from Edinburgh, both dressed casually in polo shirts and jeans, a taciturn Highlander from the Highlands and Islands Division and a professor of psychology from the

University of Edinburgh. This last person, dapper in a turquoise waistcoat, was taking copious notes – despite the meeting not having started. Richie saw that he seemed to be writing random squiggles and surrounding each squiggle with a box. He then drew arrows from each box to the next, as if charting a course for the investigation that only made sense to him.

The Highlander yawned and scratched his head, having only arrived by car from Inverness minutes beforehand. He greedily drank coffee from a large thermos on a side table. After twenty years, they had a name.

'Gentlemen, we're here to re-examine the death of a woman in Inverness. Hence,' the superintendent indicated the taciturn Highlander, 'the presence of our colleague from Inverness.' He barely glanced in the other man's direction, and then opened a blue file that lay portentously before him. 'The chief constable's orders, gentlemen. If there is a link between this fatality and what's been in the papers, we're to find it. No excuses. No stone unturned. Her name was Klara Marion Lillie.'

The superintendent looked round the table. The psychologist was still writing random squiggles, and drawing boxes around them. 'We know that her death was caused deliberately and, although it was fully investigated at the time, nobody was apprehended.' He seemed to find this oversight distasteful and pursed his thin lips, almost making them disappear. 'The link with Holy Cross is that Klara lived in the village for several years before moving to Inverness. She died five years after she moved from Holy Cross,' he said, speaking slowly, his sparkling eyes encompassing them all. The psychologist drew another box, another squiggle and linked the two with a neat line. 'Soon after her move to Inverness she married a local man, Rory Bell, and changed her name from Lillie to Bell. Two years after that he gets drunk one Friday night and was run over by a bus. He died from internal injuries in Raigmore Hospital three days later.'

The psychologist seemed struck by this fact. He doodled, fiddled with his pen and sighed. The superintendent regarded him sourly. Bringing in a trick cyclist at this stage seemed an affront to good old-fashioned detective work, but the chief constable had been insistent. Big Mac stared out the window, shirt buttons at full stretch, and sucked his teeth.

'Klara was only in Holy Cross for a relatively short period of time,' the superintendent resumed. 'Long enough, however, to make herself mightily unpopular. Klara had, it seems, a volcanic temper and was a bit of a drinker. She didn't make friends, she only made enemies. No doubt in the course of our enquiries we shall learn more about her period of residence in the village.' He aimed this last point at Big Mac who nodded.

'Before she came to Holy Cross, Klara lived in Stirling, where she'd been born and brought up. She seems to have had a series of part-time jobs, but held none of them down for very long.' He paused, looking around the table. Big Mac was, he noted approvingly, writing a list.

The psychologist had completed several pages of notes that he now laid out like a mosaic. He shifted one page a few decisive inches and asked, 'Why did she move to Holy

Cross? Do we know that?' He had a flat Birmingham accent and fat jowls that shone in the bright overhead light.

'We assume, for reasons of employment. She was offered a job in Holy Cross.' The superintendent consulted his notes, shuffling pages into some sort of order. He laid them in a pile and placed his hands across them. 'In a quarry just outside the village. A rather large quarry, so I understand, now closed. She landed the job of office manageress. Sadly for her, it didn't last. After less than a year, she was back on the dole. Less than four years later she moved to Inverness.'

The psychologist paused from his scribbles. 'Do we know why?'

The inspector shrugged. 'We assume that Klara had already met Rory Bell. From what we know so far, it seems she moved straight in with him.'

The Highland policeman, whose name Richie hadn't caught, coughed and spoke up. He had a lilting voice, made slow with weariness. 'In the last year of her marriage, police officers were called to the Bell household four times.' The psychologist's pen was poised over an empty box. Big Mac's eyes were still fixed on the window. 'Every time, drunken arguments. They were each cautioned twice.'

The psychologist nodded sagely, as if this answered some other question, and hunched over his squiggles.

'After her husband's death,' the superintendent resumed, 'Klara's behaviour became worse. She was arrested on a couple of occasions for being drunk and disorderly. Fined both times. It also appears that she didn't work again. Perhaps, by then, she was unemployable.' Here the

297

superintendent raised his sparkling eyes from his notes. 'She died *precisely* one week after the last sighting of the black cat in Holy Cross. She was, let me see, thirty-nine years old. Twenty years ago, almost to the day.' His eyes fixed them individually in turn.

The psychologist was now drawing circles and connecting the circles to the boxes in an increasingly complex geometrical pattern. 'How did she die?' he asked. The superintendent looked disapprovingly at his waistcoat.

It was Richie who replied, finding voice for the first time – the only one amongst them who had put two and two together. 'She burned to death. Someone, or persons unknown, poured petrol through her letterbox.'

The superintendent's sharp eyes rested on Richie for a moment and he had the sudden and unbidden thought that he was being *noticed*. The village bumpkin who had turned his back on the bright lights and pieced it all together.

'By all accounts she probably had it coming,' said the Highlander. He was again refilling his coffee mug from the thermos. 'There was trouble with local shopkeepers. Unpaid bills, that kind of thing.' He returned to his seat and flipped pages of his notebook. 'The post mortem put her death down to smoke inhalation. The fire didn't really take hold and the fire brigade was on the scene pretty quickly. The attack took place at night, so she was probably asleep. Blood toxicology indicated that she was drunk.'

'So, we now have a link to Holy Cross,' continued the superintendent and turned his eyes back to Richie. 'A tenuous link, perhaps, but a link nevertheless. Maybe it's just mere coincidence, maybe it's more than that. Klara Bell née Lillie was murdered a week after the black cat was last seen around Holy Cross. Sergeant, perhaps you can explain?'

He was aware of turning faces, of the psychologist's pen poised mid-squiggle. 'The black cat seemed to me to be no more than village folklore,' he began, remembering Mara's trilling denunciation of his ignorance. 'But several centuries ago it triggered a major persecution of East Lothian witches. At their trial, the sighting of a large black cat was taken as definitive proof of witchcraft activity. Therefore, the defendants were all found guilty. Like Klara, they were burned to death.'

But it all seems so pointless, he thought, *reconstructing the past as a motive for a more contemporary crime*. 'The minister in Holy Cross was the first person to see the black cat this time around. Last Friday. He reported the sighting to me. Although he didn't say so at first, the Reverend Kennedy believed that sightings of the animal would signal a re-emergence of the witchcraft cult. It sounded far-fetched, but he had been warned about this by his predecessor, who died before he could be more specific.' He remembered the dappled elm and warm sunshine shafting through its branches, an assignation with Mara making him querulous and disbelieving. 'At first I didn't take it seriously. However, a witchcraft symbol had also been carved onto an outside wall of his church. That nagged at me because it suggested that something was going on.'

The psychologist's pen was poised over an empty box. Richie took a sip of his tepid coffee. 'The villagers, of course, all said that nothing had happened twenty years ago. Everyone who was in the village then is absolutely certain of that. Everyone kept saying that nothing had ever happened here. *Here*! That's why we didn't make the connection. We were only looking *here* in East Lothian. It seemed to me that if something had happened, it didn't necessarily have to have happened on our doorstep.'

Again, in his mind's eye, was the falling child, his angel's wings folded – a small bird leaving the nest too soon. From the tenement where he fell he could have seen across the rooftops to the Castle Esplanade where, centuries before, the witch fires burned bright. The child who played with fire and whose death *there* had made Richie move *here*, the lateral thought that they were looking in the wrong place.

The psychology professor now had his fingers to his temples. 'You suggested, sergeant, that we should concentrate only on suspicious deaths caused by fire. What led you to that specific conclusion?'

This was the tricky part; the place in the narrative where madness took over: how the truth could be three-dimensional; how you could look at it from different angles, and see multiple facets in an absolute fact. 'The minister was right that the black cat held some significance. But I couldn't help but think that maybe, just maybe, he was wrong about what it actually meant. It might be nothing to do with local witchcraft, even if it exists. But, like centuries ago, it might be seen as definitive proof that someone was guilty of witchcraft.'

'That's just absurd.' This from the Highlander.

The psychologist was still doodling, boxes and circles now joined by a growing complexity of arrows. 'But fire, sergeant. Why fire?'

'Because the punishment for a witch was to be burned to death.'

The Highland policeman slumped back in his chair and turned mute eyes to the superintendent. In a distant part of the police station a tea trolley was clattering down a corridor.

The professor again rubbed his temples. 'Yet you specifically requested that the scope of the enquiry should be limited to Scotland.'

Richie raised his eyes to the Highlander, staring down his incredulity. 'In Scotland, the means of execution for a witch was fire. In other parts of the British Isles, witches were hanged. If someone had been found guilty, *in absentia* as it were, my supposition was that their execution would be carried out under Scots Law.'

The Highlander exhaled breath, having drunk either too little or too much coffee.

'Execution?' The psychologist wasn't being incredulous, merely precise.

'She was executed, in my view, because someone believed her to be a witch.'

'Smoke inhalation,' corrected the Highlander.

'Whatever,' replied Richie. 'The fact is that she died in a fire.'

The superintendent folded his fingers together and laid them on his file. 'Klara Lillie left the village five years before her death. She was unpopular. She had no friends locally, at least none that we know of. She moved far away and changed her name through marriage. After her husband's death, she kept her married name. When she died, she died as Klara Bell. Nobody in Holy Cross would have known of her marriage, her change of name or, frankly, her demise. It would hardly have made the news. The estate she lived in was troublesome. There was vandalism and a high level of petty crime. Fire-raising wasn't uncommon.'

Richie had spoken to Tam Cronin the evening before. Tam, the village know-all, remembered Klara in perfect and unadorned clarity. Not a witch in the literal sense, he'd said, just a bad neighbour. She'd pick fights, not pay for things in the shops. The children threw stones at her. He wasn't sorry, or surprised, to hear of her death.

The superintendent was now businesslike. 'Twenty years ago, the assumption was that Klara died because some local kids had it in for her. She was unpopular on the estate. A harridan, certainly. Alcoholic, certainly. Abusive, certainly. Now we know, or we have to presume, that the real motive for her murder may have been, well, more *unusual*. That's why we have Dr Samuels to help us.' He indicated the psychologist who seemed to be enjoying himself immensely, a fat smile on his cherubic face.

Richie was thinking about Adam Campbell, how he would have known Klara; perhaps taken pity on her, maybe kept in touch with her, perhaps heard about her death. Maybe that's why he'd been suspicious.

'There's something else,' said Richie, feeling suddenly tired. He had no idea what they were confronting or whether

302

you could reopen a murder enquiry after so long. The dust of years covered most tracks. 'The last witch in the south of Scotland was burned near here. A place called Spott. It's near Dunbar,' he added for the benefit of the detective from Inverness. 'In 1698 to be exact.' He let out a long breath.

'Her name was Marion Lillie. They even had the same name.'

Rosie drove first to collect groceries in Haddington and then to the butcher's in North Berwick. She exchanged pleasantries with everyone she met but was seething inside. Once again, Jack had done exactly the stupidest thing at precisely the wrong moment.

'Oh, come on, Rosie, their money is as good as anybody else's.'

'You should just have turned them down. You could at the very least have asked me.'

'You were in the bathroom. I *couldn't* ask you.'

'I was having a shower, Jack.' Even in the midst of combat, Rosie needed all relevant and irrelevant facts to be correct. She drummed and bunched her hand on the table for emphasis. 'Anyway, who the hell does she think she is, phoning up at the crack of dawn!'

'She said it was urgent and she did apologise for phoning so early.' The words Clare Derby had used were *I regret the necessity of calling at this hour*. Jack supposed it was an apology of sorts.

'Did she say *what* was so bloody urgent?'

'No.'

'And you, of course, didn't think to ask.'

'It was seven o'clock, Rosie!' Jack waved his arms about. He was utterly exasperated. 'They've been coming here regularly for years.'

'Yes, Jack, and booking months and fucking *months* in advance. This time it's bloody Clare Derby phoning in a mad panic at sparrow fart.'

'I still don't see what the problem is.'

'The problem, Jack, is that you don't ever, *ever* think! I just don't want us to be involved.'

'Us?'

'Me. Just me. Fuck it, I don't know. I'm going out.'

She left, feeling miserable, although it really wasn't his fault. It was just that she could feel pointing fingers and a weight of unresolved doubt lying heavily on her shoulders.

The pub's provisions bought and stored in the back of their sturdy Renault van, Rosie turned the key in the ignition. She sat for some minutes with the engine running staring down North Berwick High Street. Then, with a sigh, she turned the engine off and climbed back out. There was no hurry. Jack had made the booking, let him sort out the function suite. Rosie had listened to the early news; she'd never heard of Klara Lillie.

Instead, she sat on rocks on the east sands and stared out to sea. It was one of her favourite spots for contemplation, the beach stretching to a rocky headland and the closing holes of a golf course. Waves broke at her feet and sucked at the sand. The rhythm and hiss of the water made her calmer. Seabirds called and wheeled and at the margin between sea and sand a fat seagull waddled. She drew up her legs and put her chin on her knees. She needed time to think.

Further down the beach a teenage girl was throwing a stick into the water for an Alsatian to retrieve. The animal bounded into the waves, picked up the stick in its mouth and dropped it at her feet. Then she threw it again and the dog, with mindless excitement, bounded back into the sea. She smiled at this simple scene; it was both ordinary and innocent. *Now*, she reflected, *I am neither*.

A mile offshore was the white trachyte plug of the Bass Rock with its haze of surrounding seabirds. She had visited the island once, years before, and climbed through a cacophony of noise. Seabirds had soared around her on the sea thermals and dived for fish in the dark coastal waters. Two plants, bass mallow and sea beet, are indigenous to the island. Neither has any known medicinal value, or none that Rosie could fathom.

On the higher points of the island are religious and secular remains; a chapel dedicated to St Baldred, the island's first inhabitant in the eighth century, and a small castle, subsequently a prison, garrisoned by Mary Queen of Scots and Cromwell. The Bass Rock has seen its share of piety and casual cruelty. It was the final destination for rebellious Covenanters. Later, a Jacobite garrison held out on the Bass Rock for several years despite the best attempts of William of Orange to dislodge them. Rosie narrowed her eyes at the audacity of the Jacobites who successfully deceived the King's commissioners into believing they had bottomless supplies of food and wine when, in fact, they were starving. The King's men, believing that the rebels could hold out indefinitely, gave them their freedom – not knowing that all their supplies had been used up. They lived, but the earlier Covenanters weren't so lucky. Rosie still remembered the screech and smell of the place, the dizzying height of the sheer white cliffs and, far below, the ebb and surge of dark water.

Klara Lillie. The news report was short but specific; the police were reopening their enquiries into the death of a woman in Inverness: a woman who had once briefly lived in Holy Cross. A death, Rosie had to remind herself, that had happened before she and Jack moved to the village. It should hold no significance for them. *Me!* she reminded herself, not us. I was warned, not him. Medicine-fucking-*bloody*-woman, my supernatural powers confirmed by an old man's flatulence. And Jack, damn him, invites the circus back into our pub. She felt like crying but was unable to summon tears. Something had dried up inside her; she felt hard and brittle, unable to discern sense or conjure raw emotion.

Instead, she unfolded her legs and stood up, stepping back from the water's edge as a larger wave tumbled and sucked. The beach was now deserted, her only companions a pack of squabbling gulls thrashing in the water over some scrap of food. Further out, gannets swirled and dived. Each year they individually return to the same nesting spot on the Bass Rock to meet their mate from the year before. Gannets, like Rosie McLeod, are monogamous.

She filled her lungs with sea air and screamed three words.

'I am innocent!'

The gulls screeched and took flight. Her eyes remained fixed on the basalt rock with its history of death and piety.

But was she so innocent? She wasn't sure now, not really. But if not innocent, was she then guilty? And if so, pronounced guilty by whom? Her arms still ached from the effort of lugging demijohns to the water main at the edge of the village. Among the ingredients in Rosie's colourless liquid had been generous portions of clover and dandelion. She was precise in these matters, despite Clifford McIntyre's initial despair. He had also taught her responsibility, as had her mother; she couldn't, *responsibly*, leave out either plant. As she knew, every male ejaculation weighs approximately five grams and contains about 226 million sperm. Not that the process of reaching orgasm had happened personally to her for some time, of course, and which was why her colourless mixture also had several other ingredients. Sperm comprises a rich mixture of nucleoproteins and various minerals including sodium chloride, potassium and, in particular, lecithin. In terms of content, the human brain and semen – in particular the head of the spermatozoon – are virtually identical. Rosie first learned that biological fact in her second year at university. It seemed to explain much about male behaviour and the thinking parts of men's minds.

The fact of their identical surnames had removed some incredulity. There was an acceptance now that Richie's version of events could hold some validity. A coil of evidence linked past and present; even the policeman from Inverness, now brimming with coffee, was attentive.

'The madness of reason is to assume sanity in others.' Dr Thomas Samuels capped his pen and looked for a few moments at his intricate notes. 'If this version of events is true, then what we're dealing with is a delusional individual with a most interesting psychosis. Someone, no doubt, who believes that what they did was *right*.'

'An insane person,' suggested Big Mac, who didn't like clever words.

'Yes, but insanity of a particular kind. A neurotic knows that two and two is four, but worries about it. A psychotic knows that two and two equals five, and is certain about it. This someone clearly believed that the black cat was still the perfect proof of someone's guilt. He truly and utterly believed it. Klara Lillie, unkempt and unpopular, fitted the bill admirably. That someone also kept tabs on Klara for the best part of five years after she left the village. That combination of strategic thinking and delusional behaviour is extremely unusual.'

'Then let's start with mental hospitals,' suggested Big Mac.

The psychologist was anxious to be off, to transcribe notes and to consult his books. 'I doubt you'll find him there. He may, of course, be dead. Twenty years is a long time.'

'He?'

'While psychosis is more common in women, this kind of murderous delusion is more common in men. I say common but, of course, it's thankfully uncommon. It involves a

308

supreme level of fixation and precise planning. He kept tabs on Klara over a period of years having marked her down in the highly unlikely event of a black cat ever being spotted. Let's not forget that point. The black cat is a hugely rare phenomenon.'

'He had her marked down?' Big Mac had turned his eyes from the street outside. His buttons strained and heaved.

'Provisional planning, inspector. This wasn't a schizophrenic randomly lashing out with a knife. This was carefully and, I repeat, provisionally planned. If the animal hadn't been spotted near Holy Cross, Klara Lillie might still be alive.'

Richie felt hot and tense, taut sinews in his arms and legs. He also felt inexplicably lethargic. There was also something at the back of his mind that troubled him, something unresolved; a fact overlooked or a refracted shard of memory. The overhead light felt over-bright.

'Someone who is delusional can believe in things that are patently untrue, often accompanied by hallucinations or feelings of paranoia. Delusions of this sort are a common symptom of, say, bipolar or schizoaffective disorder.' The professor, warming to his subject, had lapsed into mumbo-jumbo. 'In extremely rare cases, the delusion can be highly grandiose – in this context, that's actually a medical term.' The professor's jowls shone happily. 'I will, of course, provide a report in due course.'

'In due course,' echoed the superintendent, wanting answers a lot sooner than that. 'How's about first thoughts?'

The psychologist shifted uncomfortably in his seat.

'Criminal psychiatry is not a precise science and, as I say, this brand of delusional behaviour is extremely rare. I can't emphasise that fact enough. In this case, the individual took the psychosis a step further by organising and carrying out a murder. To him, he was exacting his own form of justice.' He stacked his notes in a neat pile. 'I'd like to review the available literature before hazarding any more judgements.'

'Then guess,' said the superintendent. His eyes sparkled. It was an order, not a request.

The professor sighed. 'It's likely that our man will be a methodical person – neat, a little obsessive perhaps. Not obviously mad,' he said for the benefit of Big Mac who was again looking out the window, 'although, *mad* is not a medical term with any meaning. Depending on the level of delusion, it's possible that there may be no outward signs of criminal or personality disorder. If the delusion is absolutely specific, as it seems to be in this instance, then he may never have come into contact with either the police or mental health services. This is his one precise fixation. It's entirely possible, that he could be an upstanding member of the community.'

'A family man?' asked Big Mac.

'Perhaps.'

'A loner?'

'Perhaps. I don't know.'

'But still dangerous?'

The psychologist disliked being pushed into early diagnosis. Like any branch of forensic criminology, the art of psychological profiling couldn't be hurried. He needed reference material to compare similar cases. Well, what few similar cases as there were. 'I don't know,' he admitted. 'Trauma and stress can cause brief psychotic disorder although, in this case, the disorder appears to have lasted for years. That suggests an abnormality in the limbic system – a trauma to the head, perhaps? A car crash, something like that. That's a line of enquiry you might usefully pursue.' He paused to look again at the geometric pattern of his notes. 'If the individual hasn't received antipsychotic or atypical antipsychotic drug therapy then, yes, he could still harbour the same delusion. At this stage, I simply don't know. He may, of course, have died in the interim.'

The superintendent's steely eyes had not left the donnish psychologist. 'Maybe he has and maybe he hasn't. Let's presume, however, that he is still alive.'

The psychologist had conjured a leather case from under the table and, anxious to be off, was filling it with his squiggled notes. 'The grandiose part of the delusion is that he is both judge and jury. He chooses who lives and who dies. He then waits. If the black cat is seen in the area, they die. If the black cat isn't seen, they live.'

Richie again reminded himself that the truth could be multi-dimensional; that something mad might seem equally sane depending on your perspective. He also reminded himself that it was once a crime not to believe in witchcraft.

'But the black cat has been seen again,' said the superintendent.

The psychologist had pushed back his chair, and now placed his leather case on his knees. 'The psychosis we are

311

dealing with involves a high level of delusional precision combined with an equally complex level of provisional planning. After all, the greatest and most overwhelming likelihood is that the black cat won't be seen again.'

'Meaning what?'

'*If* he is still alive, and *if* he hasn't received drug therapy, then my initial view is that he will already have chosen his next victim.'

Chapter 20

The herb is called with the men of Chaldea, Elios, *with the Greeks,* Matuchiol, *with the Latins,* Heliotropium, *with Englishmen, Marigold, whose interpretation is of helios, that is the Sun, and tropos, that is alteration, or change, because it is turned according to the Sun. The virtue of this herb is marvellous: for if it be gathered, the Sun being in the sign Leo, and be wrapped in the leaf of a Laurel, or Bay Tree, and a Wolf's tooth be added thereto, no man shall be able to have a word to speak against the bearer thereof, but words of peace.*

The Book of Secrets of Albertus Magnus

Rosie also knew that sperm contains more phosphorus than any other part of the body except the brain and, although relatively rare in nature, it is the body's sixth most abundant element. Excessive semen emission can cause phosphorus deficiency or, in severe cases, deprive the adrenal cortex of vital lipids. Many sufferers of cortical dementia are, or have been, habitual masturbators. It won't make you go blind, your mother was wrong about that, but the loss of vital minerals, particularly phosphorus, can lead to tooth decay or chronic fatigue syndrome. Clover and dandelion are, of course, good sources of phosphorus and Rosie didn't want anyone to suffer unnecessary fillings.

But, of course, correct dosage was Rosie's real problem. Herbalism is largely cumulative; St John's Wort, for example, might be effective for depression, but not immediately. Herbs take time to work compared with the faster molecular approach of mainstream medicine. She had railed against those prevailing wisdoms, preferring more fiery approaches. Clifford McIntyre had nearly given up on her. Prune juice, that old standby, taken in quantity can cause diarrhoea. Mistletoe, comfrey and coltsfoot contain carcinogenic chemicals. An overdose of liquorice root, effective against gastric ulcers, can cause heart failure. Marigold and yarrow can produce allergic reactions. Yes, dosage was a concern but she didn't have the benefit of time.

Rosie's thoughts were interrupted by the pub door being thrust open to reveal the stately galleon of Clare Derby, her billowing skirts momentarily concealing Adrian Mountjoy trailing in her wake. She advanced purposely on the bar.

'Good morning!' she boomed heartily.

'Mrs Derby, what an unexpected pleasure.' Rosie, smiling sweetly, had by now turned up the pub's heating to full blast. Like the East Lothian Conservatives, she had concluded that events could also be turned to her advantage.

'Quite so,' replied Madam Chair. 'You've met our parliamentary candidate, haven't you? Yes, but of course you have.'

Rosie turned her eyes to Mountjoy, dapper in grey suit and blue tie. His slicked-back hair was neatly combed. 'I trust you're well, Mr Mountjoy? No lasting damage?'

He shook his head. 'Fully recovered, thank you.'

Madam Chair laid her clipboard down on the bar and looked around. At that time of the morning the bar only had a scattering of matronly women drinking tea. The *Fox and Duck*, being family-friendly, catered to all sections of the community, even the elderly.

'It was, um, a most unfortunate incident,' said Rosie.'

An incident,' said Clare Derby, 'that we must put behind us if we are to proceed forwards.' Her attention was focused behind the bar on the old photograph of Jack and Rosie, the newly-weds with their arms around one another in the bright new dawn of the *Fox and Duck*. 'Which is precisely why we're here, Mrs McLeod,' boomed Clare. 'To tie the loose ends together, so to speak.'

'Loose ends?' echoed Rosie weakly.

'This morning, Mrs McLeod, we will be holding our last press conference before the election. We want to capture votes, to set the agenda. We want to get *noticed*, Mrs McLeod! Do you understand?' Clare Derby was now looking speculatively at Mara, who was carrying in a box from Rosie's van. 'I do hope that we don't have a repeat performance,' she intoned in a loud voice.

'The function suite's all set up,' said Rosie. 'You know where it is, Mrs Derby, don't you? Mr Mountjoy,' she added, to his evident pleasure, producing one of Tam's leaflets from under the counter, 'perhaps you could *very* quickly explain to

315

me what your Party's economic policy is.'

'Good gracious!' said Clare. 'We haven't found another supporter, have we?'

'An undecided, floating kind of supporter,' replied Rosie, putting on her new reading glasses.

'It is rather complicated,' said Mountjoy.

'Nonsense, Adrian!' Clare Derby's booming command set teacups rattling. 'I'll make sure that everything is hunky-dory in the function suite while you elucidate this lady on our economic policies. But quickly Adrian! We don't have all day.'

However, economics had never been Rosie's strong suit, and the bald procession of facts that Mountjoy now presented washed harmlessly over her head.

'I am, I'm afraid, a bit of a Europhile,' he was saying, touching his snappy tie and rocking on the balls of his feet. 'To me, the course of history points firmly in the direction of a new Europe. A partnership of nations, if you will. Unlike some of my colleagues, I see economic policy as a pan-European issue. To create equality of opportunity within a stable political framework. I'm not quite in the Conservative mainstream, to be entirely honest,' Mountjoy said with a small laugh.

'A visionary,' suggested Rosie.

'Well, hardly that. I simply believe that greater European integration will produce long-term economic benefits. The twin dynamics of new technology and the global economy mean that —'

'Despite a referendum, strict economic isolationism is not

possible.'

'Precisely, Mrs McLeod!'

'Rosie, please,' she replied. 'I read it in your election leaflet.'

'Oh.'

'Actually,' she suggested, producing a jug filled with colourless liquid from under the counter, 'perhaps you'd like a glass of iced water? It's awfully hot in here.'

The Holy Cross health centre is set a little way back from the High Street, situated close to the visitor centre. Patients and tourists therefore compete for spaces in the small car park that they both share. Archie Murray was the practice's elder statesman, although real authority was vested in Patricia Harris, secretary and receptionist. Fiercely efficient, she was the undisputed queen of her domain. Habitually perched at the end of her thin nose were half-moon glasses, over which she would balefully size up the sick and the lame on the other side of the reception desk. Her steel-grey hair was pulled tight in a bun at the nape of her neck and her unpainted lips displayed only rare sympathy. Patients and medical staff treated her with cautious civility, as one might a volatile substance or unexploded bomb. Although she rarely lost her temper, she always seemed just on the point of doing so. Her expression suggested that, unless you were terminally ill, you had no business wasting the doctors' time and, if you were dying, why bother them at all? As he approached the health centre, Archie Murray heard a melodic whine coming from inside the building. Pat Harris, to his surprise, was humming.

'You're in a good mood,' he said.

The noise stopped. 'Shouldn't I be?'

'No, no. It's just that you were humming.'

'Don't be ridiculous!' she said crossly, adopting her more usual countenance. 'Doctor, I *don't* hum, not at work. It's undignified.' She looked at him sternly over the top of her glasses. 'And Dr Reilly won't be coming in today.'

'Oh. He's not sick, is he?'

She looked to a small notebook by the phone. 'No. He just said that he couldn't be bothered.'

Archie Murray frowned. 'Probably one of his little jokes.'

'He doesn't do jokes, does Dr Reilly. Not normally.'

Padraig Reilly was dull dependability personified. Archie peered round the corner of her reception desk to an almost empty waiting room. 'Maybe so, maybe so,' he agreed. 'Pat, where have all our patients gone?'

Dr Samuels had consulted his squiggles and what source material he could immediately dig up from the university archive. He'd spoken at length to a colleague at Cambridge and to a psychiatrist at the London School of Tropical Medicine. All agreed that it pointed to a precise, but reptilian, delusion.

It was a fair analogy, he reasoned, because an alligator will eat you, or your children, without compassion or remorse. Its limbic system, crude and uncaring, offers no emotional response. Your pain is of absolutely no concern to the alligator. Our limbic systems are altogether more

318

complex. Alligators feel nothing whatsoever for us, yet we make the alligator a protected species. It should be grateful, except that it isn't.

His supposition of a brain trauma seemed the most likely explanation. The textbooks and his medical colleagues agreed on that. Something traumatic to damage the limbic system; to shift perception of right and wrong. To make killing seem right and proper. An industrial accident, perhaps? A road accident? The nature of the psychosis suggested intelligence and cunning. How else could you feed such a grand and precise delusion and get away, quite literally, with murder? The flawless precision of the crime surpassed anything in the professor's experience. This wasn't a serial killer feeding his psychosis for sexual or emotional gratification. This was a serial killer who had most probably killed only once – and who, but for the coincidence of the black cat, might never have committed a crime. A specific victim, chosen years beforehand, and precisely murdered. Yes, a trauma to the head causing just a small chemical change in the limbic system.

Usually there were facts or scene of crime evidence to go on – material facts on which to base considered judgement. It was a step-by-step process. First you evaluated the criminal act itself. You assessed the victim. Then you evaluated the specifics of the crime scene alongside police and medical reports. Only having completed the spadework could you develop critical offender characteristics and advise detectives on their investigation. In this case, there was no crime scene evidence beyond the bald fact of petrol through a letterbox.

All the usual talismans of criminal investigation were missing; there was also the dead weight of twenty years.

As he'd pointed out to the police, such a specific delusion might never have required medical intervention. If still alive, he might therefore harbour the same delusion – particularly if untreated with antipsychotic drugs. These therapies are designed to bind to dopamine receptors, thereby affecting the limbic system of the brain and taming the alligator it contains. Heady dopamine, the neurotransmitter that is friends with everyone. Without it, the reptile's jaws are absolved from all pity.

One of the most imaginative ingredients favoured by Rosie was, among a great many other things, an inexcusably large dose of phenylethylamine, a chemical naturally released in the brain when we are in love, which Rosie was and always had been, despite carpet slippers. She felt cheated and sullied, on the brink of great age, and having to compromise her integrity for self-preservation. She saw her husband in the back yard, ferrying in sacks to the kitchen. Biting her lip, she decided that she owed him an apology.

'Jack, I'm sorry. I shouldn't have lost my temper.'

He was unloading a sack of potatoes from the back of the Renault. 'That's OK. I suppose I wasn't thinking straight either.'

'Well, it *was* seven o'clock. Bloody Clare Derby. Her fault, not yours.'

He hefted the sack onto one shoulder and carried it into the kitchen. She followed him and perched, frowning, on one of Sammy's steel work surfaces. Apologies from Rosie were rare indeed – and where had she been at dead of night? He'd woken in the darkness to find an empty space beside him – an empty, *cold* place. She'd obviously been gone for some time. He fervently hoped that she hadn't been up to no good, but felt in too good spirits to bother asking. The sun was shining, the Conservatives would soon be gone, and his expensive purchase was secreted upstairs.

'Soon I'll be forty,' she said.

'I rather know that, Rosie.'

She sighed. 'Actually, I'm rather sorry about that as well. The way I've been banging on and on about it. I've not been very fair on you.'

To receive two apologies in as many minutes was new ground. 'You don't have to be sorry for what you feel,' he said, noticing her puffy eyes and dulled expression. 'It's only natural to have mixed feelings about being forty. I know I did.'

'Did you? You didn't let on about it.'

'Well, it kind of made me assess things. What I'd achieved, or not achieved. That kind of thing. Anyway,' he added brightly, 'it's not the end of the world, you know.'

'You've said that to me already. Jack, I *know* it's not the end of the world.' *But it might be*, she thought. Me. Not us. 'Actually, there's something else. I should have told you about it sooner.'

'Something else?'

'It's better if I show you.' She bit her lip, frowning.

Yes, phenylethylamine, a substance of abuse favoured by

321

children and depressants everywhere, although its medicinal use originated in the New World among the Olmec, Maya and Aztec. The word derives from the Olmec. The Mayans called it kakaw. The Mayans used it for money, Casanova used it as bait. Moctezuma, the Aztec emperor, fortified himself with cacao, mixed with cinnamon, chilli powder, pepper and maize before visiting his harem. Christopher Columbus brought cacao beans back to Europe on his fourth voyage. Chocolate is a good source of phenylethylamine, a soothing chemical that recreates the feeling of love. It's why those who've been jilted can find solace in a chocolate bar – Rosie had eaten a family-size bar in North Berwick earlier. Abandonment causes phenylethylamine to dry up, creating a chemical imbalance that can lead to depression. A chocolate bar repairs that imbalance although, as any doctor will tell you, it shouldn't be taken to excess. Rosie, true to form, had bought enough cocoa the day before to build a chocolate skyscraper and, carefully purified and distilled, emptied that too into the water system.

'One condition, Jack.'

'Which is?'

'Just don't *bloody* tell me that I'm being silly!' She took his hand and led him to the beer garden. In the march of circumstance she now needed another person to confide in.

News of Klara's death caused a ripple in the village, but not a seismic earthquake. It was as if the villagers, publicly cast as satanists with a flatulent minister, were able now to take the mere allegation of murder in their stride. A murdered woman, of course, who was living in Inverness at the time and was therefore nothing to do with them. A very unpopular women, remembered the older inhabitants, shaking their heads. This wasn't their problem, so there was no need for exoneration. A deeply unpopular woman was dead, and so what? No, the sun was shining and it was too nice a day to worry about anything.

Certainly, that was Archie Murray's view as he whistled his way through morning surgery, an off-key sound that found more melodic echo in a thin whine from reception. Padraig Reilly still hadn't come in for work, unusual for someone so punctilious, and wasn't answering his phone. But, thought Dr Murray, not much need, given the sudden affliction of good health that seemed to have overtaken the village.

He then heard a gale of laughter from reception – a raucous and wholly new sound for the Holy Cross medical centre. Patients didn't, by and large, come to his surgery to laugh. Normally, they sat, heads down, and read antiquated copies of *National Geographic*. Usually, they hardly spoke to one another, even to close friends. He assumed that the intimacy of illness made people a little unnerved.

By the time Archie reached reception – this completely unexpected noise requiring immediate investigation – he found that the waiting room had been engulfed in hysteria. All told, there were about a dozen people, an equal split of men and women, and all were lolling in their seats in various aspects of helpless laughter.

He went across to the reception desk behind which Pat

Harris, in crisp white uniform, was safely seated.

'What's going on?' he asked.

'Someone burped,' she replied and, to his astonishment, broke into a high-pitched giggle: a sound that he couldn't remember ever having heard before.

Archie Murray surveyed the hilarity of his waiting room with complete bewilderment.

'I still don't see what's funny,' said the doctor.

'That's the point,' replied Pat Harris between sobbing exhalations. 'It isn't funny.'

The function suite had been set out with two rows of chairs facing the top table. Behind the top table, the curtains that Jack had rehung were, for dramatic effect, pulled shut on the orders of Clare Derby, who had a good eye for drama. The bar was closed. Madam Chair wasn't in the habit of handing out free alcohol to journalists, but there were flasks of tea and coffee and a jug of water on the top table. Because of the closed curtains, the two camera crews in the room had been obliged to rig up their own lights that now flamed on the top table, further adding to the theatre. Sitting at attention at the top table were Clare Derby and a grinning Adrian Mountjoy. He felt positively ebullient.

Arranged in front of them were journalists and columnists from most of the major newspapers, summoned at short notice at the prospect of further revelations from Scotland's most iconic village. They held notebooks or pocket tape recorders; they murmured speculation to one another. All knew that a murder investigation was being reopened and, while demonic forces weren't suspected, deranged motivation was hinted at. A tenuous link with a half-forgotten death had been established; a new version of old events to investigate.

Clare Derby was also smiling. 'I rather feel,' she whispered to her parliamentary candidate, 'that we are about to grab the agenda.'

Humorous response is generated in the left side of the cortex which analyses whether something is funny. Signals transfer to the frontal lobe and then to the right hemisphere of the cortex which, being responsible for intellect, decides how funny it really is. Electrical activity then spreads to the sensory processing area of the occipital lobe and, lastly, to the motor sections of the brain that trigger the actual physical response. Laughter is then produced via circuitry that connects several areas, all of which are central components of the limbic system. Laughter also produces significant chemical effects, in particular reducing levels of both epinephrine and dopamine. Rosie had concluded that if this could be achieved artificially, the result might be quite amusing. In large dosage, this chemical imbalance can also be achieved relatively quickly if the right ingredients are, say, added to a glass of tap water.

For the second time in a week Adrian Mountjoy was speaking to an audience at the *Fox and Duck*, although this audience did all seem to be awake.

He had donned his glasses. They winked and shone in the

bright lights, making him appear resolute. He recalled the sounds of pleasure that had seemed to come from the beer garden, followed by drunken assault in the very room – the very *spot!* – where he now stood. The pretty barmaid had earlier set up the room, shifting chairs to Clare's precise commands. Now, the sun was shining and, sharing Clare's confidence, they had an agenda to grab.

'Ladies and gentlemen,' he began and automatically took off his glasses. 'I'd like, if I may, to read a short statement after which I'd be delighted to take questions.' The assembled disbelievers switched on microphones and checked sound levels.

He looked around the room, automatically rocking on the balls of his feet. In his left hand was bundled a sheaf of notes, pencilled by himself and Clare not minutes before.

'Holy Cross is at the epicentre of our country's consciousness. It is an icon of what being Scottish is all about.' He waved his glasses at them, feeling oddly discontented with this last sentence. It sounded portentous, yet conveyed nothing. He looked again at his bundled notes, largely written, he now noticed, in Clare Derby's hand. There were only a few minor corrections in his own handwriting. Until that moment he hadn't realised that he was, in fact, speaking another person's words. He should *really* have been more assertive with Clare earlier – but it had been too beautiful a morning, and the pretty barmaid had been a distraction, bringing in pots of coffee and plates of biscuits.

'Holy Cross is in all of our hearts. Its message of hope

and mystery is in our bloodstream. It is at the centre of this county and this constituency… a constituency I sincerely hope to represent. No, a constituency that I *will* represent.' At this, he noticed that several journalists looked doubtful, having a more positive belief in opinion polls. Again, he had a sense of merely being a cipher; the words sounding hollow and make-weight; wallpaper words to explain how his indiscretion had uncovered a possible murder. He stifled an urge to giggle at this thought and sipped water from his glass.

'Less than a week ago, a black cat was seen near this village. A very black and very, *very* large cat.' He had departed from his notes to inject a spot of humour; to make himself appear self-deprecating, a politician who didn't take things too seriously. 'I should know because I am one of only two people who have seen it. The other person was, as you know, the village minister. He confided to me that the animal held significance for the village. He knew that the cat held some superstitious echo from long, long ago. Although I didn't give that much credence, his church had also been vandalised with a satanic symbol. I don't, being a Conservative, know much about such things.' Mountjoy waved his glasses, relieved to hear responsive laughter. 'In the interests of this community, and in the interests of the truth, I decided to do something about it.'

'Do something?' asked someone in the front row.

'Questions at the end!' boomed Clare and looked accusingly at Mountjoy. He merely smiled and replaced his glasses, then flicked lazily through his notes. He could feel warm sunshine through the curtains on his back, a rising sense of purpose in his heart. To Clare Derby's mounting dismay, Mountjoy then laid his carefully prepared speech notes face down on the table. From now on, Mountjoy had decided, he was going to be his own man.

'You promised, Jack. Remember?'

'I know I did.' He was on his haunches by the crippled tree, fingering the jagged artwork at its base. XIII. Hardly noticeable. 'Why didn't you tell me about this before? For God's sake, Rosie!'

'Because *before* you wouldn't have believed me. You'd have told me to stop being so bloody silly. Actually, I wouldn't have blamed you.'

He scratched his head and, putting both hands on his knees, stood up slowly.

Rosie was pacing to and fro across the small beer garden. 'Do you know something, Jack? I've always bloody thought that something happened here... maybe because everyone, but fucking *everybody*, was so damned sure that nothing had happened! I don't know, Jack... a feeling, you know? It's been gnawing at me.'

Jack managed to corral her as she paced back across the garden and put an arm around her. Encased within his embrace, she quietened and snuggled close. 'I didn't know what to make of the tree, not at first. It seemed so petty and senseless. Then it occurred to me that it was actually a message.'

'This?' He gestured to the tree stump with its faint

markings.

'Yes, but a message for me personally.'

'A strange message,' he said and rubbed his chin.

'But that's just the bloody point, Jack! Who else around here would know what that symbol means? Eh, Jack? Exactly! Nobody! Bloody no one! Just me, because I'm the local *fucking* witch!' She trembled then took a deep breath. 'A warning, maybe… well, that's all I could think of at first. A message for me personally, although I couldn't make head or tail of it. Then, whoever did *this* also vandalised the church. At that point I knew I was right.' He felt her tremble again, her eyes still fixed on the small desecration to their beer garden. 'The mark on the church, you see, was also a message, just in case I didn't see *this*. After all, no real reason why I should… the tree dies, it gets cut down, and the evidence is disposed of. A tree, don't forget, that isn't supposed to grow near a witch's house. That was also part of the warning.'

Jack opened and closed his mouth.

Rosie saw his blank expression. 'A friendly or unfriendly warning for Holy Cross's local witch.'

He spluttered. 'But it's just a joke, Rosie! Nobody takes it seriously —'

'*He* does! Somebody around here bloody well does take it seriously!'

She was right; until he'd heard of Klara's death, he wouldn't have believed his wife. 'Jack,' she said to his shoulder, her words muffled, 'I believe, *really* believe, that someone is after me. Please don't tell me I'm being silly.'

Mountjoy boiled with confidence; vigour and conviction fizzed from his eyes. He had no need of Clare's disingenuous words; he was a politician on the brink of destiny. His purpose was to succeed; to bind delicate phrase with guileless meaning: to make his audience believe that what he had caused was done with decent purpose and that he, Adrian Mountjoy, was the right and proper person to represent the county in Westminster.

'I broke a confidence and for that I am sorry,' he said softly, his audience sitting forwards. 'I have apologised sincerely for that lapse to the Reverend Kennedy. However,' he said in a louder voice, startling Clare Derby who was always worried by ad-libbing politicians, 'it was a confidence that simply had to be broken. There is no question of that in my mind.'

'Couldn't you have just told the police?' said a blonde woman in the second row who Mountjoy vaguely recognised.

'The minister had already gone to the police,' he reminded her. 'They merely said that they would keep an open mind. In other words, do nothing. By then, of course, I had also seen the cat and, I assure you, it was black and very, *very* large.' This time, nobody laughed. 'It distracted me, you see, and that's why I had the car accident.' He replaced his glasses and picked up his discarded sheaf of notes. He looked through them, page by page, and to Clare's annoyance again replaced them face-down on the table. 'I felt that I had no option but to leak the minister's allegations to the media. I felt in here,' he said, tapping his tie with a manicured finger, 'that there was a greater truth to be found. The police were doing nothing because there was no evidence of a crime. It was the media, don't forget, that prompted this new police enquiry. That enquiry, as you know, has now found evidence of a ritualistic murder.' He looked round the room, feeling flushed. 'The community deserves the truth! We deserve the truth! Most of all, Klara deserves the truth! That's why I broke the minister's confidence and that's why we are here today in Holy Cross.'

Adrian Mountjoy wanted to say more but felt detached and lethargic. However, he was at least saying his own words and not those of his Party Chair. He felt light-headed and, again, amused by the theatrical situation he was now in. He laughed, a little self-consciously, and put a hand over his mouth. He was spouting words, his words – not those dreamed up by Madam Chair in the dead of night. He had never considered for one moment that the minister could have been right. 'Breaking that confidence is leading us to the truth. As a politician, I truly believe in the truth.'

His audience wasn't sure whether or not he had finished, the politician once more rocking on the balls of his feet.

In the silence, Madam Chair decided that Adrian had said enough and called for questions, if anyone had any. Several hands went up.

It was a young man in a grubby suit who spoke first. 'Mr Mountjoy, don't you think that holding this press conference is in, well, rather bad taste? The police have only just released Klara's name. Nobody knows for sure yet if there is a link between the village and her death.'

'No.' He believed in giving succinct, straight answers. Again, he felt a sense of the ridiculous and the lethargy of having completed a good job. His words had been better than Madam Chair's; an affirmation of his political skill.

'Just "no"?'

'Is that a question?'

'Yes.'

Mountjoy, frankly, couldn't be bothered with the grubby youth. He'd again spotted the blonde reporter in the second row with her arm raised, and recognised that she was an anchorwoman for an evening news programme. Mountjoy felt joyful and playful; perspiration gleamed on his forehead. The publican had been right; it was hot in the pub and hotter still under the lights – the reason, probably, why he'd drunk several glasses of iced water.

'Yes, you, madam, in the second row,' he said, suppressing an urge to giggle and waving his spectacles in her direction, 'with the dyed blonde hair.'

The delusion of madness was to assume sanity in others. That's what the donnish professor had said, his jumble of geometric notes presumably making some kind of personal sense. You could, of course, turn the dictum around – the delusion of madness being to assume your own inalienable sanity. Richie still felt lethargic, unable to concentrate. Some thought process was missing, a connection yet to be made. A jagged shard of dislocated memory still hung just out of sight; a small fact missed, or a binding link to a previous

332

insanity. *But was it really so mad*? he thought, driving back to Holy Cross from Haddington. Deliberately crashing a jetliner into a building was patently insane, unless you believed in salvation. Smoking cigarettes was utter madness – bloody Mara and her fags! – but millions do it. Speeding in a car is sheer folly, but who is entirely innocent of that one? *Perhaps*, he thought, *it's just a case of choosing our own insanities and calling the final warp and weft our individuality*. Burning a witch was clear madness, but it had been common practice. Hundreds had died; East Lothian was infamous for it.

Mara had bored him rigid on the subject. Sometimes they burned Protestants, sometimes Catholics – it just depended on who was calling the shots. Old scores were settled – who since time immemorial had been doctor, pharmacist and midwife – and local wise women now found that it was a job with uncertain prospects.

'Did you know,' Mara had asked, 'that women then started giving birth on their backs?'

No, of course he didn't. Male doctors replaced the wise women, you see, and squatting was no longer considered decorous. The Highlands, on the periphery of the civilised world, burned hardly any witches.

'Satan,' Mara had said, munching an apple, 'obviously had trouble crossing the Antonine Wall... or thought that all Highlanders were so God-fearing that venturing north would be a waste of time.'

In Hungary, the punishment for a first-offending witch was to stand in the town square wearing a Jew's hat. He

333

hadn't known that either. Later, dispensing with this nicety, Jews and witches were burned across most of Europe. It was just, she said, a case of choosing your scapegoat. Then it was easy-peasy. Most countries – including Scotland – allowed judicial torture. Who *wouldn't* confess? She shrugged, throwing the apple core into his pedal bin: it was social context that gave it credence.

'We all need scapegoats,' she'd said, 'whether it's Catholics, Rangers football club, immigrants, single mothers, Muslims, black or white. By defining the scapegoat, we define ourselves.' She emphasised this point by tapping his shoulder. 'In the Alps and Pyrenees they burned witches, in Spain they burned Jews – for the simple crime of being either a witch or a Jew. In 14th and 15th Century Germany, it was the Jews who suffered; by the 16th century it was the witches. In the 20th century, it was the turn of the Jew again, the cycle of persecution turning full circle.'

And someone still believes in scapegoats – the cherubic professor reaching this conclusion with cheerful certainty – a small and harmless insanity, but for the return of the black cat. A grand delusion given wings by coincidence. A specific delusion precisely executed, the professor had said, rearranging his notes and twirling a biro through his fingers. The puzzle lay in the exact nature of the delusion; psychosis was rarely so precise.

'It was just pre-Christian religion, Richie. Ordinary people trying to make sense of the world. Trying to make sense of their place in it. Isn't that we're all still doing?' She looked wistful, finding solace in his eyes.

334

To flourish, Christianity had to stamp out the old religions. All Saints Day was plonked down on Halloween to cover paganism with Christian purpose. Christmas Day was plonked down on wiccan's winter festival.

'Christian imperialism, Richie. The new god usurping the old gods.'

The wiccan faith believes in Diana, she explained, the moon goddess, and Cernunnos, the horned god. *Soooo*, Christianity invents a new version of the devil and gives him horns. Overnight, hey presto! Cernunnos becomes the devil. Therefore, witchcraft was satanism. Therefore, it was evil. Job done.

'Christianity,' she said more softly, 'has blood on its hands. Gallons of it. Whole oceans of blood! It's a strange thought, isn't it? Christian tolerance? Poppycock! Actually, witchcraft has no concept of the devil. That's the contradiction. Satanism is perverted Christianity.' She was quiet for a few moments. 'The last person to be prosecuted for witchcraft in Scotland was a middle-aged housewife, did you know that?'

'Centuries ago,' he'd suggested.

Mara shook her head. 'She was jailed in 1944, for knowing a bit too much about the war effort.'

It was ridiculous, of course, that someone could still believe in an old religion and arcane justice. Mara also said that it was *him* who had found Klara. Richie, the psychotic adding two and two and then finding, by some abrupt shift in natural law, that the correct answer was five. A shift in a natural law or a blow to the head, although the professor wasn't certain. Brain damage, he'd said, twiddling with his pen, can affect both personality and perception – how we view ourselves and the world around us. It can subtly shift the burden of our certainties. Someone brain-injured can see a box in the corner of the room and know that it's a television. But, the professor said, they may have no idea what a television is. Circuits in their minds have been dislocated, chemicals flowing to the wrong receptors. Think of the brain as an egg, he'd suggested. Then think what happens when you drop it.

'It scrambles,' Big Mac had said.

Yes, a trauma to the head was the most likely cause. Other forms of psychosis are *never* so specific.

Richie parked on double yellow lines outside the *Fox and Duck*.

Inside, Sammy was helping out in the bar, a tea towel draped over one shoulder. At several tables were matronly women loudly drinking tea. Teacups clattered; there was much good cheer, despite the news reports. At the bar, drinking beer, were a couple of middle-aged men, including one of the village's GPs.

Richie was immediately aware of stilled conversation and turning heads. Uniformed policemen in the *Fox and Duck* were a rare sight. One of the spinsters whispered something to her companion who loudly cackled. Pretty soon the whole room had joined in, turning the sedate surroundings of the pub into a demented bird colony.

'It's been like this all morning,' Sammy confided at the

bar. 'God knows what they put in their cocoa last night.'

Richie surveyed the hilarity, feeling oddly elated himself. 'Actually, it's the McLeods I want to talk to.'

'Trouble?'

'Just routine.'

Sammy gestured with his head. 'They're in the beer garden, I think.'

Richie found them outside, with their arms around one another in affectionate embrace, their twin gaze encompassing the desecrated tree stump. They both turned at his approach; Rosie fearful that she was going to be arrested for chicken pie, Jack fearful that his wife was about to be arrested for exotic tea and home-made wine.

'She didn't do it,' said Jack gallantly. 'It was a mistake. If anything, I'm to blame.'

'Do what?' asked Richie. 'Blame you for what?'

Jack was aware of a sudden pain in his foot. 'Nothing whatsoever,' said Rosie. 'My husband has an overactive imagination, that's all. Nobody has done anything at all, have we, Jack?'

Instead, Richie put a consoling hand on her shoulder. 'Mrs McLeod, I don't quite know how to say this. Maybe it's best if you sat down.'

Obediently, they sat at one of the beer garden tables. Jack's foot throbbed and his eyes were watering. 'It may be nothing to worry about. But we think that you might be in some danger,' said Richie, as sudden mayhem erupted behind closed curtains in the function suite.

337

Chapter 21

Adrian Mountjoy was once again aware of falling curtains and the oblivion of temporary silence. But thankfully there was no pain this time, unlike his last outing to the *Fox and Duck*. In the darkness, he felt serene and invulnerable, his mind a disconnected maze of short-circuiting nerve endings. He had last been aware of television cameras and of not quite knowing what they were; they had pointed, like guns, but had ineffectual glass over their muzzles. Underneath the enfolding curtains, Mountjoy was laughing like a drain.

He remembered making an absolutely innocuous remark to the pretty TV reporter, who took it completely the wrong way. Christ, she hadn't even bothered to touch up her roots! Why shouldn't he remark on that fact? He felt safe under the curtains, finding the whole ludicrous misunderstanding terribly funny.

'I beg your pardon!' The girl had been aghast, framing each word with outraged precision. Others in the room were making up their own minds about her hair. Heads craned in her direction.

'Oh, don't get your knickers twisted,' said Mountjoy, holding up both hands in a gesture of conciliation. 'It was meant as a joke.'

'Like it was a joke when that young lad lost his job?' said a grubby youth in the front row. He was now writing furiously in his notebook, having taken no previous interest in proceedings. 'Are the police going to charge you, Mr Mountjoy?'

Mountjoy's eyes, behind his spectacles, were twinkling dangerously. 'Life is a joke, young man.'

'You've been reported for dangerous driving, Mr Mountjoy. A young man has lost his job because of you. If you think that's a joke, it's in very bad taste.'

Madam Chair was making mewing noises beside him, quite unable to forge a link between brain and voice box. Adrian – *her* Adrian! – was falling like a novice at the last hurdle. Her hands fluttered ineffectually on her clipboard.

Mountjoy rose to his full height and stared intently at the reporter. Again, it all seemed so pointless and utterly amusing. Perspiration formed on his forehead and ran into his eyes. He took off his glasses and, dizzy and disorientated, ran a trembling hand across his forehead. 'We in the Conservative Party do not suffer from bad taste,' he said, realising immediately just how foolish this sounded. He had intended to say something clever and crushing; instead he was talking drivel. There were stifled giggles from the floor.

He now felt nauseous and hot and put both hands on the table to steady himself. 'You, sir,' he said softly to the young reporter, 'are a cretin and a wanker!'

This was political indiscretion on a grand scale.

'*What* did you say?'

'You heard me,' said Mountjoy, who had now taken off his glasses and laid them down with a shaking hand. 'That's what I was called last week by another long-haired creep.' The camera lights blazed down on him; they were now hurting his eyes. He was aware of perfect silence, all eyes on the politician who was looking sick and defeated. 'Right here in this pub, in this very room, before he assaulted me.' His voice was coming from a long way off, the words disjointed and indistinct. 'You remind me of him, that's all.'

'Right, that's it!'

The young reporter pocketed his notebook and pushed back his chair. He had every intention of leaving right then, already penning in his mind the first words of what would be a coruscating article on the Conservative candidate for East Lothian. Mountjoy was swaying on his feet, both hands on the table. He was clearly unwell. Unfortunately, in his haste, the reporter pushed his chair against one of the TV lighting tripods which gracefully toppled over. Mountjoy was aware of an arc of light, and then the sound of heavy-duty light-bulbs loudly detonating.

The youth leapt forwards in fright. Someone shrieked.

Mountjoy, utterly disorientated, took a step backwards and reached for something to steady himself. His hand found contact with the curtains and, for the second time in a week, the bewildered politician found himself falling. *The oblivion of defeat*, he thought miserably, then found this idea hugely funny.

Coincidentally, Rosie had once owned a black cat, although it was very small, and was eaten by an eagle on the Christmas morning she was given it. That was also the Christmas she stopped believing in Santa Claus. One minute, the kitten was on a scrubby patch of grass in their Sussex back garden, a round ball of black fluff, peering fretfully at her new world; the next, she wasn't anywhere to be seen until, looking up, Rosie saw large and predatory wings disappear over the farmhouse roof. She was at an age when she knew that bad things happened, but still believed that Christmas Day was somehow exempt: guns fell silent, everyone had enough to eat, and pestilence was postponed until Boxing Day. Her parents tried to console her by saying that eagles weren't native to Sussex, searching fruitlessly in flowerbeds and, then, in the surrounding fields. In a way, that day had become a metaphor for her life: that in unexpected ways good things can be randomly snatched away. It felt like that now: sagging boobs, carpet slippers, a dreaded birthday – and the revelation of a precise delusion. Richie laid out what facts he knew, including Samuels' half-formed hypotheses.

Jack and Rosie listened in rapt attention, distracted only

once by a blonde TV reporter with badly-dyed roots, Rosie noticed, who had taken a wrong turning and accidentally found herself in the beer garden.

'I'm sorry, officer. Richie.' Rosie didn't quite know how to address Mara's superhero. 'We don't often get trouble here.'

'Particularly Conservative trouble,' added Jack who now had the task of rehanging the function room curtains for the second time in a week.

Mountjoy was resting upstairs in their spare room, still giggling to himself, while Clare Derby composed herself on their settee, a handkerchief clutched to her nose and an expression of blank incredulity on her face. 'Must have been something he ate,' she suggested. 'He's usually so reliable. Accountants *are* reliable, don't you think?'

'I wouldn't know,' replied Rosie. She didn't know many accountants.

The press conference had broken up in disarray. There was little that Madam Chair could do to stem the tide. She'd demanded that a doctor be called. 'Food poisoning!' she'd declared loudly and repeatedly. 'He's ill!'

Mountjoy, under his heavy velvet curtains, merely thought that the whole commotion was very amusing. He was safe under there, and was disappointed to be pulled free and led upstairs like a badly-behaved child.

'I do wish,' the young policeman was saying, pointing to the tree stump, 'that you'd told us about this sooner.'

'But tell you what?' Rosie replied with a touch of indignity. 'That someone had banged a nail into our tree?

That I'd then discovered some scratch marks? Come off it, please!'

She had a point, he conceded. After the Haddington conference, the Highland detective wearily climbing back into his car for the long drive north, the superintendent being driven back to Edinburgh and reluctantly giving a lift to the happily beaming psychologist, Big Mac had motioned Richie to follow him into his overheated office. If someone has been chosen, Big Mac wanted to know, did Richie have any ideas? – and although Richie didn't yet know everyone in the village, he knew most people, if only by reputation, so there was only one obvious name. Richie knew all about Rosie, gleaned from Mara and gossip, and her wiccan sobriquet in the village.

It now appeared that his suspicions were correct. If there was a link between past and present, it seemed entirely possible that Rosie McLeod could indeed be the object of unwanted attention. 'You should, nevertheless, report all crime.' It was part of his credo, he supposed, although the words sounded prissy. 'You believe that this was a warning?'

'Is a warning! *Is!* Present tense. Yes,' she added with a sigh of exasperation. 'Actually, I was going to report it... what with that woman's death. As of this morning, I decided that, just maybe, I might be taken seriously.'

'I just wish you'd told me sooner,' he repeated.

'What? And be laughed at? Treated like a sad and menopausal crone? Not bloody likely!' Rosie, sitting at one of the beer garden tables, was nursing a very large gin and tonic. The business in the function suite had completely unnerved her, despite it being entirely her fault, particularly with everything else that was going on. She again felt pointing fingers and a dark figure on the edge of reason.

'But there's something that I don't understand,' she said and pointed at the dead tree. '*This* was done weeks and weeks ago. Copper takes a while to do its dirty work.' Mara's Batman, pristine in crisp white shirt, removed his cap and placed it on a wooden table. A lock of hair hung over one eye and she had the sudden temptation to push it back into place. 'There can't therefore be any connection with the black cat. That's what I don't understand. If it is a warning,' she added, no longer feeling sure about anything.

'Mrs McLeod, the cat was seen near Dunbar about six weeks ago. It didn't make the newspapers.'

'Ah, well there we are,' she said in a small voice. The dark figure had moved closer. She looked again at the tree and wondered whose hand had killed it, and for what purpose.

'But someone knew, didn't they?' said Richie and again felt the shard of refracted memory move behind his eyes. 'Mrs McLeod, could I ask you something?'

She shrugged almost imperceptibly.

'Why would someone want to warn you?'

She had asked the same question many times of herself, and then had an overwhelming urge to laugh, although she'd kept well clear of tap water for some hours. 'Hey, maybe because he likes me.'

The policeman's lock of hair had again fallen across one eye and Rosie once more resisted the temptation to push it back. She felt old, nearly old enough to be his mother. Nearly, but not quite. Mara had gifted her that salvation.

'Could I ask you something else?' he then asked. 'It's probably unimportant, but do you have a middle name?'

This, of course, had been another source of anxiety. Startling and heart-stopping. She'd never even heard of Klara until that morning, and Rosie's middle name had been in the family for bloody, *fucking* generations, a bad joke now returning to haunt her. 'Lillie,' she said miserably and drank back her gin and tonic.

Archie Murray examined the hapless Mountjoy in the spare bedroom above the pub and pronounced him fit enough. The symptoms had been non-specific but all-encompassing; sight and hearing had been impaired. So too judgement. However, although his pallor was porcelain, his hands had stopped shaking. He had also lost the ghastly sense of amusement as cascading curtains had once more descended around his head. It had seemed funny, yet not funny. He had felt safe under the heavy fabric; returned to a warm, safe womb. He shuddered, the doctor peering into his eyes with a small light. He remembered another light toppling and the sound of exploding bulbs.

Clare Derby flapped in the background. Mountjoy was regaining some composure; circuitry reconnecting with returning memory. He felt let down; he felt that he had let himself down; let everybody down. Returning memory was all unpleasant memory; in a moment of flippancy he had allowed gold nuggets to slip through his fingers. There was a taste of curtain dust, like defeat, in his mouth.

'I could do a blood test,' suggested the doctor. 'In the circumstances, I'd recommend it. To get to the bottom of things, as it were.' At this, he was reminded sharply of chicken pie and the minister's brief affliction. 'Apart from that I'd also recommend bed rest and plenty of fluids.'

Mountjoy nodded, feeling wretched. 'I really am most terribly sorry,' he said, inching his feet from the bed and testing his weight on the floor. He still felt light-headed and unsteady. He was frightened by needles at the best of times, and this was probably the worst of times. 'No blood test, doctor, thank you.'

'Then there's nothing more I can do,' said Dr Murray, rising from Mountjoy's sickbed and folding his stethoscope into his large bag. 'Don't overdo things, that's my advice. Remember, plenty of fluids.'

Mountjoy regained the vertical and shook his head. He was feeling better, back in control: that, for the time being, was enough. 'I'm sorry, Clare,' he said to the large woman who was sailing in circles in the corridor outside. 'I really have been awfully silly.'

'You were ill, Adrian.' She came into the room and laid a hand on his shoulder. 'It can't be helped.' There were tears in her eyes.

She escorted him downstairs, through the clutch of matronly women who were now drinking white wine, still cackling, and past a smaller number of journalists who had remained in the *Fox and Duck* on the off-chance of an interview or explanation.

'Food poisoning!' boomed Clare Derby, leading him by the arm to the comfort of her car. 'Food poisoning!' she boomed again, before closing the door, making sure that everybody had heard.

Archie Murray heard her retreating voice as he packed up the tools of his trade, followed by slamming car doors and a car roaring off. He found Rosie in the beer garden nursing a large drink. She was by herself. Jack had followed the policeman back to his car.

'Ah, Mrs McLeod.'

'Dr Murray, we really must stop meeting like this.'

He was standing at the kitchen doorway, at the far end of the beer garden. 'I've just been attending to our Adrian Mountjoy.'

'*Our*?'

'Our Tory candidate.'

'And how is *our* Tory candidate?' She had refilled her glass of gin, hoping that it might take her mind off other things. The dark shape at the ends of her mind was taking human form.

'Don't mock, Mrs McLeod. The afflictions of the sick are not to be made light of. Actually, he seems much better. I've suggested bed rest. Not, I suppose, that he'll pay a blind bit of notice.' He laughed wheezily and put a hand in one pocket to jiggle change. 'Perhaps,' he suggested, 'I should have performed a chicken-dectomy? On our political candidate.'

'I thought you didn't believe in chicken pie?'

It had been a morning of revelation for both of them. 'Usually, Mrs McLeod, my surgery is full of the sick and the

347

unsick. The sick who really are ill, and the unsick who have vivid imaginations or simply want a few days off work. This morning, the unsick were missing.'

Rosie merely raised her eyebrows. 'Good health is such a blessing, doctor. Don't you agree?'

'They were laughing,' he said, an edge of surprise in his voice. 'They were ill and yet they were laughing. In much the same way,' he added, 'as our political candidate.'

'*Your* candidate, doctor.'

Again he laughed wheezily and jangled change. 'Mrs McLeod, I do wish that you liked me just a little bit.'

'Actually, I don't dislike you. I just dislike your assumptions. Anyway, isn't laughter supposed to be good for you?'

Well, not always, as Rosie knew, and the doctor probably didn't. Take, for example, the strange case of the American man who kept fainting during *Seinfeld*. During one episode he fainted several times and had to be rescued from his mashed potato by his wife. It transpired that several of his arteries were blocked and that his fainting episodes were due to dramatic falls in blood pressure. The condition was dubbed Seinfeld syncope by his doctors. On the one hand, his fainting episodes led to speedy diagnosis and successful treatment. On the other hand, television comedy could have killed him.

He looked at his watch. 'Well, I suppose I'd better be off,' he informed Rosie, 'on the off-chance that I have any patients to see.'

She escorted him through the bar where a party spirit was

rapidly developing. The morning matrons were still cackling, wine bottles proliferating, and now joined by several of their men folk who had inexplicably decided to quit work before lunch or, even better, not go to work at all. It was too nice a day to spend behind a desk; the *Fox and Duck* had chairs outside and a much-improved beer garden, now that the proprietors had sensibly decided to chop down those idiotic trees.

Archie Murray looked round the room and then at the small, dark woman beside him, no longer sure about Rosie McLeod, or the limits of her science, or whatever it was.

Chapter 22

The twelfth herb is named of the Chaldees Colorio, or Coloricon, of the Greeks Clamor, of the Latins commonly Salvia, of Englishmen Sage. This herb, being putrified under dung of cattle in a glassen vessel, bringith forth a certain worm, with whose blood, if any man be touched on the breast, he shall lose his sense or feeling. And if the aforesaid Serpent be burned, and the ashes of it put in the fire, anon there shall be a rainbow, with an horrible thunder.

The Book of Secrets of Albertus Magnus

Mara also couldn't quite believe what was going on. The pub was crowded. Weekends were rarely this busy. Moreover, everyone seemed to be in high spirits, laughing and joking, and buying drinks for complete strangers. She vaguely recognised several people from the village who weren't regular patrons. A few were in suits, ties unbuttoned, who had driven back from offices in Edinburgh. Most were dressed casually, and hadn't bothered going to their offices, and seemed in no hurry to leave the *Fox and Duck*. Even

Mara felt curiously elated. News of Klara should have put a dampener on the village; instead, everyone felt released. It wasn't yet time to size up the implications; today wasn't a day for remembering ancient sins, or for recalling a dismal former resident. Who cared, quite frankly, whether she was alive or dead? It was a day to be alive, and to savour the moment. It was a day to drink wine and beer and laugh uproariously at jokes that weren't very funny. It was day to tell loved ones that they really were loved ones and, perhaps... who knew what might happen when the kids were in bed? Mara glared at her employer, putting an unlikely two and two together.

'Rosie, what the hell have you done?'

Rosie paused from swilling glasses. 'Whatever makes you think that I've done anything?'

Rosie's shuttered eyes registered guilt. Down the road was a police car, discreetly parked, its two uniformed officers maintaining a close eye on the *Fox and Duck*. They too were much struck by the jollity in Holy Cross, presuming that everyone in the village was a little mad.

Mara persisted. 'Rosie, what the hell is going on?'

'Precisely nothing, that's what.'

Before Mara could remonstrate with her employer, they were joined on the other side of the bar by the village cricket captain who ordered several pints of lager. Rosie noticed that several other cricketers were at a corner table, although her husband wasn't one of them.

'I heard that the Tories were in town,' he said.

'Were. Past tense,' said Rosie, as Mara moved down the

351

bar to serve other customers. 'They've now ridden off into the sunset.'

Liam laughed. 'I heard about it. God, it's hot in here.'

Rosie had forgotten to turn down the main thermostat, which she now did, and opened several windows. On her return to the bar, Liam was quenching his thirst on a long glass of water, served to him by Mara.

'Your pub seems to have become a favourite haunt of the Tories,' he said, finishing the water and picking up his pint of lager.

'It certainly feels like we're being haunted by them.'

He laughed again, having now finished his glass of water. 'But I take it you are going to vote?' he asked.

Rosie wasn't going to pass up on that opportunity. 'I don't know who I'm going to vote *for*,' she replied, 'although I do know who I'm going to vote *against*.'

'That sounds ominously like spite.'

'Actually, it is spite. Pure and simple.' Clare Derby had been maliciously wrong to suggest that Jack had behaved improperly in the beer garden. It was because of bloody Clare that she had baked her pie and laced her home-made wine with additional ingredients. It was Clare Derby's fault that Jack had given them away. Everything, in fact, was the fault of the Conservatives. 'Anyway, I thought you had a job to go to. You're a computer geek, aren't you?'

'I'm a graphics designer,' he corrected. 'Computer games. You know, VirtualPlayCorp? My view is that too much work makes Jack a dull boy. Not your Jack, of course. Sporting hero, and all that. Me? I decided to take the day off.'

Rosie recalled the firm's name from its futuristic frontage. 'Oh, yes. Games where children can decimate whole planets from the comfort of their sofas. Achieve world domination between watching *The Simpsons* and eating chips.'

'You're a cynic, Mrs McLeod.'

'Rosie,' she said, leaning on the bar. 'I only insist on doctors calling me Mrs McLeod.'

'You don't like doctors?'

'No, but they don't seem to like me.'

He then noticed a stack of unopened letters by the cash register, several in gaudy envelopes. 'Somebody's birthday?' he asked.

'Mine,' she said flatly. 'I'm going to be forty.'

'Ah,' he said. 'Is that good or bad?'

She thought for a moment. 'That,' she replied, 'might depend on today.'

It was all down to timing, so she now thought. So long as Klara's link with the village remained undetected, he had whatever time he needed. Now that her death was out in the open, the forces of law and order would be closing in. Lines of enquiry were being established, so the young police sergeant had told her: it's only a matter of time. She now supposed that this might change his timetable; speed up whatever plans he had made. At the back of her mind, his form was taking solid shape. It had moved several steps closer during the day; now his brooding presence filled her imagination. She was on autopilot; cleaning glasses, smiling as best she could: functioning. She was wary of friends and strangers. She was easily startled; the pub door banging was enough to make her jump.

Mara, passing by to the cash register, looked again at her sharply. Having already been poisoned twice, she now recognised the ambiguous symptoms. The spinal tingles, the hot flushes. A disconnection from her surroundings. *Jesus Christ!* Surely Rosie hadn't poisoned the whole village? But what else could explain sudden joviality in the middle of a murder investigation? Strangely, however, Mara's was an ambiguous feeling: it was also a simple joy in being alive, of discovering love, and made poignant by news of another's death. She didn't remember Klara Lillie although her mother did. Bloody battleaxe, had been her comment, from the sanctity of her knitting needles. Nobody liked her. Nobody.

'Rosie, what the hell is going on?' Mara now confronted the older woman. She gestured across the room where a darts match was generating much loud banter.

'They're happy enough,' Rosie replied defensively, not quite answering the question. 'Perhaps it's something contagious.'

'Perhaps,' hissed Mara, 'it's something we've all drunk. Right, that's it! Rosie, outside! Fag break!'

Rosie couldn't immediately think of anything to say. 'But I don't smoke,' she eventually protested.

'Well, you do now,' said Mara and hustled her employer towards the door. 'God, Rosie what have you done?'

Mara pulled Rosie away from the pub and down to the river, away from prying ears camped at tables outside the

Fox and Duck. Rosie seemed hunched and diminished. She came unwillingly and slowly, as if each step was an effort. Her legs felt heavy; she stumbled, and would have fallen if Mara hadn't held on tight.

Rosie sat down heavily on a bench by the river and dragged deeply on one of Mara's cigarettes, immediately feeling sick. She hadn't had a fag in years; the smoke buzzed in her mind, making her befuddled. That she could do without. The phantom was close and closing in; she could almost smell him. 'I just want him to stop chasing me. But nobody would have believed me. Not you. Not Jack. Not the police.'

'Who, Rosie? For God's sake, talk to me!'

Rosie exhaled loudly. 'Strictly between ourselves, I'm now under police protection. From whom, I know not. But not a word, OK?' Unexpectedly, she laughed. 'It seems that I'm now in the tender hands of your superhero. Maybe,' she added, 'he'll have to sleep in my bedroom.' But the laughter was forced: the shadow was still there. Protection or no protection, he was close by, watching. She shuddered. 'Actually, I have you to thank.'

'Me?'

'The bloody tree! The bloody tree that Jack cut down! You spotted the copper nail, didn't you? Jack wouldn't have seen it or, if he did, he wouldn't have known diddly-squat about what copper does to trees. You, Mara, gave me the first clue. All I had to do was look a little harder.'

They walked alongside the river while Rosie told her everything that she'd previously explained to Richie. Rosie was restless and confused; her usual brittle energy seemed drained. Her face was colourless; behind her eyes was pain. Yes, the dark figure was close now; she could feel his breath on the back of her neck. His eyes held neither pity nor sympathy; reptilian eyes. He would do what he had to do; his eyes held nothing but blind purpose. He wouldn't hear her pleas or her cries of pain.

Rosie stopped by the river and looked into its depths. She pointed, a sudden smile returning to her lips. By the far bank, under an overhang of grass, a lustrous cricket ball was languidly turning in the current. 'Someone out there is after me, Mara. That's all I know. Me, don't forget, being the local witch.'

'It is in the water, isn't it?'

'What is?'

'Whatever you've put into it, that's what! Come on, Rosie, you have done something, haven't you?'

'Self-preservation!'

'What exactly *is* in the water?' asked Mara, this time loudly.

'A bit of this —'

'Rosie!'

She sighed. 'Mostly garlic, nettle and foxglove. Oh, and lots of chocolate. Pretty harmless, really. A few other things too, I suppose.'

'Harmless?' echoed Mara.

'Abso-*fucking*-lutely harmless! Mara, you have to understand! Please, *pretty-please* understand! Yesterday nobody would have believed me. I was on my own. I just wanted him to back off. I thought maybe... well, how can you kill someone if you're happy?'

'Happy?'

Rosie gestured back to the pub. 'They *are* happy, aren't they? How can you plot mayhem with a smile on your face?'

'Rosie, you're mad!'

'Probably.' The younger woman was no doubt right. She felt mad, frightened of shadows. God, she wanted it all to end. 'But you do understand, don't you? Well, at the very least, *sort* of understand? I may be mad, but there's been some method in it.'

'Not really, Rosie, no.'

The older woman reluctantly nodded, the merest downward tilt of her chin. 'It's what I thought you'd say. But, Mara, just believe one thing. The stuff in the water really is harmless, you have my word on that.'

By way of reply, someone in the public bar burst out laughing and was then joined by several others.

Mara was quiet for some moments, then pointed south towards the Lammermuir Hills. 'Look,' she said, 'a rainbow.'

Despite herself, Rosie again smiled. Rainbows always reminded her of childhood. She remembered once travelling by car, sitting in the back seat, coming back from visiting one of her mother's relatives, and they were on a motorway. Rosie had never liked this relative, a large woman with bushy eyebrows who frightened her. Partly it was her size. On a previous visit Rosie had fallen asleep on her sofa and been nearly sat on, which could have been fatal. Being squashed dead by someone's bottom, Rosie had thought, wouldn't be a nice way to die. Partly also it was her booming voice, like Clare Derby's, and the piercing way she would stare at Rosie, until she realised she'd been asked a question and had somehow blotted it out.

Mostly, however, it was her inedible food that Rosie and her parents all had to gamely eat. Being large, she served monumental portions of overcooked carrots, mushy potato that was neither properly mashed nor firmly boiled, and meat that didn't come from any species that Rosie recognised. They were all expected to eat heartily, which wasn't easy. Like many of her parents' relatives, Rosie had no idea how she was related to them, and still doesn't, but didn't want to ask in case she was a close relative and she might grow up to look like her. That was a really frightening thought. So, it was always a relief to escape unscathed and usually hungry back to their farm, where her mother would cook Rosie beans on toast.

That was the journey during which Rosie saw her first rainbow, or the first one she can remember. It was arched over the motorway; one end of it lost between low hills, the other in a scabby council estate. Her mother tried to explain about rainbows being all the different colours of light, but clearly didn't really know, and couldn't tell Rosie why light sometimes goes haywire and splits up into all its different colours. Rosie also didn't know if there were pots of gold at the end of rainbows, and didn't like thinking about all the drug addicts in the squalid council estate fighting over it.

But rainbows still made Rosie smile, reminding her of

being young and remembering that, out of a bad day, magical things can sometimes happen. 'It hasn't even been raining,' said Rosie.

'Well, it must have been raining somewhere.'

Rosie looked at the sky; a dark fringe of clouds gathering on the horizon, a faint breeze blowing them closer. 'It always is,' she replied.

Mara threw her spent cigarette to the water where it dimly fizzed and was carried downstream. 'OK, Rosie, I *sort* of understand. But no, I don't agree with what you've done. Rosie, you could go to prison! I also don't agree with your definition of harmless. The water, Rosie! What you've put into it!'

'Just don't bloody drink it! Tomorrow, OK. Today, not OK.'

A dark idea pushed to the front of her mind. 'You won't tell on me, will you? Please? No telling your superhero. Our little secret, Mara! I did it for the best,' she added lamely, looking at the gathering clouds and the arch of the rainbow, and wondering what the best now was, and whether it could still apply to her, because she could feel him beside her, taking visible form in her mind; a petrol can and matches in his hands.

Chapter 23

*The herb is named of the Chaldees Olphanos, of the
Greeks Hiliorion, of the Englishmen Vervain. This
herb, as the witches say, gathered and put with grain
or corn of Peony, healeth them that be sick of the
falling sickness. If the powder be put in a place where
men dwell, or lie between two lovers, anon there is
made strife or malice between them.*

The Book of Secrets of Albertus Magnus

There was still an unshifting shard at the back of Richie's
mind. It hung, just beyond reach, in a tributary of memory. A
grand delusion, made specific by an accident of psychosis.
Think of an egg, and then think what happens when you drop
it. A scrambled psychosis that they had failed to unscramble.
There remained this other fact, the nagging certainty of
something missed: a dislocated tendril between now and
then.

He phoned Mara when he came off duty, and she
immediately came round, and listened while he spoke,
recognising his need to unburden. What had happened was a
crime on a grand scale, on a scale that dwarfed the village's

previous petty larcenies. A precise crime, without compassion. This wasn't random schizophrenia, he said. He chooses in advance and then he waits. Rosie McLeod, another Lillie, might be next. At one point he went to the sink to pour himself a glass of water.

'Don't do that,' she said.

'Why not?'

'Not tonight.'

She instead opened a beer and handed him the bottle. He was too tired to ask why or to argue.

The chubby professor believed it to be trauma-induced; the pattern of psychosis too grand and exact for any other diagnosis. A car crash, perhaps? Mara shook her head. She couldn't think of anyone.

But the fragment was taking shape, its bright edges coming into focus. 'If Klara was so awful, how come she ended up in Holy Cross? That's what brought her here. That's when he chose her.'

She laid her head against his shoulder. Her hair tumbled across his chest. In the silence of the night he stroked it gently and reverentially. He saw in his mind's eye the falling child in a place that wasn't here, but near here, and the grief of final parting.

'I love you, Richie Scott,' she said when he had run out of words. Her demons had been caged; the child at the window still remembered grief and loss, the car skidding on the drive; the woman could now look back now with detachment. It was history, a closed book. 'Even my mum approves of you.'

361

'I didn't think she liked me.'

'She has other reasons.' The world seemed now too large and dangerous a place to travel in alone. 'She thinks that I may decide to stay here.'

Like many others in the village that night, the proprietors of the *Fox and Duck* were also being unexpectedly amorous and, to Rosie's surprised pleasure, with one another. Her pursuer might be on the threshold but, for the moment, he was held at bay by a police car parked outside her front door. On the eve of her birthday, having not been wanted for months and bloody months, Jack now pressed himself to her with urgent passion. There again, what with demijohns of colourless liquid in the water supply, his evident arousal wasn't *that* unexpected.

'We should do this more often,' she murmured. The dark figure at the back of her mind now seemed uncertain. He had drawn back; he no longer filled the depths of her vision. He was diminished; she still feared him, but feared him less.

'How could we, what with you running around like a demented gibbon?' He helped to remove her skirt and planted kisses across her neck.

'That was my description of *you*! Find your own bloody insults, Jack McLeod!' She fumbled with shirt buttons, the unusual rush of passion making her clumsy.

He pulled off his shirt and dropped it on the floor. 'Rosie, you've been impossible for months. Sex with a gibbon isn't my idea of pleasure.'

It didn't seem to be a problem now as she removed the

362

last of her clothing and lay beside him, feeling his lustful hands upon her. God, she needed this. 'You bought carpet slippers,' she reminded him. It still seemed a crime of sorts.

'Reading glasses!'

'You know I've always had bad eyes.'

'No, you haven't, Rosie. Not always.' His hand glided between her thighs and poked about. She closed her eyes as beams of pleasure blossomed.

'Have I been that bad?' she asked, almost a gasp as his lips settled on her breasts.

'Worse. Worse than worse.'

'Oh God, Jack, I'm sorry!'

'That's the third time you've apologised today.'

'Jack, can I ask you something?'

'Do you really have to?' His lips moved to her other breast and suckled greedily.

Although it was becoming almost too much to bear, she really did have to ask. 'Love, Jack. Do you love me?' Bright lights burned in her eyes; she was on the verge of orgasm already.

'You've asked me that several times just lately.' Jack looked up from his devotions. 'But, yes, of course I do.'

'Not, *of course I do*. That sounds insincere.'

'Then, yes, I love you.'

'Even with reading glasses?'

'Even with slippers. Let it go, Rosie. Life ticks onwards. You can't stop it.'

She sighed. He was, as always, quite right, resuming his duties on her body and sending sparks of pleasure up and

363

down her spine. But she wanted him inside her, to know that, old and wrinkled and on the final precipice, she was still truly wanted. 'Jack,' she said reasonably enough, 'you've done foreplay. Are you ever going to get around to fucking me?'

A loud hammering on the pub's front door dismally answered that question.

Beside him, Mara's even breathing marking life, Richie lay awake. His mind was oddly disjointed, random thoughts spilling over; coils of memory eddying and swirling. He couldn't stop the flow. He had one arm around Mara's shoulders, holding her close. She might yet choose to leave Holy Cross, leave him; but now, maybe, she might stay. She had chosen him. God, even her mother approved! Well, maybe not of him, but of her right to choose. It was all choice, just as Klara had been chosen.

Klara had come to Holy Cross because she was marked out. But that somebody hadn't chosen her after she'd arrived in the village. That somebody had chosen her *before* she'd even set foot in the place.

He sat up rigid.

'What's wrong?' murmured Mara from beside him, turning onto her back with a small sigh of protest then, as he switched on the bedside light, asking more loudly, 'What is it, Richie?'

But by then he had pulled on boxer shorts and was down at the sharp end, dialling Archie Murray's emergency number.

364

Templar Place is an unpretentious street in what is otherwise a remarkable village. The terraced houses are pebble-dashed, neat gardens fronting onto the quiet street. He wasn't there, of course. At least, he didn't appear to be. There were uniformed police officers front and rear. If escape was on his mind, it was cut off. Richie and two CID officers were at the front door, a finger on the buzzer. Neighbours, alerted by blue lights and activity, appeared at doorways, looking fearful, and stood as silent witnesses as two officers broke through the front door. It splintered easily on its hinges, sagging inwards. Another police car, siren wailing, blocked off access to the main road.

Two officers clattered upstairs as the rear door was also kicked in. Other officers filled the small back garden. Richie went for the front room, switched on the overhead light and drew the curtains against inquisitive eyes. He saw at once the room's particular order.

On the walls were pictures of Highland Scotland; rivers and glens, the high peaks of the Grampians, a small loch blazing in sunset colour. In one picture over the fireplace was a herd of deer, faces turned to the painter, taking flight across a heather hill. They were hung just so, regimentally spaced. Two armchairs were arranged on either side of a closed-off fireplace, cushions neatly plumped. The fireplace contained a gas heater; it was switched off. In an alcove by the fireplace was a small bookshelf. Nothing unusual, local history mostly. On another shelf was an ornamental ashtray; a golden cross at its centre. Similar ashtrays could be purchased anywhere in the village.

He wondered at the neat simplicity of the room, with its cosiness and murderous occupant. It gave away few clues, and held no character. Footsteps clattered back down the stairs. The house was empty.

At the back of the lounge was a dining table that looked out over a small, manicured garden that was being criss-crossed in a blaze of police torches. The room must once have been two rooms, a second door leading to a passageway that led to the kitchen. The dining area was also lined with pictures; more scenes of the Highlands; a trout jumping from a stream, a broken castle with torn battlements, a winding lane leading between high hills. Around the polished oak table were arranged four high-back chairs, each exactly placed. On the table was a white envelope, carefully sealed. In a neat hand it was addressed to:

"Rosemary McLeod
The Fox and Duck
Holy Cross"

On Rosie's doorstep at dead of night was Richie Scott, back in police uniform and looking exhausted. The lock of hair was again over his eyes. This time there was no temptation to push it back; she was immediately afraid, the shadowed figure rushing back into focus, his crocodilian eyes bright on her back.

'It's over,' he said simply. 'We know who it is.'

Rosie took this news with great sobbing gulps, sinking to

the ground in transfixed disbelief. She was giddy; her legs couldn't support her weight. It must have been raining: she could feel water against her knees, hear an echo of faraway thunder, remembering the rainbow earlier and how it's always raining somewhere. She clutched her nightgown around her, hugging herself, taking deep wracking breaths. Jack and Richie held onto her arms, pulling her gently upright, then led her upstairs. She sat slumped at their kitchen table and sobbed. A glass of brandy was placed in her hands.

'Who?' she asked at length, choking back more tears.

'Tam Cronin.'

They both stared at the policeman. Jack tried to laugh feebly. 'Jesus, you're not serious.'

'Tam?' said Rosie in a small voice. 'He wouldn't... he couldn't...'

'That's just ridiculous,' said Jack.

Richie reached inside his tunic. 'He left you a letter.'

She took the single photocopied page and laid it on the kitchen table. Then from her nightgown she extracted reading glasses.

Dear Rosemary

This letter is my apology and my last confession. I've always liked both you and Jack and never really wished you harm. I'd always hoped that Klara would be the first and last.

I never really believed that the black cat would come back. I prayed that it wouldn't. Rosemary, as the village witch, it would mean that I would have to kill you. Your middle name was the final proof. But I didn't want to do it, please believe me. I tried to warn you, I really tried. Twice, Rosie, twice! The tree and the church!

Then came news of Klara and I knew that the police would eventually come for me. They nearly came for me twenty years ago, but nobody took the old minister seriously. Anyway, this morning, I decided that killing you didn't now much matter. The police would be onto me and, I couldn't help but notice a police car outside the pub. Carrying out your punishment would have been difficult.

I still declare you guilty, Rosemary, but I also don't want to spend the rest of my life in jail. I therefore also declare that you sank, so I hope you can forgive me.

Kindest regards

Tam

PS Please do me one last favour and vote for Mountjoy. He needs all the support he can get.

She laid the sheet of paper on the table and shoved it roughly away from her, as if it was soiled and infectious. He'd even had the effrontery to sign it *Kindest regards*! God all*bloody*mighty! Her hands were trembling and she thrust them into her lap to still them. She felt incredulous and sick. Jack fussed behind her, swilling more brandy into her glass.

'My God!' she said simply.

A numbing sense of grief and new life coursed in her veins. The brandy had reached her mind, numbing it. She felt impervious, alive, and then fearful again.

'Where is he?'

'Not at home. But we'll find him. Sooner or later.'

She looked again at the handwritten note. 'The bastard actually wants me to *forgive* him!' Her voice was incredulous and on a rising curve. 'Jack, all those fucking, bloody years and he was planning all along to kill me! Jesus-fucking-Christ!'

The policeman blinked to clear his head. 'He also tried to warn you.'

'Frankly, I don't give a shit! He was planning to *kill* me! Oh God, Jack!' She clung to him, feeling wretched, sobbing again in loud gasps.

'Tam was manager of the quarry when Klara first applied for the job. It was him who chose her, before she'd even moved here. When she left for Inverness, he must have kept close tabs on her, just in case he had to kill her.'

Rosie took the brandy bottle from her husband and shakily poured another large measure into her glass. Then she reread Tam's letter, marvelling at its taut simplicity; the swirl of neat handwriting concealing dark purpose.

The policeman continued: 'He'd been in a motorbike accident two years before Klara came to the village and suffered a head injury.' This he had learned from Dr Murray. 'It appears that he was never quite the same after the accident. Found it hard to go on working at the quarry. After Klara left, and the quarry shut down, he went onto incapacity benefit.'

'I didn't know that,' said Rosie. 'But I utterly refuse to feel sorry for the bastard!'

'What does he mean about you sinking?' asked Richie.

Rosie blew her nose and took a deep, ragged breath. 'Once upon a time, officer, they used to throw suspected witches into running water.'

'Richie,' he corrected.

She smiled through tears at this. 'If they floated they were guilty. If they sank, well, that proved their innocence.' She paused to tip the brandy glass to her lips, holding the glass in both hands. 'But as often as not, when they were pulled out, they were already dead.'

'So, he's declaring you both innocent and guilty?'

'He did try to warn me,' she replied, a headache now throbbing behind her eyes, and she started to cry again, crying for no reason now, or for a whole lot of reasons put together. She remembered shouting her innocence at the Bass Rock. God, was that only this morning?

Richie suddenly felt deadly tired. 'Is there anything I can do?'

But had it really only been this morning? It seemed an eternity ago. She looked at her watch and realised that she'd reached the end of the world. 'You could wish me happy birthday,' she replied.

Tam's body was found the next morning by a local man walking his dog. He was floating face down in a weir outside Haddington. His body was recovered by mid-morning and taken into Edinburgh for post mortem examination. Toxicology found fatal dosages of painkillers, sleeping tablets and Belhaven beer. It also found unusual residues of other elements, most commonly found in plants and herbs, several indigenous only in parts of Africa and Asia. He also seemed to have ingested an extremely large amount of chocolate. Tam had broken the alcoholic habit of a lifetime and swallowed his pills with the help of a glass of water, but taken in moderation and too late to improve his mood.

Chapter 24

Here are ended some secrets of Albertus Magnus of Cologne upon natures, virtues, and effects of certain herbs.

The Book of Secrets of Albertus Magnus

In their lounge above the *Fox and Duck*, Mara raised a glass of champagne. Jack was pouring champagne into Richie's empty glass. Rosie was sitting on the settee, legs daintily crossed, and airily waving her new acquisition.

'Trapiche!' she intoned, grinning like a Cheshire cat.

'From Colombia,' added Jack, 'where all the best drugs and emeralds come from.'

Rosie held her ring to the light where it greenly sparkled. 'He's also taking me to Rome, the romantic old fool! I've always, *always* wanted to see Rome.'

'The Trevi Steps.'

'Fountain, Jack! It's a bloody *fountain!* God, honestly!'

On the mantelpiece was a line of cards and in the fireplace a vase of red roses. 'You're very lucky,' said Mara, looking at the flowers.

Jack saw the angle of her eyes. 'I could have bought her

one red rose for each of her birthdays —'

'Don't say it, Jack!'

'But it would have bankrupted us,' he finished anyway.

Yes, she supposed that she was lucky. She was alive, the best gift of all, in the company of those who, each in their own way, had helped to save her. 'The only blot on the landscape is that my bloody husband is organising a party. The one saving grace is that it's not a *surprise* party. That really would have been too much! In our very own function suite, tarted up for the occasion and catered to by Sammy. You're all invited,' she added, twirling her fingers so that her new ring again caught the light.

'Well, it's a milestone,' said Jack. 'You've got to have a party. You don't have to come, of course. We'll just have the party without you.'

'Practically obligatory,' agreed Mara and looked across the room at Richie. His usual lock of hair was hanging down. Abruptly, she crossed the room and pushed it back into place. 'You really are a scruff, aren't you?'

Rosie smiled. She'd wanted to do the same thing and had wondered if Mara thought the same. 'One day you'll be forty. One day you'll have some bloody lump of a husband organising damnable parties.' She smiled at him, the great burden of age now lighter on her shoulders. The fallen page of the calendar now seemed less substantial.

'Well, maybe,' said Mara. She raised her glass again but this time to Richie who smiled back and raised his in return.

'Young love, eh?' said Jack, still on his rounds with the bottle.

'We were young once, Jack.'

'We still are. We still bloody well are! Crying shame about Mountjoy though.' Jack winked at his wife.

Earlier they'd seen live coverage of East Lothian's returning officer mounting the platform steps, the large figure of Clare Derby at the edge of the frame, her clipboard clutched tight. They'd closed the pub for the day, while plainclothes detectives interviewed them, and police photographers took close-up shots of the defaced tree.

'He got what he deserved,' said Rosie. 'Precisely bloody nothing!' She hadn't voted for him, of course. The Socialists had retained East Lothian with an increased majority. Clare Derby had looked close to tears.

'But still,' said Richie, 'if the minister hadn't confided in Mountjoy, and if Mountjoy hadn't gone to the media...'

'... Then I'd probably be dead,' replied Rosie flatly. 'I know that! But he did what he did for political gain. He didn't give a shit about anything else! I utterly refuse to feel grateful to him.' She looked round at everyone, daring them to disagree.

Worse, some chubby don in a lurid waistcoat had arrived at the pub unannounced. *He was a victim too*, he'd said. He was ill. A psychotic who should have been on medication. *That doesn't damn well make him innocent!* she'd stormed back.

A *delusional* bastard, according to Richie, probably caused by falling off his motorbike – an accident that had happened before she'd even met Jack. Thank Mara, not me, Richie had added, holding up his hands. She helped me piece the bits together. Tam who must have placed the quarry's job advertisement and interviewed the applicants. He chose her for her name, not her competence – or lack of it – and then, who knows, her difficult character might have offered further proof. She should have lived; instead she died.

Dr Samuels was writing a monograph on the bloody man, turning his complete bastardom into explicable illness. *Witchfinder General* was his working title, so he'd told Rosie. Rosie thought the title banal as she hustled the protesting don to the pub door. *Complete Fucking Loony!* She'd loudly suggested might be a better title. She had no intention whatsoever of reading it. Well, maybe she might. She did sometimes, very occasionally, change her mind.

According to Samuels, relayed to her by Richie, Tam could live with the murder of Klara, but not with the thought of apprehension. It compromised his delusion and made him fallible; no longer someone meting out righteous justice, but a common criminal who might be wrong. He must also have liked you, he said. She'd snorted then laughed then cried. He liked us all, she'd replied.

'Actually, amidst all this birthday cheer, I have a present for you,' Rosie said to Mara and fetched a long thin box from the mantelpiece. 'My mother gave it to me. Now I'd like to give it to you.' She held it out in both hands, making the presentation seem formal. 'It's a kind of apology. Well, you know. It's also a good luck present. To both of you,' she added for Richie's benefit, but found that she was crying again. She'd done a lot of crying and laughing during the day. Her emotions had swung randomly, hormones whizzing in every direction. She could have visited her scullery, and boiled up something comforting, but hadn't. She could even, God forbid, have visited Dr Murray, but didn't much like the idea of being patronised or, worse, made to feel sorry for herself. She was innocent, the Bass Rock could testify to that. But only just.

'It's OK' said Mara, pulling off golden paper. 'Everything's OK now.'

Rosie's glass was empty and she gestured irritably to Jack to refill it. 'It's just, well – he was always so nice to everyone.'

In Mara's hand was a translucent moonstone necklace, its stones reflecting light in her eyes. In an instant, she recalled her own journey and the freedom of flight. She too had been gifted new life, and glanced sharply at Rosie, wondering about the strange potency of her talents. 'Rosie, it's beautiful,' she breathed.

But Rosie's thoughts were elsewhere, a small crease on her forehead, the lines around her mouth forming neat quotation marks, as Richie fixed the necklace around Mara's neck.

The markings on the tree. Tam practically lived in the *Fox and Duck*. Even when they weren't there, *he* was there. Day and night, propping up the bar with his just-so pewter tankard; the font of all local wisdom and source of all gossip, salacious or otherwise. Rosie now supposed that his close attention over the years was less about Belhaven beer and more with keeping tabs on his next possible victim; to assure himself of her guilt and to make sure that she didn't try to escape. *But why would I have done*, she thought? *I didn't realise that I'd been declared guilty until a dead tree offered an implausible clue*. Tam, of course, had easy access to the beer garden. He also knew everything and everyone. He would certainly have known about the earlier sighting of the cat near Dunbar. All he had to do was choose the right moment, with a hammer and nail in one pocket and a sharp knife in the other. A warning, just in case the cat ventured towards Holy Cross.

Once it had, and his plans had to be put into action, he also vandalised the church for good measure. He didn't have any family. In a way, the *Fox and Duck* was his family. Yes, a friendly enemy, who had tried to warn her, caught in his own crossfire.

Just so long as nobody, but absolutely-*bloody*-nobody, had the temerity to ask her what flowers might be appropriate at his funeral.

About the Author

Charlie Laidlaw teaches creative writing, and lives in East Lothian. He is a graduate of the University of Edinburgh and was previously a national newspaper journalist and defence intelligence analyst. He has lived in London and Edinburgh, and is married with two children. His other novels are *The Things We Learn When We're Dead* and *The Space Between Time*.

W: www.charlielaidlawauthor.com
T: @claidlawauthor
F: @charlielaidlawauthor